THE SHADOW

OF

TYR

BY GLENDA LARKE

The Mirage Makers
Heart of the Mirage
The Shadow of Tyr
Song of the Shiver Barrens

The Stormlord Trilogy
The Last Stormlord
Stormlord Rising
Stormlord's Exile

The Forsaken Lands
The Lascar's Dagger
The Dagger's Path

THE SHADOW
OF
TYR

THE MIRAGE MAKERS
BOOK TWO

GLENDA
LARKE

www.orbitbooks.net

ORBIT

First published in Australia in 2007 by Voyager,
HarperCollins*Publishers* Pty Limited
First published in Great Britain in 2007 by Orbit

9 11 12 10

Copyright © Glenda Larke 2007
Map by Perdita Phillips

The moral right of the author has been asserted.

A CIP catalogue record for this book
is available from the British Library.

ISBN 978-1-84149-608-5

Typeset in Minion by Palimpsest Book Production Limited
Grangemouth, Stirlingshire
Printed and bound in Great Britain by
Clays Ltd, St Ives plc

Papers used by Orbit are from well-managed forests
and other responsible sources.

MIX
Paper from
responsible sources
FSC
www.fsc.org FSC® C104740

Orbit
An imprint of
Little, Brown Book Group
100 Victoria Embankment
London EC4Y 0DY

An Hachette UK Company
www.hachette.co.uk

www.orbitbooks.net

This one is for my sister
Margaret
with thanks for all the
good memories

Acknowledgements

Many thanks to those who helped bring this book to its published state; and no, I never tire of thanking the same people, because I owe them so much!

My agent, Dot Lumley; Voyager associate publisher, Stephanie Smith, and all the team at HarperCollins Australia; copy editor Kim Swivel; mapmaker Perdy Phillips; and beta readers Alena Sanusi, Mark Timmony, Trudi Canavan, Donna Hanson. And two very special authors who helped me in many, many ways with this particular book: Karen Miller and Russell Kirkpatrick. Without their generosity of time and thoughtful assessment, *The Shadow of Tyr* would be less than it is. Thanks guys.

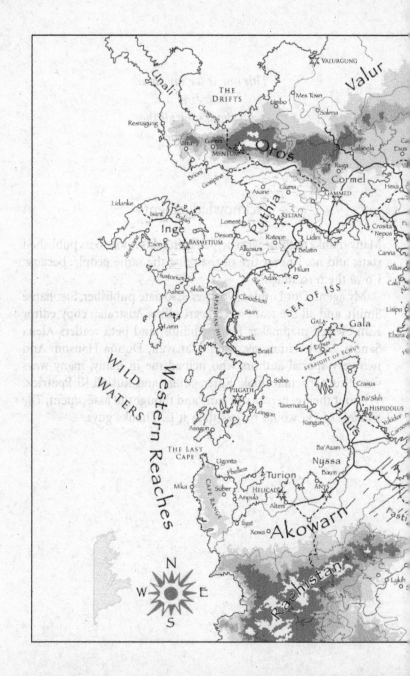

THE
EXALTARCHY

SCALE
EXALTARCHY MILES

PROLOGUE

Temellin stood on the seawall and watched the *Platterfish* manoeuvre through the moored fisher boats. In the windless waters of the harbour, four oars stroked in unison from the lower deck, while the sail hung like a rumpled blanket from the top spar. On the upper deck, a woman leaned at the railing, looking back at him.

Ligea Gayed, who was also his cousin Sarana Solad. She really was leaving him, taking his unborn child with her. Nothing he'd said had persuaded her to stay, and his sense of betrayal was matched only by the intensity of his loss. She could have chosen to rule this land alone, she could have chosen to share his rule, she could have done neither and just chosen to stay anyway. Instead, she had put her own quest for revenge, justice – call it what you would – before their love.

He understood, yet was bitterly angered, but it made no difference anyway: he loved her and always would. Mirageless soul, how was he going to live a life without her now that he had known what it was like to share one with her?

As the boat slipped past the arms of the narrow entrance and out of the harbour's embrace, the shipmaster manning the stern sweep called out something to Ligea, and indicated the limp sail. She laughed and waved at Temellin, pointing to it in turn. He knew what they were asking, and obliged because he liked the irony of it – using his own power to send the woman he loved away. A breeze sprang out of nowhere to fill the sail's patchwork of flaxen squares ribbed with leather along the joins.

She raised her hand in farewell as the boat picked up speed and slid over the first of the ocean swells. Even across the distance, he felt the emotion she let free for him to sense: that mix of love and sorrow and determination that was peculiarly hers.

As he watched, he saw Brand come and stand by her side. *Damn his eyes.* And yet he was grateful the Altani was there for her. Gratitude and jealousy, side by side . . . nothing was simple any more.

Cabochon take it, Sarana, you turn a man inside out.

A voice spoke softly from behind him, echoing his sentiments, but for a quite different reason. 'She should not go. No Magoroth should leave Kardiastan now. Not when those murdering blond bastards walk our streets and war is coming.'

He turned to look at the speaker: a crinkle-skinned fisherman weaving closed a tear in the side of an aging lobster pot, a man too ancient to sail with the fleet any more.

'She will still fight our battles, old man,' he said. 'She will be in a position to stop legionnaires from landing on our shores, one day.'

The fisherman grunted, his disbelief strong in the air. 'How much longer, Magori?' he asked. 'How much longer before I don't fear to walk me own streets again? Will these old bones last long enough for me to smell freedom on the seawind once more, eh?'

Temellin gave a grim smile. 'You look as tough as shleth leather. You'll make it.' In his heart, he wasn't so sure. It was one thing to start a war – they could, and would, do that soon. They'd been on the way to mount a challenge to Tyranian rule in Kardiastan when Sarana had brought the news of the Stalwarts' incursion across the Alps. She'd repelled them, Mirage be thanked, but to expel all legionnaires? That was another matter.

Hostages, he thought as he walked back along the seawall towards the town. *The Tyranians have a land full of ordinary Kardis to use as hostages, and they'll do it, too. How much stomach* will we have to go on fighting when they can attack the innocent in retaliation?

Sands take it, maybe Sarana was right. Maybe her help in Tyr would be crucial. Maybe without it, Kardiastan would never be free, for all their Magor power.

Power, he mused, his thoughts bleak, *even Magor power – it's not everything. It might not even be enough.*

PART ONE

LÍGEA
AND BRAND

CHAPTER ONE

The writing over the archway said simply: APOTHECARY. Most such signs would have been followed by a symbol – in this case, a herb leaf – for the benefit of the illiterate, but no such drawing graced this entrance.

Ligea Gayed knew why. Merriam of Istia, apothecary and herbalist, was renowned for her greed and her exorbitant charges. As the illiterate rarely had enough money to pay for her services, Merriam did not bother to tell them of her existence.

Fortunately, the cost of a consultation was irrelevant to Ligea; all that concerned her was that the Istian woman was not just an apothecary, but also the best midwife in Tyr. And she *needed* the best. She had to find out what was wrong. And, more importantly, how to fix it.

For a moment she leaned against the archway, delving within for the courage to find out. *Too much to ask of an unborn child,* she thought, sliding a hand over the slight bulge of her abdomen. *To have his essensa travel as my guide across a whole land – how could it not leave him wounded? He should have been safe in my womb, not asked to become an insubstantial shade. Perhaps it has scarred his very soul.* And yet, if he hadn't done that, they would both have died. *Gods above, why do you never give us easy choices?*

She sent her senses to touch on the occupants of the rooms on the other side of the door under the archway. Two people: one a woman seeping avarice into the air like the stink of sweat, the other a man whose lack of passion spoke of stoicism and acceptance – a slave, surely. Only slaves exuded that kind of staid forbearance. It was what kept them alive.

Ligea took a deep breath and raised her hand to knock. She had to know, damn it. What had she done to her son by the choices she had made?

The slave answered, his greeting rudely abrupt. 'Yes?'

'I wish to see Merriam of Istia.'

'And you are—?'

She said the first name that came into her head. 'Estella.'

'That's all?'

'Estella of Corsene.' Another lie, but she had the right colouring for a Corseni.

He looked her up and down, the contempt in his glance indicating that Merriam's clientele did not usually come clad in artisan's clothes and wrapped in a tattered shawl. 'Domina Merriam charges two sestus for a consultation, potions extra.'

The amount was outrageous, and an apothecary was not usually addressed as domina, but Ligea dug in her pouch and extracted the coins anyway. He plucked them out of her fingers, still unwelcoming, but stood back to allow her entry.

The space on the other side of the door was small and mean, curtained off at one end, the only furniture a shabby divan. The air was redolent of alchemy, heavy with the smell of herbs and the smoky fragrance of burning incense.

'Wait here,' he said and disappeared through the heavy woollen curtain. She flung off the shawl she'd worn to help conceal her identity and dropped it onto the divan, then bent to undo her sandals. No one came forward to wash her feet, so she did it herself in the bowl provided.

She heard the murmur of voices, but resisted the temptation to enhance her hearing. A moment later, the man beckoned her through the curtain.

Shelves laden with jars lined the walls of the inner room; a brazier and a mortar and pestle were among the items sitting on a bench and bunches of fresh herbs hung from the ceiling.

In the middle of the floor, a narrow table was covered by a thin pallet and a cloth. A stool had been placed underneath.

The woman waiting for her was tall and scrawny, with a narrow, pinched face; her demeanour had the warmth of a marble pillar.

Hells, Ligea thought, *she looks more like an embalmer than a midwife. Probably scares babies into taking their first breath.*

'I am Merriam. Why are you here?' The staccato of her Istian accent was sharply unpleasant to Ligea's ears.

'I wish to know if there are any problems with – with my pregnancy.'

'How many months?'

'Four – no, almost five.'

'Loosen your wrap and climb onto the table. I will examine you.'

Ligea stared pointedly at the man.

'He's only a *slave*,' Merriam said, her contempt thick in the air.

Ligea did not move.

Merriam snorted. 'Timon, leave us.'

Once he'd disappeared into the next room and Ligea was lying on the table, the woman began her examination, her touch impersonal and assured, her questions probing. Had there been any bleeding? Did she vomit in the mornings? How was her digestion? Her water? Finally she listened to the child's heartbeat, and then Ligea's own, using a hollowed-out piece of gorclak-horn pressed to her skin. After she had finished, she pointed to a nearby door and shoved a pot into Ligea's hand. 'Pass water into this,' she ordered.

When Ligea returned, Timon took the pot into the next room. She had no idea what he was doing with it and didn't ask.

'My services for delivery,' Merriam said as they waited, 'cost eight silver sestus for a daytime birth. Extra one sestus if I must go out after dark.'

'That's a lot of money.'

The midwife shrugged indifferently. '*My* patients do not die of afterbirth fever. What price do you put on your life?'

'I won't be in Tyr when the baby is born.' She'd just have to hope that when the time came she would find someone as skilful as this woman apparently was, for all her coldness. 'I do have a question now, though.'

Merriam's lips thinned. 'Don't ask if it's a boy or girl. I don't know. Nor do I care.'

'It's not that.' She touched the scarring on her face and hesitated, at a loss. How could she describe being submerged in the Ravage? Finally she said, 'When this child was less than four months along, I suffered a physical attack. I was also possibly, um, poisoned. I nearly died. For a day I hovered close to death. Will that have – have *damaged* the child?'

'If it had, you would have miscarried.'

The lie was potent to Ligea's senses. 'I paid good money for the truth, midwife! Do me the courtesy of speaking it.'

Merriam stared at her, surprised by her assertiveness, and not pleased. 'Worry won't do you any good. Truth is, I don't know. Beaten mothers can deliver healthy children. Or deformed ones. Poisoned mothers can have crippled babies. Or not. The gods dispose such things, and who knows the mind of a god? All I can say is that this child lives; I have heard its heartbeat.'

Hells, why did I come? I might have known I wouldn't get the assurance I want. Still she persevered, wanting answers. 'There are times since then when I feel that all is not well with him. He weakens and I have to—' She groped for words to explain how her son had faltered and faded within her, not once, but four or five times, each time to such an extent that she'd known he would die unless she intervened to heal him. The last time it had happened was just the evening before, as she and Brand had sailed into Tyr harbour from Ordensa.

Before she could think of a way to explain, Timon came back into the room. 'Nothing amiss,' he said, wiping a forearm across his mouth. 'Clear, and unsugared.'

Merriam nodded and turned back to Ligea. 'Your health is good.' She sounded bored. 'Your baby is normal. Its heart is strong. I foresee no problems. This is your first child. First-time mothers worry needlessly. Do not listen to the arrant nonsense other women say about such things. If you are further troubled, go to a temple and pray to the Goddess of the Unborn.'

Ligea stifled a sigh. *I am a fool. How did I expect her to help anyway, even if there was something wrong?*

However, as she slipped out into the street once more a few moments later, her shawl well wrapped about her head and face, worry still chafed her mind. She knew the feelings she'd had weren't nonsense, arrant or otherwise, and she certainly wasn't influenced by women's gossip. She'd felt her son slipping away; she'd coddled his tenuous hold on life and brought him back. Again and again. Perhaps they'd both pay for her intervention. Perhaps she should have let him go.

But he was all she had of Temellin.

Gods, if he *were* born alive and well, she'd call him Arrant just to remind herself of how silly she was, imagining things.

I will try and keep him safe, Temellin, I promise.

She walked on, never thinking to cast her sensing abilities behind to the apothecary's. There were too many other things abrading her mind. Tonight she would go to the Meletian Temple, but not quite for the reason Merriam had suggested. She wanted to take a good look at the Oracle. And tomorrow, tomorrow she would tackle Arcadim, her moneymaster . . .

'Never met her before,' Merriam said to her slave, Timon, 'but I do remember her from somewhere. Just can't think where. Strange that I'd forget someone with a face as badly scarred as that.'

She began to enumerate all that had bothered her about her visitor. 'Dresses like an artisan, but has the accent of the highborn. And the arrogance. Didn't question the cost, so she has money. Yet didn't book me for the birth. That's odd. Wrapped herself well in her shawl. Didn't want to be recognised, I dare say. Maybe she will be hiding out on some country estate when the baby is birthed. I wonder why her hand was bandaged?'

She tapped the side of her nose. 'Secrets, Timon. And secrets are always of interest to the Brotherhood. Perhaps she's the highborn wife of a general who hasn't been home for a good many months. I *wish* I could remember where I've seen her before.'

She considered for a moment, then made up her mind. 'Not much to go on, but I have a hunch she's important. Fetch me pen and ink and a papyrus scroll. I shall write to Compeer Clemens. After all, you never know what information might be useful enough to earn us some money, do you?'

'Guards?' Brand asked her.

'Only two,' Ligea whispered. 'One at the back, circling right. The other standing still, on the other side of the temple.'

'The priestesses?'

'Asleep. In the building beyond the temple.'

'How come?' he asked. 'Surely the Oracle should be tended day and night by a priestess in case one of the gods has something to say!'

'That's what they tell the public, yes. In practice – why sit up all night when you know damn well the Oracle is a sham? There is one young man in the temple itself. He's awake. Probably the acolyte who tends the lamps.'

I wish Magoroth power included the ability to make myself invisible. Or even make an illusion or two. But it didn't. She couldn't be too reckless with her use of power, either, or she'd end up weakened and vulnerable.

She felt a pleasurable excitement, the stimulus of adventure. No one visited the Meletian Temple in the middle of the night, yet here they were, like thieves on their way to rob a counting house, dodging among the treasury buildings that surrounded the Pilgrim's Way.

'And the four-legged night watch?' Brand persisted.

She smelled the fear he deliberately unfurled for her. The temple hounds, Pythian ridgebacks reared to hunt mountain bears, were the reason that the temple only had two guards at night. The dogs tore intruders to pieces. She glanced at Brand but couldn't see him properly in the darkness. 'They've got our scent. They'll be here in a minute.'

'Ocrastes' damn. I didn't need to hear that.'

'You didn't have to come.'

'Blame Temellin. He's the one who said I had to look after you. When, of course, he ought to have been asking *you* to look after *me*. You're the one with the Vortexdamn power.'

She tried not to feel annoyed that he had insisted on coming with her in the first place. Experience told her a protective man was usually more hindrance than help.

Confound this baby, she thought. *He changes everything, even Brand.* Then, more incredulous: *Temellin asked* Brand *to look after me?*

She waved a hand at the back wall of the building they were passing. 'This looks like a good place. Stand next to me, back to the wall, so I only have to worry about what comes at us from one direction.' She pulled out her sword and called the light into the blade. Other buildings, heavy with statuary, loomed up out of the night as if beckoned by the glow.

'What *are* these places?' he asked.

'The treasuries. Erected by other cities to store their votive offerings and sacred vessels and stuff like that. You've never been to the temple before?'

'No. Why should I?'

Of course not. Silly question. He didn't worship any of the gods of the pantheon, for all that he often swore by parts of Ocrastes' anatomy.

'I might start really soon, though,' he added, 'with a prayer for protection against ravening dogs . . .'

The hounds flowed out of the dark, silent and swift. She felt Brand's fear thicken. 'I have a ward in place!' she reassured.

'I just wish I could *see* it.' He gripped his sword in a two-handed grasp. And then the dogs were upon them.

The leader of the pack, a large brindled beast, launched itself with jowls drawn back into a teeth-baring growl. And slammed hard into the invisible wall of the ward. Brand flinched. Every other dog in the pack suffered the same fate an instant later, until the area in front of them was a mass of snarling, yelping animals nursing bruised snouts and forepaws.

'I think my hair just went grey,' Brand said from between clenched teeth. 'Why is living in your vicinity always so damned *dangerous*?'

She tried to wrap the ward around the confused animals, but they scattered and re-formed a short distance away. When she moved the ward in their direction, they scattered again, breaking up to approach in a semicircle. Slowly this time. Silent. Bellies low to the ground. Eyes fixed on prey.

The pack after the bear.

She was forced to bring the ward in closer to block them off on all sides.

'Ligea, um, what are you doing? This is *nerve-racking*!'

Worried, she said, 'They seem able to sense the ward now.'

'No wonder, after breaking their noses on the wretched thing! Where the hell is it anyway?'

'In an arc around us.'

'Ah. So, in effect, *we* are imprisoned, rather than the dogs. Great.' Brand, as usual, putting his finger on her errors.

She sighed. 'I thought I could just curl the edges of the ward around to corral them, but they wouldn't stay still long enough.'

She didn't get any further. The pack leader hurled itself at the ward. This time it didn't leap into it, but *up*. She had a bare second to think, *Goddess, he's going over the top* – before the hound slammed into her chest.

Her sword went flying. The weight of the animal sent her crashing to the ground. All the air in her lungs whooshed out. The dog somersaulted over her to land awkwardly somewhere behind.

Winded, she was helpless. She doubled up, desperately fighting for breath. She could only watch as the other dogs tried to follow. Fortunately, they lacked the pack leader's powerful haunches and failed to clear the ward in a single leap. Their feet scrabbled at the top of the ward. Brand beat them off with his sword as they grappled for purchase on the invisible. Even hampered by his inability to see the warding, he managed to block their attempts to heave themselves over the top.

She groped desperately for clarity. Where was the leader of the pack? *Shit! It must be somewhere inside the ward . . .*

She wanted to tell Brand she was in trouble, but her body, focused on inhaling, wouldn't cooperate. Still rolling on the ground in breathless pain, she grabbed at the power already in her cabochon and raised the warding higher.

Limping, the pack leader circled into her view. She aimed her cabochon at it, but wasn't fast enough. The dog sprang at her throat; the beam of power went astray to gouge a hole in the treasury wall.

She expected to die. Knew she was going to have her throat ripped out. Had time only to think: *How ridiculous. A Magoroth dying because she was winded.*

And the hound jerked to a stop a hand span from her face. Its jowls dripped saliva on her chest. She could smell its dog breath. The growl in the back of its throat was pure animal fury. Its yellowed teeth meshed together, aching to close on her throat.

Brand, feet planted on either side of her body, hauled frantically on its collar. The hound strained as it leaned into her, its bulk and the powerful muscles of its shoulders pitted against a man with a withered arm.

Finally recovering control, she aimed her cabochon and sank the gleam of its power into the beast's chest. It collapsed onto her, dead, driving more breath out of her lungs. Brand, suddenly relieved of its pull, sat down with a thump, hauling the corpse away as he fell.

Sweet Melete, all that lasted only a moment. Less time than it takes to light a votive lamp, and I almost died.

She sat up, gasping, and stared at Brand, at the dog lying between them. A leather collar. That – and Brand's strength and speed – were all that had saved her. Brand stared back, breathing heavily.

'What the hell just happened?' he asked finally.

'I didn't build the ward high enough. The dog landed on me. I was winded. Sorry.'

'*Sorry?*' Words failed him.

She groped for her sword with shaking fingers and stood up. The other hounds still milled around outside the ward. 'They'll want to come and sniff their leader's body. Move away, Brand. I'll make two holes in the ward, one for them to come in on this side and one for us to leave on the other.'

This time nothing went wrong, and within minutes she had the leaderless hounds corralled into a tight group against the treasury wall. Some whimpered, others began to howl.

'The howling will bring the guards,' Brand said. He was still pale with shock.

'Head towards the temple steps.'

He grabbed her arm as they ran. 'Ever thought of an alternative career as a gladiator? Or perhaps a job in charge of the Exaltarch's circus lions? It would be safer.' His shock had manifested itself in anger and he didn't bother to hide it.

She ran up the steps past the caryatids into the temple proper without answering, and he followed.

Oil lamps were lit on all the altars and in front of the main statue of Melete at the end of the stoa. She stood still for a moment, cocking her head. 'The attendant is in one of the rooms of the sanctum.' Then, to forestall his next question, added, 'That's the walled area behind the statue, not open to the public. We need to be quiet.'

She headed to the sanctum door behind the main sacrificial altar, but the door was latched on the inside. She knocked.

'*What*—?' Brand remonstrated, *sotto voce*. 'You just told me to be quiet and now you want to go *knocking on the door*? Would you like a horn fanfare as well?'

Ligea drew her sword. 'Close your eyes,' she said.

He looked as if he were about to argue, then thought better of it and not only shut his eyes, but turned his face away.

A male voice from inside asked, 'Who is it?'

Pitching her answer to sound childlike, she said, 'I have a message . . . the Priestess Antonia.'

A youth opened the door, and had to fling up his arms to

protect his eyes from the overwhelming brilliance of a fully lit Magor sword pulsing with power. He staggered back.

She stepped into the sanctum and Brand, following, shut the door behind them. She turned light to pain, a sudden stab to pierce the young acolyte through the stomach.

Vortex, I hate doing that.

While the acolyte was still doubled up, Brand grabbed a robe from a hook and flung it over him so he would not see them.

'Behave yourself,' she said in the youth's ear as she banished his pain, 'or there will be more agony like that. Not a word out of you, understand?' The lad shivered under her grip. When he didn't reply, she shook him. 'Understand?'

He nodded, his fear swamping her. He couldn't have been more than fourteen or so.

Damn it all, I feel like a school bully . . .

She warded him where he stood, enclosing him in walls that were less than a hand span from his body. He wouldn't even be able to raise a hand to take off the enveloping robe. 'If you don't make a sound, the Goddess will release you before dawn's rising,' she said. 'Fear not, for you are favoured by Melete herself.'

Behind her Brand snorted. She grabbed his arm and hauled him through a series of connecting rooms to the back of the sanctum. He was broadcasting his emotions and she knew he wanted it so. She was disconcerted; his turmoil formed a background to all she sensed. Frustrated anger, thwarted desire, deep-rooted distaste for – what? All she was doing? But most of all, an overriding fear. For her. She had almost died, and he couldn't forget it.

'Brand,' she said, quelling her exasperation, 'you have to hide your sentiments. I can't deal with all you are feeling right now. If you can't stop, then I'll go on alone.'

His emotions blanked out, as suddenly as a snuffed lamp. 'I'm sorry,' he said. His face was stony.

No explanation. No excuses. She nodded to indicate her satisfaction with his emotional silence, and changed the subject. 'Last time I was here, I had the mother of all headaches thanks to that

bitch Antonia and her drugs, but I think I remember the way.'
She pointed to a nearby door. 'That's the room where the passage
to the Oracle starts.'

Inside, it was dark, and smelled fusty. She used her sword,
considerably dimmed, instead of a lamp. She closed the door
behind them as they entered, and built a ward across it to keep
it that way. They looked around in silence. The floor was of intri-
cately patterned mosaics. A few cupboards were lined up against
the walls. There was no other visible door. The walls, made of
dressed stone, had a frieze of carved lion heads at waist height.

Brand raised a questioning eyebrow.

'It's the right place,' she said. She swung her sword around to
illuminate her investigation of the corners and the floor.

'Shine it here,' Brand said suddenly, indicating one corner.
'The floor is scraped.' An arc had been scored across the mosaics,
as if an ill-fitted door had been repeatedly opened and closed
across the tiles. Yet there was no door immediately adjacent.
Brand reached out and touched the stones of the wall, then
rubbed his fingers along the line of mortar. 'It's not real! Except
for the frieze,' he said. 'The rest is just painted wood. It must be
a door. No handle, though.'

'Try turning the lion's head,' she suggested.

Brand fumbled at the closest carving in the frieze and, with
an unpleasant grinding sound, part of the wall shifted to reveal
the outline of a door – which then caught on the floor. He yanked
it open, to reveal a stone stairway leading downwards.

A blast of foetid air swept out. Brimstone, mould, musty damp.
The noxious smells of alchemist shops and stagnant bogs. She
quelled a shudder. It brought back too many memories of the
last time she was here.

'Vortexdamn, that stinks,' Brand muttered.

Together, they looked down the long flight of steps into darkness as black as coal tar. Nothing moved. A faint murmur of
sound, muffled and obscure, came out of the blackness.

'Let's go down,' she said.

CHAPTER TWO

Rathrox fumed. He sat in the anteroom to the Exaltarch's audience hall, a picture of cool patience, but that was just an overlay to the inner scowl of his rage. Bator Korbus was keeping him waiting. After all he had done for the man, he was left waiting in the anteroom like a lackey with a petition.

The saying 'Trust no word from the mouth that sits below the crown' had the truth of it, he reflected. *The bastard wasn't always emperor. It's time he remembered that.*

Bator Korbus had once been just another youth in the legionnaires' training camp, along with Rathrox, and a Legate's son, Gayed Lucius. Three youths with little in common, companions simply because they were billeted together. Rathrox had not forgotten one iota of it.

Gayed Lucius had come from a military background, his family following his Legate father on his provincial postings. As a successful officer's offspring, Gayed had been both moderately prosperous and well used to a military life.

Bator Korbus, on the other hand, had been much wealthier than a mere Legate's son. His grandfather had been a senator. His was a highborn political family, and the wiliness of a political animal was in his blood. However, Bator had an older brother destined for a political career, so he was packed off to the legions. Bator and Gayed had forged a close friendship from the very beginning. Bator needed someone to help him acquire the arts and knowledge of a military man; Gayed had grown up in the provinces and needed someone to impart to him the polish and the knowledge of a young man of Tyr. Where Rathrox Ligatan fitted in was less obvious.

Rathrox was the son of a farm controller. As a child, he'd discovered how easy it was to manipulate the farm slaves; all he had to do was threaten to make trouble for them with his father. Before he was ten years old, he was glorying in the power he had over people who could not retaliate.

His five older brothers, however, had been the bane of his life. Although unimaginative in their teasing and taunting, they could still make life a misery for their scrawny, undersized brother. In self-defence, Rathrox learned other strategies. Knowledge, he realised, was the source of true power. With knowledge you could preempt, or blackmail. With knowledge, you could earn yourself respect. With knowledge, you became a thing of value.

By the time he was sixteen, he'd become an indispensable part of the farm management and dreamed of becoming somebody to be reckoned with in the wider world. A farm, no matter how large and prosperous, was not sufficient arena, not even when he was in charge of the delivery and sale of farm produce to the markets of Tyr and had numerous contacts in the capital. Not even when he was beginning to develop a network of informants.

Then a disaster undermined his future. A scheme of his to humiliate one of his brothers turned sour, and the youth – just eighteen – died. His father, enraged, discovered Rathrox had been the instigator of the stupid stunt his brother had tried to perform, and he was sent to the military officers' training camp.

Rathrox looked on it as an opportunity rather than a disgrace, but it wasn't easy at first. He was patently not military material. He lacked the physical stature and the coordination. He had no interest in the physical feats of other recruits. What he did have by then was considerable knowledge of his fellow men and how to manipulate them. Gayed Lucius and Bator Korbus soon discovered that if you needed anything, from a clean woman on your cot to a small luxury, Rathrox was the man to supply it. A little later, they realised that the information Rathrox could offer them was far more valuable than the commodities he procured. Still later, they realised his true worth when they saw Rathrox Ligatan could actually *make* things happen.

After the first all-too-convenient death that benefited them, the three young men were linked together for life.

As soon as he was able to do so legally, Rathrox left the army and became Bator Korbus's scribe, a euphemism for the work he actually did, which varied over the years from spying to assassination to information gathering. Bator's steep rise through the ranks to General, closely followed by that of Gayed Lucius, was just as much due to Rathrox's machinations to ensure the presence of the two men in the right place at the right time, as it was to Bator's and Lucius's skills on the battlefield.

Until the invasion of Kardiastan. Conniving to have his two friends in charge of the invasion was the first major error of judgement Rathrox ever made, and it was a huge one. The invasion was a monumental failure, and the shoulders burdened with the shame of that defeat were those of Bator and Gayed. The careers of both might have ended there, in Kardiastan, if Rathrox had not arranged the kidnapping of the daughter of Miragersolad, and used her as a lever to force her father into betrayal.

Kardiastan had never again threatened the might of Tyrans; the land had been brutally subjugated, its elite slaughtered, its youth sold into slavery. Bator Korbus had usurped the credit for Solad's act of betrayal, even though he'd been back in Tyr by then. Eventually, he'd overthrown the Exaltarch and taken his place.

And the child they named Ligea was raised by Gayed Lucius to become a compeer of the Brotherhood, an agent of Tyrans, and the spare sword in the belt of the Exaltarch, ready to be used against the nation of her birth.

Sitting there waiting to be called into the Exaltarch's presence, Rathrox remembered.

If not for me, you would never have become the Exaltarch, Bator.
And fumed.

Yet now you keep me waiting. Your head grows too big for the

*wreath crowning your brow. Have a care, Bator. I put you there
and I can bring you down if it is in my interest to do so ...*

'Magister?'

His thoughts interrupted, he looked up, but it wasn't his expected
call into the Exaltarch's presence. Instead, the High Priestess of the
Cult of Melete had entered from the main hall. Dressed, as usual,
in white, and wearing that preposterous piece of jewellery that was
the symbol of her rank around her neck, she looked like a cross
between a brothel madam and an older version of Melete herself.

He rose to his feet. 'Reverence.' He inclined his head in respect
of her office. He may have commanded the Brotherhood and
the Exaltarch's civil service, but he didn't deliberately upset
Antonia unless he had good reason. She possessed a nasty tongue,
a long memory and many followers. 'The Exaltarch has asked
for your presence too?'

'Apparently. I suspect it has to do with the annual prophecy
for the city. That is a mere three weeks away, and I need time
to write the poetry and prepare Esme.'

He swallowed a smile. He wouldn't have called her verse
'poetry', himself. 'Ah, yes, of course.'

She seated herself complacently, confident that the summons
was routine.

He said, 'When I saw you, I wondered if it might concern the
trouble at your temple last night.'

She gave a quick frown. 'Hardly serious enough to involve the
Exaltarch, Magister. I don't know what you heard, but a dead
dog killed by lightning and an acolyte who breathed in too many
orlyx fumes is all there was to it, with no connection between
the two.' Her hand moved up to play nervously with her pendant.

Rathrox watched. *She's uneasy about it, though. I wonder why.
I don't remember a storm; she's lying. Hiding something. I shall
send someone to investigate further.*

'You know, there's something I don't understand,' he added, after
the silence threatened to become embarrassing and he had decided
it might be worthwhile annoying her after all. She could be indiscreet, and therefore informative, when she was irritated. 'You told

me once that there is a cave behind the face of the Oracle. Why did the Cult of Melete ever start to use a young priestess to translate the muttering in the first place? One of your number could have hidden in the cave and pretended that Melete spoke Tyranian!'

She glanced at the Imperial Guards on duty to make sure they could not hear, then said in furious protest, 'The gods once truly spoke to the Selected! You have only to read the past histories to know that. Then – then they stopped speaking to us, but we continued the tradition of having a Selected. One day Melete at least will return, if not the others; I know it. And we will be ready.'

He stared, wondering at her naivety. 'Antonia, today's histories will record Esme's words as true, just as past scribes recorded the supposed words of their Selected of the Oracle as the true words of Melete.'

Her expression pinched with anger. 'You mock the Goddess, Magister.'

No, Antonia, not the Goddess. Just you.

How could a woman, who happily connived with the Exaltarch to deceive the public, be so silly? He wouldn't mind betting the first High Priestess who started this whole Oracle deception had known exactly what she was doing. Probably thought using a Selected of the Oracle meant more visible power for the temple priestesses.

Fortunately, he was saved from answering Antonia's accusation by the summons for them both to enter the audience room.

The Exaltarch was looking at an amulet when they entered, turning it over and over in his hands. 'Lovely piece of work,' he said by way of greeting, 'if somewhat large. The King of Akowarn sent it for me to wear on my biceps. I think he is trying to pay me a compliment.' He held it up to show the size. 'He is suggesting I marry his eldest daughter.'

'Doesn't he know you are already married, Exalted?' Antonia asked.

'Perhaps he expects me to divorce. And he is offering a very attractive dowry, too. I think I shall accept.'

'The Fasii will not be happy,' Rathrox murmured, referring to the family of Bator's third and present wife, Eriana.

'Oh, I shan't *marry* the girl. Just bring her here, procure the dowry and fob her off repeatedly with one excuse or another. After all, what's the King going to do? Attack Tyr? Stop paying his vassal taxes? He'd never dare! But this is not what I brought you here to discuss. Rathrox, I want to know what you have heard from the Gayed woman about her progress in Kardiastan.'

'The last message I received said she was about to leave Madrinya for the Mirage. She intends to bring down the rebel movement from within.' He felt a moment's smug pride. 'I knew she'd do it. She'll be the Mirager yet.'

Bator put the amulet down and seated himself, indicating they should do likewise. 'Do you mean to tell me she's lost contact with our authorities there?'

'Well, yes, for the time being. But by now she will have identified the rebel leader and found a way to enter the heart of their hiding place.'

'And you are sure she won't be seduced back to their way of life? They must know she is one of them by now; she has that jewel set in her palm.' He frowned, the harsh lines of his face settling down into petulant creases. 'I always said we ought to have had it cut out of her while she was still a toddling babe.'

'And I told you Solad said removing the jewel kills the person. The one time we did it, as an experiment with another child, that's exactly what happened. Yes, they will know she is one of them, obviously, as soon as they spot it. And I suspect they have welcomed her with open arms because of it. There are few enough of them left, thanks to us and Solad's treachery. There's no reason they should guess she's Solad's daughter, any more than she will ever find out unless we tell her. And no, she won't betray us.'

He smiled, enjoying the acumen of his own past planning. 'Exalted, why else did we wait so long, but to make sure of that? She loves her country and serves her Exaltarch. She revels in her life in Tyr and the things her wealth buys her. She hated going to Kardiastan, and she can't wait to come back. And she's in love with a Stalwart tribune who's fighting his way into the Mirage even as we speak.'

'She still honours her adoptive father,' Antonia added. 'I often saw her praying at his tomb.'

Rathrox nodded. 'It was the perfect moment to send her to wreak havoc on the country of her birth; couldn't have been better. A little younger and she may well have been more interested in finding out who she was. Now she just wants to be with the tribune and get them both back to Tyr, covered in glory.'

'Then my idea of having the Oracle speak to her was a good one,' the Exaltarch said, nodding in satisfaction. 'Any woman would be flattered at being singled out for attention by the Meletian Oracle of Tyr, even one as hardened as she is.'

Rathrox had his doubts whether the promises of wealth and adulation, made by the Oracle at Bator's instigation, had meant much to Ligea, but he wasn't about to argue the point. 'Of course. Nothing less than brilliant.' Perhaps that sounded sardonic. Hurriedly, he added without – he hoped – any hint of sarcasm, 'It gave her even more to come home for.'

'The moment you hear from her again, bring me word. I am anxious about the Stalwarts. If she is in the Mirage, perhaps she will be able to send word of them. If she has learned the secret of crossing those strange sands – what was the name of them again? The Shiver Barrens? – then she should be able to send a message out.'

'Of course, Exalted.'

'And now there is this matter of the annual prophecy.' He picked up a scroll from a side table and handed it to Antonia. 'Here are the details. I would like the Oracle to speak of the need for young men to join the legions and for the wealthy to donate money to our coffers in order for us to defeat the sorcerers and numina of Kardiastan. I expect the trademaster to be admonished because our shipbuilders have insufficient wood. I expect the Imperial Historian to be urged to write a history of my military successes. I expect the Prefect Urbis to be encouraged to supply more tax money in the coming year. I expect the Assorian moneymaster to be told non-citizens should show their gratitude more . . .'

CHAPTER THREE

Arcadim Asenius fingered the note he had hidden in the sleeve of his robe. Just two lines, unsigned, neatly lettered, on a small piece of papyrus delivered earlier to his counting house.

Come and see me tonight. Don't tell anyone I am back in Tyr.

A handful of words, but enough to make his stomach churn. The lettering was Ligea Gayed's, and when a rich patron of the Asenius Counting House requested your presence, you obliged. So he was now sitting in a curtained litter being borne through the streets on his way to the Villa Gayed.

I should have turned down the opportunity to manage Ligea's affairs, right at the beginning. It is against the Great God's order for a woman to behave as she does...

And yet he liked her.

He wondered at himself. How could he, an Assorian money-master, enjoy the company of a Tyranian woman who was the antithesis of all he thought a woman should be? She was immodest. She behaved like a man. She wasn't even that attractive, although she ... He hunted for the right word. She *fascinated*, that was it. She fascinated.

You silly old fool. She fascinates the way a snake fascinates its prey.

The litter lurched and swayed. He grimaced in exasperation and clutched at the sides. They must be approaching the necropolis and the fools of litter bearers had started to run, fear lending them the energy. *Idolaters.* If only everyone believed in the One True God, the world would be a less *fearful* place.

The pace slowed as they mounted the steps up the hill, and then turned into Senators' Row. An anachronism, that name. There were no more senators in Tyrans, not since the first Exaltarch had seized power almost fifty years before. There was no Advisory Council now, either. The present Exaltarch, Bator Korbus, had done away with them too. Arcadim tried to push that thought away. It was all part of a recurring nightmare for an Assorian: when one man gathered all the strands of power into his hands, he looked for scapegoats if things went wrong and who better to blame than people who were both foreign and rich?

There was no torch burning outside the Villa Gayed. The linkman, holding his own brand high, pounded at the door in the gate. Arcadim clambered out. His shaved head felt cold in the cool of the evening air and he coughed as he breathed in the smoke from the burning pitch. 'Wait for me,' he told the men, 'no matter how late I am.'

The slave who answered the door was expecting him. She washed his feet in the entry hall and just as she was patting them dry with a towel, Ligea appeared. He rose to greet her, started to smile – then saw her face. Shock choked his throat. His welcome died unspoken, his inner thoughts emerging as a more chaotic *God of my fathers, what has happened to her?* Not even six months since he'd last seen her, and she was now rake-thin, her face gaunt and – *gouged.* A deep, puckered crater scarred her cheek as though flesh had been ripped out and thrown away. And what in all of God's Elysium had she done to her hair? It was usually gold-streaked, falling in curls from a clasp high on her head. Now it was plain brown, roughly cut short, as straight and lustre-less as hemp fibre. Hades, his own beard, curled and perfumed and threaded with pearls, was more attractive.

He was appalled. If he'd passed her in the street he would never have recognised her.

'Welcome, Master Arcadim,' she said.

He licked dry lips and wondered what to say to a woman who must have been to Hades and back since they'd last met. He settled finally on a neutral, 'Welcome back to Tyr, Domina. I am sorry to see you have had some, er, trouble in Kardiastan.'

She raised her hand to her cheek. 'This? Yes, I am afraid so.' She shrugged and led him into one of the inner rooms, where yet another shock awaited him. Her Altani slave was lounging on a divan, a goblet of wine in one hand, very much at home. He rose as Arcadim entered, but the casual movement spoke of the superficial manners between equals, not the obsequiousness of a slave or even the deference of a lowborn citizen. His slave collar was gone and, even more puzzling, one of his arms appeared to have been withered.

Ligea said, 'You know Brand of Altan, I believe?'

Arcadim floundered. What the Hades was she doing, expecting a guest to greet a slave, or even an ex-slave, as an equal? 'Not officially, no,' he said, 'although he has delivered your messages to my counting house on occasion.' He bowed low to display the tattoo on his shaved pate – the all-seeing eye of God – in ritual greeting, then addressed his next remark to the Altani. 'As a member of a family who made their initial wealth gathering salt and soda from dry lakebeds, I'm always glad to see people come up in the world.' *There. Let them make of that what they will.*

The Altani grinned at him. 'But as Ligea's man of affairs, you are as suspicious as a pinch of that salt about to be dropped into boiling water.'

Arcadim betrayed his surprise at the audacity of the reply by being just a shade too slow to answer. 'Something like that, yes,' he said as they sat. But he couldn't relax. This was all *wrong*. His business acumen, gathered over a lifetime of deals and haggling, jangled its warning. The Altani was neither timid nor embarrassed. *Don't take him lightly*, the warning said, *there's nothing withered about this man's wits.*

'Master Arcadim,' Ligea said, 'thank you for coming. I asked you here this evening because there is going to be a major change in the way we interact, if you wish to continue as my money-master. We have much to discuss.'

Thoroughly alarmed, he replied, 'I hope I have not given offence, Domina, that you would consider changing your man of business.' He indicated the scrolls he carried. 'I have here the accounts of all that has taken place in your absence. I am sure you will find them in order.'

'I am sure of that, too,' she agreed, waving away the scrolls. 'Leave them on the table and I will go through them after you have left. Right now, I have a question. Do you regard the business done on behalf of a patron such as myself privileged?'

'Of course.' His alarm was clanging so noisily inside his head it could have been a port bell rung to signal the approach of an invasion fleet. 'Assorian banking families have attained our present position in the Exaltarchy because we are trusted. To be worthy of that trust, we maintain the strictest confidentiality.'

'What if those who represent the Exaltarch were to ask you to divulge information?'

Arcadim liked to think of himself as being in the prime of life, his swollen joints notwithstanding, but when she asked that question, he felt suddenly aged. Far too old to be worrying about treason. He hedged. 'What – what kind of information do you mean, Domina?'

'Where one of your patrons is hiding his money. Where the person concerned hides himself.'

His confidence slipped still further. 'As far as I know, none of my patrons is in hiding.'

'Ah, but perhaps you don't know that one of them is guilty of rebellion.'

He paled, desperately rummaging through his thoughts trying to identify which one of his patrons had been so incredibly stupid – and so fiendishly clever that Arcadim had not had an inkling of what they were doing. He took a deep breath and settled for far more disclosure than was comfortable. 'Compeer,' he said, giving her the Brotherhood title to indicate that he knew she must be questioning him in that capacity, 'don't ask it of me. I cannot disclose such information, not even if you were the Magister Officii himself.' His guts roiled and he had desperate need of a lavatory. Damn it, why did his bowels always let him down when he was stressed?

'You would hide the treason of one of those who use your services?' she asked, relentless.

'I know of no such treason. If one of my patrons has been so, um, *indiscreet*, he failed to inform me of it.'

'Treason is a little more than indiscretion, Arcadim. Had you known, would you have told?'

'I would refuse to manage the affairs of a traitor.'

'And the knowledge you had of his affairs?'

'Confidentiality is our creed, Domina. How can I deny the creed we live by? We would not knowingly channel money in our control to treasonous activities. But Assorian bankers, or moneymasters as you call us here in Tyr, do not divulge confidential information. Normally we are not asked for it. The Magister Officii, indeed the Exaltarch himself, is aware of this. After all, neither of them would be happy if his own moneymaster were to leak details of *his* financial dealings.'

'You know the Brotherhood has ways of encouraging people to tell the truth.'

He felt faint. 'In this case, I don't think they would learn anything to their advantage, Compeer. I don't even know to which one of my patrons you are referring.'

'Myself, Master Arcadim. Myself.'

He stared at her, eyes wide with shock, heart thundering in his chest. 'Is – is this some kind of test?'

'No, far from it. I want you to sell all my property, including this house, and convert it into gold and silver or pearls before my assets are seized. You must do this with a minimum of fuss. The longer it takes the Magister Officii to hear what I am doing, the better. And he is not to know I am back in Tyr.'

Arcadim's eyes grew wider. *I don't think I want to listen to this. I'm sure I don't want to listen to this.* His panic broke out in the form of a line of sweat along his shaven upper lip. 'Domina, I – I am sorry, but in that case I would like to resign as your moneymaster.'

'You disappoint me, Arcadim.'

He tried to keep a grip on his panic, to hold it in, but it was as elusive as a handful of coins escaping his fingers. Desperate, he said, 'If you do this, and there is a suspicion I might have knowingly aided you, my monies will be forfeit, and my life and that of my family likewise.' To his horror, he felt tears form at the corner of his eyes. He plunged on. 'Domina, I am not a man of action. I am a fifty-year-old banker who is at home only in his counting house. My joints bother me in damp weather. My wife nags me to find pious and thrifty wives for my sons. My sons nag me to find pretty women who will not nag to be their wives. My daughters nag me for handsome husbands who will not beat them. My slaves steal from me and gossip about me behind my back. Those are all the problems I need. I don't want to die of fever in the Cages!' He resisted the temptation to wipe his face with the sleeve of his robe. Confound the woman; to think he used to like her!

'Arcadim, Arcadim, do you know why I left my money in your hands all these years? Because you were willing to take carefully considered risks. I want you to take another.' She smiled at him, but on that scarred face, a smile was terrifying. 'At the moment, every Assorian moneymaster has his coins in the same purse, and the purse is that of Bator Korbus's Exaltarchy. Your position here can be as uncertain as the Exaltarch's digestion.'

She poured wine from the carafe in front of her into a pewter goblet, handed it to him and then refilled the Altani's. 'Look around you, Arcadim. There are already the rumblings of rebellion in Kardiastan and Quyr and Altan. Soon there will be rebellion right here, in Tyrans. Where will Assorian money-masters be if that rebellion were to succeed? You need one of your number who deals with the rebels to tell you what is happening. Imagine if such information enabled Assoria to shrug off the shackles of vassalage!'

Arcadim was out of his depth, unable to find footing. His heart spiralled down, spinning out of control as panic spilled from the last vestiges of his hold.

He put his goblet, untouched, down on the low table in front of him. Wine slopped and he barely noticed. 'Domina, I think it's best you seek another moneymaster.'

He went to stand, but she leaned forward slightly, holding her hand out, palm upwards. There was a gemstone there, as yellow as a citrine. He thought she wanted him to look at it, but when he reached out to pick it up, he realised it was set into her skin. Even as he watched, it started to glow and with it, her whole skin took on a golden sheen.

Panic leaped into terror, a gut reaction to something he could not understand.

'Watch, Arcadim.' She held her open hand over his goblet. Light sprang out of her palm, hit the goblet *and the pewter melted*. The goblet collapsed into a misshapen mound in a pool of wine that hissed and steamed where it came into contact with the metal. She said softly, 'I can kill with this.' The Altani still lounged on his divan, picking at a bunch of late-season grapes.

Arcadim sat dumbly, staring at what was left of the drinking vessel. 'Are you – are you threatening me, Domina?'

'No, Master Arcadim,' she said, and he thought he detected a wisp of sadness in her reply. 'Gods, no. I am trying to show you the power available to the rebels.' She crossed to a side table and returned with a sword, the short blade of which looked as if it were made of frosted glass rather than metal. 'Arcadim, my friend, of all the statues in this room, which would you find hardest to sell?'

He pointed at one without hesitation. 'That one. It's a poor copy of the Pelotonius discus thrower at the stadium. And it's poorly painted, too.'

'I kept it for sentimental reasons, because General Gayed liked it. But that's a sentiment that has lived past its time.' Casually she raised the sword and it began to glow, with the same strange golden light that still brushed her skin with colour. When the tip of the blade pointed towards the marble statue, a beam of light joined the sword and the head of the discus thrower like a ray of sunlight. And the head exploded. Marble chips scattered across the floor in a circle of debris, some of them skidding as far as Arcadim's feet. Marble dust hung in the air; they all coughed. Wordlessly, Brand rose, fetched another goblet and poured some more wine for Arcadim. The moneymaster gulped it gratefully.

'Arcadim,' Ligea said, her tone deceptively soft, 'I have power that you can't even dream about. I could walk into Bator Korbus' palace right now, and assassinate him in his own bedroom.'

'Is that what you are going to do?' he asked, meeting her gaze. 'Assassinate the Exaltarch?' His fingers gripped one of his strings of beard pearls. He silently recited the family genealogy it represented, anything to give an appearance of calm. It didn't help.

Almighty God, he thought, and it was a prayer, not a blasphemy, *help me. Show me she is not something beyond the beliefs of my fathers. That she is not something I am not permitted to believe in . . .*

'No,' she said. 'There is more to a successful rebellion than killing one's predecessor, as well you know. If he were to die now, there would be another scrambling to step into his sandals. Like Devros of the Lucii. Or Laurentius, the Prefect Urbis. There could be chaos and a civil war as highborn families fought over the Exaltarch's seat for one of their own. The barbarians at our borders would take advantage of the confusion to sack our cities. Bator will die, yes, but in our time, when we are ready to replace him with a stable government.' She leaned back. 'So, Arcadim, will you continue to be my moneymaster and help me lead the Exaltarchy to a more gracious future?'

He swallowed and seized on the one word that struck him as the most incongruous. 'Gracious?'

She said softly, 'I am sure you have read the philosophies. Didn't Cassenes the Wise say that the best government is one that rules graciously? By which he meant a council or senate or ruler who bestows on all under their power, not the force of legions, not the strength of the sword, nor even the disinterest of the Law, but the grace of their equality as men.'

His thoughts seethed, and out of their tangle he pulled the

one that bothered him most. 'Are you a goddess? Or an immortal?' *Please don't tell me that all I have ever believed in is a lie.*

'That is something you will have to decide yourself, Arcadim. Give me your decision tomorrow. If you wish to continue as my moneymaster, bring all the papers I must sign for you to sell all my property and I will give you the details of what I want done. I will want you to make certain purchases, and to set in place a method by which we can communicate in secret.'

'You – you would trust me not to betray you?' By this time he didn't care that they both noticed the way his hands shook.

'Ah, Arcadim, your terror and your disbelief and your distress leak into the air around you like wine from a cracked jar, but I see no intention to betray. There is nothing you can hide from me.'

Words came unbidden to his mind: *And there is nothing thou canst hide from the One True God . . .* He stood up and sweat trickled down his neck to soak his robe. Eternal truths, that's what he needed. *There are no such things as goddesses. The whole pantheon of Tyrans is the heresy of idolaters.* Aloud he said, 'Very well.'

She nodded as she stood and gestured for him to precede her to the door. She didn't speak again until they stood together in the entry hall. 'Arcadim, I wish – I wish I had the time to sit with you and persuade you to my way of thinking with words. I do want your choice to be free of fear. You have my word: I will not harm you in any way if you ask me to take my business elsewhere.'

'And if I dare to tell the Magister Officii all that you have said here this evening?' No sooner had the words escaped his mouth than he wished to take them back. Was he *mad* that he bandied words with a – a what? Some kind of supernatural being? *But the Holy Writ says: 'There are no gods but Me . . .'*

She smiled. 'Even then. There will be enough deaths to lay at my door without yours being one of them. Arcadim, if you do not support me in this, there will come a day when you will rue your short-sightedness simply because of the lost opportunity. The grace of equality, Arcadim. Think about it.'

The slave woman came into the hall to fasten his sandals for him. He sat on the entry stool, wishing she would hurry. He wanted to leave as fast as he could. As he sat there, he glimpsed the Altani in the room they had just left, sweeping up the marble chips. A freed slave. He glanced at the woman kneeling at his feet. And noted only then that she, too, did not wear a slave collar.

Ligea smiled at him. 'Yes,' she said. 'That's right.' She touched the woman on the shoulder. 'Leave us, Dini, please,' she said. When the woman had gone, she knelt at Arcadim's feet and tied the remaining sandal herself.

Arcadim sat where he was, staring at her, trying to absorb the enormity of the idea that was flooding his senses. 'Almighty God,' he said at last. 'You want to end slavery.'

She nodded.

'Have you *any idea* of what that will do to Tyrans? To our wealth? To our agriculture?'

'Not really. That's one of the reasons why I need you. But equality means more than just the end of slavery.'

'The vassal states,' he whispered.

They stared at one another for a long minute as she continued to kneel there, her task finished, in the position of a supplicant. Yet there was nothing demeaning in her posture, and he knew she did not consider herself to be humbled. His breath caught in the back of his throat. She knows the Assorian love of symbolic gestures, he thought. Oh God, she is a dangerous woman. She has played me like the strings of the lute. This whole conversation . . . She is a compeer of the Brotherhood. She had access to everything the Brotherhood ever knew about Assorians. What a fool I have been.

Almost in echo to his thought, she said softly, 'When Tyrans invaded Assoria, your youngest brother was one of those who resisted. He was eighteen, a handsome, hot-headed lad. He was taken alive and sold as a slave, you found out that much. But a slave loses his name when he is enslaved, and is given another of the slaver's choosing. So those who try to trace him through the records can never find out what happened . . .'

'His name was Athenqual,' he whispered. 'His Assorian name. We were told to mourn him, as if he really had died. We didn't have a body to offer to the sacred crocodiles, so instead we burned his clothes and threw the ashes into the sacred river. His name was written into the Book of the Sundered at the Temple.' He raised his eyes to meet hers. 'I don't know what *you* are. But I do know what slavery does to an Assorian enslaved to one outside his faith. It's the expunction of a living man. His elimination from records. His separation from the Law. His sundering from God.' He drew himself up, squared his shoulders. 'I don't know who you represent, but if what you do will free my country from its vassalage to the Exaltarch, or even just free Assorian slaves from non-believers, I will be your moneymaster.'

She stood up too, serious. 'I will do my best to see that you profit by this. And likewise with every other Assorian moneymaster you bring to our side as time goes by.'

But that was going too fast for Arcadim. 'Domina, there is no way Assorian moneymasters will support you if you threaten to outlaw slavery in Assoria. Slavery is part of our culture, our history, our religion. The Great God Himself endorses slavery as a reminder to us of how easily all we own can be taken from us. So that we remember that God alone stands as our salvation.'

'I assure you, when a vassal state is free from Tyr's rule, it will choose its own path. Its own laws. We have no plans to impose a different set of rules on another empire in place of this one! We merely want to dismantle this Exaltarchy and deal with a single piece: Tyrans.'

He hoped she would take his quick intake of breath as admiration, and not the gasp of disbelief that it was. He stood and bowed to show his tattoo. 'I will bid you goodnight, Domina Ligea. I shall return tomorrow evening with the papers for your signature. I believe the Exaltarch's trade adviser will be more than interested in buying this villa. He's been after it for years . . .'

CHAPTER FOUR

Ligea stood still for a moment as the door closed behind Arcadim. She was worried and felt physically ill. *How can I do this? I am only one person and I want to bring down an empire?* She sighed and walked back to where Brand was leaning on his broom.

'Well, who'd have thought it,' he said softly. 'The way to the man's heart was to promise the end of slavery – this from an Assorian with one of the largest number of slaves in the whole commercial quarter. Ocrastes' balls, the man even has a slave whose sole job is to pat his cat!'

Ligea nodded thoughtfully. 'Let me guess. They're all Assorians.'

'Yes, that's right. They are.' He shot her a sharp look. 'You're saying, what, he buys them to *save* them?'

She smiled.

He shook his head at his own obtuseness. 'Vortexdamn, you had that all planned. You knew he would cave in over the slavery issue. All the other was just the pounding of the steak to tenderise the meat!'

'I had the Brotherhood check out his personal history before I employed him.'

'And you knew he doesn't hold with slavery?'

'On the contrary. He wouldn't know what to do without his slaves! The Assorian economy runs on slavery just as much as Tyrans' does. However, the worst thing that could happen to an Assorian would be enslavement by someone who does not follow the One True God. The slave would then be unable to fulfil the daily requirements of his faith, you see, and would therefore be cut off from God in the afterlife. *That's* what is at the heart of Arcadim's hatred of the slave trade – the idea that Assorians can be owned by non-believers. His brother's name was expunged from the family records because he could no longer be considered an adherent of the faith. That's why Arcadim buys so many Assorian slaves: to save them from Hades and give them a chance at eternal life in Elysium.'

He was startled at the notion. 'Elysium? Along with all the gods and goddesses of the Tyranian pantheon?'

She laughed. 'No. You are missing the point. Assorians don't believe any of our deities exist. In their eyes, Elysium is occupied only by their One God – and all his deceased followers who have lived according to the rules of their faith. The rest go to Hades, along with the rest of us heathens once the Vortex of Death has done with us. Not, by the way, to be confused with our idea of the seven layers of Acheron. Hades is a *much* darker place.'

'Ah. A vengeful deity, indeed. Punishes you for something you have no say in, like being enslaved by a non-believer.'

'Worshipping Melete is much easier. But not as cheery in the end, perhaps. Elysium sounds like a better place to live through eternity than Acheron.'

'Boring, I imagine.'

'Perhaps. Were you joking about the slave for the cat?'

'No. But that's not as bad as that magistrate friend of yours, Pereus. He has a slave whose sole job is to make sure that no bird sings in his garden before he rises in the morning.'

She snorted. 'Difficult job, I imagine.' She tilted her head, considering. 'You must know a great deal about the households you've visited with me over the years.'

'What's a slave to do except chat to the kitchen maids when his mistress is occupied elsewhere?'

She stifled a sigh. Would Brand ever stop needling her about her past as a slave owner? She managed a cool, 'What indeed?'

He changed the subject. 'Did Arcadim realise you were expecting a baby, do you think?'

'No. What man ever notices things like that? If you were to ask him about me, he would say I looked appallingly thin.' She touched the swell below her waist. 'It's not that noticeable yet.'

'I trust the babe isn't affected by all this use of Magor power?'

She froze. Had he guessed she was worried sick? She said, 'I did ask Temellin about that. He said Magor women use their power as usual throughout pregnancy.' *But it's not usual to become an essensa, or to plunge into the Ravage. Oh, little one, stay with me . . .*

He looked sceptical, so she changed the subject. 'Tomorrow, I'll ask Arcadim to arrange for your back wages to be paid. A transfer of funds to Altan would be best, I think. Then you can be on your way. Before you leave for Altan, though, I want to pick your brains on everything you know about slaves and the houses you've been to, and the slave trade.'

'Fine. I'm not leaving for a while, anyway.'

She had been about to say something concerning booking a berth for him on a vessel to Altan, but that made her frown and say instead, 'Ah – um, I thought it was settled. You would collect what is owed you, and then go home, a free man. To raise a rebellion, or brats, or goats, or whatever.' She didn't say what was in her heart, aching to be said: *And I will miss you, dear friend.* He had been her slave, her companion, and finally – so briefly – her lover. The idea that he was going to walk out of her life, that she would never see him again, might not have had the tragedy of a death, but it had much of the pain.

'It *is* settled,' he agreed. 'It's just the timing that's wrong. I will go after the baby is born, when he is one month old, and not before.'

She sprawled on the divan and watched him while he resumed cleaning up the marble chips and dust on the floor. 'You're of the opinion that you will be of estimable help in the birthing process? How many babies have you delivered, my Altani friend?'

'One has to start somewhere.'

She laid her hand over her womb. Arrant. Her son. He might be born twisted or deformed, or worse still, not born at all . . .

Brand, noting her abstraction, paused in his sweeping. 'You think about Pinar's son sometimes, don't you?'

Pinar. Remembering, she had to swallow back bile. Her cousin, Temellin's *wife.* Twisted by jealousy and increasingly irrational, Pinar had suffered no compunction about seeking Ligea's death. As a consequence, Ligea felt no remorse at the way Pinar had died. But the child the woman had been carrying?

'He haunts me,' she admitted. 'He accuses me in my dreams. Accuses me of turning him into a monster by giving him to the Mirage Makers. In my waking hours my guilty conscience is easy enough to disregard, but at night? It takes on a life of its own to control my dreams, the bitch that it is.' She paused, then added, 'When he is grown, I hope I can go back and . . . speak to him somehow. Find out if he thinks I did the right thing. Stupid, I suppose. How would I change anything if he told me what I had done to him was unconscionable?'

She shrugged to hide the unease that gnawed at her peace of mind, failed, and turned back to more immediate matters instead. 'So, why are you so keen to stay here longer? We agreed it was best for you to go home to Altan.' She could have added, 'To build a life for yourself separately. So that you can forget your love for me,' but she left those words unspoken and said instead, 'It will be increasingly dangerous for you here, and you do not have Magor power to keep you safe. I can pay to have a midwife when my time comes. I do not need you.'

And it's just as well you cannot read lies, my friend, for that is a huge one. I need you more than I could ever say, but I have no right to ask more of you. I have stolen eighteen years from you already . . .

'I may not know much about birthing a child, but I am quite sure that every woman needs a friend at such a time. Besides, Temellin asked me to stay.'

'I don't believe it. The man is jealous of you! He reeks of it. He would *never* ask such a thing.'

THE SHADOW OF TYR   41

Brand raised an amused eyebrow in her direction. 'And am I in the habit of lying to you?' he drawled, using the broom again.

He wasn't, of course. She knew a lie as easily as most people recognised a smile. She pulled an exasperated face in his direction. 'All right, all right. So he asked you to stay. This was while we were in Ordensa, I assume? And knowing Temellin, he probably also told you that if you let your thoughts as much as stray in the direction of my bedroom, he'd see you sold back into slavery quicker than you could blink an eye.'

He grinned at her. 'Not exactly. It was more along the lines of using his Magor sword for some surgical rearrangement of my body parts. As usual, he had a persuasive way with words.'

'Persuade *you* of anything? Huh! Temellin's threats have nothing to do with why you haven't climbed back onto my pallet since the Ravage attacked me.'

He stopped his sweeping to answer, serious now. 'No. It had everything to do with the way you two looked at each other when he came to help you. After he saw what the Ravage had done to your face.'

For a moment they were silent, sharing memories, and pain. It was true. She hadn't wanted Brand after that. It hadn't seemed . . . right. Not to either of them. 'I'm sorry,' she whispered. 'But that's all the more reason you should leave. Why take any notice of Temellin? You don't even like him!'

'Not in the least,' he agreed. 'He's an arrogant, highborn Magor bastard. He had no cause to treat you the way he did. He should have believed in you. Even with all his enhanced senses, he couldn't see what you really are. He couldn't see the hell you went through, thinking you would be the one to die, not Pinar.'

But you saw. The man who had no reason to trust the bitch who'd kept him enslaved had continued to have faith in her, believing that one day she would be the woman he thought she could be.

Aloud she repeated her apology, 'I'm sorry.' *Sorry for not loving you the way you love me.*

He made a dismissive gesture, as if it didn't matter, when they both knew it did.

'You haven't answered my question. Why stay?' she asked.

'Temellin had the truth of it. A woman about to have a baby needs someone with her who loves her. It's as simple as that. And Temellin loves you enough to make sure there is someone, even though that person is a man who made him jealous – who, indeed, gave him reason to *be* jealous.' His smug self-satisfaction wafted in her direction. 'Make up your mind to it, Ligea, I'm not going anywhere until after the brat is born.'

She opened her mouth to protest, and then closed it again, aware of the overwhelming relief she felt at the thought of him being there.

He grinned again and patted her hand. 'Nice to have a man to rely on, isn't it?'

'Oh, shut up,' she said and snatched her hand away.

'Say something intelligent, then. About what we do next.'

'Men!' she grumbled. 'One of you is bad enough, but put the two of you together and you think you rule me. Well, you don't.' She took a deep breath. 'Next? Next I want some slaves to think about escape. Not just any slaves, but a few special men you can help me identify. After that, I am going to do what I believe Bator Korbus did to me: I am going to make cynical use of the Oracle and its prophecies.' She swallowed. 'Vortexhells, Brand, there is so little time before Favonius returns with his tales of what I did to the Stalwarts – after which Rathrox will scour the whole of Tyrans looking for me if he suspects I have returned. I don't know how I can do all this in a couple of weeks. Three at the most.'

She felt panic flutter in her chest. *How could I have ever thought I can bring down an empire?*

CHAPTER FIVE

Brand sat back in his chair at Ligea's desk and read through the list of names he had just scratched into a wax tablet. The sigh he gave when he reached the end originated from a deep-felt worry.

'Vortexdamn, Ligea,' he said softly to himself, 'for all your power, we are still only human.' Yet another sigh escaped him as he smoothed out a name, and entered another in its place.

His writing was poor. Back in his boyhood before his parents had died, he'd been tutored, but that time was followed by the vicious dark hole in his life, the two grim years, when he'd been passed from one perverted slave owner to another, when it was all he could do to keep his body alive and his spirit willing to live. When all he'd learned was how not to die. After that he'd belonged to Ligea and, well, it had never occurred to her he might like to write anything, and it had never occurred to him to ask. The hard years had taught him *not* to ask and not to expect.

Still, he was at her side when she went to school and, later, when she'd attended the Academy debates and scholarly discussions. As a result, the education Brand had received was better than most Tyranian citizens, even if his lettering remained poor.

It was not his writing skills that bothered him; it was the list itself. Ligea had asked him to write down the name and owner of every slave he knew who might want to swap their present slavery for freedom. They had to possess some skill her rebellion would find useful: soldiering, or blacksmithing perhaps, or handling horses.

Brand's problem was that few slaves spoke candidly of their feelings. If you wanted to escape, you didn't talk about it. Frustrated, he rose and went to the balcony that overlooked the villa garden. The late desert-season sun, filtered through evening clouds, burnished the water of the fountains and painted the marble statuary and colonnades with the half-tone russet hues of the leaf-fall.

At a guess he would never live anywhere as beautiful as this again. He would never feel as safe. And yet one part of him wanted to board the next galley for Altan. One part of him wanted desperately to go home, even though he knew it was no longer home. He was thirty years old, and he'd been taken from Altan when he was just ten; what could there possibly be for him there now?

He looked down at his withered left arm. He had dreamed once of being a soldier and fighting for Altan's freedom. He knew there was already a rebellion there, in the Delta. Slaves told each other stories – and tales of a slave uprising spread as fast as light at moonrise on a cloudless night. Wish fulfilment, perhaps. You couldn't be free, but you could dream of those who fought for freedom. You could pretend that one day it would be you.

The insurgents of Altan called themselves the Gharials of the Delta. Named after the long-snouted crocodiles of the rivers, they lived on the floating reed islands where the Great Altan River debouched into the Sea of Iss, and they even dared to blockade the ports of Altan on occasion. Minnows, some said, not gharials, but even minnows could bite. However, as Brand contemplated his useless arm, he wondered if they'd be interested in a one-armed soldier with no experience.

Yet he knew he must leave. If he stayed, his love for Ligea would end up turning him into a bitter old man who had never achieved his true potential. It would drain him, that love.

Put it behind you, and go on. But it would hurt. Excising part of yourself always hurt.

As he looked down on that garden he remembered the girl who had owned him, ten years old to his twelve, imperiously ordering him around as though he were a dog without rights. An autocrat even at that age – and yet one who occasionally asked his opinion and then listened to what he had to say. Who was *interested* in him, in his opinions and thoughts. Who sometimes followed his advice. Who never held a grudge, even when he subtly mocked her. Clever enough to know when she was mocked, though, of course.

The two years before he came to the Gayed family had made him forget that people could care about him. Ligea had restored his faith in others. She had returned his pride. Ligea, without even knowing what she did, changed him from a frightened, beaten boy without hope, into a youth who knew his own worth and believed in a future. And, gods, how he loved her for that . . .

'Are those serious thoughts of yours worth a sestus or two?'

He turned. She had come into the room and was at the desk, perusing the list of names. 'Sweet Elysium, there must be a hundred people down here!'

'Numbers aren't everything.' He took a deep breath. He always told her the truth, and he wasn't about to change that now. 'Ligea, I won't make promises to them that don't have a sunbeam's chance in Acheron of being fulfilled.'

'I've just heard from Arcadim. He's found a farm, just what I was looking for, at the foot of the mountains. Remote, and with an owner who can't believe his luck that he's found someone gullible enough to buy such a far-flung place so distant from any decent markets. We will hide the slaves there.'

'And how do we get them out of Tyr in the first place?'

'Well, I have a few ideas, especially since we had a good look at the Oracle the night before last. The annual prophecy for Tyr. That's not quite twenty days away; I can see possibilities there.'

His heart skidded sickly.

She smiled, and briefly appeared young and mischievous. He felt a familiar tightness in his chest. *What I wouldn't do to have that look on her face all the time.* But there was no going back.

Not now. He conceded, 'At least we found another way into the Oracle cave. One that doesn't involve meeting up with Pythian ridgebacks.'

'In the meantime, you can start sounding out some of these slaves.' She ran a finger down the list and read the notes he'd added beside each name. 'This fellow, for example. Gevenan. I wonder how across all the Seas of Iss he managed to keep his Ingean name? That already makes him interesting. He sounds ideal. Ex-soldier, some kind of officer, angry at his enslavement when the Tyranians invaded his island, and now a horse-handler. That means he will often be found exercising the horses under his care down on the beach. Or maybe he deals with the feed merchants at the hay markets. You'll find a way to talk to him. Same with some of the others. Cracius, leatherworker at Domina Curia's villa. He will buy at the leather market.'

'But what would I tell him? Or Gevenan? I have to offer them something better than a myth of freedom.'

'I'm not offering them a myth! I'm offering them a way out of Tyr, out of slavery and into a paying job. Isn't that enough?'

'No,' he said, and wondered at her ignorance. 'Freedom is no good to you if it only drags muck behind it. What if they get caught? A good master might just whip you. A bad one kills you. The worst ones kill your family and your friends and your fellow slaves as well. Praetor Antonius murdered half-a-dozen stable boys to punish Gev for trying to escape, and then scourged him as well. Ocrastes' balls, Ligea, you *know* this happens; I don't need to tell you.'

She stared at him, not answering, and the silence lengthened.

And he asked the question they were both thinking. 'What – what would you have done?' *Whipped me? Sold me? Let me go?*

Her whispered answer was tortured. 'I don't know. I – I never believed you'd go.' And then an angry, 'And you shouldn't have asked that question. Not now. We've been through too much to go back to what was.'

His gaze dropped. 'Yes. You're right. It was an unfair question.'

'So, are you saying that all I offer a slave won't tempt them? Regular pay. Ultimate citizenship of a new Tyrans. Pride in themselves. The end of slavery.'

'Ligea, those are just *promises*. They will have to believe what you say is true, or at least *possible*. And even I am not sure I believe in your success. How can I convince *them*?'

The horror in the look she gave him took him by surprise. She asked, 'You saw what I did, single-handedly, to the Stalwarts' legion – and you *still* doubt?'

'Yes. They were exhausted men without resources, not the whole might of the Exaltarchy.'

'Temellin believes I can do it.'

'*Does* he? If so, he's a fool. Or was he just unable to stop you? Anyway, he's never been to Tyrans. I have! I *know* what you face.'

'And you think I will fail?'

'Oh, Goddess,' he whispered, and released his hold on his raw anguish. 'Yes. Yes, I do. I believe in *you*, Ligea – but you are only one person. And they are a mighty empire. There are eighty thousand citizen legionnaires in the Exaltarch's armies; you told me that once. Twenty thousand of them in Tyrans. One full legion right here in Tyr.'

'And another five hundred thousand scattered from one end of the Exaltarchy to the other who are not citizens. Yes, I know. But no ruler has ever risked bringing a non-citizen army to Tyrans, you know that. And I don't believe they ever will.'

'Does it matter? There are still enough men in Tyrans to squash any army of yours! *And* you're pregnant! Ligea, I don't believe it can be done.'

She sank down in a chair opposite him and bent over, hiding her face in her hands. 'Oh, Goddess, Brand, am I an utter fool to have started this? Is all this just a delusion birthed by my wretched hubris?'

He went to kneel at her feet. 'Ligea,' he said, and he heard the ragged edges of his pleading, 'do what you told Arcadim you *could* do. Go to the Magistrium right now, tell Rathrox you have just arrived back from Kardiastan and you need to see Bator

Korbus immediately. He will take you there. You could kill them both before either was aware anything was wrong.'

She raised her head to look at him. 'Do you think I don't *know* that? Do you think I'm not tempted?'

'Then why don't you?'

'How many other ten-year-old Altani boys will end up slaves for the rest of their lives because no one of power would put an end to slavery?'

He winced. Damn her, she still had the ability to skin him raw. 'That was unfair,' he said.

'But true. Killing a single man, or two, won't change anything! It won't help Kardiastan. Or Altan. It would just be a pleasant revenge. Gods, Brand, my life was bought with a near genocide of the Magoroth when I was three years old. I have to do something to make it right. Otherwise, where is my worth?'

The misery in her eyes had the power to hurt him still. He took her hands in his. 'Ligea. It's not too late. You can turn around even now and go back to Kardiastan.'

She didn't seem to take in what he'd said. 'Brand, sometimes I want to see them dead so badly, it hurts. But if I assassinated Rathrox tomorrow, I would damage my chances of success. You see, I *know* him. I know his faults and his weaknesses. He's not nearly as good at his job as he thinks – for twelve or so years it was *my* senses that made the Brotherhood as successful as it was, not his bullying or his torture. If he dies, he will be replaced by someone I may not even know. Possibly someone a great deal better at the job. And I lose my edge over the Brotherhood.'

He was unconvinced and must have shown it, because she said, 'For example. When he hears from Favonius what I did in Kardiastan, he will not make the assumption that I will return, as another might. He'll think I will seek to rule there. He'll be so sure of that, he won't jump to the conclusion that a Magoroth in Tyr is me, even though he is going to recognise the power for what it is. By the way, once I start using my power, he will have the legionnaires searching for people with a gem in their palm. Eventually, when he doesn't find Magor, he will start torturing

Kardi slaves. It won't do him any good, but he'll continue until there's not a Kardi left alive in Tyr.'

He grimaced. 'So what do we do?'

'You can start a rumour around the pothouses of Tyr that all Kardis will be killed unless they leave Tyr on the day of the whirlwinds.'

'And if I am recognised as your slave?'

'Just tell them you didn't go with me to Kardiastan.'

He still wanted to beg her to give up, to go back to Temellin, but she reached out and placed her fingers over his lips. 'I know I will probably fail. I know the idea of me becoming Exaltarch was just a stupid moment of arrogant dreaming. I know I may achieve very little. I also know *that I have to try*. Because I have power, I have to try. Who else can? If I can't do it now, how will Kardiastan ever be free? Every time Temellin wins a battle, Tyr will send more legionnaires to replace those who died. If I can't succeed here, how many generations will have to pass before slavery will be recognised as the iniquity it is?'

Hells, he thought, *she's right.*

An autumn sunrise on the estuary coast meant a hoary sea, a slate-grey sky and skin-reddening cold. The beach that might be pleasant with warmth at midday was bitter with wind under the dawn sky. And yet it was a busy place. Ligea had been right; the city's horse-handlers brought horses down to the sands for exercise. Brand grunted. Trust her to know something like that, to have remembered what he'd forgotten. Her Brotherhood training, he supposed.

He glanced across at her, shielding his nervousness. He was glad she was with him, because he knew that Gevenan, as a trained army officer, could be crucial to their plans, and he had no faith in his ability to read the man – yet he was worried, too. He worried someone would realise who she was.

Still, she would be hard to recognise. The savage scar on her cheek, obliterating the symmetry of her looks and as knobbly as rough-cast plaster, had become the focus of attention. Her figure was gaunt, her hair uncoloured, and that made her appear older. She wore the drab clothes of a lowborn woman. She even held herself with less assurance. There was a slump to her shoulders that went with the persona she had donned. Brotherhood training, he knew. This wasn't the first time she had worn a disguise.

He glanced away from her to watch for Gevenan, and saw him riding towards the beach, accompanied by four stable lads on their mounts. Gevenan was a stocky man, all muscle and sinew, his skin scarred in so many places it resembled an ill-made mosaic. He went to ride past the spot where Brand and Ligea waited at the gap in the dunes, then reined in when he recognised the Altani.

'Brand?' He slithered off his mount without even glancing at Ligea. 'Brand! I thought you were still away. Well met, my friend! It is good to see you again.'

They clasped wrists in genuine delight. Then he noted Brand's lack of a collar. 'Ocrastes' balls! The General's sham-whelp sodding *freed* you?'

'She did indeed.'

'You lucky son of a bitch. So what are you doing now?'

'Planning rebellion, actually.'

Gevenan stared at him, glanced at Ligea, then back to where his stable boys were waiting. 'Well, what are you lot of shifty layabouts waiting for?' he asked, scowling at the lads. 'Start with five times at trot along the beach, single file, then twice at half-pace canter and another twice at trot. By that time I should be with you. And if any of you little bastards start racing I'll skin you alive.' As the boys rode off, Gevenan, still holding the reins of his own mount, turned back to Brand. 'Are you flipping pickled? And who's this piece of sweetness and light?' he added, shooting a penetrating look at Ligea.

She glowered.

Brand was just relieved. Her assertion that she would not be recognised had been right. Gevenan had never come face to face with her before, but he had seen her many times, especially at the chariot races. He was used to Brand being in attendance on her. Yet her identity never occurred to him.

'A friend of mine from Kardiastan,' Brand told him by way of introduction.

Gevenan nodded and Ligea acknowledged him with a nod of her own.

'You'd better make damn sure she's a good friend when you so casually speak of rebellion in front of her. Brand, what is it you're doing? Finding an easy way to suicide?'

'We're planning to start a rebellion to bring down the Exaltarch and rid the empire of slavery. We have the financing. We have the safe haven to plan and train. What we do not have are the people. We need men like you, to train others.'

Gevenan stared at him. 'Have your brains mushed since you got rid of your collar?'

'They were still there last time I looked.'

'You're trying to *recruit* me?'

'That's right. Can't think of a better man.'

'You're asking me to run away and train, what, a few miserable ex-slaves who can wield a soup ladle and a garden hoe? What do you want them to do, eh? Stick a few feathers from their dusters up some legionnaire arses?'

'Something like that. Although we might do better with men more used to wielding a blacksmith's hammer or a firewood axe.'

'Ah, you great Altani barbarian – what in all of Acheron makes you think I want to end my wretched life burned at the stake outside the walls of the city?'

'You've been telling me for years that if only the opportunity would present itself, you'd be out of the Praetor's villa like a bunny rabbit with a fox nipping at its balls. I'm offering you the opportunity. And this.' He dug into the pocket of his wrap and fished out a coin. He held it up for Gevenan to see.

'A full *gold* sestus?' Gevenan swallowed. 'Sweet Melete. Where did you get that?'

'I told you, we have financing. And this is yours, your first full year's wage. All you have to do is leave the city on the north road in about a month's time.'

'That's *all* I have to do?' Gevenan asked, his voice laden with sarcasm. 'And I suppose I can just ignore the legionnaires on my tail the moment I'm found missing. Do you know how valuable the Praetor thinks I am? My horses win his bloody races! And then there's the matter of the retribution.' He waved a hand at the boys on the beach. 'This new lot might not be much to your eyes, but they have as much right to life as you and me. And how do I get out of the city gates wearing this' – he tapped the slave collar welded around his neck – 'with no authority letter?'

'You'll have an authority letter with a Magistrium seal. Not just for you, either, but for any stable lads accompanying you. But I don't think there will be anyone at the gate to stop you. There is going to be utter chaos in the city at the time, with the citizenry fleeing in all directions. In fact, I suggest you take all the Praetor's horses with you.'

'Now I *know* you're blithering moondaft. Brand, you'll have to give me more information than this. Who would I be fighting *for*?'

'For yourself. For freedom. For the right to be a citizen and have your labour paid for.'

'A *name*, Brand. A name.'

'No, not yet. Not until you are heading north. But I will say this: you will have plenty of proof that the rebel leader has divine help.'

Gevenan laughed. 'Jumping Ocrastes! You're more than just a tile or two short upstairs, aren't you? What should I expect – Melete herself to step down from her plinth in the temple?'

Brand gave a grim smile. 'Keep your ears open. You'll know what I am talking about when the time comes. And the day to leave Tyr is the day of the whirlwind. I'll give you more details closer to the hour.' Brand held out the coin.

'You're giving this to me *now*? Without even my agreeing to this scheme?'

Brand grinned. 'You'll be there. I haven't the faintest doubt of it. If there is anyone you want to bring along, do so. The only proviso is that they be the kind of people we can use.'

Gevenan took the coin, but his amusement was sardonic.

'You've just said goodbye to your money, my friend, along with your wits.' He turned to go, but as he turned, his gaze met Ligea's.

There was a long silence as they assessed one another. It was Gevenan who moved first. He raised his hand and touched the dip of the scar on her face. 'Did the bastards do that to you?' he asked.

She shook her head. 'No. But it's the scars that no one sees that hurt the most, anyway.'

He nodded and indicated her cheek. 'That one's nothing. You've still got all the pieces that matter, believe me.' His grin was appreciative.

She stared him down, the force of her personality pinning him like a speared fish. 'You be there,' she said, 'on the day of the whirlwind.'

There was no promise of a friendly reception in her tone and his grin disappeared. 'Why should I?' he asked, his belligerence more sneer than threat.

'Because you bear an Ingean name.'

He studied her for a moment longer, then looked back at Brand. 'Watch yourself, Brand. Grit in the gut, always makes 'em cranky.' He mounted his horse and continued down towards the sea where the others cantered their mounts along the sands.

'Can he be trusted not to betray us?' Brand asked.

'Oh, yes. Betrayal never even occurred to him. I suspect he was more worried for you than anything else. He likes you. At worst, he'll simply keep the money and do nothing. But he hasn't made up his mind yet. Tell me, what was that last remark about grit supposed to mean?'

'Grit in the gut – horse talk. Means the animal is feisty and hard to handle. It was a compliment, of sorts.' His gaze followed Gevenan, his eyes full of shame. 'Why do I feel so damn dirty?' he asked as he looked back at her. 'I feel I have betrayed a good man.'

For the briefest of moments he again saw the bleakness of her soul in her eyes, before she looked away to gaze on the sea. 'That's what violence does to people,' she said flatly. 'It besmirches you.

And a war is the worst violence of all. What I will do here and you will do in Altan – we call it rebellion, but it *is* war. And wars kill innocents, and leave the perpetrators sullied for all eternity.' The wind picked up, tugging at the edge of her robe and she wrapped her cloak tighter about herself. 'I ask myself, half-a-dozen times a day, whether what I do is right. I scour my motives when I lie in my bed at night, wondering. Wondering whether the old Ligea is still there, with her callous indifference to those around her. Wondering if . . . if I will be able to live with the innocent blood on my hands at the end of it all.'

She turned away from him to walk back to the city.

He followed her, his thoughts dredging up visions of the future. *Win, Ligea, and the slaves will be worshipping at your feet. Lose, and you don't have to wait for Rathrox – the slaves will crucify you. The whole of Tyrans will vilify your memory . . .*

CHAPTER SIX

Rathrox Ligatan strode down the Via Meletia towards the East Gate in a pall of bad temper. It would have been pleasant to envisage himself as a commanding figure, parting the crowds by virtue of his stature, but in his heart he knew he resembled no more than a scurrying insect that instilled fear, not respect, in those who recognised him. His unprepossessing assistant Clemens, hurrying short-sightedly at his side, did nothing to redeem his image.

The man was a cretin. Why in all seven hells had he ever chosen such an idiot to be his compeer flunkey? He was no more than a pen-pusher with a good memory, a sly blatherer. And he, Rathrox, had mistaken the memory for intelligence, the slyness for cunning and the blathering for eloquence.

Gods, he must be growing old. A scrawny old man, whose teeth were rotting. But he still had power, damn it, and he could still make strong men cringe. When a slave staggering under the weight of a bundle of firewood blocked his way, he lashed out with his arm and sent him flying. It made him feel better.

He unclenched his jaw. 'Say that one more time, Clemens. Slowly and clearly. You are a compeer of the Brotherhood! Don't you know how to deliver a coherent report, you fool?'

The man took a deep breath and tried again. 'It started nigh three weeks ago, Magister, at the Meletian Temple. An acolyte youth reported—'

'Yes, yes, I *know* that! I asked you to investigate, even though

High Priestess Antonia said it was nothing. Did you ever prove it was more than the wild ramblings of a lad who breathed in too many orlyx fumes and wouldn't admit to having plundered the temple supply of the drug?'

'Um, well no. Except that the lad swore—'

'Utterly unimportant. What else?'

'A few days after that, the Goddess appeared in a whorehouse near the Butchers' Gate. The customers there are mostly sellers from the wholesale market – stall owners and such. Lowborn, of course.'

'Go *on*, you incompetent clod.' As if he didn't know of the place, and its clientele.

'We questioned as many as we could find afterwards. They all said the same thing – this glowing woman suddenly turned up in the reception room. Just like that. There were twenty or so customers awaiting their turn, a few slaves serving food and wine. The brothel-keeper was there as well.'

'What did she look like?'

'Like the statue in the temple, they said. Taller than a man, anything up to twice as tall. Although I can't see that could of been right. She would of been bumping her head on the ceiling—'

Rathrox winced at the grammar and Clemens stuttered to a halt. Another glare was necessary to start his babble up again.

'Long golden hair. Dressed in white. Clutching something in her hand just like the way she is at the temple, a scroll, I reckon. Most of them reckoned she was just a golden glow, not real and you could of put your hand through her, although not all of them agree and I'm damn sure none of them tried. Most of 'em had their noses pressed to the carpet by this time anyway, peeing in their robes, I reckon.'

Rathrox gritted his teeth. 'And just what made you think all this twaddle is worth Brotherhood attention?'

'We didn't at first. They use orlyx crystals at the brothel, too. We wouldn't even of investigated at all, if we hadn't of had five or six other reports trickling in since. Same sort of stuff. A golden goddess who never spoke. Always at night. Usually in the open street, rather than places like the bawdy house. Via Securia, Via Locusta, Via Solaria, the Forum Astium in the Snarls. All poorer quarters. Via Securia is portside and Via L—' Another exasperated scowl stopped him.

'That's all?'

'Yes, Magister.'

Rathrox stopped and looked around. They were in a marketplace selling fruit and vegetables. It was late morning and there was little produce left. 'Where to now?'

Clemens pointed ahead. 'I believe the statue is that way, Magister, where all those people are standing.'

He strode on, Clemens scuttling to keep up, until he reached the edge of a crowd. 'Clear a path for me,' he ordered.

Clemens cupped his hands around his mouth and yelled, 'Make way for the Magister Officii! Make way! Magister coming through!'

A path opened up with almost miraculous suddenness, and Rathrox proceeded, Clemens trailing behind like a pig on a string, until they reached legionnaires guarding a statue on a plinth at the other end of the marketplace. Rathrox looked up at the statue as the soldiers saluted him. The sculpture was of Melete. The gold leaf of her hair flaked in patches and the paint of her red robe had cracked and faded to pink. Only the bright blue pigment of her irises had stood the test of time. Her unpainted skin glowed softly with gold light.

'What happened here, legionnaire?' Rathrox asked the nearest guard. He tried to sound bored, but his heart raced in shock.

'Don't rightly know, Magister. People found her glowing this morning when they came to set up the market. And there's some kind of barrier round her. Can't see it, but it's there.'

Rathrox reached out his hand and, even though he had been warned, still felt horror at the impossibility of it. There was an invisible wall between them and the statue. 'Did anyone try to break it down?'

'Yes, Magister. Chopped at it with an axe. But we couldn't even put a dent in it. Goes all the way round the back too . . .'

'Melete's blessing the city with her presence!' an elderly woman cried out from the crowd. 'We should be kneeling at her feet in awe, Magister!'

Closer by, a market stallholder muttered, 'Happen it's a warning. An earthquake coming, maybe. Wait till the city's fore-telling tomorrow, you'll see then.'

'No, she's telling us to treat 'er better, that's what,' said another man. 'Look after Melete 'n' she'll look after us, right enough.'

Rathrox hid a snort. The gullible would believe anything.

Just then the crowd parted again, murmuring approval, and the High Priestess Antonia appeared with an entourage of priest-esses from the temple. She gazed at the statue and the enrap-tured expression on her face doubled Rathrox's annoyance.

He grabbed her by the elbow and hissed in her ear. 'Reverence, it's got to be a trick—'

'You should show respect to your deity!' she said in a furious undertone, pulling her arm out of his hold by dropping to her knees. The surrounding crowd began to follow her example.

Rathrox turned to Clemens. 'Let's get out of this.' As they walked away from the crowd he asked, 'And you, Compeer – do you believe in the Goddess?'

'Of course, Magister.'

'And do you think this is the doing of the Goddess?'

Clemens hesitated.

'Come now, Compeer, you are one of the Brotherhood. Surely you have an intelligent opinion?'

'I – I'm not sure, Magister. There – there doesn't seem much sense to any of it. I reckoned maybe it was the work of that zealot sect down in the Snarls, trying to convince everyone they should spend more time on their knees at the temple, but we couldn't find no evidence. Then I reckoned it might be the Meletian priestesses, hoping to bring people flocking to worship, along with their purses, of course.' He shrugged. 'But if Priestess Antonia hasn't said nothing to you . . .' He gasped, pursing his plump lips in surprise.

'What is it?'

'The *dogs*. At the temple. The night the acolyte said he couldn't move and the Goddess spoke to him. They – the dogs – were encased in an invisible cage . . .'

'Who said so?'

'The temple guards.'

'What happened to it?'

'The cage? It disappeared. Suddenly. As if someone had just clicked his fingers and made it go away. That's how the temple guards described it.'

Rathrox shook his head. What the sweet hells was going on? If there was one thing he *didn't* believe in, it was that the gods made personal appearances. At least, not any more. He wasn't even sure they ever had. Some of the other incidents might have been haze-dreams, or wild gossip, but not what he'd just seen. He walked on, thinking.

Golden glow . . .

Why did that seem familiar?

Kardiastan. Of course. People who glowed gold. Or green, or red. But that was twenty years ago. More. And the gold ones, they were dead now, weren't they? Except for Ligea, of course. And she wasn't here, and was loyal to Tyr anyway.

He turned to Clemens. 'This is some kind of Kardi magic. One of their blasted numen must be in the city. They're trying to unsettle us.'

'Kardi? There's not many of them about, is there? People don't like Kardi slaves. They are too rebellious, for a start, and there's been all those rumours about them being numina. And as for freemen – well, they don't seem to leave Kardiastan much. You don't hear about too many Kardi traders here, for example.'

'No, you don't. So if someone does turn up, you should hear something. Especially if it is a woman.'

Clemens nodded thoughtfully. 'It may be nothing, but I had a report about a pregnant Corseni the other day. A poorly dressed woman visiting an expensive midwife, one of my informants. The woman's behaviour was odd, so I tried to check her out, but none of my Corseni informants had ever heard of her. What if she wasn't Corseni, but Kardi? After all, who can tell one brown-skinned barbarian from another?'

'Get a proper description. Find out if she had anything strange about her hands. The numina have gemstones inserted into their palms, sometimes with the skin grown over the top. Try to find her – offer a reward. I want all city gates manned all day from now on, and everyone is to have their hands checked, coming in and going out.' He hesitated. How in all the seven layers of Acheron did you arrest someone who could burn a hole through your chest with their unholy jewel? 'Better still, send Legate Valorian to me to discuss this. We have to work out a strategy to deal with such numina.'

'Yes, Magister.'

As Clemens continued to pace alongside him, Rathrox waved his hand in an irritated fashion. 'Well, be off then. Get started!'

Clemens gave him a startled look. He needed to go in the same direction as the Magister anyway.

'Run, Clemens, run!'

Clemens started running down the street. Rathrox smiled. He needed to smile at something.

Hadrin shuffled along the paths between the burial vaults of the necropolis. His lantern had gone out, the cheap candle stub burned to the end, the acrid smoke of its last flicker still tickling his nostrils. He scarcely noticed. Unrelated thoughts streamed through his head and, like clouds in a windy sky, they never held their form for long.

The wine he had drunk earlier in the Green Bear Pothouse on the Via Ursa warmed his belly nicely. Didn't need no lamp, he didn't. Didn't believe in ghosts, or shades, or whatever you liked to call them. He was the necropolis watchman, and proud of it. Kept the place nice and tidy during the day, just as he was supposed to. Cleaned the weeds from around the graves, all except the herbs, of course, and at night he made several rounds at different times, to make sure all was well. He knew the paths as intimately as he knew the bench where he always sat in the Green Bear.

They'd been talking all kinds of stuff in the Green Bear this evening. That was because it was the annual foretelling day on the morrow, when the Prefect Urbis, him that governed the city under the Exaltarch, went to the Oracle to hear what the coming year would bring and what he should do about it. Some said there was going to be a real shocker of a prophecy this year, what with Melete appearing all over the city.

That wind had a nip in it. Usually people avoided the necropolis at night, but there had been the odd attempt at grave robbery. Barbarians, of course, who had no respect for anything, even the dead. Ocrastes' balls, was that a light there *now*, tonight?

A ray of brightness moved along the paths between the vaults. The hairs on his arms rose, his mouth dried out. He'd never seen such a light before: more like pure moonlight. Worse, it sought him out and then skewered him, pinned him to the spot with its intensity, rendering him almost blind.

A voice came from its centre: 'Hadrin.'

He quaked, speechless. By the many heads of Ocrastes, hadn't someone been jabbering in the pothouse about strange lights? He hadn't paid much attention. Gods preserve him!

He shaded his eyes, and thought he saw a glowing figure on the pathway. There was no doubt in his terrified mind: this was Melete. She disseminated light as cold and as beautiful as the moon. Her golden hair swirled around her face, long and luxuriant. He couldn't make out the features of her face, the light was too bright, but otherwise she looked just like her statue in the temple at the end of the Forum Publicum. She held something; a sword, he thought. Something not quite right about that. The statue clasped a scroll, didn't it?

She spoke. 'Hadrin. The task I perform this night is not your concern. Go home and cover your eyes. Seek not to see the business of gods.'

He prostrated himself, forehead to the flagstones. In truth, his knees would no longer hold his body upright. When he finally raised his eyes again, the figure had vanished. He scurried to all the home he had, the watchman's hut at the entrance gate, where he dived onto his cot and pulled the sacking over his head. He stayed that way till sunrise, swinging wildly between delight that a goddess had appeared to him, and trembling fear at the very thought of the same thing.

His garbled story in the pothouse that morning might have been dismissed as the ramblings of a man made crazy by his nocturnal wanderings in a graveyard, except that a group of young highborn revellers returning home late had reported seeing a glow of light moving up the cliff at the back of the necropolis. 'Like the glow of moonlight,' one man said.

And then there was all that happened later on that day . . .

CHAPTER SEVEN

Ligea, dressed in dark trousers and tunic and wearing a pack on her back, hauled herself through the slit in the cliff above the necropolis and into the cavern beyond. It hadn't been a difficult climb. The cliff face sloped; there were ledges and holes, and plants grew here and there to offer handholds. The toughest part was to find the particular cleft she and Brand had identified as a way of entering the cave complex beneath the temple. She had to use her cabochon, lighting her way by its glow.

It was a relief to stand finally on the cavern floor and call the light into her sword. Everything was quiet and, apart from the Eternal Flame burning in the connecting cave, in darkness. She brushed off some dirt and leaves and sucked at a scratch on the back of her hand, cursing all thorn bushes.

She found a hidden corner in the folds and crannies of the rock walls of the cave, extinguished the light in her sword and settled down in the enveloping darkness to wait. Once, she would have enjoyed the thrill of anticipation, the way excitement made her feel more alive, but not now. Now, too much depended on her. Favonius could turn up at any time with news of her treachery for Rathrox. Now there was Arrant. Even though he had not come close to death again, her cabochon periodically did relay knowledge of his weakness to her. His infirmity. His *something-not-quite-right*. And so she worried – and in her mind, even as she mocked her silliness, she named him Arrant as a talisman against the arrant stupidity of worrying about something she couldn't alter and which might never happen anyway.

Dawn brought a feeble light into the cave through slits and holes in the cliff, but no activity. It wasn't until late morning, by which time she was drowsy with boredom, that she heard voices in the main cavern where the Eternal Flame burned. Two young women, by the chatter. She enhanced her hearing.

'Esme is feeling ill again,' one was saying.

'She's always ill,' the other grumbled. 'She says it's the fumes.'

'She's ungrateful. I would give *anything* to understand what the Oracle said . . .'

'*Would* you, though? Fancy having to live in the High Priestess's villa the way Esme has to! I'd be too scared to open my mouth. And Esme never gets to go anywhere, or speak to anyone else. It'ud give me the shivers, that would.'

'Maybe – but only those who can understand the Oracle have a chance to be High Priestess one day. And think of *that*, Valaria! A villa of your own. As much jewellery as you could ever wear. The pick of all the men in Tyr—'

'I might've known you'd get to men sooner or later. Do we need more orlyx, Ania?'

'No. There's plenty next to the brazier. Here, give me a taper and I'll go and light it. You sweep the floor.'

Ligea tracked the Priestess Ania with her senses as the girl made her way into the narrow cave behind the Oracle and back again. After that, a desultory conversation commenced, centring around the debatable attractiveness of a male acolyte at the temple to Ocrastes on Galetea Hill. The faint headiness of orlyx began to drift through the caves, borne on discernible draughts of air. A few minutes later, the two women left and the caverns were quiet once more.

At last.

Ligea stood up and emptied the small cloth pack she had brought. From a flask, she poured water onto a cloth, which she then wrapped tightly around her nose and mouth, hoping it would be enough to protect her from the haze-dreams of the burning orlyx crystals. Then she stuffed everything back in the pack and hurried through to the main cavern.

By the flickering light of the Eternal Flame in its huge bronze bowl, the stone lion that was the Oracle appeared to be struggling to escape the rock face, a beast imprisoned in the cave wall trying to wrench itself free. The dark holes of its eyes and nostrils and mouth dribbled fumes that gave life to the human-like face. The mane rippled. The eyes watched. The nostrils flared. The jaw moved. Incomprehensible words spilled out.

Closer up, the lion shape was less distinct, the face more nebulous, but the acridity of the vapour caught in Ligea's throat and her thoughts tumbled, out of control. Her vision blurred. The Oracle exhaled powerfully against her cheek, the puff blowing her hair away from her face. The stone chin, finely balanced, wobbled.

Standing as far back as she could, she clamped a hand over the wet cloth across her nose and hurried to build a ward in front of the lion's face – but several hand spans out from the rock so that fumes could still pass from the cave to the main cavern. The smell was foul. *A tomcat's noxious breath*, she thought.

Still hurrying, she squeezed through the unobtrusive entrance to the cave at the back of the Oracle, and then warded the way in, just in case. Inside, the flow of air from under the floor was heavy with the sulphurous stench of the underworld, mixed with the smell of the orlyx. She found the brazier and extinguished the burning crystals with the rest of her water. Fortunately, fresh air flowed in from above, to whip most of the vapours straight out into the main cavern.

Less dangerous, but almost as annoying as the fumes, was the continuous murmur of the Oracle. She even caught herself listening intently, as though she could make sense of the words if only she concentrated a little harder. And yet she knew it was no more than the wind whistling through a crack in the rock. She and Brand had even located the particular fissure to blame.

Damn it, why was it so *easy* for people to believe the gods were whispering to them? Why believe that the inhabitants of Elysium *wanted* to talk to the earthbound in the first place?

There's got to be something better out there than this – this silly superstitious nonsense. One day, maybe I'll have time to think about it.

'Well, I'm going to shut you up today, anyway,' she said, addressing the fissure. 'See what you make of that. And it serves you right for allowing so many people to be so deceived for so long . . .'

Sweet hells, what am I doing talking to a hole in the rock? I hope the fumes aren't driving me crazy. And it was a damned pity cabochon healing didn't work with headaches.

She rummaged in her pack and drew out a reed-woven sack filled with uncarded wool. She stuffed it into the crack and the sound vanished. *There! See how easy it is to silence the gods?*

She removed the sack, restoring the status quo. It wasn't yet time to render the Oracle speechless.

She took the stool from under the brazier and sat on it, careful to position herself where she had plenty of fresh air. Confident that she would not be seen, not when she sat in darkness and the fumes from the cracks in the floor of the cave distorted everything by creating their own illusions of movement, she looked through the Oracle's mouth at the Eternal Flame and waited.

Another half hour passed before she again heard voices out in the cavern of the Eternal Flame. Esme and the High Priestess Antonia. She unwound the wet cloth from her face.

Now it begins, Antonia. Let's see who wins this time around, you – or me.

'Are you sure you remember everything?' Antonia was asking as they entered the main cavern.

'Yes, Reverence,' Esme replied.

'Then seat yourself. I shall return with the Prefect Urbis and the others. Remember, breathe deeply.'

Ligea's anger rose. The bitch wanted the girl to appear to be in a trance, half unconscious on orlyx fumes. It was a miracle Esme could remember what to say after breathing in that stuff.

Esme didn't reply. Obediently, she sat on the stool to one side of the Oracle. Her profile was exquisite. She had doubtless been chosen as the Selected One for her beauty – but her hands trembled in her lap. Impossible to think of her as anything more than a pawn in the hands of the unscrupulous, just as Ligea had once been.

Ligea had not been going to speak to her, but the rush of compassion she felt was both unexpected and overwhelming. In the midst of all the horror that was to come, perhaps she could help one individual. The thought was enticing. Besides, it would be fun to subvert the instrument of those who practised deception.

'Esme,' she whispered.

The girl's head swung towards the Oracle, her expression appalled. She tried to speak but it was a moment before she could utter a word. 'Who speaks?' she stammered at last.

This will be good practice. Now let me get the tone just right . . . 'Melete, Goddess, Patroness of Tyr, addresses you.'

Esme flung herself from the stool, to lie flat before the Oracle. '*Lady!* Lady, forgive . . .' The terror in her voice was so extreme, her fear so intense, Ligea felt a pang of horror.

Oh hells, what have I begun? 'Forgive you for what, child?'

'For not being a good Selected of the Oracle! I always should be able to understand your words. But I can't! I tried and tried and tried, and then the High Priestess took pity on me. She said she would come and listen early in the mornings, and then she would tell me what you said so I could repeat it . . .'

That bitch of a priestess, Ligea thought. Making Esme feel inadequate, preying on her feelings of unworthiness. 'Esme, you are forgiven.'

The girl, still prostrate, started to weep.

Ligea felt the beginnings of panic. Damn it, she should never have started this. Her misplaced compassion would ruin everything if Esme couldn't pull herself together. 'Rise, child, and take your seat. Your Goddess requires something of you.'

Vortexdamn, is what I am doing any better than Antonia's lies? Don't kid yourself, Ligea. This is just as dishonest . . .

'Anything! Anything!'

'Then seat yourself.'

Esme struggled up, her whole body shaking in her shock.

'Calm yourself, Esme. And listen.'

The girl managed to nod but she couldn't control her trembling.

'Antonia put her own words in the mouth of the Oracle, not mine. That was not your fault, and I do not blame you. Today there will be no words from your lips. Today it will be my voice that speaks.' *My lies that are heard. My deception. Damn it, this is harder than I thought it would be.* 'All you have to do is be still.'

'Lady . . .'

'Hush, Esme. One day perhaps you can undo the wrongs that were done here in my name. Until such time, I ask nothing of you.'

Esme sobbed quietly for a while, but managed to gain some vestige of control by the time the High Priestess returned with the blindfolded Prefect Urbis of Tyr, Laurentius Maximus. Ligea peered out through the lion's mouth, watching as others crowded into the cavern in their wake. When their blindfolds were removed by their priestess guides, she recognised them all.

Behind Laurentius came Trademaster Lettactes, the pompous head of the Trade Guild and reputedly the richest man in Tyr, if you discounted the man next to him, Javenid Baradas of Assoria, the Reviarch, most senior of the moneymasters. Inscrutable would be the best word to describe Javenid. He wore the bright scarlet robes of his position, and his shaved head shone like polished marble. In bold contrast to the deliberate baldness of his scalp, the locks of his long grey beard cascaded to his waist. Pearls had been threaded onto the beard hairs in eight long strings, each string representing a family genealogy, each pearl a male ancestor, extending back to the time when the One True God Himself walked Assorian soils and swam the sacred river in the guise of a crocodile.

Sethicus the Imperial Historian was next, stumbling along with the aid of a walking stick; she knew him as an elderly pedant who took pride in the accuracy of his recording of history. As a result, his work had not always pleased the Exaltarch. Some of his annals had been banned from public reading, even within the walls of the Academy of Learning, and Tyr wagered money on whether Sethicus could stay alive long enough to die a natural death.

After him came the Legate Valorian, commander of the city's legion and the city guard. She'd never met him, but she knew he was beloved by society's matrons for his social skills and charm, and Favonius had once told her that, although he was a vain hedonist with an insatiable appetite for virile young athletes, Valorian was yet much respected for his military skills and bravery. With him was Seamaster Mescades, the middle-aged commander of the Tyranian home fleet.

After them was Arbiter Cestonius Loyad, the chief judge, learned and honest, but not known for the compassion of his decisions. And lastly, the only man without a priestess guide and a blindfold. A man she knew all too well.

Magister Rathrox Ligatan.

Her stomach heaved. Her fingernails dug into her palms.

I should have known he would be here. Obvious, when she thought about it. The Exaltarch would want someone he trusted to report back to him.

She sat, rigidly still, her breathing suddenly uneven. This was the man who had sent her to capture and imprison her own cousin, Mirager-temellin. The man whose schemes had killed her mother and turned her father into the most vile of all traitors. The man who had mocked her as she grew up – and moulded her to be the instrument of destruction of her own people.

Get a grip on yourself, Ligea.

She could kill him so easily. One bright beam from her cabochon, sent through the mouth of the Oracle, and he'd be dead on the floor. And probably all those now gathered in front of the Oracle, except Antonia, would think it was the anger of one of the gods that had killed him. And even Antonia may wonder. Revenge could be so sweet. But would the confusion be enough to give her time to flee? She couldn't be sure.

No, the time is not right. Not yet.

Antonia indicated Esme where she sat on the stool, her eyes downcast, her expression rigid. The High Priestess may have thought the girl in a trance, but Ligea's senses told a different story. Esme was petrified.

'Prefect,' Antonia said, 'you remember Esme, the Selected of the Oracle? She will be revealing the words of the Goddess Melete to you, should the Goddess bless us with her gracious presence today. Or if one of the other blessed deities were to do so.'

'Of course,' the Prefect said. 'Who could forget such a beauty and one so honoured by the gods?'

One blast of her cabochon . . .

Stop thinking about it. You are not Compeer Ligea any more. You will do what is best for everyone, not what gives you the most satisfaction.

'Then let us pray to the Goddess, that she may grace us with her guidance,' Antonia said.

Ligea stuffed the sack into the fissure behind her and the Oracle's voice abruptly halted. Rathrox frowned and looked at the High Priestess. Antonia's eyes widened in surprise. Esme began to rock to and fro like a devastated child.

'Antonia,' Ligea said, her voice loud and unrecognisable even to herself as it resonated through the stone of the Oracle's face. 'On your knees before your Goddess. Prostrate yourself in supplication, for you have lied.'

It was Esme who moved first. She flung herself down before the Oracle while Antonia, her mouth a circle of astonishment, stood paralysed. Several priestesses squealed and sank to their knees; the remainder followed a second later. The men were slower to follow, but follow most did, until only Antonia and Rathrox and the Assorian moneymaster were still standing. Ligea strove to isolate their emotions from the welter of shock and fear. Antonia, she realised with surprise, was not only appalled but almost as terrified as Esme.

Vortexdamn. She thinks I really am the Goddess, and it scares the shit out of her. Now that *is funny.*

Rathrox's feelings were harder to ascertain. He kept himself under rigid control at the best of times, and even now it took her a moment to identify the thread of his shock, inextricably mixed with suspicion. He was not about to be so easily deceived. The Brotherhood, after all, were experts at lies and betrayal.

Ligea felt the cold of fear. *If he knew how to get in here without wrecking this entire deception, he'd already be on his way.*

'Do you think to defy your deity?' she thundered. The High Priestess collapsed to her knees, all of her pride melting into a misery of guilt. The moneymaster remained standing and so did Rathrox, who glared at the Oracle.

'Kneel, Magister!'

'Magister,' the Prefect hissed, tugging at Rathrox's wrap, 'have respect for the Goddess, for pity's sake. Are you *mad*?'

Rathrox glowered, but he knelt. The look he sent Antonia boded ill for the High Priestess, but it was the Prefect he addressed. 'Dominus,' he said, 'there is something wrong here. This is not the normal way—'

'Do you question your Goddess, Rathrox Ligatan?' Ligea roared.

'You're no deity,' he said in angry protest, and climbed to his feet once more.

Ligea sent a beam of power from her sword spiralling out of the Oracle's eye. It brushed Rathrox's clothing, slicing through the fold of his wrap to sear his skin at the hip, before slamming into the bronze bowl of the Eternal Flame. Carefully she slit the vessel in two. Each half fell away to hit the floor with a ringing clang, and then rocked gently until the sounds died away. The Eternal Flame continued to burn, flaring up between the broken pieces, like the centre of a flower between the petals. The faint hiss of its fire was now the only sound.

One of the priestesses fainted. No one moved to her aid. Several stifled sobs in the loose ends of their wraps. Rathrox paled as he stared down at his side. A wisp of smoke curled from the severed edges of the cut in his robe. He sank down onto his knees once more. To Ligea, his fear was a tangible thing.

She *delighted* in it.

Cestonius the Arbiter faced the Oracle nervously with a bowed head. 'S-Sweet M-Melete, we mean you no, um, no disrespect. W-We are unused to you addressing us in so direct a manner. Please f-forgive our, um, rudeness. We wish only to serve you and our city.'

'Then listen to my words, Cestonius. And heed them well, for you all have angered me with your lack of humility. And you must suffer the consequences.'

One of the priestesses burst into sobs. No one took any notice.

'Your city will pay the price of your arrogance and deceit,' Ligea said, her voice as cold as she knew how to make it. 'On the day of the whirlwind, the unravelling of the Exaltarchy will begin. People of Tyr, leave the city on that day, or risk doom. Slaves of Tyr, seek your freedom. The reign of Bator Korbus will end and a new prosperity will come with a woman's touch and you will bow to a woman's feet, one blessed by your Goddess—'

'This, this *thing* is spewing treason!' Rathrox cried, his fury pouring out from him in black waves. 'I will not listen.'

Ligea also sensed his panic. Not fear of the Goddess, she felt sure, because his disbelief was as real to her as the smell of the fumes. He leaped to his feet and lunged at the face of the Oracle. Perhaps he meant to rip away the loose piece of the face to expose what was behind, but he smashed into the ward so hard his whole body jolted back. Reeling, he lost balance and thudded to the floor. Blood spilled from a broken nose.

No one moved to help him. He lay there in front of her ward, conscious, struggling to rise, dazed, bloodied.

'Forgive him, Domina,' the Prefect whispered, fearing for his city. 'He doesn't understand.'

'He is doomed,' she replied. 'And on the day of his death, he shall understand who brings him to his doom.' She paused, and then turned her attention to the others. 'Sethicus.'

The historian jumped, alarmed at being singled out. 'Goddess?'

'Listen well, for you hear the beginning of new history today. Write the words truly.'

He bowed his head in reverence. 'It shall be done, Domina.'

'Lettactes.'

'Yes, Lady? How may I serve you?'

She didn't know the head of the Trade Guild personally, but she knew his reputation as a wily trader of enormous wealth and few scruples. It was easy to guess his weakness. 'Be prepared to serve the new order, or die a poor man.'

He stared at the Oracle in shock. 'What – what new order?' he asked.

'You will know it when it arrives.' He wanted to ask her more, but she cut him off. 'Legate Valorian. Seamaster Mescades.'

The two military men clapped their right hands to the breast and raised their heads to gaze into the eyes of the Oracle. 'Goddess,' they said simultaneously.

'A man of war must choose his side carefully,' she said.

'We are loyal!' Valorian protested. In spite of the coolness of the cavern, perspiration dripped from the ends of his curled hair.

She replied, 'In your future, a time will come when you will need to consider that loyalty with care. Loyal to whom? Sometimes an excess of loyalty is foolish, should a leader fail to earn the loyalty given him. Remember these words, for I will one day remind you both of them, and ask you to make decisions.'

Rathrox dragged himself to his knees. 'This can't be the Goddess! Don't believe her—' he began.

Ligea bathed him in the light of her cabochon, flooding it with pain. He collapsed again, rolling into a foetal ball. She turned to the moneymaster. The man had continued to stand through it all, his elderly figure ramrod straight in his red robes. 'Master Javenid.'

The Assorian tore his wide-eyed gaze from Rathrox to stare warily at the lion's head. Then he bowed, deliberately presenting a view of the all-seeing eye of his God tattooed on his head. 'I practise another faith,' he said. He was nervous, but not fearful in the sense of most of the others. He did not believe he faced a goddess. His scepticism matched that of Rathrox, but with more puzzlement than anger. 'I serve the One True God.'

The Prefect and the Arbiter winced, obviously considering this an insult to the Goddess.

'I would not wean you from your God,' Ligea assured him. 'I would say instead, guard the prosperity of your people with your wisdom.'

He inclined his head. 'I always try to do so.'

'That is well.'

She addressed the Arbiter again. 'Cestonius, it is time for the judiciary to consider the legality of slavery and the rights of slaves.'

He looked perplexed. 'Slaves have no rights, Lady. They – they are outside the Law.'

'Exactly. Direct your thoughts to the justice of that, if you would. I command it of you.'

'As – as you wish,' he said, floundering, with no understanding of what she meant. He licked his lips and sent a desperate look at the Prefect, who seemed equally bewildered.

Damn it, she thought, *such men are beyond understanding the iniquity of slavery. How can I deal with someone who can't even imagine anything else, let alone conceive that what we have now may be wrong?* She suppressed a sigh and turned her attention back to the Prefect Urbis, addressing him by name. 'Prefect Laurentius, the day of the whirlwind comes. Abandon your city on that day until the anger of the gods has passed you by. Heed my warning.'

He didn't reply. She felt him struggle to comprehend, and fail. He, too, was sweating; beads of moisture ran down his neck.

She was suffused with a sense of futility. How, by all that was holy, was she ever going to pull this off? Was she moondaft to imagine she could bring down the Exaltarch and slavery?

Ravaged hells, here I am with everyone at my mercy, and I should be triumphant. Instead, I feel overwhelmed. 'Go,' she said.

No one moved.

She snapped at them, 'All of you, be gone from this sacred place. Profane it no longer with your doubts and disbelief.'

The military men were the first to move, but when the

seamaster reached out to haul Rathrox to his feet, she added, 'No, leave him.' Mescades hesitated, but in the end he left with the others. Antonia paused too, not to look at Rathrox, but at the Oracle. When it remained silent, she followed Esme and the other priestesses who were, by then, on their way out, helping the one who had fainted.

Ligea pinned Rathrox down with a further wave of pain, then withdrew power from her two wards. They winked out of existence. She unblocked the fissure and bundled the sack back into her bag, which she slipped over her shoulder. Then she returned to the main cavern, pausing only to check with her positioning senses that everyone except Rathrox had indeed gone.

He was still curled up, groaning, only semi-conscious, his fingers digging spasmodically into the floor of the cavern. She left him there and went to the vessel of the Eternal Flame. Using the power of her sword, she righted the two sides of the bowl and welded them together. She didn't try to disguise the join between the two pieces. *Let it be a reminder to them, every time they look at it.*

By the time she finished, she felt the beginnings of fatigue depleting her strength. Her headache was worse. *Hells, I didn't realise that would take so much power.* Or was it just the damned fumes that were making her so weak?

She knelt down at Rathrox's side. Just seeing him was enough to bring back the bitterness, the rawness of her sense of loss. If she killed him, would it take the pain away? The temptation was overwhelming. Such an easy revenge. Such simple justice for all the evil he had done to her, and others. He had taken everything from her, and she could take his life.

But she wanted him to know. Wanted him to know who did it. She built a ward to make sure he could not surprise her. 'Rathrox,' she said. 'Wake up.'

He groaned, but nothing more.

'Wake up, you compeer bastard, and listen to me. You are about to die and I want you to know who's doing this to you.' She put her hand through the ward and shook his shoulder.

He groaned again, but still didn't stir. She doubted he heard her.

Her head pounded, and she was overtaken by a wave of nausea and debilitating weakness. It had to be the fumes. She picked up her sword and stood up. She had to have fresh air. But first, she'd just kill him.

Footsteps – she heard footsteps. Someone was coming down the passageway from the temple and her positioning powers had told her nothing. She gazed at her cabochon. The gold had dimmed. She was so damned weak.

I'm being poisoned. Oh, cabochon, Arrant!

She fled in the opposite direction, her thoughts a jumble of chaotic concern for her baby, as she ran towards the adjoining cave where she could find fresh air and escape.

Moments later, she was outside again, on the cliff side, spewing up the contents of her stomach before she even remembered she hadn't killed the Magister Officii after all.

CHAPTER EIGHT

Brand was bored. He was also a little drunk. He had spent the morning visiting a variety of pothouses in areas of the city where he was not known, starting rumours of how Melete was going to make a personal appearance at the annual Oracle prophecy. It had been Ligea's idea, to ensure that there was no way Rathrox and Antonia could cover up what happened. Last he'd looked, as a result of his rumour-mongering, the crowd waiting at the temple was large enough to spill out of the main gate. Soon they would all know what had happened inside. Even if none of the invited guests said anything, one of the priestesses surely would.

He now sat propped against a vault, at the back of the necropolis, in among the oregano and thyme. It was sunny, and crickets and cicadas sawed and vibrated in the grass, refusing to acknowledge leaf-fall was already signalling the close of the desert-season. In another three weeks or so, the first fresh snows would fall in the mountains, and the snow-season would officially commence.

The monotony of the insect songs was more effective than any lullaby, and only Brand's worry for Ligea kept him awake. He always worried about her. He couldn't help himself. Blast the woman, why couldn't she just do normal things for once? Like settle down and wait for her baby to be born? He sighed, acknowledging that was an unfair thought. Ligea had not been granted a normal life from the time she was three years old.

But this idea of hers, to become the Exaltarch, it scared him halfway to Acheron. They had spent days thrashing out ideas and plans and possibilities, and it *still* scared him. When you freed a lion from the cage, you were the first one in its path. She could not know what she was unleashing on the world.

The first part of the plan hinged on their ability to get their slave recruits out of Tyr. Trouble was, he still wasn't sure how many were eager to try. He wasn't even sure he had convinced Gevenan to join them.

He had spoken to the horse-handler on numerous occasions since the morning they had met on the beach, and the man had been willing enough to listen. However, the only commitment Brand had received in return, said with a sardonic grin, was, 'I'll decide when I see this whirlwind of yours.'

'Damn it,' Brand told a small lizard that came out of the grasses to stare at him. 'Gev's a bloody cynical bastard.' The lizard regarded him, unblinking and silent. 'Yeah, I know. Just like me.'

At least he wouldn't be around for too much longer. He didn't think he could bear seeing Ligea in danger all the time. He sighed, aware that he didn't know if he could live without her either, but he did know he had to try.

Until I've lived alone and free, I won't know myself.

And yet . . .

He looked up at the cliff and saw her climbing down, competent, sure-footed and entirely fearless. And still he wished he could persuade her not to do this.

The lizard crawled up onto his sandal and sat there, sunning itself. He said softly, 'Enjoy the warmth while you may, little one. It won't last. The cold always comes.'

A few moments later, Ligea was flinging her pack down on the ground beside him, startling the lizard into frantic escape. 'I'm so tired,' she announced, and sat beside him, back to the vault.

'Thought you would be.' She was always tired and hungry after using her powers. He handed over a packet of meat pastries, the still-warm gravy oozing deliciously out of the sides.

'Oh, lovely!' She selected one and took a large bite. 'How was your morning?'

'Successful. A lot of people are going to believe nothing less than a description of Melete stepping down from her plinth to speak to the Prefect. They will demand to know everything.'

She sighed. 'It's almost sad. People shouldn't be so gullible.'

'My mother used to tell me that if we were strong in faith we wouldn't believe in trickery. But that's not the case here, is it? Their belief makes them more gullible, not less.'

She thought about that while she licked her fingers. 'Religion demands people have belief in what cannot be proven. Perhaps that's what makes them susceptible: the willingness to believe in things which are ultimately uncheckable. What was your family's faith, Brand?'

'We worshipped the gods of the Delta. My mother was very devout. Every morning she would weave a small basket and fill it with tokens of food. Then she would float it on the river, for the gods.'

'And did the gods find it?'

He gave a mischievous smile. 'I don't know. But I do know my friends and I used to wait downstream from where the village headman's wife floated her baskets, so that we could wade in and grab the food. She was a very good cook.'

Ligea laughed, but there was something deeper in her eyes that troubled him. His heart sank. When would the hurt stop coming? There seemed no end to it . . .

He said in sober reflection, 'Many Altani turned to the Tyranian pantheon after we were conquered. They thought our local gods didn't protect us, so why worship them? My mother was angry. She said that just because men abused their might didn't mean their gods were holy, but rather that they themselves were unworthy. She was a good woman, my mother. There were others who felt the same way, of course. I believe most of the Gharials still serve the gods of the Delta.'

'And you? What do you believe in?'

'Myself,' he said softly. 'Only myself.' *And you. I also believe in you.*

He had a flash of memory. A slave dealer's foul breath against his neck, the pain of what was being done to him, his own sobbing while he prayed to every god he could think of, pleading for rescue. And then the same scene again and again in different places, with different men, different perversions, the same pain – and always the same answer from the gods: none. For two long, sorry years.

He dragged himself back from the memory. 'If I was going to be a religious man – unlikely, I feel sure – but if I was, I think I would kneel to the Unknown God.'

She raised an amused eyebrow. 'There is such a deity? In the Tyranian pantheon?'

'No, that's just it. It's not in anyone's pantheon. It just is. He – or maybe she, or even it – has a small temple in the Snarls. It's plain and unpretentious, and there are no priests. You just go there and pray in whatever way you want. There's only one precept to follow, and it is engraved over the lintel: *Do no person harm.* I go there sometimes, when I feel the need of peace.' He paused, then asked quietly, 'So, what happened up there?' *What has made you look so – so bruised?*

She put down the remains of her pastry in sudden distaste. 'Rathrox was there.'

One part of him went as still as the lizard now basking in the sun near by. 'Is he, um, still alive?'

She nodded. 'Does that surprise you?'

'Yes.'

'I had the perfect opportunity to turn him to ashes, and I threw it away.'

He tried to keep his tone neutral. 'Because you weren't ready to plug the hole his death would leave?'

'When it came down to it, I was going to kill him anyway. But I wanted him to know it was me, and I lost the opportunity.'

He had a horrible idea that had been a mistake. It was dangerous to play games with a man like Rathrox Ligatan of the Brotherhood. *Oh, gods, Ligea, what have you done?*

He was the lizard in the sun, suddenly feeling the chill of winter.

* * *

Pain. So much pain. What the hells?

He was lying uncomfortably on a stone floor. The chill had seeped to his bones. His face was on fire. One of his hands hurt too. He stared at it: the little finger stuck out at right angles. There was blood on his clothes. He was breathing through the mouth because there seemed to be something wrong with his nose. He touched his face and winced as red-hot pain sliced inwards to his brain. His nose was twice the size it should have been.

He put his hands flat and tried to push himself up into a sitting position, but banged his head on something instead. Agony exploded along his nasal passages. Lights flashed inside his skull. He collapsed, moaning.

When he once more regained some semblance of comprehension beyond his own pain, it was to hear someone praying.

'Goddess, forgive. Melete, patroness of Tyr, forgive this humble servant for her transgressions. Melete, arbiter of wisdom, forgive this priestess for her foolishness . . .'

By all that was holy, that was *Antonia*?

With exaggerated caution he turned his head. He was still in the cavern of the Eternal Flame. He couldn't understand that. Why had he been left here on the floor like a – a – discarded carcass? Ocrastes damn them, someone's head would roll for this!

He stared, uncomprehending, at Antonia. She was kneeling in front of the Oracle, her forehead pressed to the ground, her arms outstretched in supplication. Her shoulders heaved, her voice was weepy. The hard-boiled bitch was *crying*? He tried to yell at her, but the blood in his throat choked him. Still, his coughing had the desired effect. She rose and hurried over.

'Don't try to get up,' she said, brushing her tears away with the back of her hand and leaving a streak of dirt across her cheek. 'You can hear me, can't you? You are in some kind of, um, *cage*. We can't see it, but it exists.'

He remembered then, everything. The Oracle. The Goddess. The power. The bitch who'd sent that pain through him as casually as a torturer with a knife. The woman who'd had him help-less at her feet, grovelling in front of her and the most powerful people of Tyr. Rage overflowed from his mind, burgeoned through his veins, ready to sear or torture or annihilate. He wanted someone to blame. Someone to hurt.

Who the hell had it been?

Antonia said again, 'Don't move. You will hit yourself on the – the – walls of whatever it is encases you.' She stood staring at him wordlessly, a pace or two away, her eyes alight with fear.

He recognised the look; he had seen it many times in those in his power. His eyes narrowed. 'Are you afraid of me, Antonia? You should be. This is your fault.'

But she drew herself up, with more courage than he would have thought possible. 'I am not afraid of you, Magister, but of my Goddess. And so should you be.'

He wanted to strangle her. Instead, he put out a cautious hand. It ran into something cold and invisible, like clear glass, just inches away from his face. He pushed at it, but it didn't move. He followed it around with his hand, and everywhere he could reach he met the same resistance. He kicked out with his feet, but the imprisoning wall trapped him on all sides. He could neither rise, nor sit.

Fear flowed in the wake of his anger. How long would he be trapped? Did that bitch of a so-called goddess intend him to thirst to death?

He tried to rein in the panic. Tried to maintain his cool logic. 'You *fool*, Antonia. That was no goddess. One of your priestesses must have let that woman in, whoever it was.'

She continued to stare, this time in genuine astonishment. 'You think that was a *person*?' she asked at last. 'Are you mad? No person could do what she did there. Sweet Elysium, Magister, look!' She pointed at the Eternal Flame. He twisted slightly to see. 'She split the bronze bowl in two, as easily as jelly eels are sliced with a knife! Then mended it as neatly as a bronzemaster. She's encased you in magic so that none of us can touch you, let alone release you! What mortal woman could do that?'

'The one who entered the cavern before we did,' he snarled, bending his knees up as far as he could before lashing out at the barrier near his feet. Pain radiated out from his face at the jarring of the blow. The invisible wall remained solid.

'There was no one,' she said patiently, as if speaking to a child. 'The space behind the Oracle was empty when a priestess lit the orlyx brazier. No one entered the cavern after she left. Anyone entering would have had to pass me, in the room at the top of the steps back in the temple. Yet when Esme sat on the stool, about half an hour later, the Goddess spoke to her from behind the Oracle.'

'Did Esme see her?'

'No.'

'What did she say?'

'Nothing of import. She told Esme she would speak for herself. And she did, as you heard. Magister – she was the *Goddess*. Melete herself! Merciful heaven, she could have killed us all, right then. But she *is* merciful, praise be her name! We must do as she says. She won't be so merciful next time. I will not be a party to lies any more, Magister. If the Oracle does not speak in a language we understand, I will not have Esme or anyone else put words in its mouth.'

He controlled his rage with an effort. 'Antonia, since when have you believed all this idiocy? You were one of us – which is why you are what you are today!'

She said simply, 'I heard the voice of Melete today.'

'You stupid woman,' he spat at her. He took his knife out and tried to gouge a hole in his invisible prison. 'Have you *no* sense? You hold your place here as High Priestess because the Exaltarch allows it. Displease him, and there will be someone more amenable to polish Melete's toes or whatever it is you do with your time. Have you no sense of self-preservation?' The blade slipped, nearly cutting his other arm. It had made no impression on the barrier. 'Ocrastes damn this! Woman, go get some of my Brotherhood guards with axes to break this thing apart. Tell them to bring an alchemist with acid. Anything!' He knew he was losing control. He who prided himself on his calm, on his carefully calculated plans, his logic.

'This is part of the Sacred Way,' she said primly. 'We don't allow street riffraff—'

'Vortexdamn you to Acheron! You've asked every rich man wanting to buy his way into the Goddess's good graces to come here and listen to the effluent pouring out of Esme's throat – does that make them somehow more honourable than my men? Goddess preserve me from moondaft females!'

'Don't you *dare* call on the Goddess, Ligatan! Not in this sacred place, not with your disbelief as clear as the blackness in your heart.' She took a step closer to him. 'You are in no position to insult me. None.' She turned on her heel and began to walk away.

He threw himself at the wall that encased him, bruising his shoulder, but she didn't look back.

He thought, *Oh, shit. The nameless bitch is going to leave me here to die, and Antonia's going to watch it happen. This* can't *be happening to me.*

The next day Arcadim went to see the Reviarch of the Assorian moneymasters, Javenid Baradas, at Ligea's request. As he was taken through the scribes' room of the Baradas Counting House, where slaves sat at their desks transcribing financial transactions from wax tablets onto scrolls that would eventually be bound into vellum-covered ledger books, he noted their discipline was such they didn't even raise their heads to look at him as he passed. The only sound was the scratching of their pens. Arcadim couldn't imagine his slaves behaving that way. He couldn't imagine *wanting* his slaves to behave that way.

When he was shown into Javenid's private workroom, the moneymaster looked up from his work in surprise. 'This must be an important matter, Arcadim, to bring you all the way here at this hour of the morning. Come in and sit down.' He indicated one of the solid wooden chairs in the room. They matched the rest of the furniture – all made from Assorian ironwood, family heirlooms passed down from generation to generation, as valuable as gold. The ironwood forests of Assoria were no more, vanished to supply just such chairs and desks and cupboards.

In the centre of the room was the ironwood box, the bronze-bound coffer every Assorian moneymaster possessed. The symbol of his trade, it contained his moveable wealth – the coinage, the jewels, the gold and silver and pearls. The chest itself, too large and heavy to be stolen, was locked by several huge iron keys and then, finally, by the arcane word of the family, passed down from moneymaster to heir through the years since the coffer was birthed from its forest tree. It was said that the man who did not breathe that secret word into the lock before he turned the last key would die there and then, and all that would remain of his body would be ashes.

Javenid nodded to the slave, respectfully waiting at Arcadim's elbow. 'A drink for both of us, Esacard, and once you have brought it, see that we are not disturbed.' When the slave had gone, he added, 'So, what brings you here, Arcadim?'

'It concerns, in part, what happened at the temple yesterday.'

'Ah. An unfortunate business. Unhappily for me, everyone seems to know I was present. I've even been accosted on the street to tell what I saw.'

Arcadim cleared his throat nervously. 'I suspect I may be able to explain it.'

Javenid steepled his hands. 'An explanation, eh? At last, someone with a little commonsense.'

Something in the way the Reviarch smiled told Arcadim that Javenid was not about to be surprised. He felt as if a load had been lifted from his shoulders and said flatly, 'You already know who is responsible.'

'Well, no, not the particular individual. And if you are privy to that information, I will be delighted to hear. But we are, after all, Assorian moneymasters collectively possessing at our finger-tips as much information as the Tyranian Brotherhood has at theirs. So let me guess. There has to be a highborn Kardi involved. I saw golden light and I saw Rathrox Ligatan walk into a wall that wasn't there.'

Arcadim let out his breath slowly and nodded. *Kardi*. That was the key, as he had hoped. Not immortals. Not Tyr's squalid, quarrelsome gods. Thank the One True God. He should never have doubted. Tonight he would prostrate himself before the house altar in the God's Room, and spend the night in prayer. 'Forgive my ignorance, Reviarch. I have little knowledge of Kardiastan. I had heard that their highborn ruled with magic, but my understanding is patchy. Do the Kardi *all* have such power?'

'Only their highborn men and women – they call themselves the Magor. Arcadim, you had better tell me all you know. This could be important.'

They were both silent as the slave returned with refreshments, and not until he had departed did Arcadim settle down to relate everything that had happened since he'd read Ligea's note in his counting house some twenty days earlier. He was careful never to mention details. Ligea had been adamant about that, but he wouldn't have done so anyway. The ethics of confidentiality included keeping secrets from other moneymasters too, even the Reviarch. He finished by saying, 'And so I arranged for her house and its contents to be sold, and all her other property as well. Mostly changed to moveable assets.'

The Reviarch looked at him with open surprise. 'I never heard a whisper! God Almighty, Arcadim, you are as secretive as a beetle in its burrow. How did you do all that – in what, twenty days? – without alerting anyone?'

'Ah. That's a result of something my father taught me: to always assume you will have to sell every one of your properties in a hurry tomorrow and flee for your life. I've always extended that maxim a little further, and made the assumption that any one of my patrons might have a similar need. When the Domina Ligea left Tyr, I investigated potential buyers.'

'Now that is wisdom we would all do well to emulate. What else have you done?'

'She asked me to buy her another property further away, and to buy horses and weaponry.'

'I assume she asked you to tell me all this?'

'Yes.'

'Why?'

'She wants the support of moneymasters throughout the Exaltarchy. By the way, she said to tell all the moneymasters not to leave Tyr on account of any whirlwinds. There will be no harm done to our houses or ourselves if we just close the shutters and stay indoors.'

'*Whirlwinds?*'

'That's what she said.'

There was a long silence. Then, 'You've given me a lot to think about.'

'I have written instructions for all the property sales, supposedly sent to me from Kardiastan. She doesn't want anyone to know she is here in Tyr. Especially not the Magister.'

'Good. That will protect you as well. You must never admit you saw her, Arcadim. If the Magister questions you, show him those instructions. No one can blame you for following written orders pertaining to the disposal of assets.'

'Did I do the right thing?' he asked, desperate for reassurance, but trying to hide his need. 'I could have refused to continue as her moneymaster.'

'Of course you did the right thing! We need to know what she is up to.' Javenid leaned forward, his face as grave as his voice was serious. 'Our wealth is the only thing that gives us power in a world governed by a despot and his legions; you know that as well as I do. Domina Ligea Gayed might just achieve what she has set out to do, and bring a whole empire crashing down, in which case we need to be on her side. If she fails, well, we must be ready to take advantage of the trouble she is going to cause. She is like a galley with its rudder oar broken, yawing out of control and crashing into others of the fleet. There will be damage, but there will be wreckage to pick over, flotsam to salvage. Help her in every way possible, Arcadim, without drawing the attention of Rathrox and the Brotherhood. If you lose money over this, we will all spread the loss among us.'

Arcadim heaved a sigh of relief.

'Don't be too happy,' Javenid warned him with a grim smile. 'There are others in Tyr who have a very good idea of what the Kardi nobility are capable of. One of them is the Exaltarch. And then there's every old soldier who served there about twenty or thirty years ago. And of course, there's Rathrox Ligatan. He tried to warn everyone yesterday, and was whipped down to the ground for his trouble.' His smile broadened. 'It didn't seem to worry anyone overmuch. That man has to be one of the most hated people in the whole of Tyr.'

'I hear he remains trapped in a sort of invisible cage.'

'Yes. I don't think it is going to be a permanent state of affairs, more's the pity. Last I heard, the walls of his prison were softening. He may be able to push through them some time today.'

'He'll be furious,' Arcadim said.

'That, my friend, is a very mild way of describing how Rathrox feels right now. Your Kardi patron made a big mistake when she left him alive. She should have used that sword of hers to decapitate him there and then. If she could knock the head from a marble statue as you describe, then she could have done the same to him. He will have his revenge. Beware, my friend. He may guess she is the one responsible. And if that is the case, you will be questioned.'

Arcadim nodded miserably. 'I know. She told me to tell the truth, up to a point. To say that I sold all her properties, and gave the assets in cash and jewels to her messenger.'

She had promised that the mythical messenger would even leave a trail behind him, sufficient to deceive her fellow compeers. All he had to do was lie. He thought he could do that much. As long as no one mentioned torture . . .

After seeing Arcadim to the door a few minutes later, Javenid took a moment to think about all he'd learned. He hadn't wanted to alarm Arcadim, but he was deeply afraid. He had no illusions. If ever Rathrox suspected Assorian bankers had failed to pass on information about a rebellion of this intended magnitude, the walls of Tyr would be decorated with Assorian heads in a mass murder of a proportion seldom seen in history. As Reviarch, he had to do something to ensure the survival of his people, and to ensure Arcadim's safety in particular.

He needed to think.

CHAPTER NINE

The Exaltarch was keeping him waiting yet again. Another humiliation, on top of all he had suffered two days earlier at the Oracle.
He tried not to let his anger show. Tried to maintain a little
dignity.

At last a slave came to usher him in. The Exaltarch lounged
on a divan, surrounded by slaves, a low table in front of him
laden with enough food and drink for half-a-dozen men. He
glanced up. 'Ah, Rathrox. I wondered when you would come with
your explanation for the farce in the temple. You broke your
nose, I see. Good.'

'In private, Exaltarch.' Rathrox's tone was such that one of the
slaves made a moue of surprise that any man would dare to
speak to the Exaltarch so.

Bator Korbus frowned, and a lesser man would have cringed
at the frown, but Rathrox was out of patience. And it was the
Exaltarch who capitulated. He waved the slaves out of the room.
When they had gone he said, 'You had better have a good explanation for what has been going on, Rathrox. I expected the Oracle
to speak about the matters we agreed on – I heard nothing of
that. Nothing! Instead, I heard that the Goddess herself spoke, in
riddles, it seems, and then imprisoned you in some kind of cage.'

Rathrox opened his mouth to give his account of the events,
but Bator interrupted him. 'And don't bother to give me your
rendition of the Goddess's wisdom. I have already read the historian's account. He assures me it is word for word.'

And included a detailed description, no doubt, of the Magister Officii's humiliation.

The Exaltarch's glare impaled him. 'So, did the Goddess appear, or did she not?'

'No, of course not. When has either of us believed in the Goddess?'

'*Then what was it?*'

'Not what. Who. A Kardi woman, obviously. One of the Magor. No one else could do all that: the invisible wall, slicing the bronze bowl in two with a beam of gold light, the pain she gave me. Doesn't it all sound familiar to you, Bator?' He hadn't used the Exaltarch's given name for years, and he delighted at the feel of it on his tongue. *Wake the bastard up a little to his mortality.* Somewhere in the back of his mind, he wondered at his sudden recklessness. He knew his behaviour was uncharacteristic, but the humiliation and the fury within him needed an outlet, and right then he didn't care. He added, grinding his teeth in his rage, 'One of those Magor bitches is loose on the world.'

'I thought we'd slaughtered them all. All the gold ones, anyway. We put arrows through them from the gallery of the hall at the Shimmer Festival.' Bator grinned at the memory. 'Goddess, it was like shooting pheasants, except the Magor squealed.'

'I've been thinking about that. What if more were born after that? There's been time for them to grow up.'

'Ligea Gayed?'

'What about her?'

'She was a gold. And she's grown up. Was it her?'

'It can't have been,' Rathrox scoffed. 'She's still in Kardiastan.'

'Have you heard anything from her yet?'

'Not yet.'

'And I haven't heard from the Stalwarts.' Bator frowned but said no more on the subject. 'So, who in all Acheron's mists is this bitch who wandered into the cavern of the Eternal Flame and made a mockery of my Magister Officii – no, more than that. Who *injured* my Magister both in body and in reputation, with – I hear – impunity?'

Rathrox had to make a conscious effort to relax the muscles of his jaw before he could reply. 'I don't know. But I aim to find out. Someone must know something about a woman with a jewel in the middle of her hand.'

'Ligea had skin over hers.'

'Ligea never used hers. Wouldn't know how to. I assume that anyone who has power pouring out of their palm doesn't have skin growing over the device.'

Bator Korbus leaned forward, his whole body poised like a spear about to be launched. Rathrox felt his mouth go dry, and knew he had made a mistake trying to be too familiar. Their past relationship was long gone and to presume on it might be fatal.

'Rathrox, listen to me carefully. You do not seem to realise the seriousness of what happened, which is odd, as you usually see the significance of events immediately. Perhaps this time you are just too close to the event to realise its portent.'

Rathrox paled as the Exaltarch continued, his words as cold and hard as hailstones. 'Let me spell it out to you. Firstly, this whole story was all over Tyr while you were still stuck in your magic cage, pissing down your legs. You are the laughing stock of the city. That is not an advantageous place for the head of my Brotherhood to be. You lose credibility. I should not have to tell you that.

'Secondly, the whole city is looking to the temple, the Goddess and the High Priestess Antonia for leadership, when they should be looking to *me*. And Antonia is revelling in it. *I do not like it.*

'Thirdly, there is someone out there with the power to kill me with a beam of light. We know it has a limited range, but she does not have to stick a sword in me or poison a glass of wine to kill. And she has the power to make a whole city kneel at her feet in worship. She has *power*, Rathrox, and *we do not know what she is going to do with it.*'

Bator took a deep breath and, disconcertingly, that simple act seemed to make him grow in stature. He continued, 'But we do have some clues. She urged slaves to rebellion, and she sowed the seeds of treachery in the minds of my military leaders, my trademaster, my moneymaster, my city prefect, my chief arbiter and a member of the Academy. Now I have to work out whether to have them killed or not. I want every person who was there to be followed and the first sign of disloyalty reported to me. I would kill them all right now, if I thought I could get away with it. But the mood in the streets is volatile. I dare not overplay my hand.'

'I've already ordered them watched.'

'Tell me what else you have found out so far.'

'About the woman?' His pulse beat too fast. He could feel the throb of it. 'She came in and left the temple through the cliff at the back of the necropolis. There's a narrow opening in the cliff face that leads into the Oracle cave system. We found signs that someone had climbed the cliff. We have blocked it off, of course, and the cliff is now guarded day and night. She won't have access to the temple again. Unfortunately, even though Antonia knows Kardi numina exist, she has not been convinced by this evidence. She still believes in an appearance of the Goddess.'

'Tell her to come and see me.'

He inclined his head and continued. 'The man who looks after the necropolis: he saw the Goddess very early that morning, while it was still dark. His description was not much use. He seemed to think she was seven foot tall, and looked exactly like the statue in the temple. Except for the gold glow. I asked about her hair – he said it was golden.'

'It wouldn't be if she was Kardi.'

'No. But everyone who's seen the supposed Goddess is adamant on that point. I had men go to every wigmaker in the city to see who bought a blonde wig recently. Unfortunately, it seems to be all too common an occurrence: matrons with thinning hair, women going grey, actors who play women in the theatre, men who like to dress as women. I'm tracing every single one of them, but it will take time and it may lead to nothing. Already I have at least one bought by a nameless slave for an equally nameless mistress.'

'What else have you done?'

'I have everyone – compeers, informants, legionnaires – hunting down every Kardi, male or female, in the city.'

'And basically you have no idea who you are looking for.'

The Exaltarch's sarcasm scared Rathrox and he wasn't used to being scared. He attempted to sound optimistic as he said, 'No. I do have a description of a pregnant woman, supposedly a Corseni, with a badly scarred face. Her left hand was bandaged. Perhaps in order to hide a gem. We are searching for her.'

'I have the feeling that you have very little time, Rathrox. This day of the whirlwind she spoke of: it gives me a bad feeling.' The Exaltarch poured himself some more wine and gulped it down.

Rathrox felt his stomach lurch. 'Yes,' he agreed. 'I remember too. Only too well.' The first invasion of Kardiastan. The whirling gold wind that snatched the swords and lances and shields from the grasp of the soldiers, that *flattened* men to the ground to be killed by a few hundred Kardi warriors.

'Forgive me, Exalted, but I think your best defence may be the truth. For some reason, this woman wants to terrorise the populace on a day probably not too far distant. She wants to drive them out of the city in a panic. If that's what she wants, then we should aim to thwart her. But people will flee if they think it is the advice of the Goddess Melete. If we can convince them the Oracle voice was all a trick by a Kardi numen, then we can persuade them to stay in their houses and ruin whatever plans she has.'

The Exaltarch slammed his empty goblet back onto the table. 'And have them all wonder how long before Kardiastan brings us to our knees with its numina and their magic? The moment the Exaltarchy appears weak, *I* appear weak and ripe for over-throw. Have you any idea how many of the highborn are just waiting for me to make a mistake so they can step into my sandals? That bastard Devros of the Lucii would love to occupy the Exaltarch's seat, for a start. Yes, I want to tell them the truth, but only when I can also tell them we have Kardiastan under our control. I need to be able to show them the dead body of this Kardi bitch, with her jewel in her hand. *Then*, I can tell them the truth. And that, my Brotherhood friend, is *your* business. Fail, and we could *both* fall.'

'Then may I suggest you at least speak to those present at the Oracle foretelling? Tell them they were duped. They won't be disloyal then; they'll be angry. And not at you.'

The unnatural length of the silence that followed generated still more unease in Rathrox. Finally the Exaltarch said, 'I'll have them all called to my presence tomorrow morning. But the necessity for it makes me seriously unhappy, Rathrox. Remember that.'

'Yes, Exalted.' He cleared his throat. 'Perhaps it would be best if we rid Tyr of all Kardis, no matter who. If you could issue a promulgation that it is illegal to keep a slave of Kardi origin, and that all such should be delivered up to the Brotherhood? I've already spoken to Legate Valorian about checks at the city gates and within the city itself for anyone with gems in their hand, but it might be better to cast the net even wider to include all Kardis. Perhaps if I question them, I might find out something.'

'Good idea. Afterwards, you can kill them all. Make sure it happens, Rathrox. Nothing special, no fancy deaths. Just rid the world of them as fast and as unobtrusively as you know how.'

'*All* Kardis?'

'That's what I said. However, I don't imagine there are many, if any, non-slaves. Your problem will be the one – and please the gods, there'll only be the one! – who has a gem in her hand. I am not so stupid as to suggest you try to capture her. Kill her from a distance, however you can. Lance, arrow, rip-disc, catapult: how is your problem. Just see that it does not become mine.'

'Legate Valorian is working on it. I believe he is concentrating on whirlslings.'

'Good. You may go.'

Rathrox nodded and stood. It had not escaped his notice that he had not been invited to eat or drink anything. He politely backed away, but when he reached the door, Bator looked him in the eye and added, 'I am not a sentimental man. Remember that too.'

It was a warning, and it dissipated the last dregs of the reckless courage Rathrox had possessed at the start of the interview. Ocrastes' balls, how he *hated* having to fawn at the feet of another.

As he exited the main entrance of the palace a minute later, he paused at the top of the stairs. It was late afternoon, and the setting sun painted the marble of the buildings with pink. Some thought the vista over the Forum Publicum, past the main public buildings of the city to the Temple of Melete on the hill at the other end, was a spectacle so grand it was fit for the gods themselves.

Just then Rathrox hardly noticed. His thoughts were leaping from one problem to the next, sifting through possible solutions, trying to deal with the ramifications of things that had not yet happened. He signalled to one of his own attendants. 'Tardin, I want you to go to the Prefect Urbis, speak to his scribe. Say the message comes from me, but at the request of the Ex—'

He didn't get any further. A gold light borne on a whirlwind blossomed over the temple to blast away the growing darkness.

Breath-robbing fear stopped the words in his throat, froze him in place. The wild pounding of his heart, like a battering ram at his defences, signalled the end of the life he had known.

CHAPTER TEN

Sweet Elysium, Ligea thought, *I'm responsible for all this.* This huge crowd, shuffling along the Pilgrim's Way between the temple gates and the main temple building. This mass of people, sharing a common purpose, yet bewildered rather than united.

She didn't like being in such a crowd. She felt hemmed in and assailed by emotions. There were too many people, and too much fervour. Everyone was much too volatile, and she felt it all, raw and rough-edged, closing in on her.

'Vortexdamn,' the man next to her swore in complaint to the woman with him, 'this is too slow. We'll be walking home in the dark if we don't get into the temple soon. Can't we do this another day?' Ligea glanced at him. A freeman, he smelled of yeast and bread, and the plump woman beside him had a dusting of flour in her hair. A baker and his wife.

'No,' the woman replied. 'This evening the High Priestess and her augur are making a sacrifice. They want a sign from the Goddess. So there will be sacrificial blood for everyone.'

'If you want it,' was the baker's dry reply.

Wise man, Ligea thought. Such blood was only considered lucky if the augury was a good one. Then people dipped a fingertip into the sacrificial bowl and daubed the blood in the middle of the forehead.

Ahead, somewhere in the crowd, she sensed other emotions: annoyance, amusement. She realised why when she came closer to the spot. Legionnaires of the city guard were stopping everyone, looking at their hands. If the women had their hair covered, they were asked to remove the covering.

'Oo-er, he's holding my hand,' one cheeky matron laughed, simpering, as the guard glanced at her palms. 'You going to tell my fortune then, sweetie?'

The guard winked, and waved her on.

Ligea grimaced and clutched the hood of her cloak tighter around her. Rathrox was to blame, of course. These men were looking for one of the Magor. But Rathrox wouldn't expect a couple of legionnaires to be capable of dealing with a Magoria alone, though, would he? He wasn't a fool.

Without being too obvious, she looked around. On the flat roof of a treasury building, half hidden behind the ornamental pediment, two legionnaires crouched, gazing generally in her direction. One was armed with a bow, an arrow already nocked loosely in the string. The other held what could have been a whirlsling. Both were too far away for her power to reach. She could knock them off the roof with a whirlwind, though, but a wind took time to create.

The flirtatious matron walked past the guards and up several steps to the temple ramp. Her back would have been a perfect target for the men on the roof.

Clever. All the legionnaires had to do was signal to the archers when they saw a cabochon, then allow the person to pass by. He or she would be dead before they reached the top of the ramp. Yet stupidly over-optimistic, too. No Magoroth bent on deception was going to let a legionnaire look at her hands . . .

There were still ten or eleven people shuffling forward between Ligea and the legionnaires. She was on the edge of the pavement of the Pilgrim's Way, and she unobtrusively pointed the palm of her left hand at the dusty earth a few paces away. Without allowing the power to ignite any light, she started a tiny dust devil. It swirled up a handful of dry dirt and spun giddily. She increased the power and sucked in more dust, a few leaves. The man behind her noticed the disturbance and pointed it out to the baker.

She added more power and moved the living wind to whip

at a sage bush. The spiral grew, imbibing sand and leaves and grass seeds, until it was as high as she was tall. The murmur of voices grew with it, a mutter passing along the line of waiting people like a stream over stones. Heads followed the path of the gyrating wind, a dust devil no longer.

'Goddess,' the baker's wife said in a frightened whisper. 'Glaucus, what was it you said you heard about a whirlwind?'

'There was a rumour – just a silly rumour. And that little bitty thing is not a whirlwind. It's just a dust devil.'

'Dust devils aren't that large,' she said uneasily. 'The rumour said everyone should leave the city on the day of the whirlwinds . . .'

'Melete's tits, Julia – one dust devil is not a day of whirlwinds!'

Ligea scaled up the wind and drew it closer. People began to scatter as unease became real fear. Many ran for the entrance gate, then panicked when they found their way blocked by the crowd coming in. Most left the Pilgrim's Way to seek protection among the treasuries, scrambling through the intervening herb gardens. The panic spread, just as frightening as the whirlwind, and just as fast. Mothers grabbed their children; men pulled their wives to safety, diving away from the paths. The baker and his wife dropped flat to the ground, hoping the wind would pass over them. Most ran for shelter, flinging themselves into the portico of the nearest treasury, or crowding onto the temple ramp, or heaving themselves up onto the temple terrace and hefting others up after them. The ramp spilled people from its open side as if they were oranges toppling from an overladen basket.

Ligea temporarily blocked off the emotions around her. They were too overwhelming, too stark, too ripe with terror. They made her feel too guilty. She couldn't handle that, not now. She needed a few minutes' respite from the assault.

She paused briefly, long enough to slip her sword from under her cloak and touch it to the edge of the wind. The tower of whirling air turned gold. The grasses and leaves and bushes within burst into incandescent flames. Before hiding her sword again, she detached part of the burning whirlwind and sent it spinning onto the rooftop where the legionnaires stood. For a moment they hesitated, then leaped from the roof. She could not tell if they survived the fall.

Cautiously she looked around to see if anyone had noticed her glowing sword, but as far as she could see, no one was interested in her. Terror blinded them to everything except their own safety. Over at the base of the ramp, the first two legionnaires were cowering against the edge of the temple terrace, heads ducked down to avoid the flying grit and dust.

She put her sword back into the sheath hung on a baldric under her cloak, and headed towards the ramp. The wind followed her, a gyration of light and crackling sound. She feigned a terrified look over her shoulder and began to run, screaming. The two legionnaires looked up – and bolted. Those on the ramp either scrambled to safety in the temple, or jumped down to the ground and fled. Ligea paused the whirlwind and climbed the now-deserted ramp to the stoa.

People crowded between the long peristyles that supported the roof, pressing towards the altar and statue of the Goddess at the far end. Women sobbed, children wailed. Ligea squeezed her way through the crowd to the base of the statue.

Antonia was there, protected by temple guards. The crowd around her was calm; perhaps they believed their safety was ensured by the proximity of the statue, or the presence of the High Priestess. The sacrificial table to one side was red with blood from the slaughtered lamb, and blood still dripped into the bronze bowl beneath. Antonia was lying prostrate in prayer before the statue, one hand reaching up to clutch the marble toes at the edge of the plinth. Worshippers stirred uneasily as people glanced over their shoulders at the whirlwind.

Ligea dodged behind the last of the closest of the columns. Under the cover of her cloak, she slipped her sword out of its sheath again, poked the tip out through the folds of the garment, and sent a shaft of light towards the statue. It blossomed out to envelop the sculpture in gold, until Melete shed light like the reflections of a lamp in a looking glass.

A collective gasp rose up from the devotees. The rush of emotion that followed broke through Ligea's defences. She felt it all – fear, awe, delight – a plethora of conflicting sentiments spilling into the golden glow that permeated the building in place of the dying twilight. Someone called out, 'We are saved!' Antonia looked up at the statue and her face shone, her ecstasy a palpable touch in Ligea's mind.

Moondaft woman. Rathrox must have warned her, but she still wanted to believe in the Goddess. And this a priestess who'd cheated believers for years with her damnable doggerel.

Giving one last glance behind to make sure the whirlwind was still obeying her touch, Ligea turned her attention to the lamb splayed out on the altar. She didn't know what question the High Priestess had asked to have answered in the entrails, but it didn't matter. Without moving from where she was, she tugged the lamb innards onto the floor with power from her sword. Worshippers scattered to avoid the splash of blood and guts as it hit the marble tiles. The gasp of the devotees was one of awe.

Deftly, she rearranged the intestines to form the symbol of flight, an arrow. It pointed away from the statue towards the North Gate. She opened her mouth to cry out, but the words she wanted to use were already on someone else's lips.

'The Goddess bids us flee! Look at the entrails. Tyr is doomed – we must leave the city!'

Antonia and her augur stared at the entrails in horror. 'It's true,' the priestess whispered. 'It's telling us to leave.'

But few waited to hear her. They were already abandoning the temple as rapidly as they had sought its illusion of safety, shouting the news as they ran.

Ligea snorted, and let them stream past her on either side before following. Along the Pilgrim's Way, she stopped near Gayed's tomb, the whirlwind still bobbing in her wake. She was tempted to blast the statue of him to oblivion, to obliterate his name on the plinth. She could do it so easily . . . but Antonia would report it to Rathrox and that might give him an idea of just who was responsible for what was happening. He might guess as soon as Favonius returned from the Mirage, but she still hoped not. And the more time Arcadim had to reinvest her money and cover the trail before the Brotherhood started to investigate her, the better.

'Gayed Lucius,' she said, staring at that chiselled face, once so loved, 'you are going to be obliterated from memory in Tyr.' One day she would return and blast the statue into a shower of splinters and dust.

She moved on. What she had achieved in the temple was beyond her expectations, yet it wasn't enough. Few of the highborn had deigned to be present in such a huge, undisciplined crowd, and she needed the highborn to be just as frightened as everyone else. Their slaves had to have a chance to slip away . . .

She walked to the edge of the temple grounds on the northern side. From this vantage point, she was high enough to look down on the roofs of the quarter known as the Abundantia. This was the heart of the more prosperous area of the city, where many of the richest families had their villas. Her cabochon beckoned the whirlwind and sent it out over the houses, but not before she had strengthened its colour, quickened its spin, increased the violence of its incandescence.

She had no wish to pit the strength of a wind against the walls of a solid building; instead, she simply dropped the base of the whirlwind straight into the open atrium of one villa after another. The spinning air picked up little more than water and fish and a few lily pads, or the odd piece of furniture, cushion or drape from an adjacent space, but the roar of it, the greedy force of it, the sparking fiery colour – it would frighten.

She stirred uncomfortably as she watched it do its work. *Once I was one of them . . . living as they do, believing in the same things, counting them as friends.*

Ten minutes later, she had to stop. The houses as yet untouched by the whirlwind were now all too far away, and she was too tired. She had done as much as she could there.

Goddessdamn, she thought as she walked wearily through the crowds down the Forum Publicum towards the Marketwalk, pushing the whirlwind in front of her, *how in all Acheron's mists did I end up like this?*

And then, *This is madness* . . . She was one person. In such a crowd a single arrow or even a dagger thrust could so easily turn all her dreams to dust.

The timing for the whirlwind had been well chosen. Most of those in charge of city administration had gone home for the day. By the time they knew something was wrong, the streets were clogged with people and Tyr had disintegrated into chaos. The Prefect Urbis wasn't even in the city; after his traumatic experience with the Oracle, he had removed himself and his family to his country estate.

Rathrox did his best, returning to the Magistrium to order his compeers to search for and kill any Kardi woman they found in the vicinity of the whirlwind, but he knew he may as well have asked a farmer to find a particular stalk of wheat in a grain field.

He grabbed Clemens and his personal guard and headed for the Meletian temple himself, guessing that was where the whirlwind had started. Clemens, as usual, was chattering in his ear, something about having received a message from Getria and someone called Favonius. In his worry, Rathrox took no notice.

The whirlwind had become a gyration of colour and flame and showering sparks, all the more spectacular now that the dark was closing in. Although they hurried, by the time they arrived at the temple the wind had moved and was halfway down the Forum Publicum heading towards the palace. To Rathrox's barely suppressed fury, no one was able to tell him who had been responsible. Grim-faced, he surveyed the wreckage around the temple. Much of it, as Antonia pointed out, had been caused not by the wind, but by the press of people trampling the herb gardens, or sending some of the smaller urns and statues tumbling.

Antonia was in her element, dealing with distraught citizens seeking information and guidance. Her advice was the same to all: leave the city until the whirlwind was gone. Melete had commanded it. Only in flight was salvation ensured. She herself was going soon too – she was just waiting for her acolytes to finish packing up the more valuable of the votive offerings for transport. They would wait out the crisis in the Meletian temple along the paveway to Otus.

Rathrox was furious with her. 'You should be setting an example, not encouraging people in this foolishness,' he snarled when he heard her telling all this to a portly wine merchant leading a deputation from the commercial quarter.

To his utter amazement, the wine merchant turned on him. 'I don't know who you are, Dominus,' he said, 'but you shouldn't be talking to the High Priestess that way! I'm just a simple merchant, but I know we should respect those who serve the gods. And if the Goddess tells me to leave the city, then I shall put my faith in her advice. The High Priestess *is* setting an example – of obedience to Melete!' He turned back to Antonia. 'May the Goddess bless you, Reverence.'

Fortunately for the merchant, Rathrox was distracted at that moment by the arrival of Legate Valorian and a squad of men on horseback. The Legate managed to look remarkably cool and unflurried. 'Magister,' he asked, 'what the Vortex is going on? I was told the whirlwind started here, and one of my two snipers is now lying in the portico of the treasury over there with a broken leg. The other says the whirlwind deliberately targeted them. Forced them to jump off the roof!'

Rathrox frowned. 'I don't know, Legate. But I think you should be following the whirlwind to find out who is controlling it. Look for a Kardi woman and kill her.' He pointed at the gyration in the sky. 'Get after it, man!'

'By all that's holy, Magister, it took me all this time just to get here! The Forum is packed with every blessed handcart in the city and half the wagons, and every confounded one of them trying to head for a different city gate. The Exaltarch ordered all the gates closed, but I doubt that order got through in time. I advised him to stay put, by the way. I can't be responsible for his safety in all this.' He turned to his legionnaires with a theatrical sigh. 'Men, looks as if we are heading back down the Forum again – try not to trample any citizens along the away, eh?'

Impossible man, Rathrox thought. *How ever did such a perfumed peacock get to be Legate of the Tyr Legion?*

Valorian, about to ride away, paused. 'Oh, Magister, that legionnaire who brought you the message from Getria today says the Stalwarts were wiped out in Kardiastan. Is that true?'

Rathrox straightened up, glaring. 'Get on with it, Legate!'

Valorian shrugged and rode away. Rathrox turned his fury on Clemens. 'Why the Vortex didn't you give me the message?' he roared.

Clemens knew better than to remind him he had tried. Wordlessly he dug in his tunic and pulled out the scroll in its tube, and handed it over. Rathrox snatched it from him. As he read the contents, he felt all the blood leave his face. Favonius Kyranon, he now remembered, was the name of Ligea's lover, and his message was one of treachery.

'Clemens, I am going to go back and have another word with the High Priestess.' He waved Favonius' letter. 'With this, at least I might be able to open her eyes now. In the meantime, I want you to take a squad of heavily armed Brotherhood men – with whirlslings and rip-discs, some archers too – and go to the Villa Gayed on Senators' Row. If anyone uses magic on you, kill them. If there are any Kardi there, kill them. Otherwise, I want you to arrest anyone in the house, anyone at all, and have them taken under heavy guard to the Brotherhood cells. Not to the Cages, mind, but to the Magistrium. I want you to search the villa from top to bottom and bring me every piece of parchment and scroll and wax tablet that it contains. Any account books. Anything at all that seems interesting. Bring any women's white wraps that you find and look for a blonde wig.'

Clemens looked thunderstruck. 'You – you don't think *Ligea Gayed* is the woman we are looking for, do you, Magister?'

'No, no. She knew this letter would be written, so I don't think she would risk coming back to Tyr. Why should she?' He could have added, 'when she is the rightful ruler in Kardiastan,' but

Clemens knew nothing of that, so he refrained and said instead, 'But Favonius does offer proof of her treachery. We'll see if anyone else from Kardiastan has been using her villa.' His eyes narrowed. 'I'd love it if she returned. I'd like to see her crucified at the gates, begging to die.'

Clemens's eyes widened. Ligea Gayed? *Crucified?*

The night darkened, but the whirlwind supplied plenty of light. It towered far above the highest building and must surely have been visible all over the city. Apart from the occasional burst of power from her sword to maintain its glow, there wasn't that much Ligea had to do. The whirling maintained itself: sometimes sucking in debris, sometimes winding itself tight, sometimes opening up wide like a gigantic maw on a rampage in search of more fodder. Rainbow flames flickered within as debris burned; the sparks cascaded free like burning raindrops, yet when they brushed the skin of those underneath, they burned only with a touch as cold as ice.

The light the spiral cast was enough to illuminate the chaos its presence wrought. People were indeed fleeing the city. Many tried to take their wealth with them – the streets were choked with laden handcarts and horses, even a few oxcarts spilling goods like soldiers' plunder. To avoid the carts, some of those without wheeled transport took off their sandals and walked down the paved water channels that ran along either side of the Forum.

Although Ligea had hefted the whirlwind up high to avoid harming anyone, the sight of it coming closer was enough to turn the chaos of the crowded streets into rampant pandemonium. People fled, leaving their goods behind. Children were separated from parents, wives from husbands, slaves from masters. The wild wail of the wind obliterated the screams of terror or any rational voice. Tiles were ripped from the roofs as the gyration passed, and flying debris became a danger to those beneath.

Someone clutched at Ligea's arm. A boy of fourteen or so, wearing an artisan's garb. 'What's happening? Where should we go?' he asked, his eyes wide with uncontrolled terror. 'Is it the end of the world?'

'No, of course not. Don't panic,' she said, striving to calm him. 'Leave the city by the North Gate, and wait outside till morning.' Then people pushed between them and he was swept away. She walked on, trying not to absorb the pathos of lives reduced to a few belongings, not to hear the misery of fear around her, not to be seared by the pain filling the air. *You knew, Ligea. You always knew it would lead to this.*

When she arrived at the square in front of the palace at the end of the Forum Publicum, city guards – Legate Valorian's men from the Tyr Legion – were trying to block the four main streets: the Marketwalk, the Via Pecunia that led to the North Gate, the Via Thelassa that ran along the river to the docklands and the Via Dolce that led to the Snarls.

'Go home!' a centurion was shouting. 'Stay indoors and nothing will happen to you!' His men seized a handcart from a pair of burly brothers wearing the insignia of the Wheelwrights' Guild and deliberately overturned it in the roadway, to form part of a barricade. Enraged, the two wheelwrights attacked the legion-naires. Fortunately for the former, the fight was overwhelmed by a surge of people from the Forum, frantically pushing their way forward to escape the approaching whirlwind. A group of highborn men on horseback with their womenfolk in a covered ox-wagon added to the confusion. Surrounded by their slaves and personal armed guards, they forced their way down the Via Thelassa heading for the Via Pecunia. Ligea recognised the man riding in the lead by his hawk-nose and close-set eyes: Devros Lucius, the head of the Lucii, one of the powerful families who eyed the Exaltarch's seat for one of their own.

The centurion in charge tried reasoning with him. 'Dominus,' he said, 'it is the wish of the Exaltarch that the highborn set an example and do not leave the city!'

'An *example*?' Devros cried, 'And where *is* the Exaltarch? I don't see him! Why have we been given no guidance? Where is the Prefect Urbis? Where is the Magister Officii? This is disgraceful!'

His wife poked her head out from under the wagon covering.

'The High Priestess sent her acolytes to tell us to flee, Centurion. Melete herself sent warning . . .' The sound of the whirlwind overhead drowned her out. She screamed.

Devros signalled his guards and they edged their horses towards the legionnaires. The centurion glanced fearfully upwards at the blazing whirl in the darkening sky, then back at Devros glowering at him with his eagle-like glare, and decided that it would be unwise to pit his men against one of the Lucii. Especially when it seemed likely they were all going to be swept up into the wind any minute. He pulled his men back. Ligea snatched the opportunity to slip past.

She took the access lane around to the back of the palace area, where the palace guards and the city guards had their barracks. As she expected, all was quiet. Most of the guards had long since been called out to maintain order.

Those few left on duty fled as the whirlwind dipped towards them. She dropped the whirlwind into the roof of the barracks and removed all the tiles, stripping the rafters clean, sucking up everything she could from inside the rooms. She dumped it all in the centre of the parade ground and set fire to it with her sword, stoking the flames from a distance till it was an inferno. Spears, armour, weaponry, saddlery – it all melted or burned to ash. Slaves came running, but there was nothing they could do. No one noticed the drab woman in a cloak who slunk by along the wall, heading for the gateway once more.

Outside in the streets again, she passed the palace – splitting off part of the whirlwind to send it careering through an upstairs window – before entering the wealthy merchants' quarter along the Via Pecunia leading to the North Gate. What happened inside the palace, she had no way of knowing and didn't much care. Instead of doing the same thing to all the merchant houses she passed, she just dropped tiles and other debris on the roofs of all the villas. The noise was enough to make the occupants cringe with a fear she could feel through the walls.

It was enough. No, it was too much. She allowed the whirlwind to die. The spiral loosened, the fires dimmed, the colours faded, the burden it carried vanished. She released her last hold on it, and it blew away, dust and ash and leaves drifting in a night breeze. She felt as if part of herself had also wafted off, leaving behind only a shell of what she could have been, of what she had once been.

Goddess, but I am tired.

Overwhelmed by the press of terrified people, the legionnaires at the North Gate had given up trying to close the gates to stop people from leaving, or checking those who did leave. They stood to one side, talking urgently among themselves, exuding their anxieties like quivering rabbits.

She enhanced her hearing and listened.

'You can't close a gate when the roadway is packed full of people!' one was protesting. 'If I'd carried out the order when I got it, I would have had to squash half the rich merchants of the Via Pecunia, not to mention their fat wives.'

'Their guards would have killed us anyway,' another soldier added morosely. 'But I think we'd better close it now. The crowd is thinning.'

'It was an order from the Exaltarch. We are going to be scourged over this.'

There were several bodies lying on the edge of the road, hastily covered by some cheap matting. Soldiers? People they had killed? Accidental deaths? Ligea had no idea, and didn't want to know. She dragged herself past them and out into the night, her gait that of an old woman crippled in the joints. It was no act; she felt ancient, exhausted by her own longevity. Yet she had one final deed of defiance left to carry out even now; she turned and melted the hinges to the left-hand gate, just to make sure the legionnaires could not close it.

People had collected not far beyond the gates, as if they didn't know where to go now that they had left the city. The night was moonless, but bright enough. Stars spilled from the horn of the Cornucopia constellation like glistening wet crystals strewn across the sky. Even the cloud of red dust that formed the shape of the horn cast a ruby glow as groups of city people settled down on either side of the road to wait out the night. They huddled together, steeped in their bewilderment, without purpose, or even hope. Their lassitude, washing over her with the pull of an ocean tide, made her stumble and she might have fallen if someone had not reached out and caught her by the elbow. She should have sensed him sooner, would have done so in normal circumstances, but nothing was normal now. There was too much assailing her for the more mundane to reach her core.

Thankful, she was just glad he was there.

'Lean on me,' Brand said.

'I thought we agreed to meet at the shrine down the road.' The shrine to Barcius, God of Travellers, where you could buy blessed oil and light a votive lamp for a safe trip, was not even half a mile further on.

'Yes, but I knew you would have exhausted yourself.' Brand sounded like an exasperated mother with a tiresome child, but she was too exhausted to be anything but grateful.

'Has everything gone well?' she asked.

'The Villa Gayed is empty. Nothing incriminating left behind. Slight change in plan, though. I got us a cart ride instead of just horses. It's at the shrine.'

'A cart? Why?'

'So you could rest on the way. I hired it. The driver delivered hay from a farm up north, so he was delighted to have paying passengers for part of the journey back.'

They walked down the path to the shrine in silence. He didn't bother to hide his worry, but it made her feel safe. For once, she was glad to surrender her independence. *Just for a while*, she thought. *Tomorrow I can be me again.*

CHAPTER ELEVEN

Reality impinged long before she was ready for it.

Her sense of emotions dragged her back to rational thought. Pain, intense deep-felt grief. Impossible to ignore. It came from inside the shrine itself, shrieking at her, snaring her with its need for amelioration. Brand was intent on getting her to the cart and leaving the area as quickly as possible, but she couldn't walk away from such agony.

'Don't,' she said as he tried to lead her away. 'There's someone who needs help—'

She slipped out of her sandals and mounted shrine steps silvered with starlight and cold underfoot. A man sat back on his heels before the altar, rocking to and fro, illuminated by the single oil lamp burning there. Something lay across his knees. His anguish burned at her, so solid she could taste the bitterness of it like wormwood in her mouth. Several people stood nearby, sobbing with a quieter grief. She approached across the marble floor, buffeted by their emotions.

It was a child he held, although in the feeble light she could see little else and her senses were overwhelmed by the man's pain. 'Can I help?' she asked. 'I have some skill with healing—' Behind her Brand gave a grunt of disapproval, as if to ask how she thought she could help in her present weak state. In truth she wasn't sure. She had held a little of her power in reserve for personal protection, but she needed food and rest; she needed it desperately.

The man moved without speaking, and the child's head flopped back over his arm like a rag doll. It was only then that she saw: the jagged tear across the side of the throat, right through to the spine, red and moist like the bloodied muzzle of a predator. Above that flapping gape, a girl's face, white, drained of all blood, framed with curls. No more than six years old. Her blood was everywhere, soaking her father's wrap, pooling on the floor, congealing on his hands.

She drew in a sharp breath, wanting not to have seen. Wanting not to have that evening's work reduced in her memory to its worst specific detail.

'She was hit by a roof tile flying through the air,' someone said. Almost too prosaic an explanation for a tragedy of such proportions.

Ligea stood, bludgeoned into immobility. A child. Dead. She may as well have slit the throat herself . . .

Goddess forgive . . .

This is what it is to start a war.

It was Brand who turned her away, led her out of the shrine to the cart. 'You can't do anything here, Ligea. And we have to get away. Climb in.'

She was incapable of resisting; incapable, even, of any thought except to remember what she had just seen and then revisit it again. And yet again. She clambered up into the open cart, and Brand followed. She sat huddled against a heap of empty sacks slung behind the driver's seat. Brand nodded to the man and he whipped awake a pair of sleepy horses. As he guided them over to the dirt track alongside the paved road, Ligea stirred herself enough to redirect him.

'No,' she said, and her tone was sharp. 'Stay on the paveway.'

'I am not authorised,' he began. The paveway was for legionnaires, for the rich. Not for plodding carts bringing hay to the city or returning to the farm for another load.

'*I'm* authorising you,' she snapped.

The driver looked at Brand. 'You'll pay the fine, then?'

'If there is one.'

It was a long time before she spoke again, and then it was to whisper, 'It is one thing to speak of the future and to think you can bear it. It is quite another to see it.'

'You are weak at the moment,' he said. 'You've used too much power. You have to eat something and then you must sleep. Remember your baby.' He handed her a hunk of bread and meat wrapped in a cloth. 'Eat.'

'Eat? Sleep?' She looked at him, but could not discern the details of his expression. 'Goddess, Brand, that was a child, and just one of many I may have killed tonight. Probably *was* one of many.'

'Listen, Ligea. You made a decision to do this. I don't know whether it was a good decision or not, but I do know this: once it was made, there was no turning back. Only with success will you give that child's death a meaning.'

'Acheron's hells, Brand, giving it meaning won't help *her*!'

'Perhaps it will. Who's to know? Maybe she will look back at us through Acheron's mists and know it was all for a reason . . .'

She scorned his remark for what it was: a platitude from someone who didn't believe what he said.

He indicated the food. 'Eat.'

She took a slice of meat, stuffed it between two slices of bread and ate hungrily, despising herself for her appetite, yet unable to curb her need to replenish her energy. 'Brand,' she asked, words muffled by her chewing, 'what did you say were the words written on the lintel of the Temple of the Unknown God?'

'"Do no person harm".'

'One day that will be written across the lintel of the Meletian Temple in the Forum Publicum.'

He didn't reply and, tired, she was about to doze off, when suddenly her senses alerted her to something she hadn't felt in weeks. She sat up, suddenly wakeful. 'Stop the cart!'

The driver turned around to see if he had heard aright. 'Stop the cart,' she said again, and he hauled on the reins. She sat for a moment without moving, as if listening, but it was another sense she had called into play.

'Magor,' she whispered to Brand. 'I can sense one of the Magor ... but so faint.' She stood up in the cart and looked around. There were still people out there, some walking in the darkness, others huddled against the low burial vaults that lined either side of the paveway. Tombs, where Tyr buried the dead who could not afford a place in the necropolis. She switched to the Kardi language. 'Is there someone out there who understands me?' she called. 'Please, come – I am in the cart on the paveway.'

Heads swung in her direction, pale patches in the dimness of night. Then someone stepped forward. 'I do. I understand.' A woman's voice, stumbling with her imperfect memories of a language she hadn't used in a long time.

Ligea went to the back of the cart and leaned over the tailgate. 'Who are you?' she asked, still speaking Kardi. 'You are Magor, surely!' And yet something didn't feel right.

The woman came closer. She was perhaps fifty years old, and wore a slave collar. 'I was once, but no longer,' she said. 'How did you know—?'

'I am a Magoria.'

Ligea allowed her cabochon to glow slightly and held her hand out in greeting, but the woman did not move to take it. 'I am not one of the Magor now,' she said, her sorrow so crushing it took Ligea's breath away. 'I feel nothing any more.'

Ligea flashed the light from her cabochon into the woman's opened palm. There was a green gem there, but it was crazed through with lines like a Mirage sky. 'Sweet Elysium! How did that happen?'

'Does it matter how?'

Ligea felt the bite of her pain again, as strong as if it were her own. She swallowed, forcing down the mass of fears it roused in her. *What if that was done to me?* 'What is your name, Theura?'

'Narjemah.' A brief pause, then, 'Magoria.' There was so much pride there. The bitter, wrenching pride of a woman daring another to pity her, or even to acknowledge her tragedy.

'I am Sarana.' She looked across at the edge of the road where Narjemah's companions still waited in watchful silence, their faces indistinct in the starlight. 'Are you with friends or your, um, master?'

There was a moment's silence, before Narjemah replied. 'We are slaves, all of us. We decided to escape. We heard rumours – there have been tales through all the slave quarters, all over the city, for several weeks, about the day of the whirlwinds. I even heard the Brotherhood was looking for Kardis with gems. We heard that Tyr would fall and slaves would be free if they, er, fled when the whirlwinds came. We had a bad master, and – and many reasons to take the risk.' Ligea felt her implacable determination. 'They say we should go to the Ammalonian shrine. Do you know where that is, Magoria?'

'Ocrastes' balls,' Brand said in Ligea's ear, 'the rumour has gained a tongue and a tail since I started it. Do they really think *all* slaves are going to be freed, just like that?'

She ignored him and said, 'Freedom has to be fought for, Narjemah. It is rarely granted gratis to those who have lost it. The shrine is at the twentieth milestone. We are going that way, if you wish to ride with us.'

The woman shook her head. She waved a hand at the group by the roadside, abandoning her hesitant Kardi for Tyranian. 'They may not be Kardi, but they are my friends. My family now – all I have. I do not leave them so easily, Magoria.' She looked at the cart. 'We can all fit.'

Ligea laughed. 'Ah, why not? Brand, move over.'

'I don't take more people unless I get more money,' the driver growled.

Brand sighed and fished out his purse as the slaves, in answer to Narjemah's call, crossed the road towards the cart.

Rathrox Ligatan felt ill. His insides curdled. *Ligea Gayed*. She had betrayed them. She must have found out that as a child she had been kidnapped rather than rescued.

His own plan – so carefully woven, so beautifully timed, so ingeniously executed, at least in the beginning – to have her rule in Madrinya as Tyrans' puppet, it was all in ruins at his feet.

Bator Korbus must never find out. Ocrastes' balls, he blames me enough already . . . If he ever learned Ligea was involved in the downfall of the Stalwarts, it would be Rathrox who was nailed to a cross.

And now Tyr had suffered at the hands of another of her kind. *And if it takes me the rest of my life I will bring both the bitches down in a way that will make their souls weep before they die.*

This one in Tyr, she is pregnant, whoever she is. And already worried about her baby. That's a weakness. All I have to do is get my hands on that child once it is born, and I will have her in my power . . .

CHAPTER TWELVE

'Ligea?'

Brand's voice, penetrating her sleep. Dragging her back, upwards, into a world of light and wakefulness. Into the problems waiting for her. Into a world, she realised with more than a touch of depression, where problems would always be waiting.

They had arrived at milestone twenty earlier in the day and said goodbye to the cart driver. She'd led their small group away from the paveway, past the shrine to Ammalonia and over a low hill. There, in a coppice with a spring, workers from her country estate waited with a wagon just as she had arranged. They had a fire going, and were cooking food. She sent one of them back to the shrine to direct anyone else who turned up there, hoping that in fact some would.

'Don't worry,' Brand had said, 'we're the first because we travelled all night and we used the paveway. They'll come. We passed people trudging along the road, and I'm sure there were more waiting for daylight.'

Since then, she'd spent most of the time dozing and eating, trying to recover her Magor strength. At intervals during the day, more slaves did indeed arrive, tired and hungry and afraid, looking over their shoulders for the pursuit they knew would eventually come. Now, as Brand shook her awake and she looked around, the number of people present shocked her.

She stood up, wide-eyed with surprise. 'Goddessdamn, Brand, these are all people you enticed to leave Tyr and follow us?'

He shook his head. 'Hardly.' He sounded bemused; there must have been more than four hundred people sheltering in the coppice.

'Then where in the hells did they all come from?'

'We have a saying back in Altan: "One may as well harness the flood as contain a whisper". There could be even more people arriving tonight or tomorrow. I did warn you rumours are dangerous. We just have to hope that this one didn't spread too far, or we could have legionnaire javelins jabbing at our backsides any minute.'

'I'm hoping I left enough mess back in Tyr to keep them occupied. And are these people prepared to fight for freedom?'

'Looks like.'

'Like *her*?' Ligea pointed at a small girl playing with some leaves nearby.

He shrugged. 'A few brought their families.'

'Damn it, Brand, this is no place for children. We're raising a rebellion!'

'Slavery is no place for children, either.'

She gave him a sour look and changed the subject. 'Have there been any signs of pursuit?'

'No. Dispatch riders up and down the road all day. And a mounted squad of legionnaires went past going *towards* Tyr this evening. That's all. I rather think you're right. The legions were needed inside the city walls today.'

She breathed a little easier and looked around again. 'These people have all been fed?'

He nodded. 'Took some doing, though. Your farmers brought an ox from the farm and slaughtered it. The meat's so fresh it's as tough as bear hide, but there's plenty left if you want some. I spoke to Homfridus, by the way,' he added, referring to the controller of Ligea's country estate. 'He says he doesn't have enough carts or horses to transport everyone to our new farm hideaway. Some of these people are going to have to walk to the new place. I didn't tell him how far it was.'

She heaved a sigh. 'We will have to split them up to be less obvious. Goddess, this is going to be difficult, Brand. There's only two of us! Maybe once I've spoken to them all, I'll be able to identify a couple more leaders with enough flair to get a group from here to the foot of the mountains.'

'Homfridus is a good man. Gevenan, too, perhaps.'

She brightened. 'Did he turn up?'

'He did indeed. With no less than thirty other horse-handlers and stable boys from several households – and eighty-two horses.'

'Vortexdamn! You're joking!'

'No.' He grinned. 'Several of the slave owners actually told their horse-handlers to take the horses out of Tyr for safety's sake. They were supposed to head for their masters' country estates, of course, but . . .'

They exchanged glances and then burst into laughter. 'Where are they all?' she asked when they sobered.

'The horses? I sent them – plus most of the horse-handlers – on to the estate stables to be fed and looked after. Gevenan's still here. But he could be a problem, Ligea. He's cynical and sarcastic. Keeps people on edge.'

'Yes, I figured he was a cantankerous bastard.'

She ran her fingers through her hair and straightened her tunic. 'It's almost sundown. Get them together where I can speak to them, Brand. I'll stand in the food wagon, I think. Oh, and could you find a good strong staff? Or a cudgel or something similar? But send Gevenan across to me first.'

She washed in the stream, then slung on her baldric and sword. Her anxiety was making her stomach churn. These folk were her responsibility now, hers to save or fail. And somehow she had first to get them across Tyrans to the foot of the northern mountains.

There would be those who scorned her because she was a woman. There would be those who despised her because she was Kardi. What she did in the next few minutes would determine her success, would determine the future of these people.

Why didn't I pay more attention to my rhetoric lessons as I was growing up? I can't sway a crowd!

'So,' Gevenan drawled when he strolled across to talk to her, 'Brand tells me you are the force behind all this. You really do have divine help? All that whirlwind fire and stuff, very impressive.' The air around him shimmered with his ambivalence.

Carefully neutral, she said, 'I'm glad you came.'

'You and Brand told me to bring folk who would be of help, and I did.' He gave a disparaging sweep of his hand at those around them. 'But most of this lot you've dredged up, they're just scum. Floor sweepings from a kitchen hearth, or a stable midden. And some of them have *families*, by all that's holy.' He said that as though it was a crime. 'What kind of rebellion is this, lady?' His sneer left a trail of nastiness behind, but she caught other things too: a tinge of fear, of wariness, of watchful hope.

She shrugged. 'I'm going to have to weed some of them out.'

He leaned against the trunk of the closest tree, arms folded; an insolent pose, deliberately chosen, she guessed, to show his lack of deference. 'This Ingean standing here doesn't believe all he sees, Domina. What's more, I was once a soldier, and soldiers know one another. They know how easy it is to be enslaved by a battle lost, y'see. And so they talk of things, even to soldiers who now wear slave collars, like me. Legionnaires told me tales of the Kardi Uprising. Of the highborn Kardi who can do unnatural things. And you're Kardi – I can see that much. You're Ligea Gayed, aren't you? The old General's adopted daughter. I've been a bit dense. That scar on your face, I suppose.' He unfolded his arms to flick a finger close to her shattered cheek. 'I should have recognised you before.'

'What's your point, Gevenan?'

'My point? I want to know who I'm dealing with. Just who is this Ligea Gayed, and why should I trust her? Is she just a slave-owning bitch who's chasing power for reasons of her own? A Kardi numen with a whole repertoire of vicious magic at her disposal? A handmaiden of the gods who calls the Goddess herself to rain down fire on Tyr from Elysium? Do *you* lead this rebellion, or someone else? Who supplies the gold, Ligea? You? Or some other malcontent of a highborn bastard who wants what Bator Korbus has?'

He reached out and touched the side of her neck, running a calloused thumb up and down her throat. An overt threat, deliberately rough, backed by the spill-over of his suppressed anger. 'Our lives depend on the choices we make right now, right here.'

Ironic, she thought, I know a lie when I hear it, but at the moment I wish others had that ability, not me. I wish he could read me ...

'If there truly are gods, I've never met them,' she said. 'I'm just a Kardi who will use her power to bring the Exaltarchy to its knees in order to end slavery and free my nation. That's all. There's no one else. I would like to leave Ligea Gayed behind and I'd appreciate it if you forgot her too. Now I must talk to everyone. Listen, and decide, Gevenan of Inge.'

She jerked away from his touch, and crossed to the food wagon, where people were already gathering. She climbed onto the wagon to talk to them, and gestured for Gevenan to climb up beside her. His lip curled, but he did as she asked. She could sense other things in him now. He was intrigued, wondering what she was up to. He was attracted to what she was, a woman of power, who had something to offer him. He didn't intend to betray, but there was no idea of loyalty in him, either.

She stared at the crowd, waiting for them to quieten. She let a smidgeon of power leak from her cabochon to colour her skin. In the deepening dusk, she glowed with a silvery light that the sword gradually augmented to the richness of gold. Conversation died away, replaced by shock. Only when she had them all staring at her, hushed and nervous, did she start to speak.

She began. 'You may call me simply Domina. Like many of you, I once had a name bestowed by Tyranians who stole me from my country. I am not proud of the person who answered to that name. But, the gods be thanked, even the worst of men – or women – can change and be changed. I am now here to lead you and it is as your Domina that I will do so. And it is here, tonight, in this place, that you will make the choice to follow, or go your own way.'

There was a murmur of disbelief, and she sensed their alarm. They hadn't expected to be led by a *woman*. She read their unspoken words in their emotions. *She can't be serious! Is this what we risked our lives for? A woman's delusions of grandeur?* And yet they saw the glow along her skin. They remembered the whirlwind. They remembered the promises whispered in the rumours.

She continued, 'Tonight you make a choice to be soldiers, or to support those who will be soldiers. Soldiers will be paid the same amount as a legionnaire of equivalent rank, payment to be made on the first day of each month. Those who serve in other capacities will also be paid. And when we are more numerous and when we are ready, we will fight and defeat Bator Korbus. Some of you will die. But those who see this through to the end will be forever free.'

'Let's see the gold, Domina!' someone called from the back of the crowd.

'What makes you think a woman can win against the Exaltarch's legions?' another asked from the front row, his expression a mixture of contempt and bitterness.

'Not just any woman,' she said, raising her voice. 'You will follow *me*, and I command the whirlwind!' She drew her sword out of its sheath, filled with light, and aimed it at the ground in front of her. A dust devil formed, spinning. People edged away and a rush of anxiety fanned out through the crowd. She lifted the tiny whirlwind to where it could be better seen, touching her sword to it as it passed, so that it flared into a gyre of whirling light. It was still small and hardly a danger to even a child, but she hoped she had made a point.

'My weapons are to be feared by our enemies. But the whirlwind is on your side and it will fight for you. You know its power. You saw it spin out its chaos yesterday.' *Just as well they don't know I can't do that every day . . .*

'Are you Melete, Domina?' someone asked in awe.

'No. Just a woman who has been granted power and will use that power on your behalf. Will this be an easy road? No. If you expect to be rich and powerful by next desert-season, then this rebellion is not for you. First we have a long journey to a place of safety. Then there will be years of training and preparation.'

The man in the front row, braver than most, called out loud enough for all to hear, 'We need more than just promises and a pretty wind, Domina! How can a rabble like us defeat the likes of the Exaltarch's legions? I've never held a flipping blade in me life! And there's not one of us but don't know the penalty for treason for them that gets caught. T'aint a pretty death.'

A murmur of agreement swept the group like wind across a wheat field.

She indicated Gevenan, even though his expression was grim rather than supportive. She said, 'You will be trained by soldiers like this man. You will fight with the best weaponry money can buy. And you will be led by me.' She wrapped herself in self-warding as she spoke, then nodded to Brand where he stood at the side of the cart. 'Give the staff to Gevenan.'

Brand handed it up and the Ingean weighed it in his hands, then whirled it, testing it for balance.

'Gevenan,' she said, 'hit me with it as hard as you know how.'

His eyes widened. 'You *serious*?'

The crowd hushed as they held a collective breath.

'Do it,' she snapped.

He shrugged. 'Your funeral. Or is it mine?' He swung the staff back over his right shoulder and then swept it down in a vicious cut at her arm, aiming for a point halfway between her shoulder and her elbow. It never connected. It cracked against the invisible ward she'd just put in place, and snapped. The outer half spun out over the crowd. Gevenan was left holding the stump. He shook his jarred hand and swore, his astonishment clear to all.

Ligea turned to the silent, wary crowd. 'In a moment, I will speak to you, one by one,' she continued. 'You will give me your loyalty, or you will leave. And bear this in mind: I can read a lie as easily as a scholar reads the written word.'

Before they could react to that, she dissipated the whirlwind and filled her sword with the dregs of power she had held back for this last demonstration. She pointed it at the trunk of a tree nearby and punched the beam of power into the wood. A hole as wide as a man's fist pierced the trunk from one side to the other. Splinters showered the ground. Sap oozed stickily as the gold light faded. 'That will be the fate of your enemies!' she cried.

At her side, Gevenan snorted.

No one appeared to move, yet a tremor went through the crowd. She whirled, and turned the light on Gevenan. Before he could react, she had sliced the slave collar from him with her sword.

He leaped back crying, 'Jumping Ocrastes!' The two pieces of the collar spun away into the hushed crowd. Two men picked up the separate pieces of the collar and, as one, they offered them to Gevenan. He bent to take hold of them and she felt his emotions, turbid with conflicting sentiments as he stood again, turning the pieces over and over in his hands, the symbol of his enslavement broken so easily by the woman who stood beside him.

Perhaps to hide his unease with mockery, he said under the cover of the babble of excitement that burst from the crowd, 'Do I get a sword like that one, Domina?'

She met his stare with a grimness of her own. 'I'm afraid not.'

'And if I were to ask why, when you are so damn powerful, you couldn't stop your cheek being ripped up the way it was, would you answer?'

'No.'

'Then it's to be hoped no one else thinks of that question.' When he spoke again, still too quietly to be heard by others, it was to give her his decision. Not as much as she had hoped for, but nor was it as little as it could have been. 'Don't ever take me for granted, Domina Ligea Gayed. I will follow you for now, but you will have to prove yourself, over and over again, before you have my loyalty. I'm no Brand. I don't ankle-rub my way onto a lady's lap, to be petted and teased and fed with titbits. Gevenan of Inge does not give allegiance to the first woman who comes by with a pretty blade, sweet promises and a gold coin. I'll teach your soldiers, but I'm not inclined to fight for you, not yet.'

His suspicion tainted the air about him, but she could sense no intention of treachery. 'That's enough for me, for now, Legate,' she said, keeping her tone as cold as mountain ice. He had managed to insult both her and Brand, after all.

'*Legate?*'

Her grin was feral mockery, without humour. 'I'll bet that's the quickest promotion you've ever had. And here's your first order: line up these people before me so I can talk to them one by one. I need to know if we have any potential traitors among them. The first fifteen will have their collars removed – if they want it so. The rest will have to wait until tomorrow or the next few days. Explain that to them. As soon as possible, we'll move them off to shelter for the night on my country estate, which is about half an hour's easy walk from here down the wagon track.'

'I've been wondering about that. Your estate will be the first place anyone will look, if they are after you. I don't relish waking up in the morning to find myself captured again.'

'No one is looking for Ligea Gayed yet, as far as I know. Besides, as of sunset tomorrow, this place has new owners. I've sold it. Tomorrow morning, we'll set off for our, um, training area. We'll be taking horses, wagons, food from this estate – all we need for the journey. The controller and the slaves come with us. Most supplies have gone on ahead already. Now take over, Legate Gevenan.'

'Yes, *General*,' he murmured in her ear, the nuance an overt sneer.

Bastard. She sighed as she climbed down from the cart. Nothing about this was going to be easy.

'Right, you mob of disbelieving sandal-lickers,' Gevenan shouted, 'here's your chance to see the Exaltarch get his sodding head knocked off with the pretty sword our lady general showed you! Line up to join up if you want to be on the winning side, and the first fifteen get their collars off right now—'

Brand came across to her. He didn't look happy. 'Well, you managed to impress Gevenan anyway,' he said. 'That's a start.'

She shook her head. 'The sardonic son of a bitch is just reserving his opinion. He and I still have battles to fight that have nothing whatever to do with the Exaltarchy. And what about the rest? What do you think?'

'A mixed bag. There are plenty of hero-worshippers who'd follow you to Acheron even if all you wanted to do was spit on the God of the Netherworld. And there are others who will sneak away the first chance they get. They're scared spitless by anything that smacks of the unnatural. They won't be any great loss, though, but we'll need to keep a strict watch to make sure they don't try a little robbery before they leave.'

She nodded. 'I'll identify any troublemakers as I speak to them. My farm workers will help us keep watch tonight.'

Nothing is going to be easy. Nothing.

Narjemah was the last in line. Most of the others had already started for the farm by the time Ligea came to her.

'It would please me if you came with me,' she said, wondering if the woman had deliberately hung back so as to be the last.

'I've no choice,' the woman replied, wearing her sullenness like a cloak.

'There is always choice.'

'For the likes of me? I think not. Not since this.' She indicated her cracked cabochon. 'That rumour about Kardis and the Brotherhood: if it's not true now, it soon will be. As soon as the Brotherhood realises it was Magor magic that wrecked the city, anyone with a cabochon in their palm will be hunted down and killed.' She looked back at her hand. 'I can't remove it either – that kills us, as I am sure you know.'

'How did it happen?' Ligea asked.

'Tyranians, how else?' She shrugged. 'It was a long time ago. I was fighting the legions in Kardiastan after the Shimmer Festival massacre. They took me down with a whirlsling, and crushed my hand while I was unconscious. Not enough to kill, but enough to leak my powers. To empty me out. I have nothing left there, Magoria. Nothing. I learned to live with it. In some ways it is better being here, in Tyrans, because I never see anyone else who has power . . . until now. Until you.' Resentment bubbled up. 'Now your very presence mocks what I have lost. Every time your cabochon flares I remember I am only half alive. Once you have lost the power of your cabochon, nothing has depth any more. Have you any idea of what it is like to no longer feel, for example, the – the – *saturation* of being loved and desired? No, I'm wrong – it's not like being half alive. It is like being half *dead.*'

Goddess, Ligea thought. *She's right. That's exactly what it would be like not to have power. Half dead, half blind, half deaf.*

'I don't want to go with you, Magoria,' Narjemah added. 'But I have no choice. Although I'll be confounded if I know what use I will be to you. I was just a drudge back at my master's house in Tyr.'

'I need you, Narjemah. I need you desperately. I need one of the Magor who can help me have my baby.'

The pause that followed was filled with emotion, but every time Ligea thought she understood what the other woman felt, the mix changed. Finally Narjemah said, 'You're *pregnant*? With him?' She nodded in Brand's direction.

'No. My son's father is the Mirager of Kardiastan.'

Narjemah gave a sharp intake of breath. 'Mirageless souls! You carry a Magori? An *heir* to Kardiastan? You'll have to send him back! He won't have a cabochon otherwise.'

'I need you, Narjemah.'

'To take him back?'

'There will be someone who will come from Kardiastan for him. I hope you will consider going with them. But it's not just that. It's – well, I know nothing about—' She paused, then added weakly, 'Anything.'

Narjemah gave her a blank stare.

'Being pregnant. Giving birth to a Magori. Looking after a baby.'

'Mirageless soul, you're *drained*, aren't you? You've been throwing power all over the place, without a thought for your child.'

'I did ask when I was back in Kardiastan about using power when you're pregnant. They said everyone does.'

'Maybe, but they sure as the sands are dry don't use it all up till they have nothing left! Have you any idea of the damage you may have done to the poor wee mite?'

Ligea stilled. She thought her heart stopped beating. 'No. Do – do you know?'

'No – because no Magor woman expecting a child would ever *dream* of doing what you did yesterday! Of being so – so *reck-less* with your Magor strength.'

They stared at one another, two women suddenly connected by a shared fear. 'I'll come with you,' Narjemah said finally. 'You're right. You do need me.'

By all that's holy, Ligea thought, horrified all over again, *have I just done something even worse to my son?*

CHAPTER THIRTEEN

The Quyr Mountains were a herd of white horses galloping towards Kardiastan across the skyline, manes and tails whipping in the wind, heads tossed high, ears pricked, bodies shadowed purple where muscle knotted and sinew twisted, their galloping feet lost deep in the snow . . .

Fanciful. And stupid. She had no time to be fanciful. What was it about giving birth to a baby that could turn a woman's thoughts to sentimental mush?

She stopped briefly to study the mountains that were the wall behind the farm. Still generously snow-capped by winter, the white peaks – the horses of her fancy – dipped down to the rugged slopes and canyons of the foothills. The hills, where snow was short-lived, were scantily clad with dry scrub and crisscrossed with a cat's cradle of smugglers' paths descending from narrow mountain passes unknown to any Tyranian authority. So easy to get lost up there. So easy to lose oneself. She smiled; that's how she had first met the smugglers.

As she strode on through the orchard of the property they now called First Farm, careful not to stumble on the rough furrows of the hill slope, she knew a smuggler waited for her; she'd felt him trip the ward she had erected around the perimeter. She guessed he waited at the small temple devoted to Selede, Goddess of Cunning, that graced the crest beyond the fig trees.

The presence of smugglers using paths through First Farm had been a surprise, sheer luck. She and Arcadim had bought the rundown farm in this remote spot without any idea it was the heart of a smuggling route between the vassal state of Quyr beyond the mountains, and the markets of the rest of the Exaltarchy, a route designed to avoid the hefty tax of the customs posts. And, better still, she now knew that every smuggler was a rebel at heart, hating the Exaltarch and his laws and his legions.

Ligea already knew who waited at the temple: Berg Firegravel. She'd recognised his signature the moment he pushed his way through the ward that circled the farm. She was proud of that ward; no thicker than a silk thread, and no stronger either, a little below shoulder height, it was her warning signal yet took little strength to maintain. It did not stop intruders, of course; in fact, they would see nothing and feel little as they pushed through it, but it was all she needed to raise the alarm. And in cases like this, when she was familiar with the intruder, it was even enough to tell her who the visitor was.

'General! Wait!'

She suppressed a sigh. Gevenan. Even without the message of her senses, she would have known. No one else called her general. He strode out of the olive grove on course to intercept her.

'Yes, *Legate*?' she asked as he caught up. Damn the man. He was like grass seeds caught in a trouser leg. Hard to get rid of, and so confoundedly irritating in the meantime.

'Brand said you were going to meet the Quyriot. You shouldn't do that alone! Especially not carrying money.' He indicated the purse that swung at her waist. 'These men are *smugglers*, damn it!'

'One man, and it's Berg Firegravel.' A good nickname, that. Firegravel was the Quyriot word for obsidian and Berg was dark and hardy.

'I don't care. Next time call me, or one of my men.' He turned to walk with her.

'I am well able to look after myself.'

'You're my commander; that makes me responsible for your safety.'

'I am indeed your commander; therefore you should treat me as if I know what I am doing!'

'You were the one who told me you could be brought down by an arrow, just as easily as the next man. Woman.'

She smothered another sigh. 'I do have the advantage of being able to sense aggressive intention. Berg has no such intention. And he is alone, except for that disreputable pony of his.'

'The shit-coloured one that looks like a tattered bearskin on legs?'

'See for yourself.'

The animal in question was tied up to a temple pillar, and was indeed as wretched in appearance as Gevenan had described. Real bearskins, sewn together to serve as Berg's cloak and now flung across the beast's back, did nothing to dispel the image. However, neither Ligea nor Gevenan were deceived. The pony, shaggy and unkempt as he appeared to be, was plateau-bred, capable of carrying a man over steep mountain passes in the cold without a stumble on ice patches or loose scree, and just as able to maintain a steady pace over the plains. What they lacked in speed, Quyriot ponies made up for in endurance.

'I've been meaning to ask – what are those foot strap things the Quyriots use, attached to the saddle?' she inquired as they neared the temple.

'They call them stirrups. Probably to keep the rider's feet off the blasted ground. Damned ponies are so short-legged they look like weasels.'

'Try them.'

'What?'

'Stirrups. Have some made for your own mount and try them out.'

'Why in all of Acheron would I want to do that?'

'Maybe because these Quyriot plateau people are the best horsemen I've ever seen. And it seems to me that if you had a way of bracing your feet when you launch a spear, or loose an arrow, or sweep a sword, it could only be an advantage. Make some and try them. Although I wonder if they might not be better made of metal than just leather.'

He shrugged as if he thought it yet another weird idea of hers, but she had already felt his quickening interest as he began to think it through. *The stubborn old dog. He won't ever acknowledge I might be right if he can avoid it.*

They mounted the temple steps together, to greet Berg who was insolently leaning up against the statue of Selede. Ligea had already discovered the Quyriots did not worship the gods of the pantheon and loved to show their disrespect for them. She was not altogether sure what they *did* worship; they never spoke of their beliefs except in the vaguest terms.

He was dressed, as usual, in warm woollens with beading sewn around the collar, yoke and cuffs. A wide cloth belt was patterned with obsidian. Necklaces, earrings, brooches, bangles and rings made of obsidian and glass beads glistened in the sunshine.

'Like a bloody walking pawnshop,' Gevenan muttered in her ear.

'Hoy, lady,' Firegravel said, ignoring Gevenan. 'Y'dropped your load, since I last saw yus. A lad, was it?'

'It was indeed.'

'May he ride like the wind and fart like the devil, then.'

Gevenan gave a bark of laughter.

'Thank you, Berg. I am sure he will,' she replied, wondering if every man in her life at the moment was intent on banishing all memories of polite society from her brain. 'Wouldn't you like to come up to the villa to drink to his birth, and share a meal?'

Berg shook his head. She knew him well enough to know that he felt uneasy if he ventured too far from the mountain passes. 'The mountains call me,' he said, a polite way of saying he had already reached the end of the preliminaries, and was eager to move on to business. 'But I've brought yus more fancy glass and gravel.' He dug into the bags he had taken from his horse and produced several drawstring pouches. He tipped a sample of the contents of the first into his hand. Tiny glass and stone beads rolled out in an array of subtle hues. 'Five thousand beads,' he said proudly, 'and twenty-five separate colours. And I have the larger obsidian ones in black *and* green this time . . .'

They haggled for almost fifteen minutes before they finally settled on a price that was no surprise to either of them. The Quyriots were delighted to have been relieved of the problems of marketing smuggled beads to the rest of the empire and relished the cash Ligea gave them, which they then used to fund the Quyriot rebellion. Ligea sold the items on, using a network of slave contacts supplied by the ex-slaves under her command. The profits weren't high, but they were steady and every bit helped. She was all too aware that her fortune would fast diminish if she continued to spend lavishly on equipment and horses; she didn't need Arcadim's periodic agitated messages to tell her so.

When the haggling was over, Berg produced a necklace of black obsidian beads, carved with the runes of his people. 'For your son,' he told her. 'Put it round his neck, and he'll have the blood of a Quyriot horseman in his veins.'

She took it from him, marvelling, and thanked him.

'We don't sell beads like them,' he told her. 'Never. Them's for the people of the passes: us. And yus, now, cos yus are agin those bastards of Tyr. There's stone magic in the runes. You tell 'im as he grows. Wear those beads and he'll always understand the beast he rides. Not like yus city folk.'

She doubted he knew much about cities, but nodded anyway. The idea that the Quyriots were intent on subverting her son to their ways – even though he was still a day or two short of a month old – should have been amusing. Instead, she was touched. Gevenan just muffled a laugh and looked his normal sardonic self.

'And I came t'ask how many colts yus wanted from the foalin',' Berg continued. 'You said yus was interested. Looks like bein' a good season. We got three hundred mares breedin' this year in my clan alone. Not, of course, that we want to sell all the crop.'

She blinked, impressed. 'Well, to tell the truth, we'd prefer those already broken to the bridle . . .' More discussion ensued, more prices were haggled over and logistic problems solved.

She had been delighted to discover that the Quyriot rebels were only too glad to sell plateau ponies. They were not much use to a man as big as Brand or as solid as Gevenan of Inge, but they were excellent mounts for most of the ex-slaves. Agile and strong, they could prop and turn faster than even a trained warhorse. Because they were short, they were easy to mount and less feared by men who had not ridden before. A fully grown man looked ridiculous mounted on such a short-legged beast, but that, Ligea felt, was an advantage. The legions were unlikely to take her mounted forces seriously. If so, they would pay for that mistake. Some of her men, under Gevenan and Brand's tutelage, were already proving the worth of the beasts again and again.

Once the business discussion was over, Berg again refused their hospitality, mounted up and headed back towards the mountain passes.

'A long way just to sell a few pretty beads and tell you about some pregnant ponies,' Gevenan remarked. 'Holy gods, it's *men* we want, not horses.'

'I know. And you shall have them. As soon as Arrant is doing well with this new wet nurse, I shall be off to recruit.'

'And just how do you intend to do that?'

'If there's one thing Tyrans is not short of, it's slaves.'

'And, may I remind you, legionnaires to catch them when they escape.'

She grinned at him. 'I'm more than a match for most legionnaires. I plan to concentrate on slave pens, slave auctions, slave transport – rescue and run, and hope some will stay with us to fight. I intend to build up an army of ten thousand fighting men.'

He snorted. 'Pride puts your nose so far in the air you don't see the roots that trip you up. All this takes money, as well as courage. We've been here, what, not quite five months? You've been bringing in arms and horses. We grow enough food for our own needs, and more, and the farm has ideal grazing and oats for the nags, thanks to the soils and the mountain snow-melt –

but all that buying weapons and armour, plus the iron needed for blacksmithing and the leather and the bronze – it's expensive. Bringing it here secretly doesn't come cheap, either, I'll bet, and the longer it goes on, the greater the chance of betrayal and detection. You asked me to sodding lead this rabble, to train them up, and I have. And you know what? I've got to like the bastards. They are *my* men. And I don't want anything to happen to them before we even begin.'

He stopped at the edge of the orchard, under the shade of a plum tree. 'I want to know what your plans are in detail, Legata, and if you're not prepared to tell me, then I'm going to head back to the other end of the world, where I was born and the grass is always green, and we don't call three-quarters of the year "the desert-season". We may not grow olives, but, by the many heads of Ocrastes, we sure have the sweetest apples you ever tasted.'

'Apples?' she asked, not sure what they were.

'Never mind. I mean it, Legata. I don't know how you are going to hide ten thousand men here. Nor do I know how you intend those ten thousand to defeat the twenty thousand legionnaires in Tyrans. I'm sick of not knowing what I'm training a mob of kitchen boys and stable hands *for*. You'd better have a good plan, lady, because I won't lead them to a defeat.'

She picked a switch of leaves from the tree to fan away a persistent horsefly. 'It would indeed be a defeat *if* we played by their rules. So we won't. The battle will be of our choosing, Gev. We are going to gnaw away at their edges, year after year. We are going to rob their pay wagons, set fire to their equipment, steal their horses, destroy their food supplies, wreck their capacity to replace what they lose. When it comes to battle, they are the ones who will be demoralised, fighting with inadequate weapons on empty stomachs against an enemy who won't stay still long enough to lose a battle.'

'And we *will* start the planning now?'

'Tonight, if you like.'

'I hope you know what you are doing.'

'I was once locked in a room for a long time with – among other things – a great many books. A lot of them dealt with five centuries of military history. I know what worked in the past. And what didn't.'

'Great. A philosopher-general who knows the *theory* of war.'

She refused to take offence. 'That's right. I do. *You* are here to supply the practicalities. And Homfridus deals with the logistics. You are right; we should start our detailed planning. It is time.'

'Good. Oh, and something else. Homfridus told me you wanted men to remove the statue of Selede from yonder temple. That you want a simple altar built in its place with the words "Do no person harm" written on it. What in all hells are you up to, messing with religion?'

'All part of the plan, Gev. The pantheon belongs to the present Exaltarchy and perpetuates the legitimacy of an empire based on war and conquest and slavery. Why in all the sweet hells should we – who have suffered at the hands of this empire – worship at the feet of their many-headed God of War or their Goddess of Cunning? I want to give people an alternative. Selede's temple will now be a temple to the Unknown God. People can make of that what they will. I would appreciate it if you would encourage the men to leave their offerings to the Unknown God in the future.'

He stared at her for a long moment. Then guffawed. 'And I thought I was cynical! Ligea, my dear, you sweep me from that pedestal and stand triumphant as Queen of the Cynics. Creating a new god to serve your own purposes? I would never have thought of that one!'

'I didn't. I mean, there already is an Unknown God. He has a temple in the Snarls.'

'He does? All right, not cynical, just illogical. You would send your men into battle worshipping at the feet of a god who bids them do no harm!' He chuckled and strode off in the direction of the stables.

'Who said religion was logical?' she yelled after him, but he didn't turn around.

She continued on to the villa, where the baby's wailing soon drew her wandering thoughts back to the present.

Arrant. Four weeks old. Demanding in a way only babies can be. In a way she had never envisioned. She'd thought beforehand in vague terms of wet nurses and dispatching him as quickly as possible to Kardiastan so she could get on with her life. And then had come the day of his birth. The way the memory of pain and, yes, the terror that something would go wrong, had all vanished in that first wondrous moment of motherhood when she had held her son in her arms and his tiny fist had closed around her finger. Never, never had she considered she would feel the way she did. Protective. Insecure and anxious for his safety. Savagely angry when she even *thought* of anyone ever harming him.

She looked down at her tunic where a wet patch spread into the material, prompted just by the baby's cry. *Damn it, I can't be like this. I have a war to win. I can't be thinking of him all the time. Why in all the mists of Acheron doesn't someone arrive from Kardiastan to take him away?* She had asked Arcadim to send a message to Temellin the moment she was certain of where she'd be for the birth, but no one had yet come. Back in Ordensa, she and Temellin had agreed that he should not risk sending letters, not at first, but she had expected a person.

Damn you, Temellin. He's your son. Where the Vortex are you when I need you?

The baby wailed again, more insistent this time. She sighed. The first wet nurse had not been a success and she had been forced to continue her own feeding of him until they'd found a second. This second woman, after her own child's stillbirth, had plenty of milk, but Ligea's body seemed reluctant to relinquish its role. *Damn, damn, damn,* she thought, brushing her fingers over her breast as if she could rid herself of the spreading stain. *I hate this. I should never have been a mother. What the hell do I know about nurturing someone?*

The only mother she could remember with any clarity was Salacia, Gayed's wife, who had ignored her whenever she could, and been as cold as a snow-season wind when she couldn't. Ligea could still see the pinched frigidity of her stare when her gaze alighted on her adopted daughter. There had been the slave Aemid, of course, and she had done her best – but Gayed had kept her under tight scrutiny to limit her influence.

Ligea sighed. She still suspected she had made a bad start before Arrant was even born, and not just while in Kardiastan and Tyr. Even the journey with the escaped slaves across Tyrans to this farm in the foothills had been a nightmare. She'd worried every time she used her magic that she might be harming her unborn child; she'd been sick with anxiety every time she raised a ward around their encampment at night, or blocked a road or a trail with a ward; she'd been panic-stricken when they were attacked by a force of legionnaires sent after them and she'd come close to draining her power once more. On that occasion, she'd had to destroy the arch of a massive stone bridge across the River Tyr to stop the pursuit.

After they had arrived at First Farm, she'd fretted for the rest of the pregnancy, certain she had harmed the growing child. There had been one more incident when she had nearly lost him, and the worry that he was somehow damaged had remained. It had dissipated a little after his birth when she'd been able to reassure herself that he had the normal complement of fingers and toes, all the prerequisite features of a face in the correct places and a set of lungs loud enough – and an appetite hearty enough – to keep a whole houseful of adults at his beck and call. She'd been relieved, and yet unable to put aside that niggling feeling of concern, even though she had no further basis for it. The annoying thing about being a mother, she decided, was that you could never forget you were. If she was honest, she even had to admit she enjoyed feeding him herself and hated handing him over to the wet nurse.

She entered the archway to the main entrance of the villa and hence into the family living hall. Brand was attending to Arrant, and neither the wet nurse nor Narjemah was anywhere in sight. He was holding the baby, joggling him in his arms, making absurd gurgling noises, a ridiculously inane expression on his face. Arrant quietened. She paused to wonder if Temellin would have been so tender toward her child if it were Brand's, and thought not. Temellin did not have Brand's generous spirit.

I could have loved him so well, if there had never been a Temellin.

At that thought, she looked down at her cabochon with a surprising resentment. She wouldn't have changed what she was for anything, surely, yet right then she found herself wishing she had been born an ordinary person, of ordinary parents, in some ordinary town somewhere.

Blast it to Acheron, she thought, *it's this Vortexdamned motherhood stuff.*

Brand looked up and gestured as if to pass her the child.

She shook her head. 'I am trying to stop feeding him, not continue. Where's Dulcia?'

'I've sent Narjemah to get her. She'll be here in a moment. Sure you don't want to hold him?' She heard the words not spoken, as she so often did with Brand: *Remember, he'll be gone soon, to Temellin, and you won't have him to hold any more . . .*

'You seem to be doing a good job of it,' she said sourly, thinking in turn: *Can't you understand? I don't want to care too much.*

'He'll be one month old soon, Ligea.'

She nodded, her heart lurching.

'You remember the promise I made, to leave?'

She nodded again, not trusting herself to speak. *No. Not now. How can I bear it if you go?*

'I want to leave the day after tomorrow.'

When the silence between them became embarrassing, she said simply, 'I will miss you.' *More than I can say.*

They stared at one another across the baby's head; Arrant, indifferent to them both, alternately fretted and dozed. 'Is that all you can say?' he asked finally.

'Oh, Brand, we've shared too much to say any more. You know it all. Or if you don't, no words of mine will ever be able to tell you how much you mean to me. I want you to go, I do. It's just hard.'

'Yes. Yes, it is . . .' He looked down at the baby he held. 'I've grown fond of this squalling bundle too, although I've no idea why. All he ever does is eat and sleep and scream. And, of course . . .' He held the child out, away from himself, grimacing. The wet nurse, Dulcia, came bustling in and took him from Brand, clucking her tongue and making strange noises.

Ligea rolled her eyes. Another adult who managed to sound devoid of intelligence when placed in proximity with her son. 'Take him away and feed him, Dulcia. He is about to start sounding as enraged as a bull—'

She broke off, with a gasp.

'What is it?' Brand asked, alert.

'Ward's tripped . . .'

This time she was overwhelmed, for the man who broke the thread was one of the Magor.

'Elysium's bliss,' she said, her voice breathless in her delight, 'Brand, it's *Garis!*'

CHAPTER FOURTEEN

Garis. The last time Ligea had seen him in person, he'd been eighteen years old, and he'd called her a dangerous killer and told Brand to put a blade through her. His horrified anger at the time had been understandable; he'd just seen her remove Pinar's child from the woman's still warm body and he'd had no idea she was trying to save both the baby – by giving him to the Mirage Makers – and the Mirage Makers, by giving them a new life to absorb in order to strengthen their entity.

He'd seen her again, later, but that was when she'd been no more than an unsubstantial shade, unable to talk. Poor guilt-ridden Garis. He'd been contrite then, defending her to Korden, trying to make amends. Not that Korden would listen. He may have been her cousin, but as one of only ten Margoroth to escape massacre by the Tyranians, Korden had been suspicious of her Tyranian heritage.

Garis was a little older now; another birthday had passed, and there was a new maturity about him. He brought his horse trotting up to the villa, grinning when he saw Ligea and Brand waiting for him at the gate, those tawny eyes of his dancing, his curling lashes as inappropriate as ever on the face of a youth trying to be taken seriously as a man and Magoroth warrior.

He slid from the horse in a rush and held out his left hand. Ligea took it and they stood like that, their cabochons meshed together as they flooded one another with emotions. From

Garis, the spate included his guilt and his regret and his apology, as well as his heartfelt joy at the chance to see her again.

Brand watched, and if he resented the closeness they achieved by both being Magor, by being able to communicate in ways that were not possible for him, nothing of it showed on his impassive face. She felt a sense of loss. *He will be gone so soon . . .*

'Your baby?' Garis asked, still holding her hand.

'He's well,' she answered. 'Four weeks old and as vociferous as a pack of mountain jackals. Temellin? And Aemid?'

'Both well. Shades, Sarana, I have so much to tell you! Temellin sent presents. And a letter so long he had to ask the Mirage Makers to supply more parchment for it.' He grinned at her and went unabashedly to hug Brand. 'How's the belly?' he asked, referring to the potentially fatal sword slash Brand had received across his midriff the last time they had met. Only Garis' quick thinking had saved the Altani's life then.

'Not even the occasional indigestion. Lousy doctoring though – I have a scar the size of a gladiator's belt.'

'He plays it for all it's worth,' Ligea said, laughing. 'That scar is the envy of every kid on the farm and the milkmaids think it's erotic. Anyway, come on inside, and meet the brat.'

'Ligea pretends Arrant is a nuisance,' Brand said, 'but when he's around, she gets the same sickly sweet expression on her face as the rest of us do . . .'

'Only if he's sound asleep and unlikely to stir,' she said with feeling.

Arrant was duly produced and exclaimed over, after which Garis was sent off to bathe and change. Less than an hour later, they were eating the evening meal before the sun went down, Gevenan with them. The Ingean was as confrontational as ever, unfazed by the presence of another Magoroth. 'Hmph,' he said when introduced, 'I don't blame you for growing skin over your pretty gemstone. Not exactly the manly thing to do, is it, to wear sparkly jewels in your flesh?'

Garis shrugged. 'It makes no difference to our power whether it is covered or not, so it seems only sensible to hide it from Tyranian legionnaires. They have long memories. Especially those who might have served in Kardiastan at one time or another.' Garis smiled brightly at Gevenan. 'Would you like me to demonstrate the capabilities of this sparkly jewel of mine?'

'That won't be necessary,' Ligea said and added, 'And, Gev, I wouldn't suggest that you try repeating that bit about being manly and wearing jewellery next time you meet Berg Firegravel.' *Sweet Goddess, why is he being so provocative?*

'Well, what do you expect me to say to the lad?' Gevenan complained with a wave at Garis. 'You keep telling me about the strength of Magor power, but when you introduce me to another of your kind, I find he has eyelashes my own daughter would think were too frilly, let alone a fighting man.'

'Pass me the bread, you uncultured barbarian,' she said. 'You didn't tell me you had a daughter.'

He shrugged. 'Probably a whole bunch of them scattered from one end of the Exaltarchy to the other.' He shoved the loaf of bread in her direction.

'My eyelashes are hardly my fault,' Garis said, and made things worse by blushing.

'Oh, pretty,' Gevenan said and smiled. 'Now, lad, tell me about this squabble of yours in Kardiastan. Are you going to beat the bastards?'

'Of course. Eventually.'

'How? By throwing a few pretty beams of light at them?'

Garis swallowed his ire, and tried to stop the reddening of his cheeks. 'Yes. That's right. But it might take longer than we first thought.'

Ligea felt the host of emotions he flicked her way: worry, disappointment, resignation, hope. She signalled the serving maid for some more wine. This was going to be a long story. 'Did Temellin get my messages via the moneymasters?'

'He had four by the time I left. Oh, we have put the rumour around that Ligea Gayed is still in Kardiastan, working with the Mirager, just as you asked. The Governor believes it, and he's furious. I have no doubt that he has sent word of your supposed activities to the Exaltarch.'

'Good. That will stop Rathrox and the Brotherhood looking for me in Tyrans. I worry that if they know I'm in Tyrans, they'll torture my moneymaster to see what he knows.'

'Temellin is worried sick about you. How safe is this place? Who knows about it?'

'Only Arcadim – my moneymaster. And believe me, he's not telling anyone voluntarily. The Brotherhood questioned him, of course, as soon as they knew Ligea Gayed was a traitor, but he told them that, having sold my properties, he was no longer my moneymaster. They accepted that. It made sense, after all, seeing they believed me to be in Kardiastan.

'I have a permanent ward around this place and no one comes or goes without me knowing about it. We have escape routes from here up into the mountains, and are in the process of establishing another hideaway up there in an old ruin. Our Quyriot friends are rebuilding it for us. It is impossible to find without a guide and I intend it to be our training centre. First Farm, this place, will become a supply base, where we will keep the horses, grow food, build and repair weapons and armour.'

'It's about as safe as it is possible to be,' Brand agreed.

'But I want to know about Kardiastan,' she said to Garis. 'Tell me what's happened there.'

'There's a permanent Theuros guard on the borders between the Mirage and Tyrans now. The rebellion elsewhere went well to start with: for a while we controlled all the paveways and the Rift.'

'But?' Gevenan asked cynically, hearing the reservation in Garis' tone. He was leaning back in his chair, arms folded, chewing on a twig he had used as a toothpick.

Garis, frowning, fiddled with his mug as he continued. 'The Exaltarchy started pouring in more troops as soon as they discovered the attack across the Alps had failed, thanks to you, Sarana. Our problem is that they have no rules. They don't care *what* they do to win.' The bleakness in his eyes said it all.

Pouring herself some more wine, Ligea said, with a bark of humourless laughter, 'The Exaltarchy must be in shock. They were so proud of the Stalwarts.'

'Did you know they are hunting down every Kardi they can find in Tyr?' Garis asked. 'You have no idea how much trouble it took for me to get out of the city without being found out. I came in via Crestos, working as a hand on a fishing boat. No one checked the crew, so arriving wasn't a problem. But getting *out*—! I had to create a diversion at the walls. They are checking everyone at the gates, did you know? Looking for cabochons, I suppose.'

'Yes, we know,' Gevenan said impatiently. He speared an olive with the point of his knife and waved it at Garis. 'So, Magori, just how are you going to throw the sodding Exaltarchy out of your Kardi dustbowl?' He had been itching to centre the conversation on the military side of things all evening.

Garis refused to take offence. He plucked the olive from the knife – although he must have known that Gevenan had not really been offering it to him – and took a bite. 'Temel says we won't be able to rid our land of the legions until there are rebellions elsewhere.' He popped the rest of the olive into his mouth and switched his attention back to Ligea. 'His strategy now is to try to stop as many new legionnaires from arriving as we can. We have Magoroth hiding in every port and on ships up and down the coast. If a galley arrives with legionnaires on board, we try to sink it before it makes land.'

He spat out the olive seed. 'We can't launch a full-scale attack to drive the legions into the sea. There's just too *few* of us, and so many of them. We've lost people, you know. Twelve of the Theuros and eight Illusos. Same problem with all of them – they got into a situation where they were overwhelmed while trying to protect ordinary Kardis, and ended up too exhausted, too power-depleted to defend themselves.' He reached out to the wine bottle.

'Defending ordinary Kardis?' Ligea asked, and her heart plunged even before she had the details.

He nodded. 'New tactics from the legions. When we kill one legionnaire on Kardi soil, as soon as the Tyranians hear about it, they kill the first ten Kardis they come across in the street of the nearest town or village. It doesn't matter who they are. A pregnant woman and her two small children were three of the first ten to die.' He shuddered. 'There was a bloodbath until we realised what was happening. That's when we lost Magor.'

Gevenan leaned forward, his interest sharp. 'Now that was clever tactics.'

'*Tactics*?' Ligea glared at him. 'They were innocents! Tyranian law does not support that kind of murder!'

'Tyranian law doesn't support the killing of legionnaires by rebels, either. Whoever ordered the killing of ordinary folk knew his opponent, I'll bet. In fact, I'll wager this Temellin fellow stopped harassing the legions as soon as he learned of this, didn't he?'

Garis nodded. 'He used his power to get himself inside the Governor's villa in Madrinya one night. Alone, too. He sneaked into the Governor's apartments, woke up the Governor – all without any alarm raised, mind you – and told him they had to have a chat.' He grinned, his eyes dancing at the thought of Temellin's daring. 'And to hear Temel tell it, that's exactly what they did: chat. Of course, the fact that he had his Magor sword with him, and the Governor was just in his nightgown, prob- ably persuaded the man they had things to talk about. They struck a bargain, of sorts. Legionnaires who haven't yet landed on Kardiastan soil are fair game. Temellin reserves the right to kill those still aboard a ship. But he won't harass men already stationed on Kardi soil so long as they don't harass local people. And that's the way things are at the moment.'

'That's – that's *bizarre*,' Brand said. 'Why the sweet hells would the Governor agree to that?'

'I imagine that having a man sit on the end of your bed with a glowing sword in his hand might have had something to do with it,' Gevenan suggested in a lazy drawl. 'I think I begin to like this Temellin.'

'But what was to stop the Governor breaking the promise five minutes after Temellin left?' Brand asked.

'Think about it,' Ligea said. 'All of a sudden he is ruling a peaceful province. Here in Tyr, he'll be smelling as sweet as a Tyranian rose. Legionnaires are dying on their way there, but that isn't his fault, is it? You can bet he hasn't told anyone about any bargain he's made with the rebels.'

Garis sighed. 'The disadvantage for us is colossal, though. We're hobbled.'

'So what *are* you doing?' Gevenan asked.

'Apart from sinking military ships, you mean? Well, making life as unpleasant as possible for legionnaires, unobtrusively, with as much subtlety as possible. Training ordinary Kardis as soldiers. Making weapons. Preparing.'

'For what?' Gevenan asked.

'For when the whole of the Exaltarchy rises up against Tyr.'

'Temellin could have ignored the Kardi deaths,' Gevenan pointed out. 'After all, what better way to persuade the ordinary man to rise up against his masters than to encourage those very masters to kill Kardi children?'

Garis glared at him. 'Temellin would never think such deaths acceptable.'

'More fool him.'

Ligea added coldly, 'Be warned, Gevenan. I will never accept such "tactics" from my soldiers, *never*. Remember that.'

He shrugged. 'You're in charge. But if you care too much about such things, you won't win.'

'Winning at too high a cost is not a victory,' she snapped, and turned back to Garis. 'The timing will be critical. Tyr is not going to fall any time soon. We could be fighting this war a decade from now.'

'*What?*' Gevenan exploded. 'A *decade*? I'll have doddered to a death of old age by then! Don't you dare tell me I've got to stay here earning my paltry one gold sestus every year, training a bloody army that will be in their dotage by the time we actually *do* anything – like actually fight!'

'Oh, we'll be fighting all right. I was predicting a date for the end of the Exaltarchy, not the beginning of the fighting. Think, Gev. At the moment you and I have three hundred fighting men and a couple of hundred auxiliaries! It is going to take years to recruit enough men, to find enough money to feed and to pay them, to build up several training farms like this one – until we have an army large enough to take Tyr.'

'*First* Farm. Gods, that explains the name,' Gevenan muttered. 'You think big, I'll give you that. Spell it out for me, Domina. You know I'm slow.'

'At a guess, it will take five years to build an army, trained in the mountains behind a selection of farms like this one, right across northern Tyrans. Just as we don't have all our crop stored in the one barn, so to speak. Each farm supplies the food and horses and repairs equipment for the linked training area up in the mountains behind; each has escape routes to Quyr.

'And no, in one way, I don't think big. When it comes to the action, I'm thinking small. Small groups of men – cohorts – that's sixty men,' she added for Garis' benefit, 'with their own leadership and a strong loyalty to their cohort.

'For five years they will be merely raiders. Stealing money and weaponry and armour from the legions, from garrisons, from wayhouses along all the paveways. Stealing pay wagons and tax collections. Raiding slave auctions and slave pens and slave transports. We don't touch the ordinary citizen, ever. Just the legions and paveways and slavers and anything that belongs to the Exaltarch. After each raid we retreat to the safety of the mountains. And all the time we will be training more men.'

Garis looked doubtful. 'But won't the legions find you eventually? Five years is an impossible time to stay hidden. Someone will betray you.'

'We could possibly lose a farm or two. Possibly even a training settlement in the mountains. But these mountains and the escape routes, they will be our strength. The legions don't know the mountains – but the Quyriot smugglers do, and they are more than willing to be our guides. A legionnaire who tries to follow a smuggler dies up there. That is almost guaranteed. And, apart from the advantage I have of recognising intended treachery, we have one other huge advantage: the slave network. They are our spies and our informants. We may be betrayed from time to time, but we will also be warned. Men will escape and regroup.'

'And after five years?' Garis asked.

'An uprising across the whole of the Exaltarchy at the same time would be nice. If not, well just us and Quyr and Kardiastan.'

'And Altan, maybe,' Brand said. 'We know they already have rebels there. I can try to coordinate something.'

Gevenan said thoughtfully, 'So we will fight a different kind of war. Mounted troops, quick forays, ambushes, quick retreats. No traditional battlefields.'

'Exactly.'

'Temellin has sent me to spread the idea of rebellion throughout the Exaltarchy,' Garis added. 'He's asked me to travel from here to many of the provinces and vassal states. To foment trouble.'

Gevenan snorted. 'A lad like you, still green enough to tangle his sword in the baldric when he draws it?' His glance flicked up and down, in open disparagement. '*You*? Persuade grown men to fight the might of the Exaltarch? Youngster, have you any idea of what it's like to be a slave and to know other men have the power of life and death over you, that your master can kill you on a mere whim? Because he has a touch of indigestion, perhaps? How easy do you think it will be to persuade someone *that* scared to join a feckless band of insurgents somewhere?'

'I don't expect it to be easy.'

Gevenan laughed, mocking. Finishing his wine and pushing his plate away, he leaned back in his chair. 'You'll be dead in the first month. Probably killed when a slave who's scared pissless turns you in to his master.'

Ligea, sensing other emotions, better hidden, frowned. And glared a warning at Garis, who had stopped shielding his own annoyance.

'I may be raw but I am not stupid, and I'm not defenceless,' Garis said, riled.

'No? You couldn't take on a real fighting man and last five seconds—'

'No?' Garis drawled in return. With a casual gesture, he flared the gem in his hand into a brilliant flash of light, aimed right into the Ingean's eyes. At the same time, he hooked his foot behind the front leg of the man's chair and yanked it towards him. Gevenan and the chair toppled over backwards. Still blinded, lying on his back, Gevenan had no chance. Garis pinned him down with pain-giving light. The Ingean gave a gasp.

'That's enough,' Ligea said.

Garis took a deep breath and withdrew the light. 'Sorry, but I had a really, really tough journey here, and I'm not in the mood to be mocked.'

Gevenan clambered to his feet, wincing.

'Leave us, please,' Ligea said to him.

He rubbed an elbow ruefully and nodded. She caught the slightest glimmer of a smile as he left and felt his tinge of satisfaction. She turned to Brand. 'Brand, I want to talk to Garis alone, if you don't mind. Go and see what that idiot Ingean was really up to, will you?'

She watched Brand leave the room and then said, 'I don't know what I will do without him.'

'Gevenan?'

'No. Brand.'

'Brand? He's *leaving*?'

'Yes.' She met his gaze, her expression troubled. 'Garis, aren't you here to pick up Arrant?'

He looked uncomfortable and shook his head. 'No, I'm afraid not. You haven't read Temellin's letter yet, obviously.'

'No. I wanted, um, time to myself to do that . . . what's going on? What aren't you telling me?' He didn't reply immediately, and she said, exasperated, 'Do you know how much you leak what you feel? I'm not going to eat you, you know.'

'I never was too good at hiding emotion,' he admitted. He

sighed. 'I just wish you'd read the letter first – all right, all right! Temellin wants you to keep Arrant until he reaches an age for his Magor sword. Which is usually about twelve or thirteen. In the meantime, he wants *you* to put the cabochon in the babe's palm.'

'That's ridiculous. Arrant is heir to Kardiastan! He has to be brought up there, not in Tyrans.'

'And he will be, once he's older.'

'But why wait?'

'Temel didn't explain his reasons to me, Sarana.'

'Oh, Vortexdamn the man. Garis, I've been so worried about him. About Arrant, I mean. So many things happened to me while I was carrying him. He *seems* all right, but I can't be certain. He should be back in Kardiastan, where there are so many Magoroth who could help, just in case . . .'

'Babies need their mothers.'

She looked at him, feeling helpless. What was Temellin up to now? 'Why is he sending you out to the provinces and vassal states? Surely he needs every Magori he can get.'

'Yes, he does. But he also needs Tyrans' legions to be overstretched. So do you, for that matter. He thinks that someone with Magoroth power has more chance of surviving such a journey. And more chance of persuading any rebel elements to full-scale rebellion.'

She wanted to say, *But you are so young!* but thought better of it.

A sadness in his eyes belied his youth. 'I'm married now, you know. Magoria Tavia.'

Her breath caught. 'She can't be more than seventeen!' *Sweet Melete. The necessity of breeding a new generation of Magoroth.*

But he had caught her unguarded moment of distaste. 'It's not what you think . . . no one pressured us to marry. There never was anyone else for me, not really.'

'I'm glad to hear it. Congratulations. I remember her: pretty girl with dimples.' *Vortexdamn. There's got to be something he's not telling me. The situation in Kardiastan must be more dire than he is saying.* She stood up, stifling emotions. 'All right, Garis. I guess I do not have much choice. Yet, anyway. But the first chance I get, I will deliver Arrant to his father myself. And I am going to ask Brand if he'd like to go with you – if you'll have him.'

Hope flared within him. 'I thought he was going to Altan, to join the rebels there?'

'Yes. That was his original plan. But he has a withered arm now.' *Saving me. Risking his life to pull me out of the Ravage. Gods, the courage of that!* As a soldier, he'd be limited – yet he would be of use to you. He was sold on the slave blocks in both Cormel and Pythia. He has a smattering of five or six different languages, as well as Altani and Kardi and Tyranian. He's well read and knowledgeable about so many things, and yet he has lived in the slave underbelly of the Exaltarchy. He may be only thirty – no, thirty-one now – but he has lived a lifetime . . . He will be able to help you in so many ways, and you will be able to keep him out of trouble with your powers. It sounds like a good combination to me.'

Garis couldn't hide his relief. 'I have been . . . lonely,' he agreed. 'It would be good to have a travelling companion. Especially one I happen to like as much as I like him. I hope he'll agree.'

She stood up. 'Good. Then I will mention it to him. But right now I want to go and read this letter from Tem.'

First she opened the presents he'd sent. One parcel contained clothing. Several anoudain, practical outfits in shades of brown. A pair of sandals made of shleth leather. A pair of fingerless gloves, flesh-coloured, so that she would find it easy to hide her cabochon if need be. Practical things, from a practical man who understood her so well. One item in the other parcel, though, she didn't understand.

It had been wrapped in rough-made cloth, and it looked like a lump of dark brown clay the size of an orange, dried out and hard. She touched it with a tentative finger and for a moment it gave under the pressure, like the surface of a jellyfish. She picked it up, cupping it on her palm. And dropped it as it started to move. Back on the cloth again, it was lifeless and dull, a pile of hard earth. When she picked it up once more, it softened and began to re-form. This time she continued to hold it, to watch it take shape as if an invisible sculptor was working it, unseen hands kneading the lump into the form, unseen fingers pinching and moulding. A head, a man's head. Temellin. Looking at her, so real, so lifelike, a half-smile on his lips.

She cried then, and it was some time before she could see well enough to read what he had written.

The letter was not as enlightening as she'd hoped. His love touched her from every page – but the explanation she sought was not there. Temellin said all that Garis had already mentioned, and no more. She felt the ache in him for his son, even though his distress was understated; and yet his rejection was also there. *I do not want him here, not yet*, he wrote. *There will come a time when that is right, but a baby should be with his mother. It gives me comfort to know that he is with you . . .*

When she read the last words of the letter, tears again spilled to smudge the ink. *The lump of clay*, he continued, *is from the Mirage Makers, for you. They gave it to me when I was passing through the Shiver Barrens. They said it was part of themselves. I do not know what it signifies, but I hope it is something that will remind you of us here.*

For such a short time I knew again what it was like to love and be loved; I knew it tenfold. I knew possibility fulfilled. I shall always remember that. I shall always love you.

She read the letter once again, and again. And then she picked up the clay once more. Each time she held it, it re-formed to show Temellin, and each time it was different. She saw him laughing, smiling, serious. With his face raised to the sky, with his head propped in his hand, his expression thoughtful. Each time she put it down, it became a formless lump.

Remember him, it said. *Remember him, and return.*

And each time she saw his face, it tore a little of her heart.

*   *   *

The next night she bestowed a cabochon on Arrant.

She fasted all day and spent long hours in silent prayer. Not praying to any deity, but in reverent prayer for the safety of her son, for his acceptance into the world of the Magor, for the proper ordering of the world to occur so that a child would receive his birthright. And above all praying – with deep-felt longing – that she had not damaged him by the life she had led while he was part of her.

Some time deep in the night, she brought throbbing colour into her sword, she spoke the conjurations given to her in the Shiver Barrens by the Mirage Makers, and she placed the gem that materialised in the hollow of her sword hilt into the palm of her son. He gave a sharp cry, but then snuggled deeper into sleep. By morning the cabochon was part of his body, melded to his being in ways she could not understand, and never would. It was the Mirage Makers' legacy, not hers.

Narjemah and Garis came, to pay homage. Brand touched the golden gem with wonder, tears in his eyes. Even Gevenan came, and for once his cynicism was in abeyance.

Another Magori had entered the world.

Everything's all right, she thought. *He's healthy and a Magor, and all that worry was for nothing.*

Two days later, Ligea watched Garis and Brand ride away. She and Brand had avoided speaking of their personal feelings; there had been no point. They both knew there would be a hole in their lives because the other was not there. They both knew that Temellin's absence meant more to her than his would. They both knew whose son lay in the cradle in the farm villa.

Yet, as she watched him go, Arrant in her arms, she felt the bruising of her heart. Brand had been part of her life since she was ten years old. He had stood by her even when she'd been at her worst. He'd had faith in her and that faith had never wavered. He'd loved her without conditions. He cared enough to love her child, fathered by another man. He had saved her life and given up the use of an arm to do so.

Long after the two men were out of sight, the dust kicked up by their mounts hung in the warm, motionless air, obscuring the tangled colours of the wildflowers that bloomed along the track. And somewhere inside herself, Ligea knew the pain of the bruising was nothing compared to the loss she would have felt had Arrant ridden with them. That would have sundered her soul.

'Well,' Gevenan growled in her ear, 'now that everything personal is tidied away, can we get down to work and sort out how we are going to bring down this bloody tyrant of an Exaltarch?'

She sighed. 'Soul of sensitivity, aren't you?'

He snorted. 'Me? I'm just a soldier from Inge. An island of plentiful bogs where it rains ninety-nine days out of every hundred. Where was a mud-hopping Ingean foot soldier like me ever going to learn manners?'

'Huh. Don't give me that, Gev. You were no common soldier when the Tyranians invaded your island. You have officer written all over you. Who were you really?'

'What the bloody hell does it matter? It was fifteen years ago! They sold me as a slave and took me as far away as they could. I did a year in the galleys, did y'know that? It knocks the spunk out of a man, being a galley slave. It takes everything you once were, and makes you into an animal. No, worse. Into a *thing*. An oar. A commodity whose only value is the strength of his back. A thing that grovels when one of his conquerors passes by. Have you ever seen my back, Ligea?'

She didn't speak, but neither did he. He knew she had indeed seen the lash scars that cobbled his skin.

Eventually, she asked, 'Why did you needle Garis into attacking you like that?'

He shrugged. 'I had to know if you told the truth. I had to know if all the Magor have the same abilities you do.'

'You thought I'd *lied*?'

'Well, exaggerated, anyway. I don't have your flipping ability to tell a lie from the truth, now do I? Maybe I'll end up nailed to a cross or burned at the stake because of you. I thought at last I had a way of checking one of your tales.' He grinned at her. 'No more than you do to me every damned time I open my mouth. Does the Domina forgive her humble servant?'

'Elysium's bliss! You are like a thorn under one's wrap, Gevenan. Always so Vortex-blamed irritating!'

'You want to know who I was once, Ligea? A king's general who lost a war. And a king. And a people. I lost a whole bloody *country* to Tyrans! I was already less than a man when they killed my liege and his sons before my eyes. After that, I was not a man at all. Just a slave.'

The silence dragged on while she tried to think of something to say. Finally, all she could dredge up was: 'Have you thought of going back? Finding your wife, your children? You could now.'

He said stiffly, 'I had more sense. One should never make assumptions that a woman will wait, Ligea. Or a man, either. So I sent a message to a friend, years ago, to find out what had happened.'

He didn't elaborate, and she didn't ask. It wasn't necessary; she already knew. He had nothing to go back for.

PART TWO

LÏGEA AND

ARRANt

LIGEA AND

ARRANT

CHAPTER FIFTEEN

Arrant sometimes felt he had been born on the back of a horse. His earliest memories were of his cheek lying against his mother's back as she rode. In some of those memories he was secure and happy, lulled by the jogging rhythm to sleepy contentment; in others her back was tense and there was urgency in the hoof beats beneath. Sometimes he was cold and wet and miserable, but then there'd be the happiness of being lifted down and feeling his mother's arms about him, warming him, her soft words in his ear, her strength enfolding him, keeping him safe.

He called her Mater, because that was what people said he should do, and other people mostly knew her as the Domina, but that wasn't her real name, he knew that. Gev called her Ligea when no one else was listening, and sometimes Narjemah called her Sarana, but they both said he wasn't to use those names, so he didn't, not out loud – but in his head, to himself, he thought of her as Ligea.

The second most important person in his life was Narjemah. Arrant was never too sure which of the two women he loved the most. Ligea was safety. She was magic. But Narjemah was kindly and often spoiled him with sweetmeats and presents. When he fell down and hurt himself, it was wisest to run to Narjemah; he was always assured of a hug and a treat, especially if he scraped his knees or bumped his head. His mother was more likely to tell him to stop crying and go and wash off the blood, quickly now, there's a good boy.

But Narjemah could be irritating, too; she never let him do *anything*, even though he was five years old. In fact, she was always telling him *not* to do things. 'Don't climb the tree, Arrant, you'll fall and hurt yourself. Don't go near the river, you might drown. Don't play with the slave children, Arrant, they might have lice.' Ligea said they weren't slaves any more and he shouldn't use that word. And of course he could play with them, whenever he liked.

Ligea could be much more fun. She took him swimming in the river and taught him to stay afloat and move his arms and legs so he wouldn't drown. She helped him climb trees. She brought him a pony all of his own, although he only rode it when they were at First Farm. And best of all, she talked to him as though he was a real grown-up. She *explained* things to him. Mostly he didn't understand, but it was better than treating him like a baby, the way Narjemah did.

Narjemah was old. She had lines on her face like a gourd. Although she was soft and sort of squashy compared to Ligea, she could get mad sometimes. She got mad with his mother, often – usually over him. Narjemah scolded every time Ligea took him away from the Stronghold or First Farm. Still, he loved Narjemah. She made very good cakes and she hugged him a lot. She was a Magor too, a Theura. He didn't think it was a bit fair that her green cabochon was pretty, all crazed with sparkly lines like sunlight on water, even though it didn't glow. His gold one was skin-covered and it didn't glow much either. But it would one day, when they won a big fight and his mother cut back the skin. Then it would shine gold. Maybe when he was six.

Narjemah used to worry that he didn't know what it was like to have a home. That was true: he didn't. Sometimes he and Ligea and Narjemah stayed at First Farm, which was down at the bottom of the mountain where the land went all flat like unleavened bread. He liked that, because he got to ride a lot and Gevenan was teaching him to jump over logs on his pony. If he wore his Quyriot necklet, he didn't fall off. Well, hardly ever. But Gevenan said necklets were for *girls*. Gevenan was fun, especially when he used naughty words. He said he'd once had boys of his own in a far-off place. He taught Arrant to fight with the wooden practice sword his father, Temellin, had sent him when he turned five. Gevenan said Arrant would be a fine warrior one day.

Arrant had never met his father. He knew what he looked like, though. His mother had this funny lump of clay, and when he took it in his hand, it became a face. She said that face was his father's. Sort of like the head of a statute of him, only smaller. He loved to play with it, because every time he put it down and then picked it up again, it looked different.

His mother had other things his father had sent her over the years: a necklace she sometimes wore made of Kardi agates. And a map of Kardiastan. And a clear glass bottle of coloured sand. He liked that gift especially, because if you listened *very* carefully, in a *very* quiet room, you could hear the sands singing in the bottle. They moved all by themselves, too, and made pretty patterns against the glass.

Mostly he lived in the Stronghold above the stone-cutters' village of Prianus. He liked that place, too. The Stronghold was cold in the snow-season when ice hung from the eaves like polished daggers. It was best in the desert-season when eagles nested on the roof of the watchtower and jackdaws in the crannies of the roof. Ligea said the Stronghold had been first built hundreds of years ago, by a great king of Tyrans. Before the wicked Exaltarch had been born. Everyone relaxed at the Stronghold, and ate lots, and laughed. Except the soldiers who were being trained. They had to work all the time, even when it was cold.

The smugglers often came to visit, and the one who had such a funny name, Berg Firegravel, gave him pretty coloured beads to play with. He'd given him the obsidian necklet to wear, too. He liked to wear it no matter what Gev said; it made him feel like a Quyriot horseman. When he touched the runes on the beads, they felt as old as the stones of the Stronghold, and as mysterious.

The times he liked best of all were when he rode behind his

mother to free slaves or fight legionnaires. That was serious business, and no one laughed much then. Of course, he didn't take part in any of the fighting; Ligea would hand him over to one of his bodyguards and he never actually saw anything of the battles, but it was exciting nonetheless. The long ride, travelling in the dark, having to hide and be as silent as an owl's flight through the night – he felt so grown-up and brave.

Mostly, though, he stayed back in the Stronghold with Narjemah.

One day, I'll have my Magoroth sword and I'll glow like Ligea does when she holds hers, and people will be afraid of me, too.

The horses tailed one another along the trail to the village of Prianus in the foothills, their footing sure, their ears pricked for the warning sounds that might presage a rock fall. They were fresh mounts; the ones they had ridden from Corbussia they had left at First Farm to be rested, groomed and put to graze in the far fields beyond the river.

The track linking the farm and Prianus was barely discernible, little more than a desolate ravine bottom overhung with glistening shadowed walls of black, strewn with boulders and drenched with streams. It wound its way through the many narrow defiles of the foothills to disappear – on this particular day – into patches of damp mist and cloud as the snow-season edged reluctantly towards the dry. Eventually the ravine met the cart track that led to the village of Prianus.

When Ligea had first ridden that path, Prianus had been abandoned, the nearby marble quarry disused and the cart track leading to more frequented roads largely overgrown. She had repopulated the village with freed slaves, now legitimate quarry workers who earned their living trading the marble to Tyr. They even paid their dues in the annual tax collection. Their real purpose was to be a cover for what happened beyond the village, further up the mountains towards Quyr, in the Stronghold.

As the horses picked their way that morning, Ligea moved her mount up beside Gevenan's. Arrant, as usual, rode behind

her on their specially made saddle, loosely tied to her back so
he wouldn't fall if he dropped off to sleep. 'So,' she asked, 'now
that you've had time to look at this lot, what do you think?'

Gevenan glanced over his shoulder at the riders behind them.
Most had only the vaguest idea of how to stay on a horse. They
were sore and aching and tired and scared: twenty-two newly
freed slaves, imports from outside Tyrans, not one of them over
fifteen years old, their misery written in their eyes. Behind them
rode their more seasoned soldiers, several nursing the wounds
that had been the cost of the slaves' freedom.

'Young enough to be malleable,' Gevenan said at last, the opti-
mism grudging. 'But hardly old enough to light their wicks, this
lot. Hades below, Ligea, I'm damned if I know how we can take
the Exaltarchy on, if this is the calibre of recruit you give me.
They'll be snivelling in their cots at night, hankering after their
mothers.'

She sighed. 'Sometimes I think nothing less than legionnaires
with ten years' experience and an overriding hatred of the
Exaltarch would please you, Gev.'

'I'm just practical. Ocrastes' backside, someone has to be.
We've been at this for more than five years, Ligea, and how far
have we got? Sooner or later we're going to run into a problem
too big for us to handle. Our forces grow larger and more wide-
flung. More people know about this place, and all the other safe
houses and training grounds. That's more people in a position
to betray us. Sooner or later we will fall to treachery, you must
realise that.'

'I'm not so easily deceived,' she said. 'I can sense a traitor, as
you know.'

'Yes,' he said soberly. 'So you say. I'll admit I was surprised by
that bronzesmith, the Pythian slave. I would have staked my life
on his loyalty.'

'I sensed his intended treachery the moment he made up his
mind to betrayal.'

Gevenan shrugged. 'I just have to take your word for that,
don't I? But it went against my grain to slide a sword into a man

who had never done me any harm. Just because you thought he might – at some future time – betray us.'

'I didn't think it, I *knew* it.'

'So you say.'

'Next time, I'll do my own killing.'

'Yes, you should. Ligea, the real problem is that you can't be everywhere, although you seem to do your damnedest to try. You said five years, remember? You're behind schedule.'

'Yes. I had thought that by now Temellin would be able to send some Magor to help me, but things haven't gone as well in Kardiastan as we all hoped they would, or as quickly.' She paused and considered. 'After the next snow-season, I promise. Full rebellion, Gev, from one side of the Exaltarchy to the other: Kardiastan, Altan, Cormel, the Western Reaches – in fact, everywhere from Corsene to Inge. Brand and Garis and Temellin, the Gharials and the Quyriots, we are all in agreement and there are others who will follow our lead.'

She looked over her shoulder. 'Gev, these folk are weary. Call a halt and we'll rest up for a meal.'

He nodded and turned his horse to give the order.

She twisted to look at Arrant. 'Awake, lad?'

'Yes. And I'm hungry.'

'So am I. We'll eat the bread and meat we got at the farm, all right?'

That was the day Arrant first realised his mother was mortal. That she could *die*. The day when he wondered for the first time what would happen to him if she did.

They sat on the boulders in the ravine and ate the food the farm workers had packed for them. The plateau horses, as adaptable as goats, nibbled at the bushes growing in every crevice.

The rescued youths from the Corbussian slave pens frightened Arrant a little, for all that they ignored him. They were too severe, too unsmiling, too tense. They talked funny, too. Occasionally their nervous tension would leak into his consciousness. He hated their unease. Grown-ups weren't supposed to feel like that. Freedom was supposed to make people happy, wasn't it? And he didn't understand why they were so wary of his mother. She said it was because they were frightened by the Magor powers they'd seen her use.

They're silly, he thought. *They should be glad she'd freed them.* Sometimes grown-ups were so hard to understand. His mother was often mad at Gevenan, and yet he made her laugh, all the time.

As they ate, he overheard one youth questioning Ligea's body-guard, Mole. He was called that because he had a large brown mole in the outer corner of his nostril – as big as a pancake, or so Gevenan said. It wasn't really. More like one of the rosehips that the cook used to make into jam.

'How much far?' the youth asked. He was looking up at the sky, where dark clouds promised rain and an early dusk. He struggled with his Tyranian, his tone hovering on the fringes of fear. 'We ride under the dark?'

'If the weather holds,' Mole replied, 'we'll be in Prianus come nightfall. The Stronghold's further.' He smiled at the youth. 'Somehow, I don't think the Magoria will ask you to ride all night. We've almost reached the spot where this ravine joins the track to Prianus. After that, the ride's easier.'

'What – what happen us at this place, Stronghold?'

'You can go home if you know the way and want to risk the journey. Or you can seek work elsewhere. Or you will be trained. To be a soldier, perhaps, or a horse-handler or any one of a dozen diff'rent things, 'pending on what you're best at. So as you can fight the Exaltarchy. The only thing you can't do is betray us. We kill people who do that.'

That was true. Arrant wasn't supposed to know it, but he did. Sometimes he understood things he wasn't supposed to, like that conversation about betrayal and the bronzesmith.

'Where are you from, lad?' Mole asked the youth in a friendly fashion.

'Ba'Azam in Janus. Name of me, Polvik. We cross sea to here.' His voice told how he marvelled at that. 'I not know world so very, very *big*. Water far, many *days*.'

'How did you become a slave?'

Polvik's face went dark. 'Big fort of Ba'Azam have many soldiers. S'posed make safe us from Blue-beards. Bastards of desert, you know? Acheron rot damnable souls! But legions bad too. One soldier took sister of me, she eleven only. No man want she after. Soldier give trinkets. I say, pay more.'

He shrugged. 'Big fight. They say Polvik hurt legionnaire.' He pulled a wry face. 'Sold me. Chained, with same bastards of desert. Marched to sea, sold to trader of Tyrans. New master, he take me Corbussia, want sell me again. Then you come. And *her*.' He nodded in Ligea's direction. 'Lady of numina.'

'She's no numen,' Mole growled. 'She's a Kardi Domina. And you be polite about her, youngster, or you'll have all of us to contend with. She'll do right by you, if you do right by her.'

Polvik's eyes gleamed. 'Reckon she send Polvik home?'

'Better give up any dream of seeing Janus for a while. Takes a lot of money to get back, and you'd only get caught for escaping from Corbussia. Work for the Domina. But you're free now; you can do what you want. Just choose wisely, and remember who put the collar round your neck. And who took it off.'

The lad's face darkened. 'Not forget. Not never. But . . . fight Tyrans soldier? Always they win.'

A slow smile spread over Mole's face. 'Ah, that's the glory of it, lad. They don't. Not always.'

Arrant stopped listening. Something was making him uneasy. It was an odd feeling that started in the pit of his stomach and spread outwards, causing his heart to thump and his limbs to weaken. He swung his head towards his mother, to find her looking at him. She felt it too.

She stood, calling for quiet.

Everyone hushed. When all was silent, she raised her cabochon to her ear. The golden glow of it illuminated her face, the savage indent on her cheek smoothed over in the light. Arrant thought her beautiful. It was just plain silly that some people found her scary. Her scar never troubled him, though others sighed and said it ruined her looks.

'There are people on the track to Prianus,' she said quietly. 'Legionnaires. Fifteen of them, maybe. *Damn*. They'll cut us off from the village. And the Stronghold.'

'I not hear,' Polvik said.

Ligea smiled at his disbelief. 'Arrant will confirm it, won't you, lad?'

He raised his cabochon and listened the way she'd taught him. 'Nasty men,' he said. He heard nothing, but sensed the presence of strangers whose intentions stirred a terrible unease in him. His cabochon was like that. Sometimes it worked and sometimes it didn't. Sometimes it did one thing, but wouldn't do another. When it didn't behave, Ligea always frowned, a dark look he didn't like.

'He means legionnaires,' she said, sounding impatient. She was always cross when he used the wrong words. 'We'll either have to return to the farm, or ambush them.' She glanced across at Gevenan. 'They're on gorclaks. And we only have fifteen men, three of them wounded.'

He shrugged. 'Ambush. Safer for Prianus.'

'None can escape to tell what happened, or where.'

'Still safer. We can surprise them.'

She nodded to the ex-slaves. 'You lads, you stay here with Arrant and Timnius and the horses. The rest of you, come with me – we've got to be in place before they get to where this ravine meets the quarry road, and I don't want to take the horses. Darius? How's that wound of yours? Do you think you'd better stay behind too?'

Darius grinned. He wasn't about to miss a fight.

'I can still pull a bow. Just don't ask me to run anywhere,' he said.

'Fine then. But you'd better take your horse.' Ligea took out her sword and looked down at Arrant, her face lined with worry that hadn't been there moments before. The concern sobered the excitement welling up inside him in a way no words could have done. 'Stay here with Timnius and look after the horses and the new men. You can tell them if you feel anyone coming.

If there is danger, then remember, I'm relying on you to stay hidden.'

He nodded. He liked obeying orders. That's what real soldiers did, and he liked to show he could be a real soldier too.

'And while you are waiting, you can practise your positioning powers. I want you to tell me afterwards everything that happened. All right?'

He nodded, but felt only dismay. He knew he would disappoint her. Again. She turned to go and the men, hefting their bucklers and weapons, followed in silence. He looked across at Timnius.

Timnius was a horse-handler, not a fighter, hardly older than the ex-slaves. Arrant liked Timnius because he sometimes let him help groom a horse, even though he did have to stand on a bench to reach.

'Make sure all them horses are well tethered,' Timnius ordered the ex-slaves who were now all staring at him, wide-eyed and scared. 'We don't want any pulling free when they scent blood.' He glanced at Arrant. 'All right, lad, you find a safe rock to hide behind, in case any of them soldiers escape and come this way. Any trouble, you duck down and hide, as small as a mouse, understand?'

He nodded. None of this was new to him.

He found a safe spot; Timnius approved of it and moved off to tend the horses. Arrant tried to concentrate the way Ligea had taught him, but his mind danced away as it often did when it should have been focusing. Wanting to please her, he tried to count off on his fingers the number of men he sensed, but he soon lost count. He wasn't sure if that was because there were too many, or just because his counting got muddled.

He felt a roiling of emotion, but it came at him from every direction, all mixed up: fear, anticipation, excitement, boredom. He couldn't tell if it came from Ligea's men, or from the ex-slaves, or from the legionnaires. Nothing had happened yet, he felt sure. He tried to seek out his mother's feelings, but lost her in the tangle. Then, after a while, all the emotions drifted away and he felt nothing at all.

He began to feel sleepy. The regular burp of frogs nearby was monotonous; nothing else seemed to move or make a sound. He sat propped against a boulder and looked up at the clouds, now covering the sky from one side to another, promising rain yet not delivering. Lightning made flashes behind the dark billows, so far away he couldn't hear the thunder. He dozed.

An ant woke him, crawling across his face. Before he could brush it away, a hot jab of fire poked into his mind, like a scream of pain and despair that was felt rather than heard. He sat up, shaking, but everything around was quiet. The ex-slaves were scattered among the rocks with the horses and packs, some drowsing just as he had been. Timnius stood, alert, leaning against a boulder, looking up the ravine towards the quarry road. Arrant flicked the ant away and took a deep breath to slow down his thudding heart. He knew what had happened: the fighting had started.

His mother wanted him to listen with his mind, to read what happened. But he didn't want to know, not if it meant feeling someone else's pain. Not if it meant that awful jab in his head. Still, he wanted to please her. He tried to listen, to feel, but there was nothing. Just silence, broken only by the reality of burping frogs, snuffling horses, trickling water.

He wriggled unhappily. Why did he find it so difficult? His mother didn't. And she didn't seem to get jabbed in the head, either. At least she never said she did.

Bored, he looked around for something to do. He played for a while, building a stone bridge across a rill that trickled towards the stream. That was fun.

Then he felt the emotions once more. Terror, shock, rage: it all rampaged through him, leaving him gasping, breathless, quivering. It was closer. There were big animals. Gorclaks? He tried to feel his mother, but someone else's terror consumed him. He had no control over anything he felt. Other minds came and went at random, dropping emotions into his, like boulders into a pond. The waves they made eroded the solidity of boundaries, causing pieces of his body to react in unexpected ways. His heart pounded, his mind howled, his stomach heaved.

He ran, screaming, back towards Timnius and the others, feet scudding, leaping bushes and stones. Some vestige of Ligea's training asserted itself and he screamed words, not mindless sounds. 'They're coming! They're coming!' he shouted, over and over.

CHAPTER SIXTEEN

Timnius shouted orders to the others, sending them to seek cover. Most of them took only their own horses and packs. Timnius hurled abuse after them, and a few came back to help untie and herd the remaining animals away into the brush. In the confusion, the horse-handler found time to grab Arrant and shake him to stop his yelling. 'Ocrastes' balls, will you shut up? Go and hide!'

Arrant quietened, shuddering, and turned to do as he was told. And saw his mother's horse, still tethered by the track. She would be awfully mad if the legionnaires stole it. He untied the reins from the bush and led the horse to a boulder. From there he scrambled up onto the animal's back and into the saddle. He swung its head around and headed away from the rough track.

He couldn't go far. Beyond a thin line of brush, the walls of the canyon rose steeply from a tumble of stones into a shiny rock face. Shivering, he halted the horse behind a tangle of thorn bushes. From the saddle he caught glimpses of Timnius, helped by several of the youths, hurrying to and fro untethering horses, slapping their rumps to send them away into the scrub.

The mind-stench of gorclaks grew stronger. And human emotions: a churning of fear, rage, excitement. Perhaps the mountain horses sensed it too, for they baulked in panic, refusing to leave the open space of the ravine centre. Urged away, they circled back again, eyes wide, ears pricked. Timnius, frustrated, tried to grab at their halters, thinking to lead them instead, but

they skittered off in all directions, only to regroup further down
the ravine in a nervous hoof-stamping gathering. Far-off thunder
grumbled warning.

Arrant's heart pounded. He could feel the soldiers coming, as
inevitable as a storm about to shatter a windless calm. One part
of him was tense, but he also savoured the anticipation. He wasn't
afraid. His mother would be there. She would keep him safe, she
always did. She was a Magoria. This was just another adventure,
a shivery one perhaps, but its outcome would be good. All those
horrid feelings: they weren't his. They belonged to other people,
bad people. He had to learn to push them into the background,
that's what Ligea said.

He sat still and watched, peering through the screen of bushes.
And saw the gorclaks sweep around a corner.

Dislike of the riders with their yellow hair and short tunics
gripped him. They had snarling dog faces on their cuirasses and,
in the whirl of bodies and horses and gorclaks and weapons, the
faces of the soldiers seemed as cruel as the canine snarls on their
chests. The pounding of hooves bonded to the thunder of the
storm. The ground shook with the rush of beasts. The air was
muggy with sound, saturated with cries, with galloping, with
animal panic. Noise all around, till he put his hands over his ears.

He tried to count them, but in the confusion penetrating his
mind, he couldn't remember his numbers. Eight, nine, ten, twelve
– or did eleven come before twelve? Ligea would be annoyed.
More gorclaks than he had fingers. He looked back at Timnius.

The horse-handler was still in the open, tugging at the reins
of two of the horses. And the first of the gorclak riders was upon
him. Too late, Timnius released the bridles and tried to run, but
the rider leaned down and swung his sword. It looked like a
game. Slow, casual. The legionnaire was grinning. Grinning as
the sword connected. He had been aiming for the side of the
neck, but Timnius turned his head at the last minute to look up
– and the sword slashed through his throat. Blood spurted, a
spray of red raindrops. Timnius ran on, blood spraying, wound
flapping. Then his legs faltered, as if he ran through water.

Arrant screamed, but no one heard. Pain blossomed in his mind. Timnius fell, his dying opening out like a blood-red flower, petal edges slicing their agony into Arrant's thoughts.

This was what it was like to die.

The gorclak rider made the mistake of looking back over his shoulder at Timnius. While he was distracted, the lumbering battering ram that was his mount ploughed into a panicked horse. The nose-horn, backed by the vast weight of the gorclak, ripped open the side of the animal, spilling guts onto the ground. The heap steamed there like hot stew. The gorclak swung its massive head to sweep the slaughtered beast out of the way, but stumbled over the carcass instead and crashed hard to its knees. The soldier, still unbalanced from his sword slash, went flying over its head. The next gorclak thundered into the two injured beasts. Struggling animals now barred the way of the other fleeing men.

Eight of them. This time Arrant counted them correctly. The first one – the one who had killed Timnius – was dead from his fall. The intense desire of the others to flee flamed out into the air like fire spreading across spilled oil. He couldn't feel the other legionnaires; there had been more, surely? But his awareness of them was gone.

Ligea and Mole and Koll and Gev and the others – he felt all of them, though. Even Darius, well at the back. They were following the legionnaires down the ravine, running. Except for Gevenan. The Ingean was riding Darius' horse. His emotion was like a burning coal, all hot and intense and hard.

He arrived first, bursting on the scene in a flurry of mud and sweat and panic. The snarling-dog men were still trying to untangle the two fallen gorclaks and riders. Gevenan launched a spear at the back of the closest man. He died not even knowing what killed him. The next died just as he turned to see what had happened. Gevenan swept on and then wheeled the horse to make another pass. He was using his sword and shield now, controlling the mount with his knees and heels.

Arrant thought: *too many*. He can't win.

He felt the first twinge of fear for himself. Where was Ligea?

He looked down at his cabochon, but there was nothing there. No colour. No power. But emotions – they were everywhere around him, swamping him, muddling him. Nothing he could *use*. He sat still, gripping the reins, as his mount rolled its eyes and flung its head about.

Then Ligea was there. And the ravine seemed to be full of people, all battling to live.

Arrant felt no relief. His first sight of war and it was the taste of it in his mind that overwhelmed, all the anguish and agony poured onto a pain-saturated slope until it collapsed into an avalanche of terror, submerging everything. So much pain, inextricably combined with savage pride and rage. Who felt what, he had no idea. He clutched his head, just wanting to be rid of it all so he could *think*. So that he could stop screaming. He wanted the pain to go away.

I want Ligea. 'Mater! Mater!'

And then something else drifted into his mind, touching him in wonder. And abruptly it all stopped. The pain, the confusion, the fear. As if someone had closed a door and left all the bad things on the other side. On his side, there was . . . peace. Comfort. Then a renewed terror: *he wasn't alone.* Someone was inside him, looking out through his eyes.

For a splinter of time he was beyond fright, in a realm where fear closed down thought. Then, again abruptly, another barrier shut down. The presence was gone. He had his mind back. He could feel nothing and no one, not even Ligea. His terror lingered, along with the memory of that – person? creature? – in his head. With no thought but to find his mother, he urged the reluctant horse towards the fighting. It sidled from the brush. The conflict whirled on; the smell of blood was strong.

Once, he had thought he would enjoy watching a battle. After all, it was so pretty to see the light shoot from Ligea's sword; he thought she was pretty, too, with her golden Magoroth glow.

But he knew better now. Battle was also whirling wind and noise and lots of shouting and screaming. The yellow-haired men had those horrible gorclaks, battle mounts with horns that cut human flesh like knife blades. And the smell. Voided bowels and blood, ruptured guts and horse dung, sweat and the stench of gorclak. The sounds of men about to die with spears lodged deep in their bodies. The gurgle of men trying to breathe without lungs, the rattle in throats making their last human utterance. The resonance of death and agony and parting.

He couldn't curb his distress. He hated those sounds, those smells. He hated the fear inside himself. His emotions overflowed, out of his control.

And his mother's head swung around searching for him, alarm in every line of her body. A rip-disc came whirling out of a sling towards her. Distracted, she didn't see it.

He saw her spin around and fall; he saw blood. Lots and lots of blood. When he dragged his gaze away from that, he saw a big yellow-haired man ride his gorclak at her. He was laughing and swinging a double-headed axe, leaning half out of the saddle, the axe cleaving the air towards her neck . . . He wanted to run to her, yet he knew he mustn't and the horse refused to move closer anyway. He wanted to scream, but the sound stuck in his throat—

Nothing was exciting any more. *Fear*. Fear that made your throat so tight you couldn't breathe, or cry, or anything.

The axe bounced in the air instead of hitting her. Sparks splintered forth in a shower of gold, and it was the yellow-haired man who toppled dead, not Ligea. Wounded even as she was, she'd built wards with her sword and then burned a hole through his chest.

Still the fighting spun on, but his eyes stayed with his mother, seeing only her blood, knowing she was hurting, feeling the spill of her pain before she conquered it. This wasn't just some sort of grown-up game. It wasn't fun. It was horrid.

When the fighting was over, he slipped down from the horse and ran to go to her. He had to pass Timnius' body. He slowed, staring, his panic rising once more. Timnius was so *still*. His skin was a funny colour, all pale. And his eyes were open, but they didn't move. Like the eyes of a statue. No life in them, no spark. Painted marble. He rushed on to join Ligea, his sobs caught in the back of his throat, unable to escape.

She sat, leaning against a rock. Mole was already there, winding cloth around her shoulder. She smiled at him and reached out with her free arm. 'It's all right, Arrant. It's not as bad as it looks – just a bit of blood and skin missing. Nothing I can't fix with rest and Magoroth magic.'

Scared and shamed by his fear, he took her hand and clung, swallowing back the tears. She kissed his head. Then she turned to Mole. 'Did we get them all?'

'All dead bar one, and he's a prisoner.'

'And our men?'

'Bad news. Olad's in the hands of the Vortex, Acheron accept his soul. Koll took an arrow in the leg that's a bit nasty. A few others with cuts that might need your attention some other time. Timnius died before we got here. The other lads are fine, if scared pissless.'

'Olad *and* Timnius. Vortex-blast. Damn, damn, *damn*! I thought we had them boxed in. I didn't think they would find the way in here. My mistake.' Arrant felt the pain she felt, pain that had nothing to do with her injury.

She asked, 'Can you round up the horses?'

'I think so,' Mole said. 'They don't seem to have gone far. The prisoner?'

'I don't want prisoners.'

'Do you want to see him first?'

She nodded, so they brought the yellow-haired man to her. He took one look and spat on the ground at her feet. 'Kardi numen bitch,' he said. He sounded brave, but Arrant didn't need his cabochon to sense the sickliness of fear in the Tyranian. Lots of people smelled like that when confronted by the Magor power of his mother.

'How did you find us?' she asked.

The man couldn't keep the stutter out of his voice. 'I d-don't know things like that. None of my business. Just do as I'm told.'

She sighed. 'And that's the truth, unfortunately.' She pointed at the dog face on his cuirass. 'What's the meaning of the dog's head?'

'It is our s-s-symbol. The Mountain Jackal. We are the Jackal Legion.' He tried to grin. 'A hunting pack. Culling out those who deserve to die.'

She ignored his nervous bravado. 'I've never heard of you.'

'A new name for an old legion. We were one of the best, once. We're the military arm of the Brotherhood now, and we'll sh-sh-show you what we can do. You took us because we are just a s-s-squad – a few men hunting out your lair. When we don't come back, the rest of the legion'll know where to look, won't they? And you won't beat *them*.'

The muscles around her eyes tightened. 'That's new. The Brotherhood never felt the need of a military arm before. Who's your commander?'

'Legate Favonius Kyranon. He isn't here. He'll hunt you down one day, numen b-b-bitch.'

Her emotions hit Arrant like a punch in the stomach. Her voice shook as she said, 'Favonius? He was a Stalwart! Whenever would a Stalwart join the Brotherhood? Stalwarts despise Brotherhood tactics, Favonius more than most!'

Arrant didn't understand what she meant. He didn't understand what the man said next either.

'When the quarry is s-s-sufficiently tempting. Or s-s-sufficiently hated. We remember what numina bastards did to some of our number over there in Kardiastan.'

'You were there in the Mirage?'

'Never made it. I was one of those cut off by the avalanche. You're dead meat, lady.' He smiled at her. Arrant wanted to hit him.

'You're telling me the Stalwarts are now the Jackals?'

'That's right. After the Mirage muck-up, the Exaltarch packed us off to the p-provinces in disgrace. Five years in bloody exile! But the Magister Officii brought us back a month or two ago, to deal with you.'

'What happened to Legate Kilmar?'

'He never made it b-back from the Mirage. Legate Favonius leads us now.'

She didn't say anything; just nodded to Mole, who led the man away.

'What's a numen?' Arrant asked.

She ruffled his hair. He hated it when she did that. 'Nothing you need ever worry your head about. There are no such things as numina, but foolish people will believe in all kinds of foolish things just to explain what they are not wise enough to understand. Now run along, lad, and keep out of everyone's way. I want to talk to Gevenan.'

He moved away, but then all his fears came scurrying back. The fear he might die. The fear his mother might die. The memory of Timnius dying. The memory of that – that *something* looking out through his eyes. He sidled back behind her, trying hard not to leak all his fears, and sat down.

She beckoned to Gevenan and he came across to her, grinning, but she was in no mood for his amusement. She turned on him wrathfully. 'Don't you *ever* do that again!' she snarled.

He raised an eyebrow, his grin vanishing. 'Do what?'

'You took Darius' horse instead of letting me have it! That was *insane*, Gev, and you know it. I'm the only person here who can take on more than half-a-dozen legionnaires at once. If they hadn't had that pile-up to occupy them while the rest of us caught up, you'd be dead.'

He looked her up and down and said, 'Can I mention that *I'm* the one who's unharmed and *you're* the one who's wounded? Don't try to pull my teeth, m'dear, when your own need sharpening.'

She glared at him. 'I gave you an order back there. I told you to give the horse to me – and you rode off.'

'Sorry. Didn't hear you.'

She gave an exasperated sigh. 'I can hear lies, Gev, remember? You disobeyed an order during a fight! I should—'

'Should what?' He met her fury with a derisive smile. 'Demote me? Replace me? Throw me out of your army?'

They stared at each other in lengthy silence. Then he gave a sigh of his own and crouched down so his face was level with hers. Arrant had to strain to hear what he said. 'Ligea, I ride better than you do. I got back here quicker than you could have. Simple as that.'

'You were damned lucky not to die, and you know it. I kill better than you do, Gev.'

He shrugged. 'Maybe. I did take a chance, but it wasn't stupid bravery. It was a deliberate act based on, er, on my best inter-pretation of the situation.'

'Gev – there can only be one general in an army.'

'Yes. I agree. And it's got to be me.'

The next silence was so long that Arrant began to fidget. He didn't like seeing them argue.

Once again, it was Gevenan who broke the silence. 'Ligea, you set the boundaries. You draw the battle lines. But in the fight, I command the men. It's what I do best. I was a *general*, damn it, and a damned fine one too.'

'A general who lost the all-important battle.'

'That's kicking a man in the nobs. But yes, I admit it. I made mistakes. It was the first time any Ingean army had faced Tyranian legions and our tactics were all wrong. But that was twenty years ago, and I'm not going to make the same mistake twice.'

A third silence, but this one was less hostile. In the end, Ligea threw up her hands in capitulation. 'Let me have a look at Koll's wound, then we'll ride on to Prianus. We can ask some of the villagers to come back and bury the Tyranian dead and hide what happened here. We'll take Timnius and Olad back with us.'

Gevenan won, Arrant thought in surprise.

On the way to Prianus, he kept eyeing Timnius' body, flung over the back of his horse. His arms flopped like empty sleeves dancing as the horse trotted.

As they rode into the stone-cutters' village in the gloom of dusk, Arrant felt almost happy because he knew Narjemah would be there, staying with one of her friends from her slave days. He thought of her cakes, and the way she hugged him. It would feel good to have her arms about him, calling him her little boy. He wanted to forget the painted eyes, the flopping arms, the way fear could choke you so you couldn't breathe.

As it turned out, this time he was disappointed. Narjemah hugged and then cried over Ligea, not him. Which was odd, because she was scolding her at the same time. Arrant she merely hauled off to have a bath. He had noticed before that Narjemah was overly concerned with cleanliness. He didn't always submit meekly.

That evening he was more subdued; he couldn't forget all that blood. The way the dog-man had been swinging his axe at Ligea. Her wound running red. That other *thing* sitting in his head, looking out through his eyes. He sat quietly in the tin bath while Narjemah attended to his mother, washing the wound and reproaching her all the while.

'Enough is enough, Magoria. You can't cart the boy all around Tyrans as if you were both off on some pleasure trip. While you have him with you, you don't pay full attention to yourself. That's how this happened, isn't it? It's not right, either – he could have been killed! He's a child! He's not supposed to fight *battles* at his age.' She looked at him. 'Poor wee mite. And him so brave, too. You leave him with me up in the Stronghold next time you go out.'

Ligea sighed. 'You can't teach him the way I can, Narjemah. He's the Mirager-heir; he must learn how to control his cabochon as soon as he can. You know he – he has difficulties. He needs a Magoroth teacher. Still, you're right. Ouch! Haven't you finished yet?'

'Hold still! You rode all the way back here without a murmur, I guarantee, and now you squawk when I'm as gentle as a breeze?'

'A gale out of Acheron, more like,' Ligea muttered. 'Narjemah, I actually agree with you this time. It seems Rathrox Ligatan has his wits about him. These new dogs of his are sniffing in the right direction. And I'll admit it, I had a scare today. It was too close.' She made a gesture at her shoulder. 'And I'm not talking about this.' She sighed again and Arrant almost cried because she felt so sad. 'It's time he went to his father.'

'Me?' Arrant's heart lurched sickly inside him. 'I don't wanna go!'

She smiled at him. 'Yes, you do. You know you want to meet your father. You told me so. And he wants to see you, so very, very much.'

He felt cold in spite of the warm water. She had blocked her feelings from him – or at least he thought she had; he could sense nothing – but he knew that tone of voice. It meant there was to be no argument. When she sounded like that, wheedling had about as much effect as raising a hand against the wind. 'Will – will you come too?'

'Yes, for a little while . . . Ouch! Narjemah, don't worry about it. It will heal. You know a scratch like this won't bother a Magoria.'

Narjemah clucked fussily. 'You don't take half enough care of yourself.'

'I don't have time. Ah, here's Gevenan.'

The Ingean ignored Ligea and Narjemah and came over to Arrant. 'How's the young man?' he asked. 'Washed behind your ears?'

'Yep.'

He stuck his hand in the water, decided it was too cold and lifted Arrant out of the bath, wrapping him in a bath towel. 'Got more sense than your mother, eh? You wouldn't be so silly as to get yourself grazed by a rip-disc from a whirlsling, would you?'

Arrant giggled and shook his head.

Ligea was impatient with them. 'Gevenan, I want Prianus abandoned. The Brotherhood was too close today for easy sleep here. Double the sentries along the trail and get everyone up to the Stronghold as soon as you can. Don't listen to any excuses – insist.'

'You think this wasn't just a random search?'

'I'm sure of it. They were surprised at being ambushed, of course, but they were looking for us. For me.'

'For you, meaning Ligea?'

'No, me, the numen bitch. I questioned the survivor. Besides, they were all carrying whirlslings.'

He grunted. 'You're jumping to conclusions. And you the one with the fancy schooling in logic! It's possible every legion is under orders to increase the number of whirlslings just in case they meet you. After all, Rathrox and Bator Korbus both know enough to be aware the best way to bring down one of the Magor is from a distance.'

She thought that over. 'You could be right. Still, I want Prianus abandoned. If they do find the Stronghold, well, we can defend that or escape through the back trails. And, Gev, as soon as this shoulder is mended, I'm off to Kardiastan for a couple of months. I'm taking Arrant to his father and I want to coordinate the rebellions for next desert-season.'

Gevenan accepted that, unperturbed. 'A wise decision.' He smiled at Arrant. 'But I'll miss the brat, for all that.' And he went to ruffle his hair.

Arrant ducked.

CHAPTER SEVENTEEN

Arrant sat up on the seat next to Mole, who was driving the farm cart. It was all he could do to sit still. This was the longest trip he had ever taken away from the Stronghold, and the *best*. Mole let him take the reins sometimes, and showed him how to tell the horses what to do. And there were lots of interesting things to see along the paveway.

The paveway itself, for a start. The stones were so *neat*, all laid out in rows. Of course, they weren't allowed to use the paved part. That was for important people. They used the dirt road alongside, but Ligea said that was better for the horses anyway. The mounted legionnaires who rode on the paving tied a funny sort of leather bag with iron at the bottom on to their horses' feet. Mole said it was so the hooves didn't wear down on the stones.

He had to pretend Mole was his uncle and Narjemah was their slave. She complained about having to wear a slave collar. Mole was driving them only as far as Getria and he told everyone he was a farmer, taking his widowed sister to Getria to marry a distant cousin. The idea of his mother getting married made Arrant giggle. She kept her hair covered, as a modest widow might, and that was funny too. Her wound, aided by her Magor healing, didn't bother her any more, which was just as well because the cart was bumpy.

They paid the road tax at the wayhouses and stayed in road-side tabernas, even though Narjemah grumbled about the bedbugs. The taberna owners and the wayhouse people were all supposed to check if travellers had cabochons in their palms, but mostly they forgot. As Ligea said, when you looked at hundreds and hundreds of hands month after month, year after year and no one ever had a cabochon, you must wonder why you had to bother.

They'd only been asked twice. The first time Mole showed his own hand and then pretended he was so insulted anyone would suggest his family were numina that the man at the wayhouse had apologised. The second time, when a taberna owner insisted on seeing Ligea's hand, the man had suddenly got a terrible pain in his head. He'd gone to bed after that and forgotten all about it.

Arrant had rarely enjoyed himself more. His two favourite people suddenly had all the time in the world to attend to him. Narjemah told him stories about the Magor and Kardiastan. Ligea told him about the Mirage and his father, and when she ran out of things to say, she told tales of the gods of Elysium. They played games to while away the hours spent in the cart. A pleasant stream was an excuse not just to water the horses, but to have a swim.

The only blotches on his enjoyment were the times when Ligea insisted he practise his magic. He tried – oh, how he tried! – but somehow things rarely happened the way they should.

'Looks like a taberna up there, Domina,' Mole remarked. 'Want to stop for the night? We can get from here to Getria by tomorrow evening.'

'Good idea,' she said. 'Arrant, check your bandage.'

He looked down to make sure the lump on his palm was properly covered. 'It's fine. Look, Mater, those children have a kitten. Can I go and have a look?'

'As soon as we stop. Remember to try to sense their feelings when you play with them.'

He nodded, but when he went to join the three children, their emotions remained as blank to him as a cloudless sky. They seemed friendly, though, and let him pat the kitten. When Ligea called him back to her side, she'd already paid for their night's lodging and food and Mole was asking if the taberna-keeper wanted to look at their palms.

The man laughed. 'If ever I did find a numen, I reckon they'd kill me right then and there. Tell you the truth? I'd rather not look in the first place. Your room is at the top of the stairs on the left. Two cots and two pallets. I'll send the food up when it's ready.'

'So,' Ligea asked a little later, when Arrant was hanging out of the window watching Mole unhitch the cart, 'did your cabochon work?'

He shook his head and didn't look at her.

She sighed. 'Look at that hilltop over there, Arrant. Enhance your sight and tell me what you see.'

He brought his hand up to his face and strained to bring the glow into the gem, but it nestled under the skin of his palm as quiet and as useful as a lump of river gravel.

'No luck?' she asked. 'Never mind.'

But he did mind. He minded horribly because he knew his lack upset her. He saw *fear* in her eyes.

He was so *stupid*. At times, usually when he wasn't concentrating at all, he would be hit by someone's anger, or another's joy. And he wouldn't know whose. Sometimes, when they were in a crowd of people, he would be overwhelmed by all he felt. He'd start shaking, eyes popping wide with panic. Ligea and Narjemah both tried to teach him how to block out such unwanted feelings, in vain. He had no control.

His mother never growled at him, but then she didn't have to; the way her brow creased with worry when he failed was enough to chide him more deeply than words could have done. He laboured to please her, but it didn't seem to help. Worse, he knew his lack somehow *frightened* her.

That night, as he snuggled drowsily on his pallet and Mole was downstairs checking on the horses, he heard Ligea and Narjemah whispering about it.

'I don't know what to do,' Ligea said. 'Narjemah, you said *you* could do more at this age than he can. You said all Magor children can. And he is not just Magor, he is Magoroth! He is supposed to be *better* than most, not worse.'

'He's child still.'

'He's the Mirager-heir!'

'Let him have his childhood.'

'It's all my fault and I don't know how to make it right. Please the gods, Temellin will know what to do.'

Arrant shrank into a ball under the covers. His mother blamed herself. But it was *his* fault. He knew that. There was something *wrong* with him. And he had made his mother unhappy. Maybe that was why she wanted him to go live in Kardiastan, away from her. Probably he'd make his father unhappy too ... Why would Temellin be interested in a son who couldn't do magic? A lump formed in the back of his throat, as horrid as the way he felt.

He tried to shut out all those thoughts, but they wouldn't go away. Sensing his distress and thinking he was having a nightmare, his mother laid a hand on his head. He feigned sleep and finally did drop off, tears drying on his cheeks.

And dreamed. A tentacle slid across his skin, rubbing it raw and leaving behind a slime trail that burned like fire. It belonged to a beast with teeth like lance blades, all shiny and sharp. The creature grinned at him, and dropped saliva that sizzled through his clothes to his skin. Then it whispered in his ear: 'You are mine, Arrant weakling-child. And one day I will tear you to pieces. I will eat each piece while you watch. Your tongue first.' And the beast inserted a clawed finger into his mouth, curling the claw around his tongue to get a grip so it could rip—

Arrant woke, screaming. He sat bolt upright, bathed in sweat. It was the worst dream he'd ever had. And so *real*. That creature – it was as clear to him as the cat he had patted earlier that evening. But this had slavering jaws, made slurping sounds, seeped a thick stench of nastiness ... He shuddered and twisted his hands tight into the pallet cover.

A dream. It was just a dream. And dreams weren't real.

Why then could he *still* smell it?

Ligea came in, breathing hard. 'Mirageless soul, Arrant – what's the matter? I felt you all the way downstairs!'

'A – a bad dream,' he said.

She took him in her arms, and calmed his shuddering. 'Mirageless soul, you are in a state. Whatever it was, it doesn't matter, son. It wasn't real.'

But he knew it was, somewhere. Just not here.

'Look, lad, that's Getria.' Mole pointed with his horsewhip as they topped a rise. Arrant, sitting next to him, had a good view. 'See the walls? And the tall buildings on the hills – those are the temples to Medeana, Goddess of Love and Children, wife of Ocrastes, God of War.'

'Getria is not as beautiful as Tyr,' Ligea added, looking over his shoulder, 'and it's not as large either.' Still, Arrant had trouble shutting his mouth. It looked huge to him, and became bigger by the minute as they approached.

Closer to the walls, Mole stopped the cart and pretended to be fiddling with one of the wheels while Ligea enhanced her sight and hearing to see how the guards dealt with those entering the gates.

'Not too bad,' she said after a while. 'They only ask to see the palms of people with darker skins. Arrant and Narjemah and I will sit in the back of the cart. You tell them the usual story, Mole. If that doesn't get us through, I'll create a diversion.' She grinned at Arrant and he sensed her excitement. She was enjoying herself. 'Remember that, Arrant. If you don't want people to see something, give them something more exciting to look at.'

As Mole started the horses moving once more, she said, 'There's a cart with wine jars in the gateway. The owner is arguing over the duties due at the gate. Spilled wine would be much more interesting than you or me.' She gave him a blanket. 'Here, wrap yourself up in this. Cover as much of your skin as you can.' She and Narjemah used their shawls.

Mole started grizzling as soon as the guard at the gate came to ask who he was. 'Rollus,' he said, 'carpenter. Been to Begum to pick up my fool sister here and her slave and my nevvy. Told her she should never have married that useless farmer. Worked her half to death out in the fields, he did, and now got himself killed by a goat. Gored to death by a bloody *goat*, can you *believe* it? And what the hells am I to do with a woman and another brat? Me own wife has Acheron's sulphur on her tongue as it is . . .'

At this point, the guard gave up and waved them through. Arrant was disappointed. He would rather have seen the spilled wine.

'We will stay with Sestius tonight,' Ligea told him as they proceeded into the city. 'He's one of Moneymaster Arcadim's sons. I have business to discuss. Mole, you had better ask for directions.'

Arrant had never been inside such a splendid building as the Sestius villa. Best of all, as far as he was concerned, were the mosaics on the floor. You could walk from room to room reading the story they told underfoot, all about the gods and goddesses and immortals and the heroes of old . . . all the stories Ligea had told him. There were even pictures of strange animals from the south of Altan – dogs with funny snouts as long as your arm, people riding beasts even bigger than gorclaks.

As a child, he was welcomed in both the women's and the men's quarters – spoiled and cuddled and stuffed with sweetmeats in the former, subtly questioned in the latter. Arrant, however, was already an expert at never giving anything away, and the moneymaster had ended by ruffling his hair and laughing, telling him he was a clever lad indeed.

Sestius made Arrant giggle. Instead of hair, he had a blue eye painted on his shiny bald head. And he had a beard that grew down to his waist. He'd made it pretty, too, with strings of pearls. Arrant wanted to touch them, but Ligea had said he mustn't do that. No one was allowed to touch a moneymaster's pearls because they represented his ancestors.

Sestius showed Arrant the library of the house, and told him he must learn to read and figure. 'For if you don't,' the money-master said, 'you will be only half a man. Remember that, lad: to ride and fight and swim and wrestle – that's only half of life.'

Arrant discovered he loved the smell of the library: the scent of fresh papyrus, the lingering hint of the glue they used in the bindings of the ledgers, the interesting smell of new wax on the tablets, the edgy tang of mustiness in the dark corners. He loved the look of it: the scrolls bound with ribbon, the piled-up tablets, the marble lecterns, the row upon row of ledgers.

'I'll remember,' he promised, and meant it.

After Getria, Mole returned to the Stronghold, while Arrant, Ligea and Narjemah joined a moneymasters' caravan transporting documents and gold to a town called Bryssa. There they trans-ferred to a barge belonging to the Moneymasters' Guild of Tyr, on one of the smaller tributaries of the River Tyr.

The three of them dressed as Assorians. Arrant wore a robe, not a tunic. It flapped around his ankles and he complained he felt like a girl. He complained, too, that Narjemah and Ligea didn't look right, covered up like that. Assorian women, Ligea explained, were not allowed to show their arms or shoulders or hair to any man who wasn't a part of their family. Even odder, they were not allowed to look at men, or have men look at them, unless they were family. The Assorian bargemen not only wouldn't glance at them, but refused to speak to them unless absolutely necessary.

'I shall look at you,' Arrant told Narjemah stoutly on their first day on the barge, 'whenever I like. And you can look at me, too.'

'Don't complain,' Ligea said. 'Assorian customs are to our advantage. I believe no one will ask to see our palms, because they wouldn't want to anger an Assorian moneymaster by insulting his womenfolk. As for you, Arrant, every time a legion-naire comes close, you will have to hide in among the bales of cargo. It doesn't matter if they see you; I just don't want anyone to get a good look at you. Do you think you can do that?'

As they had an armed legionnaire escort, he often had to scuttle off into one of the half-a-dozen hiding places he found on board. That part was fun. Most of the time, though, the trip was boring. During the day, they sat on cushions in the shade of canvas covers as the barge was pulled along the towpath by a team of rented slaves. They stopped at wayhouses for meals and to change the pullers. At night, they slept on board while the barge was tied up to the bank.

Once they entered the River Tyr, the journey was more interesting. When they sighted the city in the distance, Arrant forgot all about Getria; Tyr was so much better and bigger and more fascinating. He gazed up in awe at a giant stone bridge leaping its way across the land in huge arches. It curved to cross the valley and was then swallowed up by the city walls. 'What's that for?' he asked. 'Why would anyone want a road built up so high?'

'It's not a road. It's an aqueduct,' Ligea explained. 'It brings water to Tyr from the hills.'

'But there's lots of water in the river and that goes into the city. You said so.'

'It does, as you'll see in a minute. But the water is not clean. Especially in the desert-season. Look at it, Arrant. Would you like to drink water that colour? Dirty water makes you sick. The water in the aqueduct is as clear as the day it bubbled up out of the ground.'

'Oh.' He stared and stared. He'd never seen anything as lovely as the curves of those arcaded arches eating up the miles. 'It looks like a road,' he said. 'A road on a bridge. How long is it? Must be miles 'n' miles 'n' miles!'

'This particular one is about a hundred and fifty miles long.'

'How far's that?'

'Well, it would take you ten days to walk it. And is there ever *any* end to your questions?'

'Do they have them in Kardiastan?'

'No, but they ought to.'

'Then I shall build some when I'm big.'

A little further on they were halted to have their cargo checked and taxed. Ligea and Narjemah sat together, holding their gauzy shawls across their faces, their heads modestly lowered. Arrant had to pretend to be asleep, with a sheet pulled over him. No one asked to see their palms.

They passed on into the city, Arrant staring at all he saw: the gleaming temples on the hilltops, the statues, the painted public buildings. He thought of the stories about the gods, and wondered if everyone who lived here was, perhaps, an immortal at the very least.

'No,' Ligea said with a sad half-smile when he asked. 'Just people like you and me, or slaves. It takes many, many slaves to keep a place like this.'

'Why do you sound so sad?' he asked. 'Are they unhappy, those slaves?'

'Yes, I think so. Many of them are, anyway. But that's not the only reason I feel sad. I am sorry because I am not sure the city will survive the end of slavery, at least not unchanged. We are fighting for things to be different, Arrant, but change often brings pain in its entourage.'

Another thing he didn't understand. He sighed to himself. Would he *ever* understand all the things she talked about? Then he remembered: she was giving him away to his father. He would not see her again . . . At least, not till he was all grown up. He started to cry.

Ligea looked startled. 'Goddess, Arrant, don't cry over something that hasn't happened yet!'

Narjemah hugged him and placated him with a sweetmeat. 'Are we almost there?' he asked.

Ligea was confused. 'Where?'

'Kardiastan.'

'No, of course not!' She exchanged a smile with Narjemah over his head. He pouted, knowing they were laughing at him. 'Look,' she said. 'See those ships – big, big boats – up ahead?' She pointed in the direction they were taking. At first he couldn't see anything that looked like a boat, then he realised that the large wooden things ahead of them were actually floating on the water at the edge of the river.

He nodded.

'We will be going on one of those. It will take us as many days on one of those ships as you have fingers and toes – and only then will we be in Kardiastan. But first, first we will stay here a day or two, with Moneymaster Arcadim.'

Arcadim Asenius added another gold coin to the weighing dish and checked its weight. A tedious job, but one he did not trust his slaves to do, not even the ledger clerks. Who was to say they would not shave a sliver of gold from each coin and tell him they all weighed exactly what they should? He looked up as the slave knocked and entered. 'Yes, what is it?' he asked testily.

'The barge has arrived from Bryssa, Master Arcadim. They are unloading the cargo now. And your son sent some, er, guests.'

Arcadim blinked. 'Who?'

'I don't rightly know, master. Two women and a child.'

'*Assorian* women?'

'Yes, master. At least, I think so. They are dressed that way.' He didn't sound convinced.

'Well, you should not be bothering me with women's business. Tell Mistress Reveba!'

But the man didn't go. He shuffled uncomfortably and said, 'Um, one of the women told me to tell you she once owned a poor copy of the Pelotonius discus thrower at the stadium.'

A gold coin slipped from his fingers and rolled across the floor. He stared at his slave in consternation. God of his fathers, *she had come here*? To his *house*? Great God above, if Rathrox heard of this, his whole family was forfeit, not to mention his wealth. Was that eldest son of his foaming mad?

And he could not speak to a woman alone, not in his house, not without a scandal. And he didn't dare deal with her in the counting house. There were slaves there who might possibly recognise her, and although he thought he could trust his slaves

– who knew for sure? Great God, did she want to *stay* in his house?

Calm yourself, Arcadim.

He turned to the slave. 'Tell Mistress Reveba to be good enough to wait on me here. When she has arrived, show the women in.'

The man went to do as he was bade, and Arcadim took several slow deep breaths. Ever since Ligea had fled the city, he had not had a truly peaceful moment. More than five years, and still he worried. He worried the Brotherhood would uncover the truth of his continued connections with Ligea. He worried about the fate of his family. He worried about being tortured. He worried the Assorians would be banished from Tyrans forever. He worried that Ligea would lose the battle against the Exaltarchy. He worried she would *win* . . .

He even worried that God must favour the Kardis over the Assorians to have given them such magic talents.

'You asked for me, dear?'

He tried to sound calm. 'Yes, Reveba. It seems we have guests in the house. Sent by Sestius, via barge. Two women and a child. I suspect it's the, um, nameless patron.'

Her quick frown indicated her instant anxiety, but there was no time for her reproaches. Ligea was ushered in and he turned to greet her. 'This is a surprise,' he said, taking a deep breath in an effort not to show his annoyance. No, his *terror*. 'May I present my wife, Reveba?'

'I am just passing through,' she said coolly, after a polite bow to Reveba. 'There is no need to mention a name. It is good to see you again in person, Arcadim. There are some business matters that need to be attended to, and I have news for the Assorians that may be of, shall we say, value?'

He knew the temptation of information and hated himself for the way he responded to it. Like a dog pricking up its ears, he thought bitterly, or a cat twitching its nose.

She waited while he hesitated, without – he noted – introducing the other woman, supposedly a slave, or the child. Fortunately Reveba took control, and ushered the second woman and the boy into the neighbouring room, while judiciously leaving the door open between. Her command of the Tyranian language was poor, but a child was an instant connection, and as he turned to Ligea, he saw the two women smiling and talking as if they were old friends. *Women.*

He gestured to the chairs. 'Won't you be seated?'

She smiled slightly as she sat. 'You don't look happy, Arcadim.'

'You are endangering my family by coming here,' he said. He kept his voice low but didn't bother to hide his anger. 'What do you want?'

'I want to know the present status of my financial affairs, for a start. And your family has been endangered ever since you embarked on this course. This is what we both chose, remember?'

He rolled his eyes as a wave of despair swept him. 'I must have been moondaft.'

She grinned at him, annoyingly amused at a remark so uncharacteristic of him.

'Your affairs? Not as bad as I thought they were going to be,' he admitted, and rose to fetch the correct account book from the shelves at the far end of the room. 'Everything in this is coded, to disguise any connection to Ligea Gayed,' he explained as he brought it back for her to see. 'You spent so much of your assets early on, I was worried. See here? But then you started your raids to steal Tyranian money and goods. Those figures are here.' He could hardly believe he was saying this, reciting her crimes as if they were legitimate business ventures. He groaned as he thought about it. 'That helped, and so did the trade in Quyriot beads and bearskins and obsidian – that's this column here. But all of that was really only just covering your day-to-day expenses: paying your men, clothing them.'

Her stare didn't waver. 'But—?'

'It was your decision to invest so heavily in the Pythian papyrus trade that really saved you. That was astute of you, to realise that the constant trouble in Altan was going to affect the supplies from there and that the Exaltarchy would have to seek new sources.'

She shrugged. 'The heart of the insurgency in Altan is in the Delta marshes, where the papyrus grows. But that was one of the things I wanted to tell you – it's now time to sell my interests in Pythian papyrus. I have a feeling that Altani papyrus will come into its own again, quite soon, and it will be cheaper than the Pythian. Send an agent to Altan and buy out any Tyranian interests in the papyrus trade there. You should be able to do that at rock-bottom prices now.'

He said thoughtfully, 'The Pythian product is better quality. There will always be a market for it among the rich. I wouldn't dispose of your interest entirely—'

They discussed her finances for the better part of an hour. At the end of it, when she sat back in her chair, rubbing a stiff neck, he asked, 'You said you had some news for us, the moneymasters?'

She passed on news she'd had from her informants in the provinces and vassal states. He listened intently, then said as she finished, 'So, basically, there will be simultaneous revolts in Kardiastan, Quyr, Altan, Corsene, Cormel, probably the Western Reaches – in fact, just about everywhere – after the snow-melt next year.'

'Yes. The ones I named are the ones that will be fully co-ordinated. Other vassal states or provinces may take advantage of Tyr's preoccupation with these rebellions to fight their own wars.'

'And at the end of it?'

'We expect Kardiastan and Quyr to be free within a year. For Altan to have full control of the Delta. What will happen in the others is less certain.'

'And you?'

'All of northern Tyrans will be under our control soon. Getria will be ours – a year or two at the most. We will cut off supplies of grain to Tyr. And imports of wood from Valur. Not to mention the copper and tin ore that comes overland from Cormel.'

He was silent for a long time, trying not to think about how ill he felt. They had come to another watershed, another moment of decision, when all he had ever worked for could once more be in the balance. He felt that sick lurch of terror again. *Lord my God, why do you send this woman to plague me? Have I not been a good and faithful servant that I should be tormented thus?*

'You Assorians should be able to make money out of this,' she said.

'We could lose money, too,' he said. 'Not to mention our lives. You want me to pass all this on to the Reviarch?'

'Yes, of course. Wait till I'm gone before you tell him I was here, though.'

'You came to Tyr, just to tell me this? You could have said as much to Sestius and saved yourself the trouble.' *Not to mention saved me the danger of harbouring a traitor.* He shot a look of despair at Reveba in the next room. She was playing with the boy, showing him how to use the scales.

'No. I came because I want to take a ship out, as soon as I can. We need to stay here, in your house, until there is a suitable sailing.'

He winced. 'If the Brotherhood finds out—'

'No one will know unless you or one of your household tell them. And Assorian slaves are always unbelievably loyal to their Assorian masters, or so I discovered when I was working for the Brotherhood. If it makes you any happier, when I depart, I will leave by the tunnel to your warehouse across the street.'

He lost all the blood in his face. He felt it vanish, leaving him light-headed, unsure he had heard rightly. 'Tunnel?' The whisper was the waver of an old man. 'How could you know?'

'Oh, I've known for years. Not just you, but all the Assorians on this street.' She patted his knee kindly. 'Don't worry. I never told the Brotherhood.'

He shuddered. 'How could you know?' he asked again.

She held up her hand, showing him the cabochon. She had never let the skin grow back over it; the smooth gold surface was an entrance to magic he didn't want to know about. 'I felt people moving under the street, that's all.'

Just then Reveba had come back into the room, speaking to

him in Assorian. 'The boy says they are going to stay here. Won't that be dangerous?'

He waved an agitated hand. 'I'm afraid so.'

'The slaves will know she is Kardi. The temptation, Arcad! Anyone turning in a Kardi with a gemstone in her hand gains their freedom and wealth.'

He tried to find a way to reassure her. 'Our slaves are Assorian. Not one of them would deal with the Brotherhood or with legionnaires.'

She thought about that. 'Yes, of course you are right, husband. Forgive me, I am a silly woman, lacking faith. Besides, God will protect us against heathens.'

God of my fathers, he thought. *Preserve me from the absurdity of women.*

Reveba smiled at Ligea. 'Domina,' she said. 'I show . . . you room, no?'

CHAPTER EIGHTEEN

Arrant thought he was going to be sick with excitement. He and Ligea and Narjemah were to visit the port. And if that wasn't thrilling enough, they began by walking through a tunnel beneath the street. It was only short, but it was deliciously scary to think they were *under* the ground.

He was irritated, though, that they had to stay dressed as Assorians. It was such a stupid costume. How ever was he going to run if they had to flee in a hurry? He kept tripping over the hem of the robe. Still, he wasn't going to complain, otherwise Ligea would probably make him and Narjemah stay in the money-master's villa. Narjemah wanted to anyway. She was already grizzling at Ligea for taking them both along, even though they had one of Arcadim's slaves with them for added safety.

'I just feel safer if you are both where I can protect you if anything goes wrong,' Ligea said.

Narjemah looked alarmed. 'You expect something to go wrong?'

'I – oh, I don't know. I just had the odd feeling for the last hour at Arcadim's house that someone was watching the place. I didn't get any feeling that they wanted to do us harm, though. Still, I would rather you were with me. Besides, Arrant needs to see the city. He needs to learn as much as he can about Tyr; he may never return here, you know, Narjemah.'

Narjemah then pointed out, in vain, that he was only five and wouldn't remember much of it anyway.

Arrant was indignant. He didn't think he could forget it, even if he tried. Tyr was one big *adventure*. 'I'm going to 'member everything,' he told them both.

However, as they left the moneymasters' district and headed towards the river, he began to wonder how. Everything was so huge. So noisy. So smelly. So crowded. There was just so *much*.

'This is the docklands,' Ligea said when they reached the first of the waterways. The narrow arms and fingers of the River Tyr, here coerced into canals as straight as a rank of legionnaires, thrust their way into the commercial heart of the city. Buildings and ships and water and quays were inextricably interlaced. Masts poked up among roofs; rigging and chimneys jostled along the skyline; bowsprits were in danger of being knocked by laden wagons trundling noisily along the rattling boards of the wharves; oars and sails dried on racks alongside filleted fish.

The sounds and smells of the port harassed the senses even from afar. Within the actual docklands area the assault was murderous. The smell of water permeated everything, and this wasn't just the saltwater tang of the sea, either. The channels were tidal, but the river washed down the muck from the middens of the less salubrious quarters of the city. The potent stench mingled with the more exotic odours of the warehouses and chandleries: spices, fleece, hides, tannin, salted goods, tarred rope, oil, fresh fish, malt, wine – all the pungency of a great empire in one place.

And the people. Arrant couldn't stop staring. Silk-clad merchants from lands he'd never heard of, web-toed sailors from far-off islands, scale-spangled fishermen, women with painted faces, trademasters and seamasters and trailmasters – people with every shade of skin, men and women and children, free men and slaves. They came with their strange ships and their bizarre garments and their weird languages; they filled the wooden walk-ways with their produce and their haggling and their gossip.

Arrant tried to make sense of it all. He wanted to linger, but Ligea had a firm grip on his hand and thwarted every attempt he made to dawdle. Only when she found what she was looking for did they stop.

It was a small fishing smack with a single mast and a crew of eight: all weather-beaten men with red flashes in their brown hair. Two of them were sluicing down the deck; three others were mending nets and lines on the dockside, another was sealing a water cask that had yet to be placed on board.

Arrant sniffed. Fish. And something else. An animal smell, like a dirty tomcat. He looked around. There was a wooden crate on the dock, newly unloaded from another ship. Two glaring yellow eyes stared out through the gaps between the slats.

He freed his hand from his mother's so he could take a closer look. The animal within snarled at him.

Narjemah shivered. 'Arrant! Not too close!'

He tried to decide what sort of creature huddled so unhappily in the crate, but he didn't think he'd ever seen anything like it before. It might have smelled like a cat, but it looked more like a dog and it was the size of a small lion.

'Is your master here?' Ligea asked one of the fishermen.

'I'm the shipmaster,' the man at the cask replied. 'Cord's the name. If you're looking for fresh fish, we're all sold up.'

'Come away from that dirty beast,' Narjemah said. 'Who knows what sickness it may carry? And if you get too close, it could rip your arm off.'

Reluctantly, Arrant stepped back half a pace. The animal hissed at him. When it rolled back its jowls, its teeth were yellow and pointed.

Ligea turned around to speak to Kabarrab, the slave-guard Arcadim had sent with them. 'Go and wait for us out of earshot, if you don't mind.' She waited until he had moved back down the wharf, and then addressed the captain again. 'No, I don't want fish. I want a passage out of here for myself, the woman and that child over there, to Ordensa in Kardiastan.'

'This here's the *Fisherdream*. We catch fish, woman; we don't take passengers. Go pay for a seat on a coastal galley.'

Ligea dropped her voice. 'Fifty sestus apiece. For the trip and for – shall we say – discretion?'

The captain also lowered his tone. 'Firstly, what makes you

think I'd be interested in helping a body in need of discretion?'

Arrant listened, but he didn't take his eyes off the crate. The animal twisted its snout sideways, trying to reach him through the gap. It didn't sound happy.

'I have friends in Altan,' Ligea was saying. 'One such said any Altani ship that has red and white ribbing on its stern will always bear a captain to be trusted.'

'Ah. Yes, well – I'll need a name,' the shipmaster replied.

'Brand.'

'Arrant, you are still too close,' Narjemah said and hauled him away. 'That's a sedrani devil from Zaruba, I think. They are vicious. What if a slat broke?'

This time he didn't mind obeying her. He didn't think the animal liked him much, and it made him sad just to see it in such a small cage. He went to stand next to Ligea.

Cord was saying, 'That *might* buy you the discretion. Know the man well, d'you?'

She pulled her shawl back from her face a little, to show the scar. 'He lost the use of an arm at the same time as I lost part of my cheek. Yes, we know one another well.'

'One hundred silver sestus each, you said?'

'Fifty each was mentioned, I believe.'

'Seventy-five each and you have the trip.'

'That's extortionate, and you know it. You won't have to catch a fish for a year at that price. Sixty's all I can manage.'

He sighed. 'Very well. I wouldn't do it at all, 'cept for the name you mentioned. We sail on the tide tomorrow morning. First light. Best you spend the night on board. You'll need food enough for the journey, unless you've a hankering for naught but fish.' He held out his hand and she placed her own palm over his to seal their bargain.

'We'll be back with our baggage before nightfall,' Ligea promised.

The shipmaster grinned. 'My commitment would be further strengthened if I could see the shine of your money, lady.'

Arrant thought she might be annoyed, but she just laughed

and handed over the coins. They weren't short of money, he knew that much, but her trust of the man Cord surprised him.

As they left the area with Kabarrab trailing behind like a dog on a string, she said, 'You see how handy it is to be able to read the truth and emotions of those you speak to, Arrant? Cord is trustworthy. One day, you'll have the ability to sense things like that too. Of course, even honest men can have the truth beaten out of them, so we still have to be wary.'

He ducked his head, uncomfortable, knowing that it was a skill she expected him to have already attained. It wasn't *fair*: he did try, but rarely knew a lie from the truth on anyone's tongue. He scuffed his sandals along the boards of the wharf, his thoughts unhappy and rebellious.

She grimaced at the emotions he was exuding.

And that wasn't fair, either. Other boys didn't have mothers who knew how they felt all the time. He scowled.

'Ah, Arrant, I'm sorry. I don't want to upset you. I just want you to know as much as you can absorb. I look at it this way: you will understand anything that you are old enough to handle. If you don't understand, then you are too young for the information anyway.'

He looked up at her, baffled. Narjemah snorted, apparently exasperated with her. He had no idea why.

Ligea continued, 'I don't dare make too many concessions to you because of your age, lad; we're fighting a war, and you have to grow up as quickly as you can. You have to understand as much as you can. It's a tough school, I know, and I'm proud of you. For someone who's just five, you manage very well.' She smiled at him. 'Your father is going to be so proud of you, too. Anyway, let's go back to the moneymaster's. Arcadim is going to be very, very happy that we are going to move out so soon.'

She was right. Arcadim made no attempt to conceal his relief; even Arrant felt it. The moneymaster sent Kabarrab back to the ship with Ligea's baggage and arranged to have some food sent on board at his expense. He then had another long and boring conversation with Ligea about money. Arrant didn't mind that, because in the meantime Reveba plied him with food in the adjoining room and showed him the polished crystal enlarger the moneymaster used to examine coins for evidence of tampering. It made everything look big. Playing with that was fun, especially when he looked at the hairs on his skin and the dirt under his nails, and he was disappointed when the moneymaster and Ligea finished their business.

'Domina,' Arcadim was saying as they came out of the inner room, 'I haven't told anyone where any of your properties are, not even the Reviarch or my sons, and I never will. And there is nothing written down anywhere that will make sense to anyone but me. While I am safe, your secrets are safe. However, you should realise I'm, um, I'm not a hero. If the Brotherhood questions me . . .'

She nodded. 'I know. And I do not pay you to be a hero, Arcadim, never fear.'

He stared at her, as if he wanted to say something more but had lost his voice. Finally he managed to blurt out in strangled tones that didn't sound like him at all, 'The – the Reviarch has his own methods of keeping us moneymasters safe. Be – be careful.'

Ligea was thoughtful after that. Several times when Arrant asked her a question, she didn't seem to hear him.

They left Arcadim's house after the afternoon siesta, and headed back towards the ship, with Kabarrab once again trailing them a step or two behind. Halfway to the docks, she halted for a moment as if listening.

'What is it?' Narjemah asked.

'That person who was watching the house? This time he's following us.'

Narjemah grabbed Arrant's hand. 'What are you going to do?'

'Find out who it is. You two keep walking with Kabarrab. Don't look at me.'

They did as she asked, and a little further on, Arrant became aware that she was no longer with them. 'Keep walking,' Narjemah told him firmly.

Ten minutes later, Ligea caught up with them again. 'An Assorian slave,' she whispered, after a glance behind to make sure Kabarrab was not close enough to hear. 'Wearing Reviarch Javenid's colours.'

That did nothing to diminish Narjemah's alarm, which worried Arrant in turn. She whispered, 'I heard what Arcadim said – he was warning you about the Reviarch, wasn't he? What did you do to him?'

'To the Reviarch?'

'To the slave!'

'Nothing! I'm not going to upset the Reviarch by harming one of his slaves.'

'How could the Reviarch know you are here in Tyr?'

'The barge,' she said, calmly skirting a couple of legionnaires chatting at the side of the street. 'The barge we came in on belonged to the Moneymasters' Guild. The bargeman must have told Javenid enough for him to guess we were worth investigating, to guess even who we were perhaps.'

'So what are you going to do?'

'Nothing for the time being. It's not in Javenid's interest for me to be caught.'

To Arrant's increased alarm, that remark seemed to upset Narjemah even more. 'How can you be sure of that?'

'I know the way the Assorians think. I was a compeer, remember? With all the Brotherhood's information at my fingertips. It's true the Assorians wouldn't want to upset the Exaltarch, but they don't want to throw away a chance – however slim – for them to earn their freedom from vassalage. They *hate* the Exaltarchy, Narjemah. Believe me, I know. I have *felt* it. If I start to lose, Javenid will probably throw me to the Jackals without a qualm, but while there is a chance for success, he will try to sit in the middle of the road.'

'Arcadim just *warned* you about him!' Narjemah was almost crying. 'It nearly choked him to do so, but he did!'

Arrant wished his cabochon worked so that he could tell what his mother felt. She sounded so calm. 'The slave is doing no more than following us. Think of it as information gathering, and remember that Javenid knows a great deal about Magor power. At a guess, he knows that *I* know I am being followed!'

Arrant was still trying to make sense of that when they reached a crowd spilling out over the wharf to block their way. He wrinkled his nose in disgust. These men – those near him were all men – smelled of dirt and sweat and unwashed clothes, while their manners were worse than ditch-dogs. They hawked and spat and swore as they jostled one another. The closest of them, a Tyranian with a face covered in bristles like a worn scrubbing brush, carried a whip. He ran the thong of it through his fingers in a way that stirred Arrant's cabochon and made him shiver. He wished the gem had stayed quiet, because he could now sense emotions and most of what he felt was hateful.

Ligea picked him up in her arms, something she rarely did any more, and started to skirt the crowd. From the security of her hold he was able to see that everyone was watching what was happening on the grime-coated deck of a single-masted ship.

'What's up there?' he asked.

'The boat's an Issian trader. And that's a slave auction,' she explained in a whisper, her distaste obvious. 'A private slave ship selling off the dross that neither the central market nor the slave pens will accept. Remember this, Arrant.' She jabbed a finger at the ship. 'This is what we are fighting to stop.'

Obediently, he watched, although he wasn't exactly sure what he was supposed to be remembering. One of the trader's crew wrenched a slave woman up onto a block on the ship's deck. Her right eye socket was empty, and her emaciated body could hardly carry her own weight. The bidding was unenthusiastic and her final price was so low the auctioneer cuffed her in disgust, hard, as she stepped down from the block. Arrant shuddered.

By then, Ligea had already circled most of the crowd, Narjemah at her elbow and Kabarrab close behind. Another slave was produced for sale. This one was a boy – and Arrant felt Ligea stiffen like a hunting fisherbird about to spear its prey with its beak. 'A Kardi,' she said. 'No one is supposed to have Kardi slaves any more, but he's wearing a Kardi bolero . . .'

Arrant stared. The lad was older than he was, perhaps twelve. He was filthy. And hurt. He clutched his right arm to his chest as if any movement of it pained him. Arrant, revolted by the dirt that clung to the boy, felt more distaste than sympathy, and tried to hide that sentiment from his mother. He wasn't sure if he was successful.

She'll rescue him, he thought, but he was wrong. She decided to buy the boy, not fight for him. The brute with the whip was interested in obtaining the slave and so were several other men, which led to more spirited bidding.

'They want a child catamite for their blasted brothels,' Ligea muttered angrily in Narjemah's ear, another remark which meant nothing at all to Arrant. 'I know that sod with the whip. The nastiest procurer in all Tyr—' She continued to raise the price until all the other bidders, disgruntled and surly in their disappointment, gave up.

The slave owner gestured Ligea closer, demanding to see the colour of her money before he closed the bidding. 'He's suspicious,' Narjemah hissed at her, worry cutting deep lines between her eyebrows. 'You're supposed to be an Assorian woman and they don't come to places like this to buy slaves.'

Ligea handed Arrant over to her. 'Wait here,' she said and pushed her way up to the gangplank to pay.

'You got a bargain here, woman,' one of the slaver crew told her with a leer as she took the boy from the ship. 'Be as good as new when that arm mends, and years of work in him—'

She gave him a look that would have curdled goat's milk and his next words died in his throat. Arrant didn't blame him. He'd never seen his mother look so mad.

Then she turned away and started down the gangplank, her hand on the shoulder of the boy. Unexpectedly, her stride faltered. Arrant looked over Narjemah's shoulder, trying to see what had caught her eye. There was a scrawny old woman in the crowd with a slave at her side, and she was staring at Ligea, her eyes as hard as pebbles, her mouth a thin line across her face. An unpleasant feeling settled in the middle of Arrant's stomach.

Ligea walked on to rejoin them. She still had her hand on the slave boy's shoulder and said quietly in Kardi, 'Don't be afraid, lad. You're safe and in good hands now. You'll be back home in a week or two.' The boy didn't react. Arrant stared, wondering if he had even heard. He was so dirty and he *smelled*. As they pushed their way out of the crowd, Arrant pulled a face at him and poked out his tongue. For once his mother didn't seem to notice his lapse in manners. She hurried them away down the wharf.

The day before she had told him all the funny names of the vessels moored there: biremes and triremes, galleys and caiques, feluccas, liburnias and dhows and others he had forgotten. Today she couldn't move him past fast enough.

'What's wrong?' Narjemah asked her.

'That woman back there. She knows me, and she's greedy. By the feel of her emotions, I'd say she'll be hunting down the nearest legionnaire she can find. Hurry!'

Arrant cast behind them, but his cabochon wouldn't work now. Ligea spoke to Narjemah over his head. 'Her name's Merriam. She's a midwife and I went to her when I was carrying Arrant.'

Narjemah was starting to puff, and her cheeks had gone as red as ripe persimmons, so she handed Arrant over to Kabarrab. The slave pursed his lips, but a glare from Narjemah chopped short any protest he might have contemplated.

As they passed a ships' chandlers, a beam of light shot forth from Ligea's hand to engulf a large cask at the bottom of a pile stacked high outside the doorway. The wooden staves splintered into dust where the light hit them, a mess of salted meat spilled out and the entire pile stacked above subsided. Casks from the top hit the wharf and split; others rumbled off in all directions. They had to scramble out of the way themselves. The chandler rushed out of his office into the middle of the chaos, took one appalled look and called down a potent curse on the head of whoever was responsible.

After that, they ran. Ligea hauled the slave boy along. Kabarrab swung Arrant onto his back, where he clung, half excited by the urgency, half fearful because he couldn't understand what was happening. It felt like a game gone wrong.

CHAPTER NINETEEN

Kabarrab unceremoniously dumped Arrant and disappeared back down the wharf, his job done. Arrant ran past the crate with the sedrani devil inside and up the gangplank, grinning happily. They had made it safely on board! Everything was all right again.

Shipmaster Cord's regard was thoughtful as Ligea followed him up the gangplank, Narjemah and the slave boy close behind. 'Your baggage arrived,' he said. 'And your supplies. You didn't mention *him*, though.' He pointed at the boy. 'Not an escapee, is he? You got the deeds of ownership, Domina?'

Ligea held up the parchment. 'Right here.'

'You reckon on taking him to Ordensa too?'

'I do.'

'That'll be another seventy.'

'*Sixty.*' She dug into her purse. 'And how much to leave immediately?'

He chuckled and leaned against the railing. 'You couldn't pay me enough, Domina. The tide is contrary.'

'Sorry. You don't have any choice. We're leaving.'

He straightened, eyes narrowing, and made an unobtrusive movement of his hand. Several of the fishermen stopped what they had been doing and moved closer. Arrant, feeling a wave of panic from Narjemah, began to pay more attention. Just getting to the ship, he realised in dismay, had not been enough.

Cord said, 'If you are in that much of a hurry, you can get off my ship. I don't want no trouble.'

'You've got it already,' she told him. 'I've been recognised, and I'm the most wanted woman in all Tyrans.'

Cord drew in a sharp breath. 'So? That's nothing to me. You can have your damn coins back. Just get off my ship. Nobody brings trouble to my lady.' He fumbled with the purse at his waist.

'Your wh—? Oh, the ship! Well, there'll be Brotherhood Jackals searching your lady down to her keel within the hour and someone will remember that I talked to you. Cord, you and your boat are finished in Tyr. Forever. Your only chance is to run – now, before your ship has new owners.'

The wallop of Cord's rage hit Arrant in the middle like a blow. He tried to shut it out, but as usual his cabochon had a mind of its own. He sat down on the deck with a thump.

'If the Brotherhood wants her, we could earn us a fortune by reporting her ourselves, master,' one of the fishermen suggested, avoiding Ligea's eyes as he drew his fish knife from his belt.

Cord was staring at her in shock. 'Gods of the Delta, who the Vortex are you?'

Bellowed calls for guards in the distance made Arrant stand and clutch at Narjemah's leg. He would have preferred Ligea's, but she was leaning over the railing to aim her cabochon at the crate on the quayside below. The wooden slats splintered. A few moments later, the sedrani devil slunk out, lashing its tail and snarling. 'That should provide a bit of a diversion,' she said with some satisfaction. 'Never could stand caged animals anyway.'

Eyes wide with disbelief, Cord still hesitated.

'If I'm caught I'll tell them the meaning of the ribbing on your stern,' she said. 'Cord, you've already apparently thrown in your lot with Altani rebels. Don't risk a brush with the Brotherhood. Get this boat out of here before you all find yourselves languishing in the Cages.'

'Who are you?' he asked again. And then added, indignant, 'And she's a ship, not a boat!'

'I can tell you who I used to be. Legata Ligea Gayed, Brotherhood Compeer.'

Cord paled and was silent. One of the others wasn't as wise. 'Gods of the Delta protect us! There's a price on her head that would make us all as rich as Assorian moneymasters!'

Ligea raised her hand. 'Blood money doesn't benefit the dead, my friend,' she said. She bathed them all in the golden glow of her cabochon and they winced away, bodies jerking in pain.

Arrant gasped as a wave of unpleasant emotions swamped his mind.

'Come downstairs,' Narjemah said to him and pointed to a ladder in the centre of the ship leading down into the dark. She went to scoop him up. He shook his head violently. 'No! Don't wanna!' His fear suddenly became more tangible. In the dark he wouldn't be able to *see*, and he had to see. He reached out to the railing and clung. If he couldn't see maybe bad things would happen to Ligea.

Narjemah scowled at him. 'Mirage take you, child, you can be as irritating as a bedbug sometimes!'

He pouted at her, but she didn't try to pick him up again.

Ligea was still speaking to Cord. 'Now will you get us out of here?' she asked. She cut off her power, and they stared at her, limbs still twitching in reaction, faces white with shock and terror. 'I didn't want to have to do that, but I'll do it again if need be.'

Someone screamed on the dock below, and an animal snarled. Arrant looked over the side in time to see the sedrani bounding along the wharf. A loin-clad sailor in its path took a flying jump from the dock to seize the bowsprit of the neighbouring ship. He dangled over the water, his face purple. The animal took no notice. It raced up the gangplank and made straight for the mast. Within seconds it was at the top, where it teetered precariously. Several sailors jumped off the ship to the dock. The man on the bowsprit fell into the water and splashed his way to a piling.

This time Cord didn't hesitate. 'Cast off,' he croaked. Arrant still wasn't sure whether to be scared or excited. He hoped Ligea wouldn't give the sailors pain again. He didn't like that.

She glanced down the wharf. 'Make it quick, Cord.'

'Move!' he roared and the crew moved. Then he looked back at Ligea, having second thoughts. 'But we have an incoming tide and I haven't ordered tow-rowers.'

'You have your own rowers.'

'Two pairs? That's not enough against the tide! We're not a bloody liburnia with a bank of oars, we're a *fisher*. The oars are just for emergencies. And my men are fishermen, not bloody galley slaves!'

'If they want to *stay* that way, they'd better move. *Get the sail up.* You'll have a following wind.' As the ship moved sluggishly out from the wharf it seemed unlikely that there'd be any such thing, but no sooner had the sail been unfurled than a breeze came out of nowhere to fill it and send them wafting down the canal. Arrant let out the breath he had been holding. The sail was pretty: leather strips formed a pattern of squares across the flax cloth. Four of the fishermen ran out the oars, another manned the bow steering oar while Cord took the stern sweep. Arrant knew all about oars and sweeps and sails from watching the other vessels on the River Tyr when they were on the barge.

He looked back at the docks. The sedrani was still on the mast of the other ship and a crowd was gathering to look at it. No one was interested in the departure of the *Fisherdream*.

His mother smiled down at the slave boy. 'Now, lad, let's see to that arm of yours, shall we, hmm?'

Arrant stared, jealous, while she set and strapped the boy's forearm, using his torn tunic. *I'll bet he doesn't know about oars and sails*, he thought.

She must have taken away the boy's pain because he did not complain. He was so much in awe of her he could barely speak, but she did find out that his name was Palin and that he was indeed Kardi. Having extracted that much from him, she sent him down into the below-decks with Narjemah. She looked across at Arrant. 'You behave yourself, young man,' she said. 'No more nonsense, or you *will* be below decks, understand?'

He nodded solemnly. And felt bad. He wasn't supposed to be naughty when they were in trouble. He was supposed to be a soldier and obey orders. That's what Gevenan had told him.

She turned her attention to the ship.

At the stern, Cord kept glancing up at the sail as if he couldn't believe the wind was so obliging. Ligea gave him a bland smile when he caught her eye. Her skin glowed, so Arrant knew she was still using her cabochon magic. Still, they made slow progress through the ships using the tangled network of interlocking canals. It wasn't until about an hour later, when they came out into the main river, that the ship heeled a little in the wind and picked up speed. Cord ordered the oars shipped.

'Are we safe now?' Arrant asked.

'Possibly,' Ligea said. She sat down beside him and put her arm around his shoulders. 'But that lady back there on the docks? I heard her making a ruckus about us after we left. And the slave who was watching us – he will report our departure to the man who owns him, the Reviarch. If the Reviarch thinks I'm going to be caught anyway, he might go straight to Rathrox – he's an important man here in Tyr who doesn't like me – to tell him we are on board this ship. That way the Reviarch gets the credit for something he thinks will happen anyway, and the moneymasters will end up smelling as sweet as the Exaltarch's roses no matter what. I think that was what Arcadim was trying to tell me: that Javenid sometimes feeds Rathrox information to keep the Brotherhood happy.' She looked down at him ruefully. 'And you really don't know what I am talking about, do you?'

He shook his head.

'Never mind. It doesn't matter. To answer your question: are we safe? Not yet.' She pointed downriver. 'Between the city and the sea there are paveways, which means that orders and soldiers can move quickly. And on the banks of the river there are forts like the Stronghold, one on each side, and booms which block half the river.' She shrugged. 'We'll have to wait and see.'

She turned to Cord. 'Get your men back on the rowing benches if the wind dies.'

He nodded, still white-faced.

She looked across at the buildings on the far bank. 'Take a

good look, Arrant. It could be your last glimpse of Tyr.'

He did as she asked, then glanced back at her uncertainly, not knowing what she expected of him. There was an odd expression on her face; she wasn't looking at the temples, or the roofs of the palace, but up at one of the hills overlooking the river. Her features softened with a gentle sadness.

'There,' she said. 'Do you see that white villa on the crest of the hill there?'

He tried to enhance his sight and, after a few false starts, finally saw the place she meant and pulled it into focus. He still couldn't manipulate the picture correctly, though; it was much too large, with the result that he could only view the villa one small piece at a time.

He supposed it was pretty. It had a wide terrace with columns carved like ladies, who supported the roof on their heads, but he couldn't see much else. He waited for her to explain.

'Bator Korbus's chief trade adviser lives there now, and I believe he's laid down carpets,' she said, her voice heavy with disgust. Then she added, even more confusingly, 'Arcadim sold it right under Rathrox's nose . . .' She dropped her cabochon away from her eyes with a sigh. 'It was once the Villa Gayed, Arrant. That's where I lived, when I was your age.'

Rathrox salivated, as gleeful as a child on a feast day. It was worth being dragged away from his siesta and down to the harbour-master's office for this. He was finally going to catch that numen bitch.

He mentally ran through all the orders he had just given after talking to the Reviarch and the harbourmaster, checking to make sure he had covered everything. Legionnaires with whirlslings were on their way to the fort on horseback. The harbourmaster was also on his way by chariot. A messenger had left even earlier, with orders to close the booms and stop all ships. Legate Valorian and Seamaster Mescades had been alerted, and the Exaltarch informed. A chariot had been ordered for himself and Clemens.

Gods, how he wanted to see the end of this woman who had

given him so much trouble . . . whoever she was. The Reviarch swore he didn't know. All the moneymaster's informants had told him, he said, was that a Kardi female with a scarred face, accompanied by two children and a servant, had boarded a vessel in the port, and that the boat had sailed. The harbourmaster had confirmed the sailing of a single fishing vessel. Only one, because the tide was rising, not ebbing, and no one in their right mind would try to leave – unless they had numen magic.

All the forts had to do was stop one ship. And they had catapults and war galleys. Ideal for sinking a numen witch.

Vortexdamn, I hope this really is the woman we have been hunting.

The bitch had been ravaging the country from one side to another with her golden light and her damnable whirlwind. Slave holding pens and slave auctions had lost their merchandise; wayhouses along the paveways all over Tyrans had been raided again and again, losing their horses, slaves, supplies and money; tax collectors went out *knowing* there was a good chance they'd be robbed; legionnaire barracks had been raided for weaponry and burned to the ground. Whole wagons of tin and copper ore had vanished en route to Tyr, although the gods only knew how that was possible. There seemed no end to her depredations. The helots she commanded even had the *gall* to use the paveways themselves, passing along in the night and vanishing by day. Slaves gave her information, and the ordinary lowborn citizen looked up to her as a goddess or an immortal, and *knelt* when she passed by instead of informing on her!

Every time they'd sent legionnaires to search out her hiding places in the mountains, they'd lost men and horses and equipment, while the rebels melted away unseen only to regroup elsewhere. By comparison, legion successes had been tiny. A few helots killed. A few abandoned buildings found which may or may not have been used to repair weapons.

Ocrastes, grant that today I get my hands on her murdering neck. He would slaughter a bull for Ocrastes at the God of War's temple if he were successful.

'Magister?'

He looked up. 'Ah, Clemens, at last. The horses are ready?'

'Yes, Magister. But – but—'

He stared at his assistant in surprise. The man was white-faced. 'What is it?'

'There's a woman to see you. She also says she saw the numen woman at the docks. She says she recognised her.'

'She recognised the woman with the scar?'

Clemens nodded and beckoned to someone outside the room. 'This is Midwife Merriam of Istia,' he said as she entered. 'Tell the Magister all you know, woman.'

'And my reward?'

'You'll get your reward if your words prove truthful,' Clemens growled at her.

The elderly woman met Rathrox's stare with a steady gaze of her own. *Lean and mean*, he thought. 'Well?' he asked.

'The scarred woman came to see me when she was pregnant, some years ago. I informed Compeer Clemens of this. I thought I had seen her before, but couldn't think where. Today I saw her again, and remembered. I was down on the docks to buy myself a cheap slave and she was there. Domina Ligea Gayed. I didn't recognise her before because of the scar, which was still fresh then. It has faded now, and she is not as gaunt. It is her. I am sure of it.'

Disbelief flooded him. 'That can't be true! Ligea is still in Kardiastan. The Governor sends reports from Madrinya about her doings. These Magoroth women, they all look alike. Besides, when Favonius last saw her, she had no scar on her face—' His protestations faded and died.

Ligea. *He had trained her in deception.* He wouldn't have fallen for the very same tricks he had taught her, would he?

Ocrastes, *no*. He *couldn't* have been so stupid . . .

No. *No*. Please let it not be so.

Ligea?

'Domina—' Cord, hesitant and much more deferential than he had been, gestured ahead. 'The signal flag raised above the forts means all ships leaving are to be searched. Shall we—?'

She laughed. 'No, Cord. Not unless you relish the thought of the Cages and want to see your beloved lady broken up for firewood. And I've heard say that torture is commonplace in the Cages since a certain Brotherhood Compeer was sent to Kardiastan.'

'Domina, if we don't come into the wharf, they will use the catapults and she will be just that – firewood!' He was close to crying.

'Slip through the booms under cover of the mist.'

'Mist? *What* mist?'

'There will be a mist by the time we get there. The wind will drop then, though. We will have to go through with oars, or drift through. Has the tide turned yet?'

'No, still an hour before the turn. But the flow is slackening.'

'Head for the centre of the channel while the wind lasts. As soon as the mists block both forts, veer to the left-hand side, as close as you can to the end of the boom on that side. The catapults will be aimed at the middle of the channel.'

'Master!' Cord had sent one of the fishermen up the mast, and he was yelling down to the deck in a panic. 'They are launching galleys! From both sides!'

Ligea swore. 'I guess they know who we are.' She turned to Cord. 'Get the oars out.' Then she looked down at Arrant again. 'Time to go below.'

He shook his head, panicking. 'I don't wanna.'

'It will be safer. I don't have time to worry about you, Arrant. Narjemah will look after you.'

But he was stubborn, fearing the darkness below decks, fearing that if the ship sank he would be unable to get out. Fearing, most of all, the unknown. On deck, he could at least see what was happening. He put on his most ferocious face.

She suppressed a sigh, found him a place between the mast and the hatch to the fish stores and sat him down. 'You stay right here, promise?'

He nodded.

'I'm going to build a ward around you.'

'Won't we leave it behind as we sail?'

'I will attach it to the ship, so it will move with us.'

He nodded again, but felt a twinge of guilt. Warding him meant she was diminishing her power. He was being naughty, and he wasn't supposed to be naughty when there was a war . . .

In the centre of the channel, the wind dropped. Arrant could not see the galleys yet, but Gev had told him about galleys. About how fast they were over short distances, how quickly they could manoeuvre, how they had fighters on the top deck. Fighting meant deaths. And he knew now that it *hurt* when people died. It hurt him and it hurt them. He *hated* fighting.

The fishermen on *Fisherdream* began to row as the vessel slowed. Arrant tried to work out what Ligea was doing. She stood in the prow, glowing gold, concentrating. At the same time as he saw one of the galleys, still just a smudge against the blue where the river widened out beyond the forts ahead of them, mist began to creep across the water like a soft blanket of pallet-cotton. It came in from the sea and crawled up onto the banks of the river on both sides. But it was so *slow*.

Fear clenched in his belly. He knew about catapults, about hand-held ones for birds, and this kind too, that sat on the ground. Gev had asked the carpenter on First Farm to build him a toy one. Narjemah had been angry because he lobbed stones at the chickens to make them squawk. He looked up at the real forts and imagined stones sailing out over the ramparts to land on the ship.

When he looked at the water, he saw a floating fence of logs, protruding from each bank under the forts, but not quite meeting in the middle. The channel between the two anchored ends was a narrow passage of smooth water. Each of the forts had a cata-pult on the flat roof of the tower, just waiting for the moment when the ship sailed between those logs. The galleys were coming closer, but they were rowing through the edge of the mist now, their oars stirring up tendrils of dampness like smoke curling from a fire. Even if Cord did manage to guide the ship through the booms, they would still have the galleys ahead of them.

A shiver crept down Arrant's spine and raised the hairs on his arms. Fear and excitement mingled in equal parts. He wanted to sneak down the steps and crawl into Narjemah's arms, but it was too late now. He was trapped inside the ward.

And then everything happened at once. The forts disappeared behind a wall of white, and so did the two galleys. The *Fisherdream* swung hard to the left. A wind hustled up from behind to billow out the sail so fast that the mast creaked and bent. The gust blew on past the ship, pushing a narrow mist-free passage ahead of them. Cord gave the order to ship oars.

The vessel fell quiet, slipping through a sea wiped clean of ripples by the dampness of the mist. The bow split the calm surface cleanly, silently. No one on board moved. Cord, leaning into the sweep, kept his eye on both sail and the left-hand buoy, just visible at the edge of the mist wall.

And then, with heart-stopping suddenness something sailed out of the mist above their heads, crossed above the ship and disappeared into the whiteness on their right. A brief moment later, they all heard the splash. Ligea fell to her knees in the bow, exhausted. Arrant tried desperately to call his cabochon to life. If he had power, he could help her . . .

Golden light spluttered ineffectually in his palm. He looked up just as the ship slid past the boom and another rock came spinning out of the mist, low. It would hit them, Arrant knew. There was no time to do anything. They were all going to die. *Like Timnius.* He opened his mouth, but no sound came out.

In the split second left to them, Ligea poured everything she had into the wind. A bubble of moving air burst against the sail. The squares of flax blossomed, straining against the leather strips; the mast bent still further. Cord gasped. And the rock – about to hit amidships – suddenly wasn't there, but behind. It came down on the sweep with a sound like a thunderclap. The oar splintered, littering the wake with wood chips. The spume of water was close enough to splash the deck. Cord just managed to save himself by letting go of the shaft in time; as it was, he was hit on the head by the longest surviving piece of wood.

Sprawled on the deck, he looked at Arrant, dazed. Blood dripped from his scalp. People onshore, hearing the sound of the impact, cheered.

Arrant watched wide-eyed. Petrified. Ligea lay on the deck, sapped of strength. The ward over Arrant's head wavered and vanished. *And someone was looking out through his eyes. Again.*

He couldn't cope. He began shaking. He wanted to crawl to his mother, but fear nailed him to the deck. Cord scrambled to his feet, fingering his head. Blood ran through his fingers. He staggered, then bellowed into the rowing deck, shouting at the fishermen to bring out the spare sweep. The sailor with the shorter steering oar at the bow strove to keep the vessel on course, but the *Fisherdream* yawed as the sail flapped uselessly. The wind had vanished. Ahead somewhere in the mist were the two galleys with their legionnaires on the deck . . .

Ligea crawled to him. 'Arrant—?'

He'd never seen her so helpless. His fear burgeoned, wisping his thoughts into incoherence. *The mind that was not his watched.* He tried desperately to push it away, to get it out of his head.

'Arrant . . . try . . . where are they?'

He knew she was asking about the galleys. He heard the fishermen scrambling below-decks. He stared out into the mist, willing his cabochon to work, begging it. The gem flared, its power flooding in all directions. He had no control. He sensed emotion everywhere: fear on their ship, triumph in the forts, fatigue in the galleys, interest along the shore, disinterest on another vessel further upriver. He couldn't sort anything out. Their emotions swamped him, drowned him: puzzlement, indifference, anger, rage, disgust, frustration. Sensation *everywhere*. He started to cry.

The person in his head shrank, shrivelled, disappeared. His mother took him in her arms, held him tight, soothed, told him it didn't matter, it was all right. 'There was someone in my head!' he cried. 'Someone looking through my eyes . . .'

She didn't understand. 'Hush, lad,' she said. 'Hush. There's no one but us. You were feeling other people's emotions, that's all.'

The ship slipped on; the extra sweep was brought up on deck and put in place. One of the sailors climbed the mast to the crosstrees, hoping to spot the galleys. No one spoke. The fishermen dipped their oars again and began to row. Cord squinted trying to see ahead, then staring down at the water to see which way it flowed. No one was sure any more where they were heading. The gold light in Arrant's palm dimmed. The mist was cold and damp.

They waited. And waited.

And broke through the mist into sunlight.

Ligea stood, holding onto the mast, and looked around. Behind them, the bank of fog hid the forts and the city and – somewhere – the galleys. Somehow the *Fisherdream* had slipped through to safety.

'We made it, Arrant,' Ligea murmured. But before he could feel relief, they both sensed the same thing: malevolence. It came across the water like a cold wind on a moonless night: invisible, yet chilling. It fingered them with threads of hate, slipping out of the mist to surround and choke them. Arrant had an absurd vision of a spider-like creature crouched on the land they passed, casting its hunting web in their direction, its avid hunger tangible and frightening.

'*Mater—!*'

She took his hand and held it tight. 'It's all right, Arrant. He hoped to catch us – but he's failed. We're safe enough.'

'Who is he?'

'A hunter, Arrant. A hunter of men. The man I mentioned to you, Rathrox Ligatan. He is the Magister Officii of the Exaltarchy.'

Cold clutched at his heart and his shivering was inside, not visible. He strained to see through the mist. There was nothing, not even the shadow of the land, let alone the shadow of the waiting predator, but he had felt the mind of Rathrox, and he knew neither of them was safe from that man. The spider would never be satisfied until its prey had been devoured.

Neither his mother's smile nor her reassurance could vanquish his dread.

*   *   *

Ligea Gayed, who had spoken with the Oracle's voice. Ligea, who'd caged him under the temple for more than a day, left him to lie in his own body wastes, conjured up the whirlwind and wrecked portions of the city. Ligea Gayed, who had somehow found out that as a child she had been kidnapped rather than rescued.

She'd had him at her mercy in the Meletian Temple all those years ago and *let him live*, her magnanimity the worst possible insult she could have handed him. *You mean nothing*, she'd said with her forbearance, *your death is unnecessary to me, irrelevant to my ultimate victory*. The insult rankled even worse than the failure of his plan to use her to bring down the resurgence of the Magor in Kardiastan.

He felt such a curdling in his gut that he knew he would never feel well again until she was dead.

She had a son now. People with children were vulnerable. You could do all sorts of things to people who loved their children.

CHAPTER TWENTY

The further they left Tyr behind, the more lighthearted Ligea became. This bright laughing woman who played with him, teased the crew, told jokes to the freed slave boy Palin, tried to teach them how to fish, even though it was obvious she knew nothing about fishing herself – this was his mother, she was *fun* and she was *his*. There were no messengers to interrupt them, no meetings necessitating her presence, no business needing her urgent attention, no legionnaires to flee, no battles, no fighting.

Even the fishermen left Ligea alone most of the time and Palin preferred Narjemah's company. They were all too much in awe of her to intrude unless she made the first move.

Cord avoided the open ocean as much as possible, and the route of the *Fisherdream* to Kardiastan was a thread stitched through the coastal islands. When they anchored for the night in some sheltered bay along the coast, Arrant learned to dive from the deck into the sea. When the boat rocked gently at anchor, he would listen to the tales the fishermen told and the sea hymns they sang to their Altani gods. When they called in at various seaside villages to sell fish, buy fresh food and refill the water casks, he would scamper alongside the fishermen, asking a stream of questions. He climbed the mast, and mended nets. His skin bronzed as dark as a wet seal's, or so Cord told him. There was always something new to see, something new to do.

And then they arrived in Ordensa where fishing dhows fussily jostled one another in the harbour, protected by the curve of a stone seawall, and brown unpainted buildings with flat roofs lined a small river like tortoises come to drink. Arrant was wide-eyed with the strangeness of it all.

He clung to Ligea's hand, suddenly shy as they were surrounded by people speaking Kardi. He didn't have trouble understanding the language – Narjemah always used it when speaking to him, and his mother often did too – but it was odd to hear *everyone* speaking it. And, when his cabochon obligingly worked soon after they arrived, it was even odder to feel the unfearing reverence the people had for Ligea, himself and Narjemah. It made him feel uncomfortable, as if his clothes were too tight.

They stayed that night in the biggest of the brown houses, the only one that had two floors and many rooms. He found out later that the owner, the portmaster, had moved out to make room for them.

The next day, Palin was dispatched to his family; a messenger was sent to the Mirage to tell Temellin of their arrival; and Narjemah went off to search for her family. 'Don't worry, Arrant,' she said cheerfully as she prepared to leave, 'I will be back.' But he didn't like her departure, nonetheless, and fretted.

Still, there were other things to occupy him. The house was close to where the seawall began, and he loved sitting on that to watch the fishing vessels come and go from the harbour. It wasn't long before he knew all the ships and their masters by name. And when he was bored, well, he could build sandcastles on the beach that nestled on the other side of the start of the wall.

Once every couple of days, when there were legionnaires from a nearby encampment in the village, he and Ligea had to climb up onto the flat roof of their house, pull up the ladder behind them and then lie silent, concealed behind a low parapet, until the men left. Ligea didn't seem to be worried, so Arrant wasn't scared; it was all an adventure.

Then his father arrived.

Arrant was overcome with shyness. This tall, slim man – so unlike Gev or Mole – was a stranger, even though he knew the face so well. He smiled first at Arrant, saying in a strangely husky voice, 'Well met, son,' then he enfolded Ligea in his arms for so long Arrant became impatient and tugged at her anoudain. She laughed and they moved apart. Arrant, astonished, saw that they both had tears in their eyes. And then they turned towards him with shining smiles. He had never felt so loved. They flooded him with their feelings and his cabochon glowed in response. He was overwhelmed.

The man squatted down so that his face was level with Arrant's. 'I'm so glad to see you here, Arrant.'

He hung his head. He expected Temellin to laugh, but he didn't. And he didn't ruffle his hair, either. Instead he asked if Arrant had learned to catch fish when he was on the ship. And had he seen a shleth yet? What about the snakes in the street – did he know he could stroke them? They wouldn't bite . . .

Arrant mumbled answers, and sneaked a few glances at his father from under his lashes.

Temellin casually picked him up, seated himself and sat Arrant down on his lap. But he didn't continue the questions; he chatted to Ligea instead. He spoke of mundane things, occasionally including Arrant in the conversation. He was so matter-of-fact about it that, within an hour, Arrant felt as if he'd known him all his life. At the end of the day, he was eager to hold his hand and call him Pater. No, Temellin said, not Pater. That was a Tyranian word, and he didn't like Tyranian words. Just Papa would do; that's what Kardi children called their fathers.

Arrant went to his pallet that night happier than he'd ever been in his whole life. When he woke in the morning to see that Ligea had not slept on the pallet next to him as she usually did, he was unconcerned. He set off to look for her and found her sharing a pallet with Papa. They lay close to one another, the covers tangled around them. It seemed right somehow, and he snuggled in between the two sleeping bodies without waking them, his happiness complete.

*   *   *

Papa taught him how to ride a shleth and took him out sailing in a small dhow. They fished from the bridge over the river. They built forts in the sand along the beach, pretending lumps of seaweed were legionnaires and the shells were Kardi attackers. Papa told him some of the old Kardi legends about the Mirage Makers and the Shiver Barrens and the way the Magor had once made illusions.

He told one story of a woman, his own cousin, stolen from her family when she was only three in order to force her father, the Mirager, to betray his people. She was raised as a Tyranian so she would one day return and destroy Papa and the Kardi nation. She did indeed return when she was grown up, but instead of betraying Temellin, she fought to save her people and forced the wicked Stalwarts back across the mountains into Tyrans.

And then Papa told him that the woman was Sarana, Arrant's own mother, and he thought he would burst with pride.

He also learned what the words Mirager-heir meant: that one day he would be a leader of Kardiastan, just as Papa was now. He hadn't known that, and the thought was scary. But, well, it wasn't something he had to think about just yet. He preferred to think of the day when he was bigger and Papa would take him to walk the Shiver Barrens so he would receive his own Magor sword from the Mirage Makers. Maybe his cabochon would work properly then.

Papa tried to teach him how to manage it, but it still glowed only when it felt like it, not when Arrant wanted it to. Papa just shrugged and told him not to worry. Occasionally Arrant thought he caught a glimpse of Temellin's love for him, and he would bask in the feel of it before it vanished, eliminated – he guessed – by his own inability to control his power to recognise emotion.

Of course, there were times when neither Temellin nor Ligea wanted him around. They would give him over to one of Temellin's Theuri attendants, while they pored over maps and discussed fighting. Military strategy, they called it. Arrant was used to that. Such discussions had always been part of Ligea's life for as long as he could remember. He was happy enough to go off with the men who had come with Temellin: Theuri Lamin, who would take him shleth riding, or Theuri Scallis, who was teaching him to be a better swimmer. Or he could go down to the kitchens, where the cook would give him pastry to make shapes that he could bake in the oven and then eat with melon jam.

Sometimes he sensed his mother was not as happy as she tried to pretend. He would catch her in a pensive mood, and see the sadness in her eyes, or his cabochon would stir when she was near, telling him things he didn't want to know. When he asked her what was the matter, she said she was sad at the thought of leaving him. The pang of impending loss took his breath away. She couldn't leave. She *couldn't*.

For a moment he hated her, just a little bit, but afterwards he felt bad, knowing it was naughty to feel that way. Knowing he didn't really want to make her unhappy. He hugged her and told her he loved her. After that, he felt good again.

It didn't last.

He was playing with the cat on the garden doorstep. Kardi cats had funny tails, all twisted, or short, or crooked. This one had a tail that curled around in a circle to one side, and he found he could thread stalks of flowers through the loop and they wouldn't fall out. Drowsing in the sun, the cat didn't seem to notice. In the room behind him, his parents were talking.

His father had given him a lesson in using his cabochon to hide his feelings, and he was trying to do that so they would forget he was there. 'Pull all your emotions into a ball and hide them here,' Temellin had said, tapping his chest. 'Pretend it's a ball of string, all tied up . . .'

He thought maybe he was successful, because they weren't paying him any attention. If he peeked through the open door he could see them, but they never looked his way.

Ligea was saying, 'You're telling me that I gave Pinar's baby to them for *nothing*? Condemned that child to grow up as something, um, *alien*, all for nothing?'

The bitterness in her tone was ugly. Arrant stared, cat forgotten.

His anxiety swelled into something large and terrible. He tried to tie it up with the make-believe string. She couldn't be angry with Papa, could she?

When his father replied, he sounded sad. 'We don't know that yet. It's only been, what, not quite six years? Maybe he's not old enough to make a difference? All I can tell you is that so far nothing has improved. The Mirage is attacked by new pieces of the Ravage, and the old patches grow in size. We have lost part of Mirage City – even parts of the Maze. People have *died*. It's – it's not a good way to die. Once we launch the coming offensive, we will withdraw from the Mirage completely.'

'Forever?' she asked.

'Forever.'

'That child has haunted me,' she whispered. 'When I see Arrant grow, and know there was once another, with just as much right to live.'

'He wouldn't have lived at all, but for what you had the courage to do. He has a life, Sarana.' The words were comforting, but Arrant heard the barrenness of his father's tone. There was no joy in what he said, none.

'*No.*' The word was wrenched out of Ligea. 'I took his life and condemned him to – to an *existence*. But I did it for a *reason*. And now what you have told me has taken away the validity of that decision. Goddess, I am sorry, Temellin.'

Arrant felt her tearing grief, her shame, as if it were his own. He wanted to run to her, but something held him back. They were silent so long, he peeked around the doorway into the room again. They stood close together, Papa's hands on Ligea's shoulders, but neither of them seemed happy.

When his father dropped his arms, she changed the subject. 'Garis,' she said, in bright tones that didn't seem to ring quite true. 'You said you had a letter from him this morning? How is he? *Where* is he?'

'Brand's back in Altan but he left Garis in Gala. The rebellion there is doing well. The whole island is waging war on Tyrans and, from what I hear, the Exaltarch is pouring more and more legions in with less and less effect. You did know Garis' wife died, didn't you?'

'Yes. Brand wrote. Mirageless soul, Tem, she was so *young*.'

'And a child left motherless, too.'

They were silent for a while, and Arrant knew they were speaking with their emotions, even though he couldn't feel them. Then Ligea said, 'You should marry again yourself.'

'*No*,' he said. There was a long silence during which neither of them moved. 'I *can't*.'

She stirred unhappily. 'Temellin, I don't know how long it will be before I can return. Things – things are not as easy as I once thought they would be. It will be many years. Too many to ask you to wait. Too many for us to plan a future together.'

Temellin's stab of grief made Arrant wince. He looked again, to see Papa shake his head. 'Don't ask it of me, Sarana. I cannot and will not marry someone else. I've married someone I didn't want to wed once before and, as you know, it led to disaster. Pinar and I ended up loathing each other. I won't do it again. I *won't* settle for second-best. Mirageless soul' – he waved a hand at the rooms upstairs – 'after *that*, how can I think of wanting anything else? Any*one* else? The thought of you is sometimes the only thing that makes it worthwhile to open my eyes on a new day. You and Arrant. And you will come to me. You *must*. How can I go on if I don't believe that?'

She was silent. He reached up and wiped a thumb down her cheek. *Tears*, Arrant thought. *She's crying, and she never cries.* Well, hardly ever. His own eyes filled. They had been so happy; why did they have to go and *spoil* it all? Why couldn't they just all have fun?

In his misery, he jabbed at the cat and the indignant animal ran away, trailing flowers from its tail.

The good times ended when he dreamed another nightmare. Another dreaming so horrible he could hardly believe it all happened in his head, hardly believe he could *imagine* such things in his sleep.

He woke terrified, with memories of teeth and claws and spines and tusks slashing at him. Of creatures shockingly dedicated to attacking him. The night was quiet, and he was alone – yet he knew what he had seen in his dream was *real*; he knew in his thundering heart that the bestial horrors were more than just dream-creatures. Somewhere they really existed. He could taste their hate for him, sourish and corrosive in his throat. And they were *close*. They *wanted* him.

He sat up on his pallet, his throat constricting, his mind jolted from fear into blank nothingness, his emotions so tied up in knots that he cut them off rather than feel them. The ball was there under his ribs and he didn't want it like that, but it was so tightly wrapped he didn't think he could untie it.

Shivering and unable to think, he staggered out of the room looking for Ligea. Reaching the top of the stairs, he looked down. Cold, numbed, he tried to speak, but his spasming throat would make no sound.

Papa and Ligea were there, sitting close together on shleth pelts by a driftwood fire, and they were alone. He tried to speak, his mouth moved, but no words came out. *Why didn't they sense him?* Inside he felt awful. Everything was wadded up tight, painfully tight. It *hurt*.

Oblivious, Ligea was saying, 'Tem, Arrant needs help if he's ever to learn to control whatever power he has, although I think it cannot be much. You've tried to teach him and seen how hard he finds it. Don't be disappointed—'

'Perhaps you've put too much pressure on him? Perhaps he just wants to please us too much, and tries too hard?'

'Maybe. And if that's the case, how much more imperative is it that he stay with you!'

'Ligea – *I don't want him.*'

The words slammed into Arrant, stark and uncompromising. They scythed through his mind, shredding his confidence, making a mockery of the happiness he'd found with his father. He wanted to be hugged, comforted, loved. Instead, he was *betrayed*.

Ligea frowned in puzzlement. 'But – why ever not?'

'He will come to me to get his Magor sword when he's twelve or thereabouts. That's soon enough. I'll send someone back with you to help with his training. Pity Garis is not here, or I could send him. By the way, did Garis ever tell you why I sent him away from Kardiastan in the first place?'

She shook her head.

'It was because I thought he would be safer. The Ravage developed the same sort of dislike for him as it had for you. I suppose because he was with you the day you gave Pinar's baby to the Mirage Makers—'

'You're changing the subject!'

'No, I'm not. Think about what I'm saying. Sarana, dear, I don't want Arrant, and I think the reason is obvious. He goes back to Tyrans with you.'

'But you are so good with him! Better than I am. You're the kind of man who has – well, who has an affinity for small boys and an – an instinctive understanding of their minds. Both attributes I lack. I've always had to work hard at being a mother. Parenthood seems to come to you naturally. You've only known him a few days and already he adores you.'

'I don't want him.'

Arrant turned his silent cry of hurt inward. They still didn't look up, still didn't feel him. He turned and stumbled back to his pallet, his breath coming in uneven gasps of pain. *Papa didn't want him.* His own father didn't like him. He buried his head in his bolster, his misery swelling as a lump in his throat and spilling in tears. He *loved* Papa. Yet it wasn't enough. He was the heir to the Mirager's sword, and even that wasn't enough. Temellin didn't care enough to want him around.

It must be because he couldn't control his cabochon. Because he made a muck of things when he tried to help. Because Ligea had asked for his aid on the ship and he'd failed her. He was a disappointment to everyone. He couldn't tell when people lied. He couldn't sense people when he wanted to. His powers vanished when he needed them, and came when he didn't.

He refused to let his feelings seep away. He wouldn't let them know how he felt. He wouldn't let his father see him blubber, the great silent gulps heaving up from inside him. Wouldn't let him feel that anguish welling up in the silent cry: *Why can't I do anything right?*

And that was when *he* came again. The person who came into his head and looked out through his eyes. Only this time it was different. He *spoke*.

What are you doing?

The question slipped into his mind. The questioner wanted to know why Arrant was upset, but was also puzzled by the actual *process* of crying. And he – somehow Arrant knew the maleness of the intruder – was rummaging around in his mind trying to understand. There was no threat, just a friendly interest.

Arrant stopped weeping, breathtaking astonishment driving all thought of his distress from him.

Don't you know what you were doing? The thoughts emerged just as if Arrant had thought them – but he knew he hadn't.

He was indignant. 'Of course I know what I was doing! I was crying!' And then: 'What are you doing inside my head?'

I don't know, came the reply. *I just came. All of a sudden. I think maybe because you felt so bad. I've been here before, you know. Once I came when there was all that fighting and you were frightened. And then again when you were scared on the boat—*

'I didn't feel scared!'

Yes, you did so too! I can feel the way you feel. And you feel bad right now. But I can't do what you were doing. Um, with water in your eyes. That weeping thing.

Arrant was diverted. 'Why not?'

I s'pose cos I don't have a body.

'Everybody has a body,' Arrant said, not trying to hide his scorn. 'Who *are* you? What's your name?'

I don't have a name.

Arrant's scorn increased. 'Everybody has a name!'

Well, I don't. And I don't care if I don't have a body, either. I can see out of your eyes. And I can hear with your ears. That's fun.

Anyway, I sort of see things and hear things all the time, even though I don't have eyes and stuff. I listen to people speaking. That's how I know words.

Somehow that frightened Arrant. 'Go away!' he shouted. 'I don't like you! Go away!'

His shouts brought his father running up from downstairs. Temellin picked him up in his arms, soothing him, asking him what the matter was. But his father's rejection was still fresh, the hurt of it as raw as skinned knees and far more painful. He shook his head and shrank away from the comfort. The pain inside him clenched tight.

He's your father? Why don't you like him? the voice inside his head asked, interested. *He's my father too.*

This time, when Arrant shouted, he did it within his mind. *Liar! Liar! Liar!*

I'm not lying. I never lie – why should I? He's hurt you, hasn't he? And made you angry, too. I can feel it. Never mind, if he's your father, then we are brothers. And aren't brothers usually friends? You can be my friend; I've always wanted a friend. Don't feel so bad. You have me now.

Arrant blinked in surprise. A *brother*? The idea was foreign, yet enticing. He knew about brothers. He'd seen brothers in Prianus playing with one another.

Tendrils of concern and tentative affection spread through his thoughts, emotions that were not his. A brother who wanted to love him! The pain of his father's betrayal faded a little.

'Feel better now?' Temellin asked, still holding him.

'I'm all right,' he mumbled, careful to keep his emotions closed up tight. Careful to shut his father out. All of a sudden, it was easy. 'I can go back to sleep again now.' Temellin went away, but the presence of his unknown brother stayed, not speaking but just there, comforting him with his concern until he fell asleep.

Downstairs Ligea stretched in front of the fire, sated, smug, happy. She hadn't been this happy since . . . well, she wasn't sure she could remember when.

After Temellin came downstairs again, she asked, 'A night-mare?'

'It seems so. He wouldn't talk about it, though. He has his emotions shut up as tight as a rolled-up millipede – I can't sense a thing.'

'Yes, there are times when he is able to do that.' She sighed. 'In fact, I think it happens when he's not trying, too. Sometimes he is so closed to me I have no idea he is even there. It's ... weird. I worry, Tem, about him. About his Magor abilities. About everything. It's no kind of life for a boy, the one we're leading. It's dangerous. He sees things a child shouldn't see. He would be better off with you, and I don't understand why you can't see that. You still haven't explained why you don't want him, not to my satisfaction.'

'Don't *want* him? Sweet cabochon, of course I *want* him! I want you both, more than I have the words to tell you.'

'Yet you used those words.'

'I didn't mean it that way, and you know it.'

'Well, what *did* you mean? With you, he could learn to be a Mirager. He needs to learn how to control his powers. With me, he is in constant danger.'

'The dangers he faces in Tyr are things you can fight. But how do we fight the Ravage welling up beneath our feet?' He reached out and touched the deforming gouge on her cheek. 'Remember this? You were lucky to escape. Others die, more and more often now. And I am afraid for Arrant more than any other. The Ravage will seek him out, him personally. Sarana, if I take him to the Mirage he will die. It's as simple as that.'

'Then let him stay here in Ordensa. Or with someone some-where else. Someone who can train him better than I can. Narjemah will happily stay to give him some stability. She does not want to be parted from him.'

He thought about that. 'It's a possibility, but the risk is enor-mous. The Tyranian legionnaires conduct frequent searches for the Magor. Anyone with a cabochon – or a lump in the palm – is slaughtered the moment they are identified.'

'No one of the Magor is helpless, Tem.'

'No. And we usually kill a great many people before we die. But in the end we tire, and when that happens . . .' He shrugged. 'An arrow. A spear. A rip-disc from a whirlsling. He's safer with you. More anonymous.'

'Rubbish. I'm one of the most wanted people in all the Exaltarchy. So, the Brotherhood may not know I am Ligea Gayed yet, but they are looking for a Kardi with a scarred face. And Arrant is my weakness; if Rathrox or Bator Korbus get to know of his existence – and they have now met Merriam the midwife – then they will have a way to attack me.'

'You will keep him safe.'

She stared at him, baffled. Then her face changed as realisation grew. 'You're doing this for me.'

For a moment she thought he would deny it, even knowing she would identify the denial as a lie, but he said, 'Well, partly. You have no one. You are so alone . . .'

'I have friends,' she said defensively, but she was touched. The troubled concern in his gaze, the love that wafted her way, even sometimes when he tried to hide it. Vortex, she had forgotten what it was to be loved so . . . so *utterly*. The thought came to her, accompanied by an uncomfortable feeling in the region of her stomach, that now she'd been reminded she would have to learn to live without it all over again.

Never had she so regretted her decision to leave Kardiastan.

She said, trying to sound cheerfully unconcerned, 'Narjemah looks after me like a broody hen. Gevenan watches over me too, although he's more like a bad-tempered rooster defending his pile of grain. He thinks of me as a means to an end, and that end – revenge on Tyrans – is very precious to him, so he takes good care of me. But, Tem, the only person we should be thinking about here is Arrant.'

'And you think he doesn't need his mother?'

'Or a father?'

'He will come to me in time. For his sword. That is time enough.'

She took a deep, calming breath. 'Goddess, there was a time when these decisions were so easy, so blithely made. But that was before he was born. It is – harder now.'

'I know. Mirageless soul, I know.'

'This is not settled, Tem. Not yet.'

At that, he pulled her into his arms, and they embraced, loving, hurting, grieving, yet celebrating their present joy in one another. Not knowing what the future would bring.

CHAPTER TWENTY-ONE

The nameless boy – whoever he was – came back every day. Arrant still wasn't sure he wanted someone inside his head. He didn't see how a being without a body could be a brother, either.

If Papa is your father, he said a couple of days after they'd met, *then my mother must be your mother.* He was seated at the kitchen table at the time, waiting for his supper, which he took earlier than his parents. He was getting good at this speaking in the head.

No, she's not. You and me are half-brothers. My mother was a different lady, but she's dead now. I remember her, but not alive.

Arrant tried to make sense of that. *What do you mean?*

I remember things the others saw.

What others?

Oh, the boy said vaguely, *the others. The other part of me. We're the Mirage Makers. I remember what they saw, even if I wasn't born when they saw it. Your mother killed my mother, you know. While I was still inside her body.*

'That's not true! You are such a *liar.*' He said the words aloud and the Kardi cook, who was stirring the evening meal over the open fire, looked at him with raised eyebrows. He closed his mouth hurriedly. *My mother killed yours? It can't be true. Ligea doesn't kill women.* At least he didn't *think* she did.

She did that time. The boy didn't seem particularly upset. *I don't think she was an especially nice person, my mother. And she was sort of daft, too. She tried to murder your mother, but your mother killed her first. Then she cut me out of the body and gave me to the Mirage Makers so I wouldn't die. That's why I'm not a person like you.*

Arrant reeled under the impact of all this, supper forgotten. A feeling that took some time for him to identify rippled through him: shame. His mother had killed his brother's mother. Because of her, his brother was what he was. He didn't have legs and arms and a body like him, because of Ligea. His brother couldn't run and play the way he could.

He looked out of the open kitchen door to where Ligea stood talking to someone in the yard. He stared at her as if he'd never seen her before. He shuddered, remembering blood and screams and the dying of men. How part of you was . . . gone when you died. Eyes looking but not seeing, so suddenly all cold marble statue.

It's nothing, his brother said airily. *I don't mind.*

But Arrant did. And his understanding changed something, although he wasn't sure what it was. He began to speak of other things, too frightened to think about what the boy had told him. *Why don't you have a name?*

I don't know. I just haven't.

Everybody has to have a name.

Well, I don't.

Then I shall give you one. I shall call you Tarran.

That's almost the same as yours.

Well, we're brothers, aren't we? He was desperate to make amends.

None of the other Mirage Makers has a name; at least, I don't think so. Maybe a long time ago. I like it because it sounds like yours. Tarran. I've got a name!

Arrant felt his pleasure and grinned.

Arrant ached to have his father ask him to stay, longed to be *wanted.* He hung around his father with a woebegone expression on his face that exasperated Temellin because he didn't know the reason for it and Arrant wouldn't tell.

He didn't know what to do to make his father like him. He knew Papa loved his mother; it was obvious from the way he looked at her. Yet when he looked at Arrant now, it was as if his mind blanked over at the sight of him. Arrant tried to tell himself that maybe his own Magor weakness was letting him down, that maybe the love was there but he just couldn't feel it. Then he would remember those words, those tearing, horrible words: *Ligea, I don't want him.*

It *had* to be his fault. His insides scrunched into a tight ball whenever he thought about it. 'I don't understand,' he said to Tarran one day. He was outside at the time, sitting on the seawall watching one of the fishing boats unload. He swung his legs to and fro over the water. 'Why doesn't he want me here?'

Maybe he doesn't like little boys? Tarran suggested helpfully. Then, when he realised that the remark hadn't made Arrant any happier: *You should listen to them more. When they don't know you're listening, I mean. That's the way to find out interesting stuff. We listen to what people say all the time in the Mirage. How else would we understand anything? And even then, we get muddled.*

'That's not polite. Do you live in the Mirage? That's where Papa lives sometimes.'

I know. Go on, Arrant, try some far-hearing like the other Magor do.

'I'm not very good at all that stuff. Most of the time, I can't,' he admitted miserably.

Go on. It can't be such an awful thing to do, can it? I mean, we do it all the time. In fact, we sort of hear everything spoken in the Mirage whether we want to or not. Most of it's awfully silly, though. And boring. Go on – try it now.

Arrant looked over his shoulder. He could see the house they were staying in and as far as he knew his parents were inside, with several other of the Magor who had just arrived from the Mirage. One of the servants was sitting on the steps keeping an eye on him.

He sighed. 'All right.'

He focused his hearing the way he had been taught, and for

once everything happened the way it was supposed to. He heard the voices he wanted to. Ligea's words came sharp and clear into his ear: 'The Pythian rebels were grateful enough to agree to cooperate—'

Then Temellin: 'I could send Garis there from Gala, together with Brand. They've been there before.'

I don't really know Garis, but we remember him, Tarran said. *He was always fun. Then the Ravage wanted to eat him. He had to ride for his life and we haven't seen him since—*

'Hush, I want to *listen*,' Arrant said.

'If they can persuade the Pythian miners to withhold shipments of iron to Tyrans,' Ligea was saying in answer to a question from one of the Magor, 'the Exaltarch's legions will have problems with weapons supply within a season.'

'But you're still talking another year before a full rebellion in Tyrans?' someone else asked. 'So long? Why not now, this summer? We here in Kardiastan don't want to wait!'

'What's the point of being free if you are then drained by constant fighting and further legionnaire invasions?' Temellin asked. 'We've discussed all this before. A premature uprising could bring more problems than it solved.'

Ligea agreed. 'The legions are the finest soldiers who ever lived and, thanks to the paveways and the naval galleys, they can be quickly mobilised. It's no use winning the initial fight and then not having the means to keep the power thus gained. But I'm planning to change from quick forays and retreats – the kind of thing we've been doing for the past five years – to full-scale war once the snows melt after next year's snow-season. That's not a full year away.

'My forces will attack from my five strongholds in the mountains. We will seize the paveways and the bridges and the garrisons of northern Tyrans first. Ideally, war should start everywhere at the same time. That way, the Exaltarch cannot concentrate his legions in any one trouble spot. Believe me, his forces are large – but they are still spread thin on the ground.'

'So let's recap,' Temellin said. 'Where do we have cooperation?'

'The Quyriots and Altan,' Ligea said.

'Corsene to the south of us,' an unknown voice said.

'Brand seems to think Cormel will rebel if they see everyone else rebelling first,' Ligea added.

'Gala's already following your example and Pythia is a possibility, if Brand and Garis can organise it,' the unknown voice added.

'There may be others who take advantage of Tyrans' problems as time goes by,' Temellin said. 'For example, Garis says the King of Akowarn is furious with Bator Korbus. Something about insulting a princess.'

'Yes,' Ligea said. 'He said he'd marry her, brought her to Tyr, and there she sits, still unmarried while Bator makes use of her dowry. Temellin, I think I will go back to Tyr via Altan. I want to see the rebel leader there, Hotash.'

There was a long silence. Then his father said coldly, 'All sea journeys have an element of danger. Why not just send a letter back with the *Fisherdream*?'

'If I am going to be Exaltarch, I have to establish relationships with other people. The rebel leader in Altan will be an important man one day. I want to meet him. I want to talk about the future.'

'How safe are your strongholds?' someone asked, changing the subject after a strangely long silence.

'The original one is as hard to find as a shleth egg, and easily defendable,' she replied. 'The others aren't quite as well protected. However, they were chosen not just for their remoteness, but also for how easily they can be abandoned without loss of life. And, in fact, that has happened several times. The legions arrive, my men simply melt away into the mountains over the border into Quyr. They gather at a back-up location within a month.'

'Get along with you! You think I didn't see those pickle fingers of yours dancing their way into her bodice, you sly muck-sweating street sweeper? Get your backside out of my kitchen—'

Arrant sighed. His concentration had slipped and he'd homed in on some other conversation elsewhere by mistake. He waited for Tarran to laugh at the fumble, only to realise his brother had already gone.

He was like that, slipping in and out of Arrant's mind without warning, his coming and going usually governed by what was happening back in the Mirage rather than what was occurring in Arrant's part of the world. It took getting used to, but gradually Arrant was becoming aware that if he was upset, Tarran came. It was a good feeling: he could *rely* on his brother.

His father stood there on the seawall and watched them go. Arrant could feel some of his anguish at the parting, but knew it must be for his mother, not him. He'd hoped, right up to the moment of departure, that Temellin would change his mind and ask him to stay.

It hadn't happened.

A hollow place under his breastbone filled up with sadness. He refused to let it out. He would *not* show how he felt. He didn't want anyone's pity. He didn't want anyone to love him because they felt *sorry* for him.

You'll see him again soon, Tarran soothed. *It's just a few years.*

To Arrant, that seemed a lifetime.

The figure that was Temellin grew smaller and smaller until finally he blurred into his surroundings, at one with the harbour wall and the town beyond. Ligea stood at Arrant's side, watching. Narjemah and Foran, Arrant's new tutor, leaned on the railing next to her.

Cord was at the stern sweep, keeping an eye on the sail. The rowers shipped their oars now that the *Fisherdream* was away from the hazard of the shore and the breeze had picked up.

'Shipmaster Cord isn't so grumpy any more,' Arrant said to Ligea.

She took one last lingering look at Ordensa, then turned her attention to him. 'He's going home, with quite a lot of money in his pocket.'

'Why didn't Papa want us to go to Altan?' Arrant asked.

'Whatever gave you that idea?' she asked lightly. 'He was a little concerned about the sea trip, that's all.'

That's not the whole truth, Tarran said. *Temellin doesn't like Brand, and Brand is in Altan.*

Why doesn't he like Brand?

Because your mother does, Tarran said.

That didn't make sense to Arrant, but he didn't want to appear stupid so he kept quiet.

'I've always wanted to go to Altan,' Narjemah said as the *Fisherdream* encountered the offshore wind and picked up speed. 'Imagine a land that's mostly water!'

'Only the Delta is like that,' Foran said. 'The central part of Altan is as dry as Kardiastan.' Foran was an Illuser and Arrant hadn't made up his mind whether he liked him or not yet. He didn't smile much and he moved as though he was wearing rusted armour. His fingers were all crooked, too. Narjemah said that was because he was old.

At least Narjemah was returning with them to Tyrans. She had promised she would always look after him until he was grown up, but he had been worried that she might change her mind when she discovered they were not going to stay in Kardiastan. However, she didn't seem to mind at all. She'd tried to explain it to him, even though he didn't quite understand. 'In Kardiastan I feel the horror of what I've lost because the other Magor look on me with pity. Their pity reminds me every day that I am no longer complete and never will be again. I don't mind going back to Tyr. There I can sometimes forget . . .'

Tarran, Arrant asked, looking back at the coast, his fear sudden and real, *you don't think you'll have trouble coming into my head when we are in Altan, do you? Foran says it's a long, long way from Kardiastan.*

Tarran thought about that. *No, I don't think so. After all, I can come to you in Tyrans, can't I? And that's a long way, too.*

Arrant breathed a sigh of relief. He could no longer imagine being without his brother. *Why do you often have to leave in such a hurry?* he asked.

Because of the Ravage. Hey, can you go up there into the front of the ship? I like the feel of the wind. It tastes good!

Narjemah says that's cos the sea is salty. He edged past the bow oarsman into the prow of the ship. He'd already realised that everything to do with the sea fascinated his brother.

We don't have the sea in the Mirage, Tarran explained. *And we don't taste things, either. I didn't know what taste was till I found you.*

Really? That's weird! What's the Ravage?

The thing that eats us from the inside. It's full of monsters. They make us sick. The others need me cos when I am there, the Ravage is not so strong. But I don't like it. It hurts. That's why I like it here – I can't feel it any more. And when I go back I can fight it better cos I've been here.

Arrant frowned, trying to sort through that. *I don't think I understand. Monsters? You mean it's like nightmares?*

Tarran considered. *You know how you scraped your elbow the other day? And it got all sore and had that yellow stuff oozing out of it? And you had to get your mother to fix it?*

Arrant nodded.

Well, the Ravage is like that. Only it's huge and it has horrid things inside it. And it can't be fixed. He deposited a picture in Arrant's head.

Arrant's eyes went wide. 'Oh. *Oh.*' He was looking at the monsters of his dreams once more. He was shocked into an appalled silence. The creatures of his dreams *were* real. And they had threatened to eat him alive.

PART THREE

ARRANT AND
TARRAN

CHAPTER TWENTY-TWO

When he was older, Arrant sometimes thought the trip to Kardiastan sliced through his life like a Rake across the Shiver Barrens. On one side was the firm ground of a childhood that centred around his mother, the years when he felt loved and secure no matter what happened; on the other side, a life of shifting sands that had no centre, when the future threatened rather than beckoned, a time of uncertainty, made bearable only by Tarran's frequent presence in his mind.

The trip back to the Stronghold via Altan, marked by endless travelling, discomfort and fatigue, lacked the joy of the outward journey. The time on board ship was often boring, although Foran insisted on daily lessons. Arrant didn't like Altan, he didn't like the way Ligea spent most of her time with the Altani rebels instead of with him, and as a consequence, he sulked most of the time he was there.

From Altan, they sailed through the Issian Isles to the head of the Gulf of Tyr, thereby avoiding the city altogether, to disembark, unremarked, in a tiny fishing village where Cord had friends. There, they hired mounts and a guide to the next town, where they bought some horses of their own. From there, they made their way to Bryssa, mostly along dusty country roads that offered no wayhouses or comfortable tabernas. In Bryssa, Ligea contacted Arcadim's agent, and they joined another money-master's caravan along the paveway to Getria. From Getria, it was once again a long journey on horseback to the Stronghold.

It wasn't entirely an uneventful journey. Between Altan and the Issian islands, they encountered a storm that terrified Arrant into thinking the ship would sink. On the way to Bryssa, a small squad of legionnaires stopped them and demanded to see their palms. Ligea and Foran killed them all. Tarran, feeling Arrant's panic, came to comfort him, but even so, he once again felt the pain and terror of the death of strangers.

After Getria, there seemed to be legionnaires everywhere and Ligea used her positioning powers to avoid them, which slowed their progress. 'They are still hunting the Stronghold,' she said, her voice grim. 'They are not going to give up until they have found us. Foran, I am glad we'll have another Magor there – your positioning powers will help sense any attackers. Invaluable, especially if I am elsewhere.'

He smiled slightly. 'I am an Illuser, not a Magori. My powers are not as far-reaching.'

'Better than nothing.'

Arrant winced. He was the nothing.

Five months after leaving the Stronghold, as the desert-season made its long slow slide towards the snow, they rode back through its gates.

To Arrant, the building looked smaller than he remembered. Smaller and more grim.

While they'd been away, the Jackal Legion had come back in force to search for their missing soldiers. They'd reached the now-deserted village of Prianus, but failed to find the way up to the Stronghold. More by accident than anything else, they had followed the defiles down to First Farm, but the farm workers had been well primed. Homfridus lied, telling them that yes, there had been a troop of legionnaires come once before to search his farm, but of course there was nothing to find. After that, he added helpfully, the legionnaires had just headed back the way they had come, towards the mountains. 'It's difficult country,' he'd told them, shaking his head in sorrow. 'Landslips are common. A man can disappear forever up there.'

The Jackals had searched the farm, but there was nothing to arouse their suspicions. Sentries had given plenty of warning and by the time the legionnaires had arrived, the forges looked dirty and rarely used, the workshops seemed rundown and poorly equipped, the artisans were all wearing slave collars and the herds of Quyriot plateau ponies were nowhere to be seen.

The Jackals moved on, baffled.

There were still sometimes reports of legionnaires searching the farms and foothills and mountain trails, but none found the paths to the Stronghold. The village of Prianus remained empty, the marble quarry disused.

Arrant wasn't unhappy with his life in the Stronghold. Narjemah spoiled him as usual, and Gevenan or one of the other soldiers coached him in wrestling and swordplay. Gevenan also passed on much of his rough wisdom. 'A dead hero's no use to anyone,' he said, waggling his sword under Arrant's chin. 'And a fully trained legionnaire would find a lad your size about as dangerous as a dung beetle. In battle, he wouldn't even notice the nip. So learn to use your cunning, and to run like a ten-legged lizard when things look bad, all right?' Or, 'There's no honour in battle, lad, and don't you forget it. Killing your opponent from behind may not be particularly honourable, but it's a damn sight safer than meeting him face to face.'

Foran taught him to read and write and figure, which he enjoyed. In fact, the only part of his tutoring that he hated was the most important of all: his Magor studies.

What made his troubles with his power doubly frustrating was his knowledge that he did have talent – sometimes. There *were* times when he could call the colour of power into his cabochon at will, when he could far-sense, read emotions or do most of the things he ought to have been able to do. But there were even more times when he couldn't. And even when he could, things often didn't happen quite the way anyone expected.

Foran would say, 'Bathe your eyes in the glow of your cabochon, that's right. Now look at that tree growing on the cliff. Think of yourself as being right there, in front of it . . .' He would do everything Foran asked, but instead of seeing the tree up close, there was a fair chance that he would see a nightmarish brown network of lines and blurs and flowing circles instead. It was like gazing into a looking glass and expecting to see his own reflection, only to be faced with the features of a stranger.

Embarrassed by his inadequacies, Arrant asked Tarran to avoid coming when he was working with Foran on his Magor powers, and his brother respected his request. If he came at the wrong time, he slipped away again immediately. He preferred to be there when Arrant had normal lessons anyway, because he enjoyed those. He was also convinced his presence was necessary in order to correct Foran's misconceptions, and he didn't hesitate to tell Arrant so. *That's a load of city sweepings*, he would say when Foran twisted history. *We remember that. The ruler of Kardiastan at that time was Errinwith, not Gowanlin, and he didn't kill the envoy from Tyrans; the man died of a pain in the belly—*

Arrant would have to stifle a giggle and pretend he hadn't heard a thing.

They hadn't been back from Altan more than three weeks before Ligea and Gevenan rode out again. Arrant pouted when his mother told him she was going away. 'I want to go too,' he whined.

She sighed. 'Do you know how much I hate it when you whinge?' she asked. She gathered him onto her lap. 'Arrant, I miss you terribly when I'm not here, but you don't need me to teach you now. You have Foran.'

'Where are you going? Why can't I come?'

'I am going to all of the other strongholds. And their farms. Gev and I have to check them all, to see if the soldiers are well trained and ready for the war. We have to make sure there are enough horses, and weapons and armour. We have to see if all the commanders and cohort leaders know their orders. I shall be back before all the snow has melted from the mountains, I promise. But we ride to war on your sixth birthday.'

'Can I go with you then? I practise with my sword all the time, and Gev says I throw the javelin real good.'

'You do, I know. I've seen you. But no, Arrant. This war is for men, not children. Your job is to stay here and learn to use your cabochon.'

He stood on the watchtower with Foran and Narjemah and watched her leave with Gevenan and a small force of soldiers and auxiliaries. The gusting wind was cold, but the three of them stayed up there until Ligea and her soldiers were out of sight.

It was four months before she returned, just as the snows began to melt – and, as promised, she rode out again three weeks later on the day Arrant turned six.

He had expected her to spend the intervening time with him; it didn't happen. Most of the time she was with her commanders, poring over maps and talking strategy. Bored, he didn't bother to listen. His disappointment was an ache at the back of his throat, unexpressed and raw. He knew she didn't have time for him. He knew why – but none of it helped. He wanted his mother.

When she did leave, at the head of a marching column of three thousand men, he gazed down from the watchtower once more. This time he didn't know when she would return and she made no promises. Before she went, she tucked the Mirage Makers' clay head of Temellin and the jar of Shiver Barrens sand into the pack where he kept his personal treasures, and told him they were his now.

He didn't cry until he was alone on his pallet in the dark that night.

Rathrox Ligatan looked at the new reports just handed to him by the Exaltarch, and shuddered.

'This is not some small raid,' Bator said from between clenched teeth. 'We are only two months into the desert-season, and we've already had attacks on every legion stationed in the north, on every wayhouse, on every garrison, on every border customs house.'

Rathrox raised his appalled gaze to meet his Exaltarch's rage.

'And *she* is there,' the Exaltarch continued. 'A woman with a scarred face and a power we cannot fight. She is back in Tyrans.'

Ligea. But neither of them mentioned her name. 'She's only one person,' Rathrox muttered.

It was the worst thing he could have said. For a moment he thought Bator might burst a blood vessel, he was so angry. Finally he spat out, 'Every time she appears in person, her soldiers win a substantial victory. She is going from one area to another, granting that success to her helot rabble. Tell me, Rathrox, *how can we kill her*?'

Rathrox wanted to shout, 'It's your soldiers at fault! Why have they failed to kill her from a distance with a whirlsling?' Instead, he said calmly, 'The Brotherhood uses different methods from the army. When we find her son, we will have a hold over her.' He felt his guts stir at the thought. Revenge. Gods, how he wanted it . . . 'If I can still have command of the Jackals, I will find her lair, I swear. We know the general area. It's just a matter of finding a clue, or a traitor.'

They stared at each other. Two men in their sixties, seeing their whole life's work unravelling at the hands of one woman. It was impossible, but it was happening.

'I am riding out to join the army,' Bator said. 'Find the child, Rathrox. For both our sakes.' For once he didn't threaten. There was no need.

Every few weeks a note, written in Kardi, would arrive from Ligea. The three of them – Narjemah, Foran and Arrant – mapped the progress of her forces on a chart Foran had drawn, to show their slow and steady spread southwards from the mountains of northern Tyrans and Quyr. By the onset of the following snow-season, the rebels had seized the northernmost paveway that connected Tyr's sister city of Getria in the east to the province of Cormel – once the independent kingdom of Kormelya – in the west. Ligea's troops manned the wayhouses and collected the taxes. Of the cities along the paveway, Getria alone remained in the hands of the Exaltarch's legions.

In the meantime, Temellin wrote of successes in Kardiastan, Brand described how the Gharials now controlled the Delta in Altan, Garis sent word about the slaves of Pilgath who had seized that city, only to lose it several months later and be massacred to the last child.

Arrant heard it all, but he was only six and the places seemed far away and no more relevant than a myth told about the gods of Elysium. Here in the Stronghold, he fought with his wooden sword on the training grounds. Here in the Stronghold, the worst battle was the one he had with control over his own Magor abilities.

Another snow-season came and went, and Arrant turned seven. He hadn't seen Ligea in a year.

And he was still an incompetent Magoroth.

The chill of the early-morning mountain air, borne on gusts of wind whining around the stonework, sliced through Arrant's cloak to lay the cold along his skin. He tried not to mind. This was one of his tasks: guard duty for an hour a day. Alone, there in the tower that overlooked both the trail down to Prianus and the trail up to the Quyr Plateau. Although there were other guards up and down the trails, it pleased him that he was entrusted with the responsibility, surely one of the most important of the Stronghold. He felt grown-up, even though his seventh anniversary day was only two months behind him.

Because he couldn't rely on his cabochon powers, he had to scan the land, watching for movement, for disturbed animals and birds, just as Gevenan had taught him to do.

That morning, however, there was nothing untoward and he was delighted when Tarran popped into his mind. His brother was excited, he could tell. His mind gleamed and shimmered, full of bubbles like froth in a waterfall.

'What is it?' he asked, thrilled just by Tarran's feel. 'What's happened?'

They are leaving! Tarran cried. *They are going . . .*

'Who's leaving? Leaving what?' He tried to make sense of the pictures passing through his mind, but they flashed by too quickly, thought and then unthought as quick as lightning strikes.

They are leaving the Mirage.

'Who is?'

Everyone.

'Everyone?'

Yes.

'Why?'

Because the last of the Exaltarchy's legions is leaving Kardiastan. The land is free! There is no need for anyone to stay in the Mirage any more.

In spite of his own jubilation, Arrant also felt a pang of disappointment. He would never see the Mirage. He would never know the Mirage Makers – except for Tarran, of course – not in the way his parents had. All he would ever know would be a hazy shape beneath the Shiver Barrens, handing him his Magor sword.

The disappointment swelled to a pang of loss, even as he understood the stupidity of that emotion. 'I'm glad,' he said, 'for everyone. For the Mirage Makers, too. Temellin said you did not like us being there.'

Tarran hesitated, apparently striving for an explanation that would make sense to them both. *The others don't understand any of you. The way you think. The way you behave. It is – was – sometimes hard not to hurt you accidentally.* He paused, still groping for words. *I understand better than the others. Because there's part of me that's human. And because of you – you show me what it is like to be human. You are my brother.*

For one wild moment, Arrant felt an overwhelming desire to touch Tarran. To hug him. To have the impossible come true. 'I – I am glad Kardiastan is free,' he said, choking back the emotion. 'Have you – have you seen Temellin lately?'

No. He has not been back to the Mirage for a long time. From what we hear, he is still safe. Him and Korden and others of the Ten lead the fighting.

The Ten. The Ten Magoroth, Pinar and Temellin included,

who had escaped the massacre at the Shimmer Festival because his grandfather, Solad the Mirager, had sent them away.

Think, Arrant, now Temellin will be able to send Magor to help you.

Arrant shivered. Perhaps his father would come here, himself, to Tyrans. Was it possible? Arrant wasn't sure he wanted that. He wouldn't know what to say to him. How did you talk to a father who didn't want you? He dredged up enough courage to ask, 'Will he come himself?'

I don't think so. He has to stay in Kardiastan. Because of the Mirager's sword . . . and the babies. You know.

Of course. His father could never leave, not when he and Ligea were the only people who could bestow cabochons on newborns.

Arrant looked down at the wooden sword he was wearing, a practice weapon his father had given him. One day he would be asked to make the cabochons for all the future generations of Magor. Arrant the useless. Arrant who couldn't control his power. How could he ever be the Mirager of Kardiastan?

He remembered the concern in his mother's eyes when she spoke of his difficulties. He remembered his father's rejection. His stomach knotted. He swallowed back a horrid taste in his mouth.

He drew the wooden sword from its scabbard, turned it over and over in his hands, bitter tears in his eyes. His father had a Mirager's sword. So did his mother. Two people with the ruler's blade for the first time in history. And he was their son. He should have been the best Mirager-heir ever born.

He grunted in angry frustration, drew back his arm and hurled the sword away. Not into the exercise yard below, but over the outer wall of the watchtower, as far as he could throw it, as if he could fling his rage with it. He watched it fall, growing smaller and smaller, spinning as it went, until it bounced onto the rocks and shattered in the ravine beneath the walls of the Stronghold.

'I will never be the Mirager,' he said. 'Never.'

Tarran did not answer, but his love enfolded as he attempted to fill in the cracks in an aching heart.

CHAPTER TWENTY-THREE

'That's funny,' Jorbrus said, frowning. 'Isn't that one of the quarry horses? And it's not hobbled.'

The five of them – Arrant, Narjemah, Jorbrus and his two grown-up sons, Tarkis and Remolis – had just rounded a bend in the final gorge that led to Prianus. They were still a mile or two from the resettled village and marble quarry, and the horse that had caught Jorbrus' eye was cropping the grass struggling to grow among the stones along the valley bottom.

'Damn careless,' Jorbrus muttered. His breath was sour with stale wine and his temper uncertain; everyone knew he drank too much. He and his sons had been up at the Stronghold to deliver supplies from First Farm, and were now on their way down again, leading the pack ponies. Narjemah and Arrant had taken the opportunity to descend to Prianus to spend a few days in the village. Narjemah wanted to see her friends; Arrant wanted to play with the village boys. Last time he'd seen them, they'd made plans to hunt for caves in the cliffs behind the quarries . . .

'What in all Acheron have those careless fellows been up to? Here,' Jorbrus said to Arrant, handing him some twine from his pack, 'tie that to the bridle and you can lead the beast back to the village.'

Arrant obliged, happy to have something useful to do. It was a lot better than knowing himself to be as pointless as grain husks winnowed away on the wind.

As they rode on, he thought about that. Ligea had returned twice that year, just to see him. She was fighting a war, and yet she still felt she had to baby him, even though he had turned eight. So didn't that mean he was not only of no help to her cause, but was actually a hindrance?

He shifted uneasily, feeling guilty. He knew she and Gevenan were now based in Petrum, one hundred and fifty miles to the south of Prianus. Since the start of the rebellion, she and Gev had secured a grasp on the north and were now attacking Getria. She had done all that in two years, and all he had done was grow taller, like a weed.

He sighed and decided to think about something else. Would she, he wondered, be mad with the people from Prianus, like Jorbrus, for moving back to the village? They felt safe now that her army was so close, but he knew Ligea still worried about the Jackals. 'I've heard whispers,' she'd said to him and Foran on her last visit, 'rumours, really, that Rathrox knows my true identity. If that's true, he and Favonius have added incentive to find me. They will move these mountains stone by stone until they find me.'

He glanced across at Jorbrus and his sons. They joked as they rode; to them life seemed good. Remolis had his pet ferret with him, and every now and then it would poke its head out of the saddlebag to look around, as if it knew it was almost home. Even Narjemah, who hated horses in general and having to ride them in particular, began to look more cheerful as they entered the final defile leading to the first of the houses. Smoke wisped upwards from the village around the bend ahead.

'Hey, look, the water pipe's been knocked down!' Remolis pointed to where the wooden channel, which brought water into the village from the stream, had fallen off its trestle. Water had flooded the ground and the path was a soggy patch of black mud and stones.

'Maybe the horse did it?' Arrant suggested.

'Odd that no one's been to fix it,' Jorbrus said. They all reined in, staring at the gush of water. The harsh cry of an eagle split the air. Arrant looked up. Scavengers wheeled, wingtip feathers splayed, the watchfulness of their circling an eloquent expression of desolation and death.

'Oh, *gods*,' Jorbrus breathed. He kicked his horse into explosive action even as he drew his sword. His sons dropped the leads to the pack animals and raced after him, the hooves of their mounts sending the mud flying.

Arrant looked across at Narjemah and felt her fears as tense as thread about to snap. '*Don't go*,' she said, her voice full of dread and urgency. 'Wait—'

But he was already digging his heels into his pony's flanks. She cursed him and followed.

Around the corner, he found what he did not want to know.

Nothing was left of the stone huts of Prianus except blackened walls. They stank of smoke and ash and charred meat. His gaze fell to a stinking body sprawled out of the nearest doorway. A woman, her skirt rucked high so he could not see her face.

He didn't understand. His mind wouldn't catch up with all that his eyes told him. Why was her flesh so – so *green*? She was naked from the waist down, skin taut over her bloated belly. Flies swarmed and crawled, blackening the congealed blood between her legs.

His gaze wandered on in shock, to a scattering of children's naked corpses strewn down the middle of the street. Bellies as round as pregnant sows, limbs rigid and hard and black, starkly thrust up into the air like dead branches . . . Crows rose in flight, cawing their warnings, sated on flesh. And then, further on, more dead. He stared, bewildered, trying to equate the grotesque postures of these bodies with people he had known. With people who had such a short time ago been *alive*.

Jorbrus, in stricken silence, knelt beside the body of a toddler. There were cuts all over her chest and limbs, as regular as the border pattern of a mosaic floor. Arrant looked away, desperate not to see, but heard the man's whisper anyway: 'Tortured. They tortured the children.' Tarkis started wailing, a sharp keening to rival the cry of the scavengers. And then Jorbrus scrambled up and ran from house to house, from body to body. They'd had family in Prianus.

Arrant sat on his pony, unable to move. Terrified. Sick with dread. *Please let this not be true.* His hands spasmed around the reins, nails digging into his palms. People he *knew*. Children who had played with him while they were living in the Stronghold or at First Farm. His *friends*. He didn't want to dismount. He didn't want to see, or hear, or smell. He didn't want to have the knowledge that was there, clawing at his skull: the reason *why*. But he knew it anyway. The children had been made to suffer, they'd been tortured in front of their parents – to persuade someone to act as a guide through the labyrinth of defiles and gorges to the Stronghold.

'Arrant,' Narjemah said gently. Tears, melted memories of the dead, coursed down her cheeks. 'Come away. There is nothing here we want to see. Nothing.'

Tarran! he cried. *Help me!*

And Tarran came. He saw the village through Arrant's eyes, and grieved with him, wrapping him in the only thing he had to give: his love. But not even Tarran could take away the etched pictures, the stink in his nostrils, the burning acid of the memory. Arrant slid off his pony and vomited.

How could anyone do this? Tarran asked. *This – this is Ravagevile.*

The Ravage didn't do this. This was men.

'The Jackals did it.'

The voice was unexpected: high-pitched with shock and pain. Arrant's head whipped around, to see one of the village boys, Nagus, Jorbrus's fourteen-year-old nephew, staggering towards them past the ironmaker's.

Arrant had never liked Nagus. He took malicious delight in teasing the smaller children, making fun of them with the nastiness of his clever tongue. But as the older boy stood there trembling, eyes wild and wounded, Arrant's pity for him tumbled out. There, on the doorstep, was the body of Nagus' little brother. Someone had slashed open his chest and taken out his heart.

They'd laid it there on the doorstep for Nagus to find. His *heart*.

Jorbrus – tough, whiskered Jorbrus, who swore all the time and was drunk three days in every four – took the lad into his embrace and rocked him.

'Arrant,' Narjemah said quietly, 'our horses do not like this. Let's get them out of the village, eh?'

Obediently he went back to his mount and took up the reins. The animal – a Quyriot pony – did not appear to be upset, but he led it out of the village anyway, glad to have an excuse to leave the smell of death behind. Yet his unease did not leave him. Horror permeated the air, overwhelming him. He glanced down at his cabochon; it glowed gold.

'Go and round up those pack animals and tie them up,' Narjemah ordered. He felt her emotions, too: her quiet despair welling up from some deep inner place, a more desperate grief for dead friends, her concern for him. For once, he wished his cabochon did not work. He didn't want to feel all this.

Block it out, Tarran suggested.

As he started to round up the horses, he tried to do as Tarran suggested. It was surprisingly easy. Narjemah, Jorbrus, Tarkis, Remolis, Nagus: one by one he banished their feelings from his mind. Yet when the last of those unwanted emotions vanished, he realised *they had not been all there was*.

Other people. People he didn't know. Two of them. Feelings of intense interest, of anticipation. Something hard and nasty.

Tarran? Who——?

I can only feel what you do, his brother said. *I dunno who they are. That's your Magori power speaking to you.*

Arrant tied up the string of pack animals and returned to Narjemah, his stomach churning. 'There's someone out there,' he said.

'What do you mean?' she asked, looking at him sharply.

'There's someone there. Not one of us. Someone I don't know. No, not one person. Two people. They're not – not good people. They're hidden, watching us.'

'Where?'

'Somewhere behind the quarry.' He wanted to point, but she grabbed his hand and stopped him in time. He said instead, careful this time not to look in the direction he meant, 'Up there, overlooking the village.'

'Do they mean us harm?'

'I – I don't think so.'

She frowned, thinking. 'The men who did this – they must have left someone behind.'

'Why?'

'To follow whoever came here. They hope we'll lead them to the Stronghold. Fools. They underestimate the Magor. I'll tell Jorbrus. Don't worry, Arrant, he will deal with it.' She patted him on the shoulder. 'Good lad. Your powers work just when they should, it seems.'

He should have felt pride; instead, he shuddered.

'We never t-told,' Nagus stuttered some time later, as they all gathered together again, away from the houses, away from the stench of the dead. They had to coax him into speaking. He'd been hiding in the ruins of a house, living with the stink of his own family's dead in his nostrils for two days, afraid to move. 'We couldn't. None of us know the way. Them that did wasn't here – Brianus and Tomasi and all them were down south selling a shipment of marble. Gessi and Mariam and her sons had gone to First Farm to help with the pickling. They're not due back till t'morrow. And you was up in the Stronghold. None of us knew. Uncle! We would of done. We would of said it all. We would of told 'em everything. But we couldn't . . . and so they – they—' But he couldn't go on. And those from the Stronghold didn't want to hear.

'Why did they leave you alive?' Tarkis asked. There was accusation in his anguish.

Nagus turned his face away. 'They wanted me to give a message,' he mumbled. 'To the Domina, only they called her someone else. They made me learn it. They said, "Tell Ligea Gayed that Favonius Kyranon of the Jackals remembers what happened to the Stalwarts in Kardiastan."'

'Merciful soul,' Narjemah whispered. 'They know.'

It was the second time Arrant had heard the name of that particular legionnaire. *Do you remember what she did to the Stalwarts in Kardiastan?* he asked Tarran.

Yes, his brother replied, *of course. We were there. She made them turn back after they invaded, and many of them died. But she saved the Mirage. Favonius was a tribune and he worked out she was to blame. He was so angry. He was all coiled up inside, like a snake wanting to strike, full of venom. We didn't like him. His hatred was like a – a dark patch in his middle. When people have that feeling inside, they hurt.*

Hurt? They feel hurt?

No – they hurt us, the Mirage Makers. Their touch burns. Arrant, don't hate . . .

Arrant felt his brother's worry in his head like a dull ache, and wondered if what he felt for Favonius right then was hurting his brother.

He looked back at the village. There were too many bodies to bury just then, so Jorbrus and his sons were stacking them in the only cottage that still had part of its roof. Tarkis wept as he carried the blood-covered corpse of a girl. Arrant knew her: Janissa. She had taught him to play the game they called knucklebones. She'd just lost her front teeth and spoke with a lisp. He'd teased her about it when he'd seen her last.

I hate Favonius Kyranon, he told Tarran. *One day I will kill him.*

Tarran didn't reply, but Arrant could feel him fretting. *I can't help it,* he thought. *I do hate this Favonius. And he does deserve to die for what he did here.*

When Jorbrus and his sons disappeared shortly after they had all started back on their way to the Stronghold once more, he didn't ask where they went, or why.

He knew, and he was glad.

He and Narjemah and Nagus rode on upwards, alone.

CHAPTER TWENTY-FOUR

Once, they would have held this meeting in the Hall of the Magoroth in the Pavilions. There would have been an agate floor and a great beamed ceiling, while the walls would have been of polished adobe. It would have been a Kardi building, with Kardi simplicity. But the Pavilions were long gone; what had not been burned had been demolished by the conquering Tyranians. Over the many years of occupation, most of the other Kardi public buildings had vanished as well.

Instead, they had this. This huge room with its columns and statues and its cold grey and white marble. Temellin would have liked to turn all his Magor power on it, to have reduced it to rubble and dust, but that would have been a foolish gesture. There were too few buildings in Madrinya as it was.

He looked around at his fellow Magoroth, still chatting among themselves, and noticed the gaps. Selwith, dead in the battle at Asidin this past year, the only one of the original Ten to be killed in the fighting. Welmith and Kelsa, young Magoroth cousins, killed on a ship when wards broke during a sea battle. Fezani, whose head had been staked on the walls of Madrinya: no one had ever found out how the Tyranians had managed to kill him. Tavia, Garis' wife.

Temellin sighed.

There were still fifty-eight of them, fifty-eight adult Magoroth in this long marble hall, most of them young. Happy now, able to think ahead to a new future. Temellin himself felt a thousand years old, scarred and sullied by every one of those years, by every battle, by every death, by every tortured body. *Sarana, I need you here . . .*

Sarana, I need you.

He buried his feelings deep so none would sense them, and wondered if he would be able to persuade this roomful of Magoroth to follow his lead in the one thing that mattered to him more than any other.

He stood and began to speak at the first meeting of the Magoroth Council since they had gained their independence.

'We have only one further policy matter to discuss,' he said, just as the late-afternoon sun began to shine directly through the colonnaded arcades into the main hall. He strove to maintain the neutrality of his tone and hide his anxiety from those who had the power to feel it. 'And it is a serious one. As you all know, we are the first of the provinces to have reclaimed our status as a self-governing state, independent of the Exaltarchy. We withstood the might of the legions because the legions could not concentrate on us – you all know that. Rebellion throughout the Exaltarchy over the past two years, including in Tyrans itself, saved us. Rebels elsewhere have suffered even more than we have, because they have no Magor. And their fight goes on.'

He cleared his throat and looked around the small gathering. Emotions flickered around the room, invisible, yet as obvious to him as if they were sparks rising from a wood fire. Concern, worry, annoyance, doubt, cynicism – feelings to be read by all, unspoken, yet a language for all that. It was a struggle to ignore what was silently said, a struggle not to be thrown by the suspicion that danced in the air.

He continued, knowing that he was about to confirm their mistrust of his motives. 'I want you to consider whether we should now help them. In particular, help Miragerin-sarana in Tyrans, so that she will have certain victory. Then the Exaltarch will fall, and the true break-up of the empire can proceed.

'If we don't, we may find the Exaltarchy's legions landing on our shores once more.'

'Help her how?' Korden asked. His long aristocratic face was pinched with distaste.

'Send a number of Magoroth to Tyrans, the way we have sent Garis to other places.'

There was a long silence. Temellin noted the exchanged glances, the fidgeting, the deliberate dampening of their emotions. They all knew how he felt about Sarana. They all knew she was the rightful Miragerin of Kardiastan: he had told them that long ago. And he knew that everyone in that room was glad she had elected to leave. With the possible exception of Jahan and his sibling wife, Jessah, not one of them had liked her.

I wish Garis were here to back me in this, he thought. But Garis was still away, stirring up rebellion in the Exaltarchy's provinces.

'We owe Tyrans nothing,' Korden said flatly. Temellin's heart sank. Korden, in years the most senior of the Magoroth, was respected by all. Without his support, it would be hard to win over a majority of the Council. And Temellin needed consensus, for if a Mirager took action without it, he risked breaking the Covenant with the Mirage Makers. Without the Covenant, the Mirage Makers could withhold the bestowing of Magor swords and ultimately the granting of cabochons.

Temellin's stare in Korden's direction was as hard as he could make it. 'We owe Sarana *everything*. Without her, the Mirage would have fallen to the Stalwarts, and every one of our children would have been slaughtered. Without her rebellion in Tyrans, we might never have won here.'

'She was the daughter of a traitor, of the man who caused our downfall,' Markess said. Her bitterness contained the bile of loss; she was Selwith's widow.

Temellin tried to remain calm, to sound reasonable. 'She was three years old at the time, hardly responsible for the actions of her father, who was, may I remind you, our Mirager. *She* was responsible for nothing. And if her breeding *does* matter to you, then why not consider who her mother was? Wendia was the first Magoroth to die fighting legions on Kardi soil. She died with her sword in her hand. By all reports, she caused the death of many legionnaires before they overwhelmed her. Sarana, then, was the daughter of a woman we honour for bravery.'

Jahan stood, a troubled expression on his face. 'I don't think who Sarana is should enter into this,' he said. 'What we ought to be deciding is whether we want to ensure the success of the rebellion against the Exaltarch by helping the rebels in their fight. Mirager-Temellin is right. We should help those who fight the Exaltarch. Otherwise we may spend the rest of our lives fighting at our borders.'

'Rubbish,' Markess said, her flood of emotion deliberately scathing. 'The legions are never going to return here, not in our lifetime! Bator Korbus cannot risk another such defeat – his own people would turn on him. Besides, I don't think he could persuade the legions to return here, not after what we did to them.' She gave a nasty smile. 'Confronted with the Magor, their bowels turn to water.'

'Markess is correct there,' Korden agreed. He stood up as she sat down. The grey slashes in his hair and the deep modulations of his voice added to the distinguished air he exuded so effortlessly.

Blast him, Temellin thought. *How the Ravage hells does he always manage to appear so reasonable and wise, even when he is being just the opposite?*

'Mirager-temellin,' Korden continued, 'we do not need to help Sarana or the rebellion in order to save ourselves. We do not require saving. The legions are not coming back here. This decision should be made on the basis of whether we are in a position to aid others. And my answer is no, we are not. You only have to look around Madrinya. People are hurting! So many have died; there are still thousands wounded. Ordinary Kardis. There are children suffering from the effects of an inadequate diet, caused by the breakdown in trade and transport since we went to war. There are people living ten in a room because so many homes were levelled. We all know the legions tried to wipe out vale after vale – crops destroyed, lakes poisoned, buildings fired. Even trees were felled and then burned so we could not use them. Trees!' A collective shudder swept the room in response to his horror. In a land where trees rarely grew unless deliberately nurtured, the death of even one copse was a disaster.

Once again, Korden aimed his words at Temellin. 'We need to think of our own first. We need to lead our people, to make up for the years when we withdrew into the Mirage and ignored their pain. We need to tend our sick, to heal our land, to replant, to build anew. This is our foremost duty. This is *your* duty as our Mirager. Only when that is done can we consider what happens outside our borders. In fact, I would urge you to ask Garis to come home. He is needed here; we are *all* needed.'

Grief speared Temellin. He felt their approval of Korden's words – their emotion not sparks now, but ropes woven of the strong fibres of their belief. They turned to him as one, and the only pity for his predicament came from Jessah and Jahan.

There wasn't even any need for a vote.

When they filed out of the hall a few minutes later, most avoided looking at him. Out of courtesy, they curbed their feelings and muted their conversation. Most, he knew, would take no pleasure from his grief. He had their respect, sometimes even their love. Could he blame them if they cared for their own more than others fighting far-off battles? They'd had their fill of death and war and being warriors.

The room emptied of all but Korden. He remained where he was, seated at Temellin's right hand, flicking his fingernail against his exposed cabochon. It had become a mannerism with him, born perhaps of his sense of wonder that they could at last wear their cabochons openly.

'Do you really hate her that much?' Temellin asked.

'That's unfair. I don't hate her at all.'

'That's a lie. Every time you mention her name I feel your antipathy.'

'That's a different thing to hate. I don't *like* her and I don't mind admitting that.'

'Why – because she was the one who saved your wife and children from the Stalwarts instead of yourself?'

'Don't be ridiculous, Temellin. I don't like her because she is Tyranian, not Kardi, for all her birth. I don't like her because I think she is a cold-eyed bitch. I don't like her because I think she used you.'

'Used me?'

'She's the mother of the next Mirager.'

'You think she did that *deliberately*? How little you know! Korden, she could have been the *present* Mirager – Miragerin – if she had so chosen!'

'She knew we'd never stand for it.'

'You would have had to, had I refused to use my sword to make cabochons. I gave her the choice.'

Korden failed to contain the contempt he felt. 'Then you're more of a fool than I thought. Temel, she went back to get revenge on those who mocked her. She went back to obtain far more power than we were prepared to offer. That's the kind of person she is! All right, she's not the evil woman I once thought her to be, but she is still tainted by what was done to her by those men. She is not an honourable person. And I will *never* forgive her for taking the next Mirager of Kardiastan away from his birth-place.'

Temellin was silent for a long time. He fingered the hilt of his sword where it lay, poking out of its scabbard on the table in front of him. 'You are angry with me for refusing to take Arrant after his birth.'

'So angry, I dare not even let you feel my rage, because you would never forget it, Temellin.'

'So be it, but it was indeed my doing, not hers.'

Korden slammed his hand palm down on the arm of his chair. 'It was the idiocy of a man who lost his wits when he fell in love. And she connived at it! The heir should be brought up here. Trained by the Magoroth, in his homeland, among his own kind. How can he learn to lead Kardis if he never meets any? What you did, in some puerile attempt to please the woman you loved, was irresponsible and idiotic. Culpable! *And you didn't ask our permission.*'

'I didn't have to. Family matters are not governed by Magoroth consensus!'

'A *family* matter? The boy is the next Mirager! Surely that concerns us all? Surely that even concerns the Mirage Makers! It was morally wrong, Temellin. And stupid. Cabochon knows what sort of a Mirager-heir we will receive when you send for him. In fact, you'd better send for him right now; he will be safer here than in the middle of a rebellion. And at least he will learn who he is, and what his duties are. And he had better be a capable Magoroth, or I will fight to prevent him being recognised as Mirager-heir to my very last breath. And so will my family.'

He leaned in closer to Temellin and lowered his voice in volume, even as he increased its intensity. 'I have eleven children, Temel, every one of them Magor-strong. Four of my boys proved themselves over and over as warriors and leaders during the war. My eldest daughter, Erenwith, has a clever mind and enormous popularity. The next, Flavissa, is one of the finest Magoroth talents I have seen. Any of them would make a fine Mirager, and if your boy doesn't match up, then I'll be asking the Magoroth Council to make someone else Mirager-heir in the hope that they will consider one of my family. Just because leadership is usually passed down from father to child doesn't mean it always has to be that way.'

Temellin tensed. Korden had never been so blunt before, and there was more than enough truth there for it to hurt. Perhaps Arrant's talents wouldn't match up to those of Korden's children. Nonetheless, the thought of a member of the Korden family – particularly Tirgan, the eldest – being made Mirager-heir left Temellin feeling ill. He said, as calmly as he could, 'Arrant *is* being raised by Kardis, Korden. By Sarana herself, by his Theura nurse and now by Illuser Foran. Moreover, he can only benefit by the wider exposure to peoples outside our nation. Haven't we learned anything from what happened to us? Mirager-solad and those before him ignored the outside world, pretended it didn't exist, and look what happened! Your children have skills, it's true, but they look inwards. My son will know what's out there when it is his turn to rule this land. He will be a Mirager to be proud of.'

'You are a foolish dreamer, Temel! May the Shiver Barrens swallow you—'

'So you can rule as you've always wanted?'

Korden's breath caught. 'I never desired it to be at the price of your death. You must know that.'

Temellin took a deep breath. 'Yes. Yes, I know that. But you wanted it, nonetheless. And now you have revenge of a kind: you have led the others into refusing help for Sarana.'

'I didn't do it for revenge!'

'No, I know.'

'It was *right*, Temel.'

'It was betrayal.'

'Nevertheless, *right*.'

They exchanged another hard stare. It wasn't the first time they had flirted with an irrevocable schism.

Korden broke the eye contact first. He stood, nodded, and left the room. Temellin stayed behind, sitting alone in a patch of light from the last rays of the setting sun.

Sarana, he thought. *Sarana. I am so, so sorry.*

CHAPTER TWENTY-FIVE

It was raining when Ligea and her escort passed through the burned ruins of Prianus two months later, on their way up to the Stronghold. Gusts of wind sifted the drizzle at them from all directions, ensuring the shivering misery of sodden clothes and chafed skin.

She'd been warned what to expect. Narjemah had sent a message telling her. Even so, her spirits foundered at the sight of those desolate ruins and blackened beams.

Goddess, Favonius, how could you come to this? You, who once spoke to me of honour?

She rode straight through with her men, not looking right or left. *Your fault*, the stones whispered as she passed. *You should have killed him when you had the chance back in the Mirage.*

'Will we have to abandon the Stronghold?' Arrant asked her the following day. 'Narjemah says we ought to, cos they'll find us here too.'

'When I am here, I'll know if Favonius or his Jackals come anywhere close,' she reassured him. 'And if I am not around, there is always Foran. He can also sense the approach of strangers.'

Ligea felt Arrant wince and slipped her arm around his shoulders to give him a hug. 'There's no need to be afraid, really. You will be safe here. You know what the trails are like, Arrant. A twisted maze of defiles, each looking just like the last. I had to have a Quyriot guide along that route almost ten times before I could remember the way myself!'

He didn't seem comforted, and she wondered if she had mistaken the reason for his wince. Maybe he'd thought her words a comment on his continued Magor incompetence. Apart from that day at Prianus when he'd sensed the two legionnaires Favonius had left behind, his powers had been erratic. Foran had just told her that he'd burned a hole in an untapped wine barrel the day before, when he was learning how to light a candle. What should she do about that? Commiserate? Scold him? Gods, he could have hurt someone. Perhaps his lack of control could threaten them all ...

She hid a sigh. Being a mother was so damnably *hard* sometimes. Why had no one ever warned her there were so many pitfalls?

She smiled brightly and let slip her delight at the good news she carried. He didn't react, so she added, 'Cheer up – I have had such good news from your father! I actually knew a while back, but I wanted to tell you myself instead of sending a message. *Kardiastan is free.* The last of the legions left Kardi soil about four months ago.'

He still didn't react, almost as if he had already known. But that was impossible, of course.

'That's good,' he said. 'But doesn't that mean there will be more legions here, to fight you?'

'I'm hoping we will have some Magoroth help to compensate. Your father will send people, of course.'

'Will you be staying long this time?'

She thought she heard a wistfulness in his tone, but it wasn't reflected in any discernible display of emotion. It was becoming harder and harder to read him. Did he know he was hiding himself? Or was it just something he did without being aware of it? Aloud she said, 'I have to leave again soon. There is to be a slave uprising in Getria. The city should be ours soon. Next year, when you are nine, we will take Tyr.'

He didn't say anything, almost as if he didn't dare believe it. Or, perhaps, he couldn't picture life being any different.

Vortexdamn, I wish I could have offered you a better life than this, Arrant. And then, sadly, I wish I could have had a better one myself.

Life went on as usual for Arrant. He studied and trained and shared part of his waking hours with Tarran. Foran kept him too busy to miss his mother when she was gone, although, in truth, he didn't think it would have made much difference if she had been there all the time. Part of him felt Ligea had left him long ago.

She's not a mother like other boys have mothers. An unbidden disloyal thought, but he couldn't help what popped into his head, could he? Now, on the rare occasions he saw her, it was as a commander of an army, a woman whose glance barely softened when it alighted on him. This was not the woman who had played with him on the way to Kardiastan. This woman was a soldier, with a soldier's eyes. With a hardness to her muscles that matched something in her core. He might not have been able to command his power at will to read emotions, but he could feel her toughness anyway. It wasn't what he wanted from a mother. Nor what he needed.

Yet, as most of the fighting became concentrated around Getria, she was able to come back to the Stronghold more often. On one visit, she told him that his father was unable to send the Magoroth help she had hoped to receive. Her tone was neutral when she imparted this news, but he knew she was hurt.

Temellin doesn't care enough . . . The thought writhed there in his mind, twisting his memories of his father.

And that was enough to bring Tarran to him. *Temellin cares,* he protested. *I am sure he does.*

'Then why does he refuse to help us?' he asked.

We – we don't know, Tarran admitted. *Arrant, everyone left, so we don't know what's happening any more. In the old days we had the power to find out even when no one came to us, but not now. We must conserve our strength. We are fighting for our very life.*

Arrant felt those words like a blow, but didn't know what to say.

Tarran continued, *Next time a young Magoroth comes to collect their sword, we will ask for news. But that will only be what that person happens to know . . .*

Getria finally fell to Gevenan's men. The victory was greeted by jubilation in the Stronghold, but the joy didn't last. Within four months of the city's fall, it was besieged by a force that included the Jackal Legion and was led by Bator Korbus himself.

Gevenan and his men were trapped inside the city walls and the snow-season set in.

Ligea, who was in the Stronghold when she received the news, had to wait a month before she could leave because the passes were blocked with snow. As soon as the weather relented, she left with all the men she could muster. Yet again, Arrant could only watch them ride out, and both dream of and dread the day he would be old enough to go with them.

The day everything changed, just six weeks later, started normally enough: breakfast, chores, then sword practice, after which he went for his usual lessons with Foran, who was trying to coach him on how to create a wind with his cabochon. No, not a wind. Just a breeze. Just a waft of air enough to stir the feather Foran held in his fingers. And he couldn't do it.

The week before, he had managed that much; in fact, he had created a whirlwind. Unfortunately, he hadn't managed to keep a hold on it, and it had gone spinning into the fireplace. It was just bad luck that the servants hadn't yet cleaned out the ashes of the fire that had burned there the night before . . .

Foran had not been pleased. They'd both had to go and bathe.

Well, he certainly wasn't having that problem today. He couldn't even make a feather move.

Foran looked at him across the table. 'Your mother just arrived,' he said. 'I've been sensing her approach for the past two hours. I've been waiting for you to tell me.'

He sat dumbly, joy and failure warring in his mind.

'You had no idea, did you?'

It's not my fault. I do try . . . 'May I go and—?' But before he could get the question out, the door opened and Ligea strode in, laughing and aglow.

As she hugged Arrant, Foran said, 'You look happy, Magoria. More good news?'

Light sparkled along her skin like moonlight on snow. 'The time has come,' she said. 'Before the next snow-season, we'll all be sleeping in the Exaltarch's palace!'

We?

She touched her cabochon to Arrant's, and the contact stimulated his into action. He was flooded with emotions. Foran's: nervous anxiety, twinges of fear, a gentle sorrow. And hers: elation, joy, a ferocious excitement. He looked at her in surprise. *Vortex, she loves this!* Events that made everyone else feel jittery brought a shine of anticipation to her eyes. He hadn't realised that. Her elation disturbed him.

She laughed and said, 'We are finally ready – these next few days see the culmination of all my plans. My only regret is that Gayed Lucius doesn't know how I spent his fortune! Ah, Arrant – how I'm looking forward to this coming battle . . .'

He suddenly felt as if his chest was stuffed with pallet-cotton. For a moment breathing became something he had to actively think about doing and his recently eaten lunch seemed to have a mind of its own.

She didn't notice. 'I want you to understand what's going on, Arrant. You're nine now – and oh, I'm sorry I missed your anniversary day yet again, didn't I? Anyway, I think you are old enough. I have nine-year-old stable boys in my army.' She turned to where Foran had pinned his charts on the wall, beckoning him over. 'Come and look at the map.' She pointed a finger. 'We are here. This is Kardiastan here. Gala, Pythia, Cormel, Quyr, Corsene and Altan.' She jabbed at each as she named them. 'They are all at open war with the Exaltarchy. Down here, the King of Akowarn has declared himself free of vassalage and has closed his borders to all Tyranians, especially levy collectors. In Janus and over here in Pilgath, slaves are in open rebellion. Right here in Tyrans, we own the north, from Getria as far as the Cormel border.'

'Gevenan isn't stuck in Getria any more?' Foran asked.

'Not any longer. We broke through the ring and we have scattered the besieging forces with the help of my Magor power. The Exaltarch has retreated to Tyr with most of his men. The Jackals, however, are on their way here. Following me.'

Arrant paled. 'Here?' *Fighting.* Men with the light dying in the black depths of their eyes. That horrible smell of death that no one mentioned when they spoke of the glories of battle and victory.

'Jorbrus is leading them. Do you know he's been sober ever since Prianus was attacked? He's a brave man, but one who no longer cares whether he lives or dies. They think he's a traitor and they believe they have me – all of us – trapped. But tomorrow we'll be away through the back pass, leaving them an empty fort while we sweep down on Tyr.'

His heart somersaulted. *Tomorrow?*

'But won't the Jackals follow as soon as they find the Stronghold empty?' Foran asked.

'They will try. But I have plans for them. Berg Firegravel and his men will take care of the Jackals.' She grinned wickedly.

'And me?' Arrant asked. *What about me?* He felt guilty even as he asked. She had more important things to think about.

'Well, that depends on how you've progressed with your Magor abilities. I could risk having you close by so that you'd know what was going on – *if* you can look after your own protection. Otherwise, I'll leave you in Getria, along with the others from here who cannot fight. You would be with Narjemah.'

He looked down at his feet, his shame a black thing in his mind. 'I can only build a good ward sometimes. Sometimes I can do it really good.' *But not often.*

She pursed her lips. 'Let me talk to Foran. Wait outside on the training ground. I'll join you in a moment.'

Reluctantly, he went outside, and Tarran, who had been lurking inside his head since she'd arrived, said, *Hey, things are really happening, aren't they? You'll be going to live in Tyr! That'll be exciting. I rather liked Tyr, what I saw of it. Which wasn't much, actually, I suppose. How about listening to what Ligea and Foran are talking about?*

'You know perfectly well that I shouldn't. And that I probably can't anyway.' He scuffed his sandalled foot in the dirt. Overhead, jackdaws rose from the roof in a black whirl, calling to one another like yapping mountain jackals.

Go on, give it a try.

He allowed himself to be persuaded, pushing away the thought that Tarran really didn't understand about things like manners. He focused his hearing in the right direction. He edited out the sounds from the neighbouring kitchen and homed in on Foran and Ligea – all without the slightest mistake, as though he never had any difficulty with such an exercise.

Easy as making a tree with feathers, Tarran said gleefully.

Arrant refrained from pointing out that anyone other than a Mirage Maker would have trouble with the creation of a feathered tree.

'So,' Foran was saying, 'the time has come.' He didn't sound happy.

'Yes – the Exaltarchy is taking its last tottering steps.' Ligea did not bother to hide her own sense of satisfaction. 'Now, about Arrant—'

A pause followed. Then: 'What can I say? He's a bright lad with a sharp, inquiring mind. He could be a scholar if that was his destiny. Or an engineer. He has a fine grasp of all branches of mathematics, especially geometry.'

'But—?'

'He's no Magori.'

Arrant felt her anger even across the intervening space. 'With his parentage, how can he be anything else?'

'Magoria, I've tried everything and so has Narjemah. And so has he. Mirageless soul, how he has worked! My heart has ached for him. But he just doesn't seem trainable. The power is there, but it is unpredictable and unreliable.'

Another pause. Then an agonised, 'Why? Foran, why? You've worked with him for four years now. You must have *some* idea.'

'I have thought of two possible explanations, but they are both just that: possibilities. I have no real answers.'

'Go on.'

'Sometimes, when I've been teaching children to read, I have come across a student who, although very intelligent, seems to have difficulties in comprehending the written word, no matter how hard they try. I have come to the conclusion that such children have a problem with communication within themselves. The eye sees the word, but somewhere between eye and understanding there is a – a break. It's a very small break; they can see and comprehend anything else. It's just the written word that escapes them. Sometimes, with training, they can overcome this problem. Sometimes not. Perhaps Arrant's problem is similar: there is a break between his cabochon and his head. The power *is* there, waiting to be used, but his sense cannot always find and control it.'

'And the second possibility?'

'He has too much power.'

'Too *much* power?'

'It's possible. Magoria, you and the Mirager-temellin stand at the end of a long line of highly skilled Magoroth, people who have chosen marriage partners with more care for their Magor lineage than they had for their own hearts. Power has been strengthened again and again by such unions. Temellin and you – you both have more power in your cabochons than some of your ancestors had with their Magor swords in their hands.'

That's true, Tarran agreed. *Some of your forebears couldn't have trimmed their toenails with a beam from their Magor blades, not even to save their lives.*

Arrant shuddered, although he wasn't sure why.

'So?' Ligea asked.

'So maybe it has come to the stage with Arrant where there

is simply too much power concentrated in one person; too much for him to control. Perhaps we should be grateful that he doesn't get his hands on it, so to speak; he might burn himself, and us, to ash if he ever did.'

Arrant sat down on the ground with a thump; the pallet-cotton seemed to have gone from his chest to his knees.

'I don't believe that,' Ligea said flatly.

Probably another load of street sweepings, Tarran agreed cheerfully. *I don't suppose Foran knows what he's talking about. You're controlling your power perfectly at the moment, aren't you?*

Arrant didn't answer. It was true, though; just then he could hear every word, he could sense every nuance – and it was suddenly so *easy*.

'I could be wrong,' Foran admitted. 'But be wary of ever giving him a Magor sword.'

Her reply was as cold as snow-melt. 'He will have his sword, just as every Magoroth does. It is his birthright. And one day he will exchange it for his Mirager's sword.'

'I doubt that. No one will accept such a person as the Mirager. He'd have to fight for the right, and he would lose. It wouldn't come to that anyway; the Mirager holds his sword by consensus, as I am sure you know. Temellin can declare Arrant to be Mirager-heir – in fact, he has already done so – but it has to be confirmed by council when he is sixteen, and what Temellin says will mean little if the lad is found wanting.

'Magoria, Arrant is a fine boy, but I doubt that he's the stuff that Miragers are made of. Even his character lacks . . . well, independent strength, somehow. Why, he still has an imaginary friend, and he's really far too old for that kind of nonsense. He should have outgrown it.'

'What imaginary friend?'

'Didn't you know? Well, he does try to hide it, but occasionally he forgets and I hear him talking. It's not uncommon among lonely children, but Arrant has more important things to concentrate on. It's time he forgot such silly diversions.'

Does he mean me? Tarran asked indignantly. *A silly diversion?*

Arrant sighed. 'I think he must. I don't have any imaginary friends.'

There was a long silence, then Ligea said, in a neutral voice, 'Sometimes I think perhaps you were the wrong person to be given charge of my son, Foran. Anyway, it's time for you to return to Kardiastan. I shall arrange it as soon as we have taken Tyr. In the meantime, stay with Arrant. Keep him safe if he himself cannot manage his own warding. Right now I shall see for myself just what progress, if any, he has made in his Magor studies.'

Arrant stopped listening as worry swamped him.

Hey, don't panic, Tarran said. *You can do it, you know you can.*

'Yeah. I shall probably set fire to the roof tiles and scare blood-spots into every egg the hens lay for the next year,' he said. As Ligea came back outside, he tried to look less gloomy.

'Arrant,' she said, 'I want you to show me what you can do.' She was coaxing; it was a role that didn't suit her and he almost flinched away when she laid a hand on his shoulder.

'Can you focus on, um, the people in the kitchen and tell me what is happening?'

You can do it. You just did—

And once again he could, much to his surprise. There was something bubbling on the stove; the fire crackled on the hearth. 'Chop those up finer, my girl, else cook'll be after you—' 'Fetch in some more water, Filgo, and then stoke up them coals—' He could hear it all, even the ragged purr of the kitchen cat.

He told her what he heard.

'And their emotions? What is the lad Filgo feeling as he goes to get the water?'

He frowned. 'He's – I dunno. He's sort of empty. The girl chopping the vegetables, that's Kimma, she's sullen. Like someone who's just had an argument. And the other fellow there, that's Rorn. He's sort of excited. Like he's got a secret that no one else knows.'

She gave a husky laugh. 'Exactly right! I bumped into him on my way in to see you and Foran, and told him that he had to kill all the chickens for cooking because everyone would be leaving. Apparently he hasn't told the others yet. Arrant, I want you to show me what else you can do.'

She took him through the standard elementary uses of a cabochon, and he found he could do it all: suppress or enhance the golden glow of the gem and the way it tinged his skin, draw wards that held, cause pain, burn holes at a distance, enhance his sight and hearing, even manage the talent that usually gave him the most trouble of all: telling a lie from the truth. He wasn't sure who was most surprised, himself or Ligea.

Then she led him over to the rough-built stone barrier that edged the training ground. Beyond, there was nothing but the eroded fissures and rugged walls of the canyons that led southwards towards Prianus, Getria and Tyr. She waved her arm towards the cliff walls scoured by the raw savagery of time and weather, then rested her hand on his shoulder again. 'Bathe your senses in light, Arrant, and tell me what you can see and feel and hear out there.'

The wind first. He could hear its low whine among the rocks as it gusted up the canyons. He thought: *Cabochon – why is all this suddenly so simple?* Then the desolate wail of a bird of prey ... Yes, he could see it, too, bring it closer, identify it by the russet colour of its feathers, note the way it rolled, whiffling to lose the wind from under its wings so it could plunge down after its victim.

And then he felt them. Hundreds of them. Gorclaks too. And one, one who burned with venom. The air shimmered with his emotion, rippled—

'What do you feel?'

I'll be Ravage-blasted! What in the world is that?

'Legionnaires,' Arrant said, answering them both. 'A whole legion? Too many to count. I can sense Jorbrus. And there's someone there ...'

'Who?' Ligea asked, sharply attentive.

'I dunno. But he hates us.' He was unable to suppress a shiver. *Come off it, Arrant. It's hot enough today to curl hen feathers! That was because I'm scared pissless, you idiot.*

'Yes, I'm afraid he does. I can feel him too. That's Favonius Kyranon.'

The intensity of her regret caught him unawares and he stared at her, surprised.

She didn't seem to notice. 'I'm almost tempted to forget about Bator Korbus and lead my men down on him instead, right now, and wipe him and his wretched Jackals off the face of the earth.' She smiled wryly. 'Almost, but not quite. I have a larger prey; Favonius must wait for Berg. With a little luck, the Quyriots will do it for me.'

Her sorrow-relief brushed by his mind before she closed it off to his senses. Then she turned him to face her, saying, 'Arrant, there's not a single other Magoroth except Temellin who could have told me what was out there the way you just did. Those Jackals are still two days' ride away, too far for ordinary far-sensing, *yet you felt them*. You can do things most Magoroth can only do when their powers are enhanced by a sword, and some-times not even then.'

'But I – I can't usually.' His misery bubbled up; he had to be honest with her. 'I can't usually do anything much: at least, not right. Today was the first time everything has gone just the way it should for ages.'

She considered him thoughtfully. 'You know what I think? I think you're just too young to control all the power you have. You have more than most – Foran just suggested that, too – and it's too much for someone your age. When you're older, you'll be able to bend it to your bidding whichever way and whenever you like. You just have to be patient.'

One part of him knew she wanted to believe that, rather than Foran's interpretation. He hoped she was right, but in the centre of his chest there was only a sliding, sinking feeling that made him want to be sick.

Tarran, it can't happen, can it? The way Foran said? That I'll end up killing people?

Tarran didn't reply, although Arrant could feel his discomfort as he grappled with the question.

'And,' Ligea added, 'no more imaginary playmates, eh, Arrant? You have to be grown-up now.'

'He's not imaginary! He's alive, even though he doesn't have a body—'

'Please, Arrant, don't be silly. I'm surprised at you, believing in such things still. You are quite old enough to sort out what's real from what you've been making up.' She waved a hand at the defile below. 'We are on the verge of battle, and if you are going to come with me, you have to leave your childhood behind.'

It's all right, Tarran said cheerfully. *She doesn't have to know about me.*

He hid a sigh, and nodded. 'All right,' he mumbled.

They stood side by side, looking out over that rock-rough landscape, drawn together in companionship by their shared perceptions, by the oppressiveness of what they both felt: an army on the march. And then the moment splintered. People came for orders, there were things to be done, and she had no more time to share with him.

She could be right, said Tarran after she'd gone. *We Mirage Makers know you have the kind of power we've never felt before.*

'Yeah. And maybe next time I try to use it I'll end up like a wood-possum on a spit when the fire's too high,' he said morosely. '"Look, that once was Arrant; now he's a hunk of charcoal."'

Tarran didn't reply, but Arrant felt his comfort anyway.

CHAPTER TWENTY-SIX

Damn the rain. Damn the blasted godforsaken bloody mountain weather.

He had the best horse Brotherhood money could buy, and still the beast was slipping and sliding in the loose scree. He peered through the driving rain at the man on the horse ahead of him. *Jorbrus*. The drunken sot had better know where he was leading them or he, Favonius, would skin the foul-mouthed helot alive. Why the Vortex wasn't *he* slipping and sliding all over the place? How did that ridiculous mountain pony with its short legs and unkempt hair manage to keep plodding upwards as if it were strolling across a meadow in the sodding sunshine?

He glanced behind. He could just make out the first twenty or so Jackals, heads down against the rain, mounts stumbling.

He sighed and turned to yell at the guide. 'Hey, Jorbrus!'

The man ahead reined in and waited for him to draw alongside. 'It'll be getting dark soon. Is there no shelter around here anywhere?'

'There's a ruined village just around the next bend,' the man said. 'No roofs on them houses no more, but's better than naught.'

'Good. We'll stop there.' That must be the village they'd destroyed last time they came this way. They'd reduced the place to ashes, they'd tortured and killed, yet he had not found the rumoured Stronghold.

He could hear the screaming still . . .

He hadn't tortured the children himself; he'd left that up to

Crassus, one of his foot soldiers who loved nothing better than carving up living bodies. But there had been a time when he wouldn't have allowed such a thing under his command. Back when he was a Stalwart. He took no pleasure from hearing children shriek or seeing their parents beg or watching his men rape anyone they chose. But now such things were necessary and he'd do it again if he had to.

Damn you, Ligea, this is your fault. You made me what I am today. If it wasn't for you, I'd still have my honour. I'd still be a Stalwart, and we'd still be the best damn legion in the Exaltarchy.

Ah, yes. There was the stream where he'd stopped on his way out of the village to wash up. He'd plunged his arms into the iced water and watched the red blood of children swirl away . . .

Merciful Melete, what have I become?

Bitterness swelled and swamped him. The remnants of the Stalwarts, battle-hardened assault troops, had ended up as Jackals on the outside of the walls of Getria, in the mud of a besieging army. Degrading, humiliating work for dregs, not for proud men. He *hated* it. He hated *her*, loathed her with growing rage. *You did this to me, Ligea Gayed. You took everything from me.*

She'd brought his legion down, sullied their name until Stalwart was synonymous with the Mirage Muck-up, as the whole foray across the Alps had come to be known in soldiers' parlance. As if that hadn't been wound enough, she had routed the besieging troops outside Getria with her godless magic and sent them scattering. The others had returned to Tyr, their banners drooping in the dust. But not the Jackals. They had set off on her trail, and this time she would be the one to suffer.

He dreamed of the day he would cut out her gemstone and watch her die. Rathrox Ligatan had said it was a slow and painful death for one of the Magor, and the Magister should know.

Gods, how he wanted to see her writhe. How he wanted to see her beg . . .

They reached the village and stopped for the night. They made camp, cooked and then settled down to sleep. Jorbrus refused to bed down in among the ruins and disappeared to sleep else-where. 'Ghosts,' he said. His face was impassive, bovine even. Yet there was something in his eyes that spoke of horrors no sane man would want to pursue. 'Too many people died here,' he added.

Typical bloody lowborn peasant, Favonius thought. *What do a few shades of the dead matter anyhow? They can't hurt you . . .*

And yet he couldn't sleep that night. It wasn't the shades that kept him awake, if indeed there were any, but his desire to get to Ligea. She was up there somewhere, or so Jorbrus said. The man had sold her for a handful of coins. His eyes had glinted with greed and his voice was sly with glee as he'd regaled Favonius and his centurions with all he knew about the Stronghold. He'd been reluctant to volunteer to lead the legion there, but a few coins had persuaded him. He had been less helpful with regard to Ligea's abilities. 'I dunno much about how it works,' he'd said. 'The likes of me doesn't get to meet the Domina too often.'

Poetic justice, Ligea, for you to be brought down by a traitor to your cause. For that's exactly what you are, a traitor to our whole way of life. You were Tyranian, damn it!

He knew how dangerous she was. In the Mirage, he'd seen her make a whirlwind burn. Still, she had limitations. The use of magic tired her out, he'd seen that too. He just hadn't under-stood at the time what he'd been seeing.

'Will she sense our approach?' he'd asked Jorbrus.

'Not if you sneak up quiet, no. No sentries there neither, until you get to the walls.'

'I've heard her kind can feel things from afar.'

'From the next room, maybe,' Jorbrus had said scornfully. 'Legate, she's just a woman with a special sword. She can do funny things with a wind, that's true. Anything else, she has to be real close. The rest is exaggerated. Even that invisible wall she can build around herself – it takes an age for her to construct it and it don't last long, neither. You can bring her down with a rip-disc, easy.'

'And how do we get a chance to do that?'

'She comes out on the training ground every day. And there's a cliff above. An easy climb. Hide a few of your men up there with a whirlsling or two and she's yours. Easy as cracking an egg. And her men – they'll surrender the moment they lose her. By Ocrastes' balls, they were only slaves!'

Favonius liked the sound of that. But a quick death? That was too easy. He wanted her to recognise him; to know he was the instrument of her defeat.

He smiled to himself, ignoring the discomfort of too thin a sleeping pallet. The numina at the Shimmer Festival had died because Gayed and Bator Korbus had taken them by surprise, caught them without their swords as a result of treachery, killed them quickly before they had time to raise their magic walls, or so Rathrox had told him. He'd do the same . . . but he wouldn't kill her. If they used pebbles instead of rip-discs, they could knock her unconscious. Then he could chop off her hand or dig out her gem.

Somewhere in the back of his mind he marvelled at the ease with which he could speak of her death, the pleasure he felt at the anticipation of actually seeing her dead. And to think he had loved the bitch once. Gods of Elysium, how could he have been so *blind*?

When they arrived at the Stronghold late the next day, the training ground was bare, the buildings open and empty, the whole place deserted. When Favonius turned around to demand an explan-ation of Jorbrus, the man had slipped away into the gathering gloom of evening and was nowhere to be found. Favonius frowned, worry seeping, unwanted, into the chinks of his mind. It couldn't be a trap, could it? Uneasily he remembered the two men he'd left behind in Prianus after they destroyed the village. No one had ever seen them again.

'Search the buildings!' he barked. 'And find that bloody guide!'

They couldn't find Jorbrus, but they did find plenty of signs left by the exodus of men and horses. The following morning they tried to follow the tracks, thinking the rebels would be easy enough to overtake. Instead, they found the route blocked by a landslide and the cliff sides seeded with archers snapping off arrows into the Tyranian columns from hidden crevices.

The Jackals were forced into retreat. On the second day of their descent, they found the route blocked once more, by another landslip that had dammed the stream to flood the defile. They were trapped, at the mercy of a handful of men who knew the gorges and the tracks, who knew of a hundred caves to hide in and a thousand places that offered shelter for an ambush. Men who were far too wily to offer battle but who were deadly with a bow. Warriors loosing arrows down from hidden places at exposed legionnaires who had to send their arrows upwards . . .

A whisper went around the Jackals, fuelled by the glimpses they had of their elusive enemy – of their short stature, their strange garments sewn with beads, their bearskin cloaks and the jewels they wore. *They are numina adorned with the gems of Hades, shades of the underworld who can seize the souls of their enemies . . .*

It took Favonius over two weeks to lead his men to safety and, in spite of the protection offered by their armour and their curved shields, many did not make it.

His hatred for Ligea festered. He didn't care if it took the rest of his life, he would bring her down. Killing her meant nothing; death, after all, was only oblivion, or Acheron's mists at worst. Favonius meant to make her hurt while she still lived. He would find out what she most loved, and he would destroy that. If it was the child they had heard about, then it would be the child he would torture and kill.

He would take everything from her that made life worth living. He would bring her to despair and make her live out her days in misery.

Next time, bitch, I will not fail.

PART FOUR

THE BATTLE

FOR TYR

CHAPTER TWENTY-SEVEN

Arrant's head swivelled around with unexpected suddenness. He jumped like a frightened rabbit and banged his elbow on a towpath bollard. Fortunately no one seemed to notice. Foran, Narjemah, Ligea – plus half the population of the city of Getria – were intent on watching the activity along the river.

What's happening? Tarran asked, swinging Arrant's head back the other way. *Who are all those people? Where are they going? Where are we?*

Arrant stifled a sigh and rubbed his elbow. Having a brother who appeared without warning, and then took over your body without asking first – it made him jump out of his skin, every time. 'We're still in Getria,' he whispered. They had been there several weeks, preparing for the campaign and waiting for better weather. 'Those are Gevenan's soldiers and they are about to leave for Tyr now.'

Gevenan, a scowl on his face, was watching his horse being loaded onto one of the barges tied up to the towpath. In both directions along the river, soldiers were boarding other barges, lugging their armour, weapons and packs.

Mirageless soul, there's hundreds of them!

'Two thousand. And leave my head alone, you brainless idiot! I wish you'd never learned to do that. You'll have everyone thinking I've lost my wits.'

All right, but would you mind looking the other way, then? That's better. And I don't understand. Your mother is sending soldiers down the river to Tyr to fight a war? I don't have anything in my memory that matches that. Soldiers don't fight wars from river barges.

'They're not going to fight from barges! Gev is posing as a tribune bringing in a whole lot of new recruits for the legions in Tyr from a city called Nitida. It's on another branch of the river and it's still in the Exaltarch's hands.'

Isn't the river all wobbly, meandering all over the place? I remember seeing a map of the Tyr river basin, oh, several hundred years ago, and it looked like bits of curly wool.

'It is. It will take ages. That's why Gev looks like a thunder-cloud. He'll be bored out of his mind. But *we* aren't going straight, either. We'll have horses, but we will head south and east, and travel the foothills where there are no towns, until we hit the coast. Then we travel west through the other hills where the aqueducts begin. We want to arrive in Tyr on the same day as Gev.'

Why don't they just ride, too?

'Well, for a start, not everyone can ride a horse. And we don't have enough horses. Besides, Ligea says there will be too many other soldiers on the roads, all bound for Tyr. All pretending to be someone else.'

That should have been reassuring, but to Arrant the scale of it was scary. Besides the men on the barges and another thousand going to Tyr under Ligea's command, there were five thousand heading for the city in small bands from all over the country. Still others were to seize the coastal and central paveways.

He tried to explain that to Tarran. 'She doesn't want the Exaltarch to know there is an army on the march. So most people are travelling in little groups, disguised as something else. Like some of the Quyriots – they're driving our horses, disguised as traders on their way to Tyr markets.'

'Did you say something?' Narjemah asked, overhearing him.

He jumped again. 'Um, oh, just that . . . there are such a lot of them. Gev's men.'

'What happened in Prianus is nothing to what will happen in Tyr,' she said. She sounded grief-stricken. 'I remember war.

When I was a proper Theura, I fought in one. Your mother has set in motion a whirlwind she may not be able to stop.' She gave Arrant a hard look. 'You stay here with me, lad. War is no place for children. You've already seen things no child should.'

'You fought in Kardiastan?' He blinked, trying to equate Narjemah the nurse with the idea that once she had been Theura Narjemah, a soldier.

'Yes. But I was a lot older then than you are now. And trained. And I had a cabochon that worked. I killed people. It haunts me still. Arrant, don't be too eager to see what horror one man can inflict on another.'

'I'm not,' he said. And that was true. It made his stomach heave just to think about it. *But I am to be Mirager one day. How can I run away from everything just because it makes me feel sick?*

He glanced to where Ligea stood, arms folded, watching the barge loading. 'Why the horse, Gev?' she asked.

'I'll be damned if I will sit on some fancy cushioned flat boat to be pulled by a farting donkey all the way to Tyr. I will ride when I can.'

'They're mules, not donkeys,' she pointed out. 'And they'll be slaves once you reach the part of the river controlled by the Exaltarch's legions. Slaves working in shifts and moving you along twenty-four hours a day.'

'So? Gevenan of Inge will not be hauled all the way to Tyr behind slaves, either.'

She ignored that. 'Remember, no one will question you too carefully if you come across as a prosy old bore. You'll find that easy, just complain bitterly to anyone who will listen about the standard of recruits these days.'

Several of the men nearby sniggered, only to be on the receiving end of one of Gevenan's glares. He took her arm and led her out of their earshot, back towards Arrant and Narjemah. 'Damn you, woman, are you trying to make me look a fool in the eyes of my men?'

She grinned. 'Somehow I don't think that's possible. Not since you took Getria. Your men worship you and you know it.' More seriously she added, 'I'm relying on you, Gev. If you don't get these men safely to the walls of Tyr on time—'

'I'll be there,' he growled at her. 'Stop nagging. And I will ride part of the way on my horse, even if it is just down a damned towpath.' He looked at her, and Arrant wondered if he were searching for the right words to say goodbye, to say all the things one should say to a friend before you both go to fight a war. But perhaps he was wrong, because all Gevenan said in the end was, 'You were right about the stirrups, by the way.'

Gevenan turned his attention back to the barges and his men, shouting orders. Ligea hid a smile. As they began to move a few minutes later, Arrant caught a wisp of her emotions and realised with shock just how fond she was of the Ingean soldier. 'But they're always arguing,' he said in protest to Tarran under cover of the cheers of the crowd.

That doesn't mean much. She was always arguing with Brand, too. And Temellin. That's what she does with people she likes.

The remark did not make him feel any better. He didn't like it when his mother was too friendly with men other than his father, even Gevenan. And he remembered the Altani, Brand. When he'd been five years old and they'd arrived at the rebels' stronghold in Altan, a nameless place built mostly of woven reeds and thatch, the man called Brand – warned by sentries – had been waiting on the floating dock. The moment Ligea saw him, her body took on a golden sheen of joy. No one else seemed to notice, but Arrant did. The only other time he'd seen her look quite like that was the day Temellin had come to Ordensa to meet them. Worse, it seemed to Arrant that the way she eyed this Altani giant was no different from the way she had looked at his father.

Even after all these years, Arrant's memory of that moment was vivid.

Brand leaping on board as the boat docked, and whirling Ligea into his arms, laughing and hugging her, then kissing her on the lips with a passion he hadn't tried to disguise. Ligea laughing and pushing him away. Arrant seeing her happiness, feeling it as a personal stab in his heart, a betrayal.

Thinking: She shouldn't do that. Papa wouldn't like it.

He could still recall the Altani's appearance. A large man, tall and muscular and bronzed. His size had been so intimidating, it had been a while before Arrant even noticed the withered arm. Even now, his stomach churned with cold and dislike at the memory.

He didn't have time to think about it, though, because Foran came up just then, saying, 'Time for you to go back and work, young man. You need to perfect your ward-making. You aren't doing nearly enough practice. This is a *battle* we are heading towards!'

As if he didn't know. As if it didn't made him sick just to *think* about it. He just couldn't see the sense in practising all the time when it never resulted in the slightest bit of improvement.

Three days later, in spite of his lack of reliable success with ward-building, he left for Tyr with Ligea's forces.

Forbidden to speak except in a whisper, they walked under a night sky, the stars a bright splendour in the plush of moonless black. The only sound was the occasional splash; they walked ankle-deep in water. Even though the snow-season was over and the great plains of the Tyr valley were warm with a desert-season sun during the day, the coldness of that mountain water numbed their bare feet. At least the stones were water-worn smooth, easy on softened soles.

They carried no lights, but Arrant could see the stone walls on either side, waist height to the average man. An adult could have reached out and touched them both at the same time, so closely did they hem in the marching line of men. The soldier in front of him was humpbacked in the dark, his food pack and buckler making him appear misshapen as he marched through the water using his spear as a staff. His sandals were slung around his neck, his cloak wrapped tight.

In front of him was another man, similarly burdened, similarly clad, and another, and another, as far as Arrant could see. Just as there would be behind, if he cared to look.

Ants, he thought. *We're just like a line of ants marching off to make war on another nest . . . and miles to go before dawn.*

Somewhere at the back was Foran, using his senses so that they would not be surprised from behind; somewhere up ahead Ligea led them, her senses alert as well.

And here I am in the middle, because that's the safest place.

At least he had persuaded the two of them to allow him to come. Not to fight, of course. Just to be there. He hadn't really wanted to, but he knew there was no choice. Not really. Not for someone born to be a Mirager. He had to prove himself, and what other way did he have when his powers were so unpredictable?

I'm cold and I'm scared and I wish I wasn't here. It's strange, but I feel lonely even when there are people all around me.

A stray thought, but it was true. There were always other people around – yet, if it hadn't been for Tarran, the loneliness would have seeped into his bones like the cold, leaving him bereft. He was surrounded by people who were heavy with the concerns of war, rather than the needs of a nine-year-old boy who wouldn't be taking part in the battle.

And even Tarran didn't come as much as he would have liked.

That worried him. He wished Tarran would tell him more. He tried to understand, but it was hard. What was it like to be a Mirage Maker? The others Tarran spoke of seemed to be so *old.* Older, maybe, than the stones of the Stronghold. Ancient. With such strange memories. And Tarran himself had never been human, never could be human.

Arrant grappled with that. He resented the part his mother had played in it. No matter how often Tarran reassured him that he liked being what he was, Arrant grieved for what had been lost: Tarran's chance to be a man.

He walked on.

Walking. And walking. It was boring, and endless.

In the middle of the night they halted for half an hour's rest. He leaned against the parapet and looked out into the darkness of the night. They were high above the ground; star-lit fields were

spread out below in irregular shapes, like a flagstoned floor. Patches
of fallow and growing crops, meadow grass and neat orchards –
all dark and shadowy with night; farm buildings nothing more
than black blocks scattered haphazardly on the land like the
random roll of dice on the surface of a table. A distant river
looped lazily, the glint of moonlight on water betraying its presence behind the bordering lace of trees. And below him – below
there were stone arcades arching across the valley, holding this
channel up in the air, just as Mount Candidrus, somewhere in
the Alps, supposedly held up Elysium on its many peaks.

Someone passed a pisspot down the line. Ligea had threatened them with dire consequences if she caught anyone contam-
inating the water with their bodily wastes. This aqueduct brought
water to Tyr. They had to walk one hundred and twenty miles
of it unseen and when they did reach the other end, this water
would be what they drank.

Just before dawn, to seek shelter for the day, they halted on top
of a hill. Here, the aqueduct was no more than a stone-built
ditch laid on top of the land, ploughing its way straight through
a forest.

Ligea sought Arrant out, and settled down beside him, back
to a tree. 'How are you doing?' she asked.

'Cold,' he said. In truth he was desperately tired as well. His
legs ached, yet it was all he could do to stay awake long enough
to eat some of the rations he had: bread, cheese, olives and nuts,
watered wine.

'That's what being a soldier is all about,' she told him with a
sigh. 'Being tired and cold and hungry and wet. And having to
sleep on the ground. Most of the time, you're bored as well
because nothing happens. Then when it does, you wish it hadn't.'

'Have you put up a ward?' he asked.

'Right around the camp. We can sleep well. Although the
ground will be hard, I fear.'

It was, but he slept most of the day anyway.

The next couple of nights in the aqueduct were just a replay

of the first. An army of men ankle-deep in water, marching thirty
miles in the dark between walls of stone, a path as straight as
an arrow's flight. A path no one had ever thought necessary to
guard. They would leave no signs of their passing, no footprints
to show an army had gone that way across the land, right to the
walls of Tyr.

'It was you who gave me the idea, Arrant,' Ligea told him on
the first day. 'Do you remember? Last time we came to Tyr? You
said the aqueduct looked like a road built on a long bridge. And
so I had it checked. No guards until you come close to the walls.
Just the occasional artisan who walks his allotted miles every few
months, checking for leaks or problems.'

He couldn't remember what he had said so long ago, but he
hugged the idea that he had been of use, that his five-year-old
self had inspired battle strategy.

After the second night's march, when they left the aqueduct
before dawn-break to descend from an arcaded portion, Ligea
led them to a wood where her men had buried supplies to await
their coming. On the third day, they hid under the arches of the
aqueduct itself, deep in a rocky gully. Yet another night of walking
brought them to a populated area where there was nowhere to
hide.

Here the aqueduct was built tall, with three arcade levels, lifting
the water high above villas and farms and fields. Only closer to
Tyr did the land rise up to meet the aqueduct – or was it the
aqueduct stooping to meet the land? – until finally the channel
disappeared inside the city walls, disgorging water into the city's
cisterns.

That miserable last day they had to spend crouched in water,
high above the ground, unable to descend because there were
too many buildings, roads and people around. At each of the
access stairways, every mile, there was now a guard at ground
level, so no one was allowed to speak above the lightest whisper,
or sneak a look over the side. They had to be careful to sit in a
way that didn't block the water flowing down the centre of the
channel. They were forbidden to stand for fear of revealing them-

selves. Several pisspots were periodically passed down the line and emptied over the side in a quiet spot when full. Men slept fitfully under a burning sun, shaken awake by their comrades if they dared to snore.

And yet they were cheerful, these men. Every now and then Arrant's sensing abilities would assert themselves and he would feel emotions drifting in the air around him: anticipation, excitement, joy, the ache of longing.

Their origins varied. Some came from as far away as Inge. Each had their own story of how they had come to serve Ligea. Most were ex-slaves. Most were just men who wanted a way to go home, wherever home was. There were others, too, who exuded emotions Arrant didn't like. Avaricious men, who foresaw the fall of an empire and wanted to be along to seize what they could from the ruins. The feel of such raw greed made him shiver.

By nightfall of the following day, they should know the fate of the city. Of themselves. Of their distant families. Today they faced the thought of battle; tomorrow they could all face death, or the fate of traitors to the Exaltarchy – crucifixion or beheading, torture, disembowelment, enslavement in the galleys. Arrant knew; he'd heard the tales. He'd seen the dead in Prianus. There was never any mercy for those perceived to be traitors to the empire. Tomorrow many of these men would die.

And I can't help them.

If Rathrox or the Exaltarch found him, his fate would be no different. It could be even worse.

In the first light of the false dawn on that last day, Ligea left her army hunkered down in the water channel and climbed from the top tier of the aqueduct. There was no one around; her senses told her that much. *Good.*

Once on the ground, she changed her wet clothing for a dry robe in her pack, the sort of thing a lowborn artisan's wife might wear. She slung her baldric and sword, well wrapped in cloth, over her shoulder, and draped her cloak over the top to hide them. She put on her sandals and set off for the nearest barge dock.

Gevenan stood out like a beacon to her probing mind. Which meant all was well, gods be thanked. He was supposed to have arrived at dusk the night before, too late to proceed into the city, and apparently he had. She walked briskly, using her positioning powers to dodge the odd person up and about that early: a milkmaid on her way to the cows, a farmer on his way to the city with produce.

It still wasn't fully light when she surprised Gevenan on his way back from the privy in the yard of the dock wayhouse.

'Ocrastes' balls, can't I even visit the outhouse without you homing in on me like a kestrel on a mouse?' he growled, still adjusting his clothing.

'And that's all the welcome I get?' she said with a soft laugh. 'Somehow I don't exactly see you as a mouse, Gev. Is all well?'

'Never, *ever* ask me to travel with a barge again. I have never been so *bored* in all my life.'

'For an army getting to a battle, boredom is a good thing, Gev.'

'Yeah, well. As soon as it's properly light, we'll be on our way. Come and have breakfast with me in the meantime. We have time.'

'You have no idea how good that sounds. We've all been living on bread and cheese and cold water, with a few nuts and olives for variety. I swear, my feet are so cold and wrinkled I doubt they'll ever be the same again.'

'Thought a hot drink might appeal. No problems getting here?'

She shook her head as he guided her to the stools and benches of a stall on the wharf. He ordered hot milk and bread and he sat beside her, laying his dagger on the bench top. The river ambled past, the waters low and brown with mud in the beginnings of the desert-season drought. A long line of barges were moored upstream of where they sat, decks covered with sleeping shapes. Soldiers wrapped in their cloaks. Her soldiers. She grimaced, and refused to think how many would die in the coming days.

'No sign of the Jackals?' Gevenan asked as they waited to be served.

'Not that I've heard. After we are finished in Tyr, someone will have to go after them. There is no way Berg Firegravel will have eliminated them all.'

Favonius is not so easy to kill. She didn't know whether to take comfort from that thought, or to be worried. There was part of her that remembered his hard body against hers. The joyousness of their coupling. His pride. His courage. Not the kind of man to give up easily.

'I know,' Gevenan said cheerfully. 'Leave it to me. If you have any particular orders with regards to the Legate who leads them, you'd better tell me. What's his name again?'

'Favonius.' She shook her head. 'No.'

'I hear tell you were friends once.'

'That ended a long time ago on his part. On mine, it ended the day I saw what he did to Prianus.'

'Right. I'll see to it, then.'

'Good. Bator Korbus and Rathrox Ligatan are mine, though,' she added as an afterthought.

'Ah, yes. Revenge will be sweet, won't it?'

'*Justice,*' she said firmly.

His lip curled in familiar cynicism. 'Call it what you will, but it is revenge, for all that. Do you think I don't know? I'm an expert on the sweet taste of revenge.'

She was startled; he so rarely mentioned his past, even obliquely. 'You are?'

'Even a slave has ways. My king was betrayed and his two sons murdered with him. The soldiers who did the killing, they were just doing their job. I had no argument with them. But the Ingean courtier who betrayed his king? I couldn't let the bastard live out his life in complacent luxury, adviser to the Tyranian Governor of Inge. I couldn't get near him – he was too wily for that and I was a stable slave at the time – so I killed his two sons.' He paused to drink the milk the stall owner had deposited in front of him. 'Don't look so shocked, Ligea. They weren't children.'

'I – I don't presume to judge you.'

'Of course you do. All the time. Anyway, I paid for it, as you can imagine. The Governor thought death was too good for me, so I was whipped and sold as a galley slave to the worst brute of a shipmaster who ever sailed the Iss. I never saw Inge again. At the time, I considered it worth it.' He shook his head with an ironic laugh. 'Ligea, it's a lie that revenge is sweet. The two years I spent in the galley were so hellish that even the memory of them scars each day I live.' He fiddled with the hilt of his dagger. 'After this next day or two is over, you will look around at the dead, you will hear the injured screaming their pain, you will look for those you care about and fail to find them, and then you will wonder if you had a right to hurt so many people on the whim of your vengeance.'

Something caught in her throat and it was a moment before she could snap a reply. 'I do this for Kardiastan. For the land my son will one day rule. So they will be safe from Tyrans forever.' For the man I love. For the end of slavery. *Not just to feel my sword slide into Bator Korbus' flesh. Not just to see Rathrox's despair.*

'Good,' he said, as a girl came out of the kitchen with the food. 'Keep telling yourself that, and you may keep your sanity after tomorrow.' He used his dagger to saw the bread in two and handed her half.

'I was a Brotherhood Compeer once, remember? And I've seen plenty of blood spilled in the years since then, too.' *I can handle it.* She tore at the fresh bread with her teeth. 'Sweet Melete, but that is good.'

'Tomorrow, it's not just those who deserve to die who will. Not just those who kill others for a living who will end up being killed, Ligea. We are taking a *city*. A city full of *people*.'

She put down her mug, suddenly remembering the girl with her throat slashed from ear to backbone, dead in her father's arms in a wayside shrine. 'Damn you to Acheron, Gevenan,' she said.

She looked over at the nearest barge. Her soldiers, awake now, were lined up along the edge of the docks, eating their rations, watching her with respectful eyes.

*   *   *

Everyone knew the Exaltarch's legions were scouring every village and town in southern Tyrans for more recruits, a desperate search that Ligea and Gevenan had banked on to provide a way for them to enter Tyr. Gevenan, posing as a legionnaire officer, had the right uniform, all the right answers and an official-looking scroll, supposedly from the Prefect of Nitida, indicating the delivery of two thousand men, as promised.

He chatted with the legionnaires who boarded the barge with the easy camaraderie of a soldier speaking to other soldiers. When the officer asked about Ligea, Gevenan identified her as his pallet companion from a Nitidian brothel, and they both grinned knowingly. Barge travel could be stultifying. The officer didn't even bother to check her palms, or look at the supposed recruits, and he waived the usual barge tax because Gevenan was on Exaltarchy business. The string of barges moved on to the main city docks.

Ligea turned to say goodbye to Gevenan as the gangplank was being put in place. 'Good luck,' she said. Her voice was hoarse, and the words almost stuck in her throat.

He grinned at her. 'I'm looking forward to this. Rolling up at the city barracks with two thousand totally unexpected, supposedly raw recruits is going to throw every officer in Tyr, not to mention every lictor and minor military official, into a paroxysm of bad temper, blame and much scouring of records, to find out just why no one knew anything about it. The only one who will come out smelling of roses is me, and I shall be righteously indignant at not having been greeted with the thanks due for delivering a bunch of recruits the Exaltarch has been begging for.'

'Watch for my signal tomorrow morning, that's all I ask.'

But it wasn't all, not really. She wanted to say: *Don't get yourself killed. Don't be one of the deaths to lie at my door.*

In the end, she walked away with the words unsaid. To tell a man like Gevenan that you cared what happened to him was not so easy, not when the cynic lurked, ever-present, in his eyes.

CHAPTER TWENTY-EIGHT

Ligea went first to find the Reviarch, Javenid Baradas.

When she arrived at his counting house, it was still early morning, but that made no difference to the Reviarch. He was already at work. Ligea told the Assorian slave who opened the front door to the counting house to tell the Reviarch that a client of Arcadim wanted to see him urgently. The slave exuded suspicion and left her to wait in the entry hall under the watchful eye of another slave, but the Reviarch hustled in a moment later full of apologies for the delay, bowing deeply to display his scalp tattoo.

Yes, you know exactly who I am, you cunning old bird . . .

Only when she was seated in his private office, with its massive ironwood chest taking pride of place in the centre of the room, did he utter her name. 'It is a pleasure to meet you, Magoria Ligea,' he said as he took the seat opposite her. An Assorian woman stood motionless behind his chair. 'As you can see, I have asked one of my household to be present, as it is not proper for me to be alone with a lady. She is my daughter. She does not speak Tyranian.'

Ligea inclined her head towards the nameless woman and laid her sword, still wrapped, across her knees. 'I wish I could say it is a pleasure to meet you, Reviarch. Unfortunately, I feel our connection has been a mixed blessing.'

He ran his fingers down a row of pearls in his beard. 'I am not sure I know what you mean, Domina.'

'At least once you passed information about me, without Arcadim's knowledge, on to the Magister Officii. I suspect you have done it several times.'

He stilled. 'I cannot imagine what has brought you to that conclusion.'

'If you wish to deny it, I am willing to listen. I assume, however, that you – as an Assorian Reviarch – have access to the wealth of information your guild has accumulated over the years. I am guessing that you know I can tell the truth from a lie.'

He was silent for a long moment. Then he said quietly, 'I am responsible for my people and their wealth. When my house is threatened on both sides, I have always found it advantageous to sit in the middle.'

Without looking at him, she unwrapped her sword and fingered the hilt. 'Today you make a choice on which side of the house you will sit, Reviarch. By tomorrow night I intend to be the new Exaltarch.'

'You? Yourself?' He sounded more intrigued than disbelieving. 'I did wonder who you intended to put on the Exaltarch's seat. I thought you'd choose a scion of one of the highborn families. A woman will not be easily accepted let alone one of foreign blood, no matter that she has citizenship.'

'It is remarkable what is possible when one has power, Reviarch. I shall want the support of the Assorian moneymasters, both here and elsewhere. Without you all, I have no chance to build something on the ruins of the Exaltarchy. For that reason, I want none of your people, nor your property, harmed in the coming battle – which is why I am sitting here, telling you what is about to happen. I have given instructions to my forces that this enclave is not to be entered, and that no Assorian is to be harmed, but we both know that in the midst of a battle, it is also best not to tempt fate. For that reason, I suggest you warn your people to stay indoors for the next two days. Possibly longer.'

'I am grateful. My people will be grateful.'

She raised her eyes to fix her gaze on his face. 'But, as you can imagine, it also leaves me with a problem. How can I be sure that, the moment I leave this room, you don't send a messenger to Rathrox Ligatan or the Exaltarch, telling them the city is about to be attacked? Even as I sit here, I am aware of your ambivalence. I cannot trust you.'

'If it is any reassurance, I never passed anything on to the Magister in time for him to do you harm.'

Her gaze hardened with rage. 'My son and I were almost killed passing the boom in the river four years ago. It was sheer luck that we escaped when we did. We were not scheduled to leave till the following morning, and had we waited, we would have been trapped because you chose to tell the Magister we were there. Or so I believe. I would be pleased to hear differently.'

There was another long pause, then he admitted, 'I was informed you were aboard the ship and that someone else was looking for legionnaires to stop you. I assumed you knew that, and would leave immediately. I would not otherwise have contacted Ligatan. I also made the assumption your Magor abilities would ensure your survival, as indeed they did. Magoria, I was merely protecting both sides of my house. If I had not reported what I heard about you from time to time, Rathrox would have assumed I was helping you, especially once he learned the woman he was hunting was Ligea Gayed. He would never have believed that no hint of your activities ever reached the ears of Assorian moneymasters. I feared for Arcadim. He could have been tortured to reveal all he knew. That would not have helped you.'

Ligea curled her left hand around the hilt of her sword, her cabochon slipping into the hollow there. The translucent blade glowed. 'I think we have both been luckier than we deserve, Reviarch.' Her gaze did not waver from his face. 'This does not quite solve my present problem, though. I do not intend to leave the outcome to luck.' She rested the tip of the blade on the edge of the chest.

He stared at it and licked dry lips. 'I could give you my promise. And you know the truth when you hear it.'

'Yes, but could I be certain that you would not change your

mind once you have thought things over? I am afraid I must do more than just rely on your word.' A wisp of smoke spiralled up from the sword tip. The wood beneath was beginning to scorch.

The Reviarch's daughter gasped, her eyes as round as an owl's.

'Ah.' Javenid took a deep breath, but his eyes did not leave the spot where blade and wood met. 'You can be insulting.'

'Yes. But never naive.' The colour in the blade brightened, and the smell of burning wood filled the air.

He stared, mesmerised. His daughter moved restlessly, her hands fidgeting with her shawl, her expression mirroring her distress. The mark on the chest was small, but already the length of a fingernail deep.

He said, a little unsteadily, 'So, doubtless you have a solution to this impasse?'

The curl of smoke thickened. 'Indeed I have. You have one son, I believe. A lad of twelve. He comes with me, to ensure your good behaviour.'

The Reviarch wrenched his gaze from the chest to her face. His anguish was sudden and deeply felt.

'Never fear, I will keep him safe. I have no wish to gain your enmity.'

Javenid was silent.

She was relentless and pushed her sword a shade deeper into the ironwood. 'If you send any hint of information to Rathrox or the Exaltarch about what is going to happen in the next twenty-four hours, I will know about it, I will probably lose this battle – and you will never see your son again.' *See what it feels like to have your child under threat, old man?*

'And if I keep my silence and you lose anyway?' he asked in a whisper, his arrogance reduced to a father's focus on what really mattered.

She felt a pang of sympathy for him, and killed it.

'What will happen to him then?' he persisted.

'He will be returned to you, safe and sound. My word on it.' She pulled her sword out of the wood and rested it across her knees once more. The wood continued to smoulder. 'Now send a slave to ask your son to come here, dressed for a walk. When he arrives, tell him nothing except that he is to go with me and do as I ask. Address your slave and your son only in Tyranian so that I might understand.' Calmly she reached for the water carafe on a side table and poured a little into the smoking gouge she had made in his most precious family treasure.

Arcadim Asenius hated the sound of the warning bell. The old Assorian slave who lived across the road in the warehouse, rang it to signal he was about to send someone through the tunnel, someone who needed to use an unobtrusive entrance to the Asenius Counting House, and every time Arcadim heard its muffled clang from the cellar, he dreaded that the visitor would be Ligea Gayed again.

Arcadim hated thinking about her. It reminded him how precarious his very existence was, how fragile the safety of his family, how transitory their wealth if Rathrox Ligatan smelled a whiff of his treachery. No sooner did he hear from Ligea than Arcadim's stomach would begin to roil.

God of my fathers, please don't let it be her today . . .

He hurried down to open his entrance to the tunnel. And was shocked when he realised it was not only Ligea, but that Ishakim Baradas was with her. The Reviarch's only son. He couldn't think of any scenario that would account for that unlikely event. And the boy's face was a picture of sullen puzzlement. He had no idea what he was doing here, either.

'I believe you know Ishakim?' Ligea asked, as though she were introducing a friend to the host at some highborn's feast. 'The Reviarch wishes him to be kept safe for the next two days, but doesn't want to know where the lad is. Could you keep him in your household?'

Arcadim blinked, a stream of thoughts rushing through his head as he tried to make sense of that request. And nothing he came up with was at all comforting. He'd had no idea that the Reviarch and Ligea had ever met, let alone that he trusted her enough to put his son's safety in her hands.

Great God in heaven, what did I ever do to deserve this? Aloud, he said, unclenching his jaw, 'Of course. Any member of the Reviarch's family is more than welcome here. I shall have Reveba attend to it.' He waved a hand at the stairs. 'Ishakim,' he said, 'go on up and wait for me in the room at the top.' The lad gave Ligea a considering look, then did as he was told. 'What is this about?' Arcadim asked as soon as Ishakim was out of earshot.

'I will be attacking the city within the next twenty-four hours. No one should leave the house now, not for the next two days. If you and all your household stay inside, you will be safe enough. My men hope to keep the fighting away from the moneymasters' enclave. And should you see anyone over the next day or so – including the Reviarch or anyone of his household – please refrain from mentioning Ishakim is here. And give that warning to your man on the other end of the tunnel as well. I am sure he recognised the boy.'

His thoughts jumped to the only conclusion that seemed to make sense. She was afraid the Brotherhood would threaten Ishakim to find out if Javenid had any useful information. The sick feeling in his stomach began to spread. 'You think Ishakim is in danger.'

'I didn't say that.'

'Javenid is elderly, and he has but one son. He would do anything to save the lad, and that's the kind of thing the Brotherhood would know.'

'It is indeed,' she said with the ghost of a smile.

He was going to get nothing more out of her, he knew. 'What else do you want?' he asked, and knew he sounded ungracious. He was trying to hide his fear from her, knowing all the while it was useless. She read him as easily as a scroll. You couldn't hide secrets from Ligea. She had eyes that could bore to the back of your skull.

'I need to wash,' she said. 'I want that parcel I sent to you last month; it has the clothing I want to wear in it. And then I want a litter. Do you have your own?'

He shook his head.

'Then I had better leave from across the street. You can order one for me. Now show me where I can wash.'

'I'll get Reveba,' he said, his misery deep enough to drown in, and turned towards the stairs.

He saw her again after she had changed. She was wearing a robe of white, and she had applied something to the skin of her face. It didn't hide the way her scar puckered on her cheek, but the damage was less obvious. Her sword was carried in a jewelled baldric. She also wore a wig, which he had never seen her do before. An abundance of long golden hair fell over her shoulders in curling waves. That alone changed her appearance dramatically, and he scarcely recognised her. No one would ever call her beautiful, not since her face had been ruined, but he had to acknowledge that she could still look imposing.

She flung a large shawl over her head and shoulders, covering most of her upper body and face. 'Is the litter ready?' she asked.

He nodded. 'It's waiting for you at the front of the warehouse across the street.'

'Then I shall go. When you see me again, you will be the new Exaltarch's moneymaster.'

'But – I don't understand. Who will the new Exaltarch be?'

She didn't answer. Sick to the stomach, he took her down to the tunnel and she disappeared into its darkness. As he closed up the tunnel entrance, disguising it as usual behind a large banner covered in writings from the scriptures of Assor, he was assailed with doubts. *Oh, God, what if she loses? I won't be the new Exaltarch's moneymaster. I'll be the old Exaltarch's gate decoration.*

And then he began to wonder.

The new Exaltarch's moneymaster. She *couldn't* mean – no, of course she couldn't. There had never been a woman holding power in Tyrans. It didn't happen.

Oh, God, tell me she didn't mean that . . .

His stomach churned and he dashed up the stairs in the direction of the lavatory.

*   *   *

I am only one person. It took Temellin and fifty Magoroth to bring down the Tyranian forces in Kardiastan. What can one Magor do here? Am I mad?

She could die today. So easily.

She could fail. She could end her life in the Brotherhood's torture rooms. All they had to do was remove her gem . . .

Why did I ever start?

By the time the litter reached the naval building on the docks, it was already midmorning. She thought of her men, crouched at the top of the aqueduct, trying to snatch some sleep. They had to stay there until the morning of the next day. *Please let Arrant be safe. Please let them all be safe.* And with that last thought, she closed off her doubts, buried them deep where they would not intrude. There was no longer a place for second thoughts now.

She bade the litter bearers wait for her and, still largely concealed by her shawl, mounted the marble steps of the naval building. Two guards stood at the top of the stairs at the open doors, and as she approached, they swung their spears across to halt her entry.

Under the cover of the shawl, she gripped her sword hilt and called up the power of her blade. One of the huge wooden doors burst into flames at the top. She made the fire more inaccessible than dangerous; the flames burned nothing more than the paint, but she configured them so that they weren't easily extinguished, either. The guards gaped, horrified. One whipped off his ceremonial cloak and tried to batter the flames with it, but the door was too tall. Ligea slipped past, unnoticed, into the interior of the building.

More military men came running, but it was the fire that had their attention, not the woman wrapped in a shawl. She cast around with her senses until she pinpointed the location of the man she was seeking. At his door she discarded her shawl, called more colour into her sword and wrapped herself in its golden glow. Anything to blur her looks and deceive the senses. She enhanced her hearing to listen for a moment before she stepped inside.

Seamaster Mescades was standing at a table, turning a piece of beaten copper over and over in his hands. A naval officer was standing in front of him, giving a report on the efficacy of copper cladding on ramming vessels. They both turned to look at her as she entered. Their initial surprise blossomed into amazement and then a mixture of reverent awe, appalled fear – and disbelief. And the disbelieving one was the seamaster.

Ligea gave them no time for thought. She gestured at the naval officer and pointed, sending a trail of golden bubbles of light across the room to the door. Her meaning was clear. He bowed his head and clasped his fist to his breast in a gesture of submission. 'Goddess,' he whispered, and left the room. Without moving, Ligea used a wind to close the door behind him with a slam.

'You and the Legate Valorian were informed that a man of war must choose his sides with care,' she said, modulating her voice to a lower, more sensual register. As she spoke, she created the gentlest of breezes around herself. Her hair swirled in the blur of a golden haze, her robe fluttered. 'You were informed that a time would arrive when you would need to reconsider your loyalty.'

The seamaster finally managed to react. He laid the copper down. His hand was remarkably steady. 'The Magister told Legate Valorian and me that the Oracle was a fraud,' he said. 'That the words were spoken by a Kardi numen, with certain magic abilities, who posed as the Oracle.'

Ligea smiled. 'Were you convinced?'

He radiated a mixture of alarm and anxiety.

'I don't know,' he admitted. 'Rathrox may have just said it because he was put in such a humiliating position that day. Perhaps he felt that if we thought a god did that to him, through the medium of the Oracle, then he would lose authority. We wouldn't want to take orders from the Brotherhood, if the Brotherhood was despised of the gods.' He paused, then dared to look her directly in the eye. 'Who are you, Domina?'

'I don't think it matters, Mescades. Goddess, Oracle, numen?

What counts now is what I want, and what I can achieve, not who I am.'

He considered that thoughtfully. 'And what *do* you want, Domina?'

She found herself liking him, admiring his control of his fear. A rational, thinking man, this seamaster. 'I want a better world for people of the Exaltarchy. Unfortunately there will be those who will think the world I would create will be worse than the one that went before. The present Exaltarch, for example. Or Rathrox Ligatan. Mescades, you have long served an emperor who craves power, no matter what the cost. His war with Kardiastan brought Tyranian legions to their knees. So now I tell you this: I demand your service. I demand that you support a new Exaltarch.'

The seamaster blanched but did not speak.

She continued, 'Order every single naval ship in the port to sea today. Sail with them yourself and blockade the entrance to the estuary, well out to sea. Ignore any orders to return for three days, then go to the palace and prostrate yourself before your new Exaltarch.'

She probed his emotions, and felt almost sorry for him. He was appalled, knowing that any naval ship leaving port was supposed to do so only on orders from the Exaltarch. If he ordered the ships out, and Bator Korbus was still occupying the imperial seat when he returned, then he was a dead man, crucified for treason, his estate confiscated, his family destitute.

'And if I don't?' he croaked.

'I could threaten you. But let me offer incentive instead: do this, and you will be more than just the city's seamaster – you will be seamaster of the Tyranian fleet, and you will have the ear of the Exaltarch and a seat on the Senate.'

'*Senate?* When there hasn't been a Senate for, what, fifty years?'

She felt the first stirring of expectations within him, and knew she had touched strings that hummed with hope. His grandfather had been a senator until the Senate had been banished by the first Exaltarch.

She pointed her sword at the copper on the table and, with

careful precision, began to melt it. 'I have power, and it is time this land had an Exaltarch who is not a despot.'

Mescades stared at the melting metal, mesmerised. Beads of sweat had formed along his brow.

She added, 'You have a choice, seamaster. I could kill you now, if you'd think that a simpler solution. Or you could go to Rathrox – or Bator Korbus – and tell him I was here, and why. Then I would have to kill you later, and that would be a shame. A senator's robes would sit well on your shoulders. Or you could do nothing, in which case the new Exaltarch will remove you from your post as soon as Bator Korbus falls.' At least he didn't doubt that – she could feel his belief laced through with the tendrils of stark anxiety.

'What kind of man am I if I abandon my city when it is threatened?' he asked in a whisper. 'Do not ask this of me, Domina.'

'What kind of man are you if you do not save your men from needless death serving a tyrant? Tell me, Mescades, how many ships and men did Tyrans lose fighting Kardiastan? How many never made it to Kardiastan?'

The line of his jaw tightened. She had hit a nerve. 'Too many,' he admitted.

'And yet he continued to send more and more men to their deaths.' There was a long silence while he thought that over, then she added, 'If Tyrans had a Senate still, would they have allowed him to commit such folly?'

'How can ships leave without the Exaltarch's order?' he asked. 'The forts at the booms—'

'Let me worry about them,' she said. 'Begin now. I wish to see the ships on their way out of port on the next tide.' Which, she knew, gave him about five hours. She added more kindly, 'Don't think of this as treachery, Mescades, but loyalty to your city and the land it governs. Tyrans needs rescuing from the greed of a few men who no longer concern themselves with the greater good. Oh, and if it is any consolation, I suspect the Exaltarch will order you to send your ships out into the estuary entrance anyway, to be ready for an attack coming in that direction.

'I just want you to stay there – all the fleet – no matter what. My intention is to keep your ships intact and your men safe. I want to save them from the fate of those who set sail for Kardiastan and never returned.'

The faintest of cynical smiles flitted across his face. 'The new Exaltarch wishes to govern a strong Tyrans with a strong, intact navy,' he said. He looked back at the misshapen copper and poked it with a tentative finger, flinching when it scorched his skin. She felt his capitulation like the ebbing of a tide within him. A decision not to push against something that was inevitable. 'Very well. If I get the order from the Exaltarch, I will take it one step further and do as you ask. And I'll pray that you *are* Melete,' he added with dry humour, 'so I can one day tell my grandchildren that I served a goddess.'

'You're a very brave man, Mescades. You will make a fine senator.' She changed the breeze to a small whirlwind, which she sent spinning in his direction. He leaped to his feet to get out of the way. As the wind whipped around him, she left the room. He hadn't quite believed her to be a deity, but she had sensed no intention to betray. *Good*.

The naval officer she had sent out of the room had taken it upon himself to guard the door. He saluted as she came out and, through the haze of golden light, she smiled at him and gestured him inside once more. The moment the door was closed, she grabbed up her shawl, swaddled herself in its anonymity, and made her way back to the main entrance.

There, the fire was finally out and two badly burned ceremonial cloaks in a large puddle of water were smouldering testimony to how tenacious it had been. A number of sailors with empty wooden pails were standing about arguing over how such a fire could ever have started. No one took any notice of her as she slipped out into the street.

'What the sweet hells—?'

The man on watch duty in the tower near the floating booms stared hard at the ferryman's dhow coming downriver. It wasn't the boat that had his jaw dropping; ferry vessels were common enough on the lower River Tyr where there were no bridges. What had the sentry gaping was that the dhow was skimming along as fast as it was possible for such a boat to move, and yet the tide was still on the flow upstream. To make the progress of the boat even more extraordinary, it was the middle of the day when the air was as hot and as still as a baker's oven. So how in all Acheron's seven hells was the Vortexdamned thing moving?

He leaned out of the tower. 'Hey, Petrus – call the centurion, will you? There's the unholiest thing coming downriver!'

The centurion, directed up into the tower, was more horrified than amazed. One look was enough to have him reaching for the alarm bell, scowling and shouting at the watchman. 'Don't you remember that Altani vessel that sailed when there was no wind? The Magister wanted to have our hides because we let it pass!' The sound of the tolling bell rang out over the water, sending sailors and rowers scurrying for the galleys, others running to man the catapults.

The dhow, however, did not try to escape through the booms. At the last minute it *halted* midstream, the wind in its sail and the tide under its keel in sudden perfect balance. Light flashed at the end of each of the booms, and the anchoring buoys sparkled with gold. And disintegrated, shedding pieces into the air like feathers from a flock of startled pigeons. The chains rattled away into the water. The centurion screamed at the men handling the catapults to aim at the dhow.

Liberated of their shackles and caught by the current, the string of logs of each boom floated free. For a moment they threatened the dhow, but the sail soon billowed and the tiny boat began to scud upstream on the tide. Boulders from the two catapults landed harmlessly in its wake.

The logs bunched up, bumping one another, then sorted themselves out to drift with the flow, only to be brought to a halt at the limit of their connecting chains. As the end of each string of logs was still attached to the shore on either side, each boom swung in, slowly but inevitably, towards the bank. The river was no longer partially barricaded, but wide open to any vessel that cared to enter or leave.

'That's impossible,' the duty guard muttered as he watched the small boat speed away upstream, powered by a wind that bulged the sail yet never raised a ripple on the water. 'No boat can do that.'

The men gave up on the catapult and gathered at the battlements, staring as the dhow disappeared into the dock area, long before the galley even drew level with what was left of the boom buoys.

'All right, you men,' the centurion snapped. 'If someone wants to break the boom, it's so others can gain easy entry to the river. We can expect to be under attack, and soon, from the sea. I want everyone on watch duty. Delonius – mount up and take the news of what just happened to Legate Valorian and to Seamaster Mescades. We need reinforcements here, and we need them fast. Xasus – get every engineer you can find: we have to mend the booms and get them back in place. Although Hades knows just how we can do that in a hurry.' He remembered the appalling trouble they'd had once before when a boom chain had broken. A boom was a cantankerous thing to manage in mid-river, and the few minutes between the ebb and the flood of a tide was the only time when it could be tamed long enough to fix its anchorage.

Three hours later, half of Tyr's legionnaires were lining the riverbanks downriver of the city, looking seaward. Less than four hours later, the Tyr fleet rowed out through what was left of the boom and disappeared into the wide stretch of the estuary.

CHAPTER TWENTY-NINE

Arrant's fingers were blue. His feet probably were too, but he couldn't see them properly yet. They certainly felt cold enough to be the colour of day-old bruises.

After spending the last day inside the aqueduct with their feet freezing in water and their heads baking inside their sun-heated helmets, they had walked overnight the last few miles to their destination. Now it was just a matter of waiting for the dawn, and Ligea's signal to attack. 'You'll see it over the city,' she'd said.

They rested within the confines of the water channel, trying desperately to snatch a little sleep, but how was that possible when you had your feet ankle-deep in water, and no dry place to sit except on your helmet? How was that possible when you knew you might die in the morning? And was it sensible anyway, to spend what could be your last moments on earth *asleep*?

The emotions around Arrant were so potent, even he could not fail to feel them. They twisted with dark excitement, with hope and desire and fear, with tendrils of poignant memory. He felt the emotional lifetimes of adults replayed in the heads of the men who wondered if this was their last night alive. He struggled to maintain his composure in the midst of such murk, but to these men, the future was a tragedy louring, ready to consume, and the past was filled with the savagery of dislocation, slavery and inhumanity.

Arrant, don't.

He pulled his mind free of the morass to answer his brother. *Tarran, I can't help it. They think such dark things ...*

*I know. I feel them too. But you must be strong. I cannot stay
and help.*

What's wrong?

They need my strength.

Who does?

Tarran didn't reply; he was already gone. A silly question
anyway, of course. The Mirage Makers needed him. That's why
he was one of them.

Arrant thought, *I have to be strong. We both have to be strong.
Oh, Vortexhells, I am only nine!*

Foran, grim-faced, came to find him as night dissolved into
the chill grey light of the pre-dawn. 'Here – have this,' he said.
He handed over a stale piece of bread and some very hard cheese.
'At least there is plenty of water to soak it in.'

'What – what happens next?' Arrant asked, shivering with cold
and trying to nibble a corner of the bread. He didn't relish dipping
it in the water that had already run over the feet of hundreds of
soldiers before getting to him, and he'd already finished all the
water in his waterskin.

'We wait for Ligea's signal. We will find ourselves a safe place
a nice distance from the walls and watch. This is not our fight.
I'm too old and you're too young.'

That's not true, Arrant thought. *No one is too old to fight using
Magor magic. Foran could easily help Ligea.*

He knew Ligea's instructions to Foran were to keep him safe
at all cost. Yet the power of another Magor, even one who was
only an Illuser, could have meant the difference between success
and failure. Guilt churned his stomach. If he were a proper
Magoroth he would have been able to look after himself. He
could have helped. Instead, the unreliability of his powers meant
that he and Foran had to hide themselves away while real soldiers
fought a battle. *I shouldn't have come. I should have stayed in
Getria; then Foran could have helped Ligea.*

Why had she allowed him to come, then? Did she think she
would win, no matter what? He couldn't believe that. No, it was
because she knew he had to see this. He would one day rule a

nation. He had to see what it meant to go to war. He had to know the enemy next door.

He dropped his eyes, wishing he'd had a last chance to talk to Ligea. He wanted, at the very least, to wish her luck, or say goodbye, or *something*, but she had gone without seeking him again. He knew his bitter disappointment was silly. It was unrealistic of him to expect her to do so. She had a whole army to command and he didn't need her anyway – Foran was there to look after him.

Miserably, he forced himself to eat some of the cheese. It was as tasteless and as hard as ox-hide.

'Signal!' An exclamation from somewhere ahead. He looked up. A plume of golden light rose into the sky above the city. In the aqueduct, men scrambled to their feet, an army rising up to greet a day of battle, but it was *relief* Arrant felt from them, not fear. They were *glad* the time had come. Within minutes they were gone, vanished down the access stairs and ladders, disappearing into the gloom still gathered like a skirt around the city walls. And the first men had already died: the city guards along the aqueduct. He felt their terror as swords slid home.

Arrant turned to Foran. They were the only two left standing in the water channel. Foran, who normally kept his feelings subdued and guarded tight within him, was now surging with passionate frustration. He in turn caught Arrant's astonishment and they exchanged a stare. 'I'm sorry,' Arrant whispered. 'It's my fault you are here. Not there, helping.'

Foran abruptly closed off his emotions. Or perhaps it was Arrant's sensing that failed him; he couldn't tell, but the memory of Foran's rage at his need to stay with Arrant – that memory remained, to swamp him with guilt. To remind him that he was a nuisance. A burden.

'Look,' Foran said, changing the subject, reverting to tutor and slotting him back into the role of pupil. 'That's not the light of sword power she is shooting into the sky as a signal. That's water. She is trying to conserve power and it's more economical to colour water and send it skywards than it is to send light direct from her sword.'

Arrant tried to sound interested, but all he could think of to say was, 'Oh.'

The waiting was hard. For a long time nothing happened at all. It was too dark to see the progress of the soldiers as they made for the North Gate. All they could do was stare into the grey shadows of the predawn until eventually they could distinguish the gate, off to the right of the aqueduct. Foran enhanced his sight. Arrant tried desperately to do the same thing. The scene wavered in and out of focus, as irritating as watching fish through ripples on the water.

In the brief moments that he did manage to steady the picture, he could see the army from the aqueduct assembling. The city guards, who had opened the gates at first light to allow the entry of the farm carts stacked with produce for the city's markets, were now struggling to close them. The farmers appeared to have fled, leaving their carts and mules and oxen behind. Produce was spilled across the paveway. Men were fighting in front of the walls. Above, in the sky, Ligea's signal plume dwindled and vanished.

'Can't we go closer?' he asked, as frustrated as Foran. 'I can't see properly from here. What's happening?' A sudden clawing of pain ripped along his mind: a random burst of a soldier's agony against his senses. It was gone before he could scream, leaving nothing behind but the stark shadow of the memory.

'You can ward me there,' he said. His bottom lip trembled. He didn't want to feel that stab of agony again. He didn't want to see. Yet the fight drew him. The emotions churning in the distance, just out of reach, sucked at him. These were men he knew. Mole, who told him stories of his homeland in the Western Reaches. Batricus, who loved to play dice and had made him a hand catapult so that he could shoot stones at the Stronghold ravens when they came to steal the grain. Remolis, one of Jorbrus's sons, who carried his pet ferret with him, even into the battle. 'You can ward me there, while you help those who are wounded.

I promise I'll stay within your warding. Nothing can happen to me.'

Foran pinched up his mouth, considering. 'All right, all right. As long as you swear you'll stay warded even if the warding weakens. I have to be able to trust you.'

'I promise.'

'We'll get closer. I may not be a Magori, but I am a skilful healer, for all that. Perhaps I can help. Ah, Arrant, I *hate* to feel their suffering . . .'

Arrant stared at him. With those words, Foran became not just a teacher, not just one more person always telling him what to do. He was a man, made suddenly real – and just as vulnerable and lost and bewildered as Arrant himself.

It wasn't a comforting thought.

'*Look* at that, you scrawny *insect* of a helot's son! Suppose *you* tell me what is going on, *Magister* Rathrox?'

The words hacked at him, as potentially damaging as the sword Bator Korbus was now inserting into his scabbard. Rathrox felt the cut of those words, severing success from his future. Chopping, perhaps, at his neck. Obediently he glanced out of the window, and his look was stricken, even though he had already seen all there was to see. A fountaining of water, made unnatural by the gold of Magor witchery, towering into the air over the roofs. It had been like that for half an hour, since the false dawn that morning. From the look of it, the source was the water of the channels running down either side of the Forum Publicum. A signal, he guessed. Even as he watched, the gold died and the water dropped away behind the rooftops.

Rathrox Ligatan as the Magister Officii, no matter what else happened that day, was finished; he knew that. He uncurled his hands, and ran the sweating palms down his thighs. If rage could have killed, Ligea Gayed would never have drawn another breath.

He looked away from the window and met Clemens' gaze. And the blathering idiot was *pitying* him. He choked on his fury.

The Exaltarch's diatribe, venom uttered with chilling cold,

continued as slaves bent to tie on his greaves. 'You head the *Brotherhood*, Magister. You are *supposed* to save me from surprises. Yesterday you told me to expect an invasion via the river. Just now I was told that slaves killed Arbiter Matius and all his family. I sent for Legate Valorian to explain, and was told he is unavailable because he is in the thick of fighting around the barracks. With slaves? I asked. No, I was told. With soldiers from someone else's *army*. Right here in *my* city! It seems there is everything happening *except* an invasion upriver. So, Rathrox, tell me *what is going on*? My helmet!' This last was addressed to one of the slaves. The Exaltarch snatched the plumed headgear from the hapless helot and followed it with a backhanded slap that sent the man flying across the room. He landed at the feet of a centurion who had just entered. Clemens winced in sympathy, embarrassing Rathrox. *Has the man no spine?*

'Well, what is it?' the Exaltarch snapped at the newcomer.

'Centurion Belion, Exalted One, reporting from the Tyr Legion. We – we are being attacked at all gates. So far, our legionnaires are holding them off, but they are sorely pressed. And no reinforcements have come from the barracks. I couldn't get near the place. There's fighting everywhere! And armed men have secured the armoury.'

'Our men?' the Exaltarch asked.

'No, no, Exalted! We don't know who they are! They must have already been in the city, because they didn't come in from outside. At least, I don't think so.'

Bator eased his head into his helmet, looked at the centurion and pointed at Rathrox. 'Have that man taken to the Cages and imprisoned there, to await my pleasure.' He strode out, followed by his guard.

Clemens, appalled, flapped his hands in agitation. Rathrox glared at him and then at the slaves, who took the hint and scuttled away through the servants' door. He turned to the centurion. 'Tell me exactly what else you saw.'

'Magister, I have to escort you to the Cages—'

'Don't be ridiculous, you dolt. The Exaltarch was just upset.

He'll be enraged if you were really to do anything so foolish. Right now we need to find out exactly what the situation is so we can combat it.' He tried to sound reasonable, unafraid, but he couldn't keep the quiver out of his voice and knew he'd ended up sounding like a querulous old man. At his side, Clemens quivered like a startled hedge mouse.

The centurion paused, half convinced. Rathrox could almost hear the man wondering who presented him with the greatest threat if he disobeyed: the Exaltarch or the Magister. 'The Exaltarch won't even remember this tomorrow,' Rathrox said reasonably, 'and he certainly won't remember you.'

He knew the moment he added those last words that he had made a mistake.

The centurion drew himself up. 'If you would just come with me, Magister—'

Rathrox gave what he hoped was a rueful smile. 'As you wish, Centurion. Let's just hope my absence makes no difference to the outcome of this battle for the city.' He looked at Clemens. 'Clemens, you will have to get to the Magistrium and do your best to salvage the situation.' He turned towards the door, but clapped his left hand to the centurion's back as he went. The manoeuvre forced the man to walk alongside him, rather than behind. Clemens dithered, his mouth opening and closing in dismay. At the door, the Magister stopped, and waited for the soldier to open it.

As the man reached for the handle, Rathrox reached under his robe for his dagger. The centurion did not even see the blow coming. Rathrox angled the tip of the blade upwards to slip between the scales of the man's armour, and rammed it home into his back. The soldier staggered, and opened his mouth to scream. But instead of sound, blood spilled out. His fingers scrabbled blindly, looking for his sword. Then he fell forward against the door, gasping, desperately seeking what was left of his life. Rathrox eased his blade out as the dying man fought to stay upright.

'Oh, *gods*,' Clemens squeaked.

'Sorry about that, Centurion,' Rathrox said softly in the wounded man's ear. 'If you had been more sensible, this need not have happened.' He wrenched the top of the man's helmet backwards from behind, forcing his head up so that his throat was exposed. The centurion struggled, but he was choking on his own blood. The dagger blade sliced deep across his neck.

Rathrox dropped the man and stepped back to avoid the swathe of blood that splattered across the door and pooled on the carpet. *You poor fool*, he thought.

He dropped the knife and opened the door, only to find two soldiers on guard duty on the other side. 'Men,' he said calmly, stepping over the centurion and pointing back at Clemens, 'that man there just killed the centurion. Arrest him and have him taken to the Cages.'

The expression on Clemens' face made every moment Rathrox had spent in the company of that pathetic idiot worthwhile.

Midmorning. The sun was already high in the sky. The burning air of the desert-season raised heat shimmers from the stone of the streets, and clouds of insects from the fields beyond the walls.

Ligea paused at a fountain to wash her face and rinse the grime away. Her wig was tucked in her bag, the sword and baldric out of sight under the folds of her shawl. She glanced at the dusty hem of her white gown, and cursed. She would have done anything to be wearing an anoudain right then. Well, almost anything. But she might need her goddess persona yet, and no one was going to believe Ligea was a goddess without the trappings. She was tall enough for the part, but little else.

She still had power left in her cabochon, but she herself was exhausted. She hadn't slept for two days, and she had been constantly on the move. There was so much to coordinate, so many things to think of, so many separate parts to fit together. And so little she could delegate, because she was the only Magoroth around.

Ah, Temellin, I wish you could have sent me help.

She sat for a moment on the edge of the fountain and, while

she rested, ran through her chaotic memories of the last twelve hours.

Overnight, she'd built a long ward to stop the soldiers posted down at the booms from returning into the city in the morning once they heard of the attack. She'd followed that by eating an enormous meal of roast chicken and stuffed swan in an attempt to replace her dwindling energy. Then, some time after midnight, she'd warded the entire off-duty Imperial Guard inside their barracks. They were still there, as far as she knew, unable to fight.

At first light, after starting the fountain of water as the prearranged signal for attack, she'd eaten a large breakfast at a shop in the marketplace and then hurried across the Tyr Bridge to the West Gate. This gate had been the destination of those of her men from Second Farm. They were supposed to arrive in squads of ten during the night. Each squad had its leader, and they were to have crossed the whole of Tyrans on their Quyriot ponies, taking dozens of different tracks and roads, disguised as anything but what they were: ex-slaves, aching for a battle that would legitimise their freedom. A battle that would make them men in the eyes of the Law, not speaking tools to be rewarded or disposed of on a whim.

By the time she'd arrived at the gate, there was a midden of bodies – a mess of unfulfilled dreams – waiting to burden her with guilt.

As planned, the legionnaires on guard duty had been attacked at dawn by some of Gevenan's men already in the city. Also as planned, the gate had been opened to admit the invaders. By the time Ligea arrived, however, legionnaires spending the night in a nearby military brothel had heard the sounds of battle and rushed to reinforce the guards, surrounding the first wave of attackers inside the walls and shutting the gate on the rest. Those trapped inside had been systematically killed.

Their bodies piled high, leaking fluids, already swelling in the morning heat – they'd saluted Ligea with the stink of death and the accusing eyes of the slaughtered.

Gevenan's voice in her head: *This, the whim of your vengeance.*

She blasted the gate open, accepting that she might kill some of her own men on the other side. Accepting the guilt that went with that knowledge. Her soldiers poured in, swinging long-handled hammers with crushing force that dented helmets, broke ribs even through armour, and shattered the bones of arms and legs. Nothing heroic here. No god of battle to honour a brave man, no goddess to bestow her favour on a champion as in the stories of old. This was just brutal death and vicious, unimaginable pain.

She remembered leaning against a wall to catch her breath. To watch what she had put into unstoppable motion. A hammer in the hands of a Janussian becoming a weapon that crushed and battered. A terrified legionnaire, little more than a boy, trying to run from a battle he knew they could not win. The screams of men beyond agony. The sound of blows and blades on metal. The stench. Voided bowels. The sickliness of blood. The stink of a slaughterhouse.

She'd turned away then, knowing that here she had won. And yet not wanting to see the victory.

Making her way back towards the barracks to find out if Gevenan needed help, she'd discovered more she hadn't wanted to see. Slaves rampaged down the Via Conedea, a street of well-to-do merchants. They had no leaders, and many were bent on settling old scores. Marauding gangs of men – women too, sometimes – hunted prey, battering down doors, intent on looting and vengeance and rape. They'd even turned their fury on the inanimate – toppling statues, setting fire to anything that would burn. Ligea, fuelled by her own fury at needless slaughter and destruction, rounded on them with a minimum of mercy. Group after group ended up grovelling, brought to her feet by the power of her sword, crippled by pain until they swore to leave the streets. Some she'd left encased in a cage of warding as a warning to others.

In the streets behind the palace, fires were more of a problem and putting them out drained more of her power. She'd used whirlwinds to pick up water from the river and dump it on burning buildings, gradually working her way through the back-streets towards the barracks.

And now she sat on the edge of the fountain, shoring up her strength of purpose. Accepting the memories. Accepting that it was still only midmorning, and there was so much more left to be done. She sighed and rose to her feet.

By the time Ligea arrived at the barracks, Gevenan had already left. The building was in the hands of some of his men, most of them nursing wounds.

'Last I heard,' the man in charge told her, 'there was fighting in the Forum Publicum.' A sword slash had opened up his cheek from the corner of his eye to his chin. It was no longer bleeding, and he appeared to be ignoring it.

She nodded her thanks and jogged over to the Forum in front of the palace. There, the fighting was already over. Gevenan was standing on the front steps, giving orders to his men. He saw Ligea, and nodded brusquely. 'The Exaltarch's not here,' he told her. 'He left before I arrived. I gather he took the Imperial Guard and personally led them to the North Gate. I think the major battle is now down there somewhere, along the Via Pecunia. The merchants have brought out their personal guards to reinforce the legionnaires and Valorian's city guards. I've got to get down there.'

While he was speaking she laid a hand on his right arm, where a long gash, inadequately tied with part of someone's tunic, seeped blood. She started the healing process.

He didn't seem to notice. 'It's going well, Ligea. I've heard from the Quyriots: they routed the men at the East Gate and they are holding that part of the city. They are all still on horse-back, would you believe? I heard there are a helluva lot of decap-itated legionnaires over that way, and people are so terrified of the Quyriots they are staying inside their houses. That keeps the looting to the minimum.'

'Where's Legate Valorian? Did you kill him?'

'No such luck. For all his bloody perfumes and curls, he's a damned fine commander. Done a competent job of rallying his men and making some sense out of the chaos. He's down along the Via Pecunia somewhere, with his emperor. They have contained our men near the gate, I think.'

'Right. What about Rathrox?'

'One of the guards here said the Magister Officii left the palace earlier this morning. Very early. No one has seen him since. Oh, and one interesting thing. He ordered the Brotherhood not to fight. He ordered them to report to the Magistrium.'

Her heart lurched. The idea of entering that building again made her feel ill. 'I'd better check it out. Your arm should feel better now, and I've stopped the bleeding, but just because it doesn't hurt doesn't mean that it's healed. Nurse it.'

'Yeah,' he said with a sardonic grin. 'With me right-handed and all. And off to fight another battle, too. I'm heading towards the North Gate and Bator Korbus. I'll try to keep the bastard alive for you.' He signalled to two of his men. 'Go with the Domina,' he ordered.

Without asking me if I wanted company, she thought in annoyance as she headed for the Magistrium. *That man is never going to change.*

Still, the thought of being in the Brotherhood building again sent shudders of unpleasant memories through her mind. And so did the idea of meeting Rathrox. Perhaps she might even need those two soldiers now trailing behind her.

CHAPTER THIRTY

Foran set up a place for the wounded, just outside the North Gate on the dirt track to the side of the paveway. He rigged the canvas covers from the farmers' carts to provide shade, and did his best to bind wounds, relieve pain and set the healing process in motion. It wasn't long before he was overwhelmed as more and more wounded arrived from the city when the word spread about what he was doing.

All Arrant could do was watch. His frustration ran deep. The Illuser could have keyed the ward to Arrant's body, thus allowing him to come and go as he pleased, but he hadn't trusted his pupil enough to do that. The invisible cage of the warding was solid to Arrant's touch. One part of him wanted to be out there, part of the battle, being what a Mirager-heir should be. Inwardly, however, he was glad enough to stay where he was. It felt safe. And he didn't really want to be involved in the fighting. Or the healing. He didn't like feeling the anguish. He didn't like the eddies of fear and shock and despair that wafted his way in uneven, unpredictable waves. He tried to shut it all out, the way a Magoroth ought to be able to do, but – as usual – he had no control over any of it. Emotions and other people's fear came and went as they chose.

He sighed. He'd wanted to come closer in order to see better, but he had ended up not seeing anything at all of the fighting, just lots of the gore and nasty aftermath.

Midmorning, though, things changed. The Exaltarch and his

elite Imperial Guards arrived at the gate, mounted on gorclaks in an attempt to drive the invaders out. The fighting just inside the walls became more ferocious and more intense. Arrant could hear it. He could *feel* it. At least sometimes. When he couldn't, when his sensing failed, then it was even worse. Like going suddenly blind.

After fifteen minutes, the fighting spilled through the open gate. Men from Ligea's legions were retreating, fighting every inch of the way with desperate, futile courage. The legionnaires used their huge beasts as battering rams to mow down the foot soldiers. Foran glanced up at the gateway and then ignored what was happening as one of the wounded under his care began to scream with pain.

Arrant had always hated gorclaks, ever since the day Timnius had died. Their black hides as thick as metal armour, their small, beady eyes loathing all they looked at, their spurs and horns ripping open men's bodies like crow beaks cracking eggshells – if any animal could be thought of as evil, they could.

Arrant stood, his hands against the wall of his warding as he watched, his nose flat to its hard transparency. Only it wasn't that hard any more. In fact, it was sort of squashy.

Is it supposed to be like that? he wondered. His mother's wards could last for days, he knew, but she often used a sword to make them. Foran was only an Illuser. He didn't have a Magor sword, and his cabochon had less power. And then Arrant, absorbed in the battle, ceased to think about it.

Ligea's men panicked. Unable to prevail against riders on such well-armoured beasts, they turned and fled, running in all directions. And the legionnaires followed, whirling their slings, spurring their mounts to a lumbering run. And over a short distance they could be fast, those immense beasts. Rip-discs flew with a high-pitched whine that continued until they buried themselves in their victim. And a fleeing man's back, especially when many wore only leather, made such a suitable target.

Arrant watched, beating his fists against the warding, screaming unheard warnings. Soldier after soldier fell, flesh ripped or spine broken. And Foran, busy with his doctoring, did not look up.

'Foran!' he yelled, pounding on the ward. 'Look out!'

Finally Foran looked up and took in the scene, his jaw clenching as he realised how close the legionnaires were. His shock penetrated the ward to burst inside Arrant's mind, leaving him reeling.

Tarran, Tarran! His breathing sped up. He wasn't in danger, was he? Was the ward too weak? *Oh, Tarran, please come. I need to know what to do ...*

Foran called more power into his cabochon and shot at one of the riders. He tumbled off his mount. The two legionnaires behind saw the flash of red light and swung their beasts in Foran's direction. Foran blasted the second out of his saddle, then the third.

What's happening?

'The legionnaires are attacking us!'

Why are you warded?

'Foran did it! I can't get out! Can you help our soldiers?'

Arrant, don't be a tadpole. You know I have no power here. I'm just in your mind!

Foran's help gave the fleeing soldiers courage. They turned back to aid him, facing the gorclaks with only their axes and hammers and swords. Arrant watched, his mouth dry. Foran threw shaft after shaft of power, but each beam was paler. Legionnaires died, one after the other, but Ligea's soldiers died too. Several of the wounded men pulled themselves up to join the fray, desperate to help. They grabbed up their weapons and staggered away to do what they could.

Arrant, incapable of aiding them, was almost in tears. 'Tarran, I can't get out to help.'

A Magor can send power through a ward.

'Only through their own wards! This is not mine,' he wailed. Anyway, he didn't have any power.

Foran shot off another blast of red Illuser power at a rider. At the last moment the legionnaire swerved his mount and it was the gorclak that died instead, pierced through the eye. Its forward momentum carried it straight on, right to where Arrant was trapped. The animal plunged to its knees in front of him, somersaulting its rider over its head, and skidded onwards, ploughing a furrow through the soil. Instinctively, Arrant leaped back as far as he could in his warded bubble.

The legionnaire slammed into the ward headfirst. The beast met the warding head-on a split second later, and the magic *bent*. Arrant watched in horror as the horn of the gorclak stretched the ward, and visible crack lines like a dew-wet spider's web blossomed out from the impact point. Appalled, he watched as the magic began to splinter. Tiny pieces of the ward turned opaque and then vanished. The breakage started slowly, then spread faster and faster.

I'll be Ravage-blasted, Tarran said.

The ward popped out of existence, leaving Arrant standing in the open, vulnerable and alone. He shot an anguished look at Foran, but the Illuser was in no position to help. Another legionnaire was ramming his gorclak at him, and the man was furious.

You got your wish, Arrant. You wanted to help. Seems to me you'd better get to it, right away.

'How?' he asked, anguished.

That gorclak might be dead but the legionnaire at your feet is definitely not. Be quick! The others are pulling me back. We are in trouble in the Mirage.

'I need you!' Arrant drew his dagger from his belt. The legionnaire was only two paces away, and he was groaning and trying to push himself up.

I think you had better hurry.

'And do what?'

Kill him, what else? Before he wakes up enough to kill you.

Arrant was horrified. 'I can't kill him! He's a legionnaire and – and – and I'm only nine.'

If you don't do something pretty quick, you'll be dead aged nine. Hurry, you idiot, before he comes to his senses. If you don't kill, he will.

'I don't think I can stab a man to death . . .'

You're a Magoroth! Use your cabochon.

The legionnaire scrambled up, groping for his sword as he did so. There was no more time. Wildly, Arrant held out his hand with his palm outwards and thought about power, thought about killing, thought about a beam of yellow destruction.

And blew the man's head to pieces. The body remained standing for a fraction of time. Headless, as if it didn't know it was dead. Then it toppled.

Tarran warned, *They are dragging me back . . .*

There was blood in Arrant's eyes. Red sticky globs of it on his neck. Bits of brain on his tunic. The bits were like the curds Narjemah used to make for him from goat's milk, whitish and soft.

Tarran, I can't . . .

A piece of bone was stuck in his arm. It didn't hurt. He plucked it out and flung it away. He started shaking, great shudders racking his body so hard he almost fell over.

Tarran . . .

But Tarran wasn't there.

He vomited, the contents of his stomach splashing onto his feet. *Tarran? Please come back.*

No reply. He spoke to himself instead, rummaging for sanity. *Oh, Goddess, his head . . . Do something, Arrant. You have no ward and there are legionnaires all over the place still.*

That was an exaggeration: there were only three mounted guardsmen left. Five or six legionnaires on foot. None of them seemed to have noticed what Arrant had done. Five gorclaks were trotting around riderless and aimless.

One of the mounted three battled five or six of Ligea's soldiers. Another was riding his mount over the injured men Foran had been treating, crushing them to death under the hooves. The third rider was hit by a blast of red power from Foran. It splattered into his chest – but the man didn't fall. He just swayed in the saddle. He glanced at where the beam had melted a hole in his armour, hefted his javelin and rode on straight at Foran.

The Illuser looked horrified. He started to build a ward between them.

Oh, Mirage hells, Arrant thought. *His power, it's gone.* Frantic, he groped for his own power, trying to drag it into being. He raised his arm again, not knowing if anything would respond.

Tarran, that man's head, did you see? . . . Tarran? Silence. Emptiness. No one there to rely on. *Just you, you fool.* His cabochon responded and a beam of light left his hand. He misjudged the speed of the thundering gorclak, and missed the rider.

That man's head; gods, what did I do . . .

The focused beam of power sailed on and hit the city wall fifty paces away, dislodging stones.

The man's head – it just . . . vanished.

Tarran didn't hear. Wasn't there.

The javelin hit Foran in the middle of the chest. The Illuser collapsed. Arrant, his mind screaming denial, tried again. This time his beam of power broadened out into a swathe of burning gold. It hit both man and beast, but didn't stop. He hadn't controlled the reach of his power. He hadn't controlled its spread. He hadn't controlled anything. Didn't know how. The gold moved on with a remorseless mind of its own, broadening as it went, spilling power from its edges in reckless, destructive splashes.

He glimpsed the other two legionnaires and their gorclaks just before they ruptured, torn into pieces, none bigger than a legionnaire's helmet. Behind him he felt more disintegration. More cessation of life. The injured no longer moaned. And then the squelching splats of soft things falling. Blood and flesh rained down, red rain, bloodied bits of bone that bounced like hail, chunks of meat forming a circle of scarlet around him.

He stood at its centre, like the stamen of a blood-red blossom that was forty paces across.

The remaining soldiers near the gate fled. They were Ligea's men and they fled her son, scattering into the field outside the city.

And still he stood. Rivulets of blood snaked down his face,

his back, his arms; blood dripped from his nose, his chin, his fingers. It soaked his clothes. Stung his eyes.

He withdrew, shrinking himself into the quietness of a mind shut down. He no longer heard anything at all.

CHAPTER THIRTY-ONE

Ligea found the Magistrium empty. She walked through the echoing marble halls with their extravagance of friezes and statues, to investigate the side rooms with their thick carpeting. She sensed no one. In Rathrox's office, scrolls and ledgers and papyrus sheets scattered the floor like leaves after a storm. The message was clear. The man had taken what he needed and fled.

Still trailed by Gevenan's two men, she left the Magistrium and hurried on up to Rathrox's villa, but of course he wasn't there, either. Two of his slaves were dead in the entry hall. She recognised them both. One had been his man of affairs; the other, his scribe. *They knew too much*, she thought. *He was cleaning up behind him. And they'd be alive now, too, if I'd killed him in front of the Oracle that day.*

She sent the two soldiers to the port to stop him if he were trying to take a ship out, but she had an idea that they would find only a dead end. Rathrox was too wily to have left a trail behind him.

She herself headed off for the North Gate, to see how Gevenan and her men there were progressing. Once again, she was delayed by the chaos of the streets, her purpose interrupted by her need to control looting, or stop the violence, or send rioting slaves back to their homes with orders to stay there. Maintaining her dominance over the situation was not easy: to do it without too much expenditure of power was almost impossible. The colour in her sword began to dim as her cabochon lost power. Fatigue dragged at her. She was going to have to be careful. She needed to retain enough Magor power for the rest of the day; her battle was not over yet. She grabbed some pastries and a handful of shelled pistachios from an abandoned bakery, and ate them as she walked.

She didn't get to the gate. The Via Pecunia leading to the North Gate started at the palace, slanting off in a different direction from the Forum Publicum, and the whole area of the Forum in front of the palace was jammed with fighting men. The public concourse had become a battleground, seething with individual conflicts.

Ligea swore. Where the Vortexdamn had all these men come from? A glance told her they were a mix of Imperial Guards and Valorian's Tyr legionnaires on one side, and on the other . . . well, she spotted men who had come with her from the Stronghold, there were Quyriot horsemen, she recognised some of Gevenan's men from the barges, but there were also men and women wearing slave collars and hefting everything from roasting spits to blacksmith's hammers. Apparently, her forces from the North Gate had pushed Bator Korbus' men back to the centre of Tyr. The final battle for the city was being fought right here, in front of the symbol of Exaltarchy power.

She enhanced her sight and surveyed the top of the broad flight of stairs at the palace's main entrance. The Imperial Guard, with some of Valorian's men, had formed up in rows on the marble portico in front of the huge wooden doors. Bator Korbus fought with them, in the centre. Valorian was there too, beside him. With their curved shields covering their torsos, and their long spears, this wall of experienced fighting men was proving impossible to dislodge. They had the advantage of the higher ground and were using their spears to deadly effect, jabbing at the attackers who repeatedly stormed up the broad set of stairs. Less than a hundred men, and they were able to keep a whole army at bay. If a guard fell, then there was another from the row behind to take his place. However, as far as Ligea could see, not many had died.

She scanned the attackers. Gevenan was there, at the heart, rallying and directing his men. The relief she felt at the sight of him touched more than her desire for victory. *Gev*, she thought, *I would hate to see your death, my friend. And wouldn't you love the irony of that . . . Ligea caring, in a quite personal way, about your sarcastic hide.*

She took a deep breath. This was where and when it ended. This was the moment of victory – or defeat.

She threw off her shawl and the white robe, discarding them together with her bag. Clad only in a brown tunic and leggings and carrying her sword, she began to wend her way through the fighting men. She kept every sense alert to danger, open to hostile intention from those around her, but a nondescript woman was of no interest to men fighting for their lives. Only when she had nearly reached the bottom of the steps did she hold her blade aloft, calling on some of the remnants of her Magor magic.

The intense flare of light from her Mirager's sword halted the fighting around her. Bator raised his shield in front of his face. Soldiers drew back, unable to see, raising their arms to block the light.

Except for Gevenan.

He used everyone else's moment of disorientation to grab Valorian's spear by the haft. One sharp pull and the Legate tumbled from the portico. Ligea's lips curved up. *Trust Gev.* The two men grappled on the steps, ignoring all else. Ligea felt their satisfaction. *Goddessdamn*, she thought, *for all like a pair of bantam cocks trying to rule the roost. Bloody men! One of them is going to end up dead, and they are* enjoying *themselves?*

Everywhere else, a shudder went through the armies. Men were stung by the prickles of pain, as sharp as thorns against the skin, that she had stitched into the Magor light. The cessation of combat spread outwards, following the ripples of that uncanny light as it dispensed its pain. Ligea heard the whispers spread too, old soldiers' memories, imbibed by younger men around campfires: *Numen. Goddess. Immortal. Witchery. Remember Kardiastan. Remember what they said about the Kardi Uprising.*

Remember the legends about the Rift. Beware: you cannot win this fight.

But perhaps it wasn't fear that stopped the battle. Most of these men had been fighting since dawn, and now the sun hung overhead, a hot blaze heating metal, baking men in their leather cuirasses or their bronze armour. Perhaps it was just the desire to rest that halted them. To have it all end.

Except for Gevenan and Valorian.

Cursing Gevenan for forcing her to use a portion of that last reserve of power, she built a ward around the two of them, making it so small neither could move. It was Gevenan's turn to curse, his vocabulary so ripe she wasn't sure she understood all the words he used. She glared at him. Valorian just looked stunned.

'Get down here and protect my side,' she yelled at Gevenan and let the ward vanish. She was too weak to hold it in place much longer anyway. Across in other parts of the city, she felt her other wards wink into nothingness as well. She had to finish this before the legionnaires and Imperial Guards she'd had trapped behind those wards arrived.

And she had expended all she had in that burst of gold, all but one last shaft she had saved for Bator Korbus, a pathetically weak bubble of power now latent in the blade of her sword.

Gevenan sprang to obey her order, half tumbling down the stairway, Valorian's spear still in one hand, his own sword in the other. She felt his men gather at her back to help. Valorian stayed where he was, not far below the Exaltarch's feet, sprawled across several of the steps. He clutched his shield to cover his body, and his eyes gazed at her over the top. She felt his emotions, and smiled at him.

Bator Korbus stared at her. His hate curled around the edges of his shield like surf swirling on a beach. She felt the slap of it, the raging, foaming intensity.

He flung his javelin at her chest. One of Gevenan's men raised his shield in front of her, deflecting the point. A hail of spears followed it, flung by the Imperial Guardsmen, as they recovered from the blast of light and pain. Every single one targeted her.

One knocked her to her knees when it caught in her tunic and wrenched her off-balance. Around her, several men died because they had chosen to shelter her with their shields instead of themselves. She scrambled up, cursing the weak fluttering of her power.

Please, let there be no more spears, or I am dead . . .

She levelled her sword tip at the Exaltarch, knowing she no longer had enough power to kill him from more than a pace away. She ran upwards, taking the steps two at a time, her weakened sensing ability open to all the information it could garner.

'*Kill* her,' Bator bellowed at his guard. 'She's only a Kardi woman, not a damned goddess!'

Gevenan leaped up the stairs alongside her. Others sprang to follow, cutting off the Imperial Guardsmen from either side as they moved down.

She filled her sword with colour, showered herself with gold. *Colour*, she thought. *There's nothing much else there. I am about to fight a military commander with a sodding paintbrush . . .*

Yet it was enough to make the guardsmen falter.

They had seen her power. They feared its mystery. They were brave men, but they feared to fight what they did not understand. They looked out over the crowd filling the concourse, and saw an expanse of upturned faces watching. Not fighting; *waiting*.

And in that hiatus of time, Bator Korbus lost his command. She wondered if he felt it too, that wavering of spirit that went through his men.

It's kill me now, or lose, Bator . . . one chance to take back your command.

He threw himself down the steps to meet her coming up. As he leaped, he flung his shield at Gevenan. The Ingean had to raise his arm to ward off the blow, but it toppled him nonetheless. His fall brought down the two other men closest to her.

Bator levelled his sword at her chest. She had no shield. She was alone, and almost defenceless. All she had were her senses.

'Valorian,' she said in the split second available.

And on the steps, the Legate tilted his shield just as the Exaltarch jumped over him to reach her.

They spoke of it for years afterwards, those who had been there. Those who were close to the steps and who saw and heard what happened. The privileged ones, who could boast that they had seen the fall and the rise of exaltarchs.

'She used her magic,' one said. 'She sent the old Exaltarch flying through the air to land with his head at her feet and his legs further up the stairs. He looked about as dignified as a whore in a brothel with her legs apart.'

'She rolled him over with her foot,' another said. 'Alive? Oh, yes, he was still alive. She put that sword of hers to his throat and said, "Do you know who I am, Bator? Do you know why you are about to die?" He spat at her then, but she didn't flinch. He said, "I should have killed you at the same time that I slid my sword into your mother's belly." That's when she killed him.'

They were wrong, those storytellers. She hadn't killed him then. That was when she'd bent to say softly in his ear, 'Everything you had, Bator, will be mine. A Kardi numen bitch is going to rule this land, and everything you built is going to be destroyed. Die knowing that your name is going to be forgotten, because there will be nothing anyone can point to and say: "Bator Korbus did that."'

That was when she killed him.

When she withdrew the blade from Bator's neck, it was to Gevenan that she turned. He was holding Valorian by the arm, with a dagger at his throat.

'Gev,' she said mildly, 'he was the one who just saved me. He tripped the bastard up. Let him go.'

Gevenan dropped the point of the dagger, but his reluctance was obvious. She guessed his suspicion was spilling out in all directions, but she could not feel it.

She continued, 'I want you to get your men organised and the slaves under control. No looting. No more killing.'

He looked at Valorian. He was still clutching the Legate by the arm. 'And what about *his* men?'

'You two are going to have to learn to like one another. You had better start now. Legate Valorian, you are still in charge of your forces. For the time being, until such time as they take a new oath of allegiance to me, they will have to give up their swords, shields, javelins and spears. Gevenan here will organise that. They can keep their daggers.'

'Allegiance to *you*?' Valorian swallowed. He could not quite conceal his horror. '*You* are going to be the new Exaltarch?'

'I am. Get used to the idea. Gev, I want Bator's head on a spike at the palace door. And send someone to find my son and bring him to me. I shall be in the palace.'

Valorian, struggling to absorb the idea of a woman Exaltarch, finally managed to recover some of his aplomb. He asked, 'Can I assume then, Domina, that you are not Melete? Or some other goddess, for that matter?'

'*Her*?' Gevenan interrupted. 'The gods would never let her *near* Elysium!'

Ligea glared at him and turned to Valorian again. 'You've made one wise decision today already. Now's the time to make another. You can serve me, or you can retire, preferably somewhere a long way from Tyr.'

He took a deep breath and said, 'I'll serve whoever sits in the Exaltarch's seat.' He jabbed Bator with his boot and shrugged. 'Seems he just abdicated.'

She nodded, smiling faintly at the way he had worded the statement. 'Fair enough. You're a careful man, Valorian.'

He gestured at the Imperial Guards, who were already relinquishing their weapons to Gevenan's men. 'One thing I should make quite clear right now, though. Those are not my men, and never have been. They are Bator's hand-picked thugs. I would advise that you have them killed.'

She squinted against the light, looking at the men above her, trying to assess their feelings. She could discern nothing: all her power had vanished. It was disconcerting to have no sense of the mood of those around her. Disconcerting and dangerous. 'No,' she said. 'Just have them locked away somewhere for the time being. I will interview each man later before I make any decisions. Can you see to that, Valorian? You may choose twenty men of your own – men you trust – who can keep their weaponry. Gev, give him back his sword.'

She looked at the crowd. At least three-quarters of them were kneeling. *Kneeling.* To her. She found the notion suddenly repellent. Mostly they were silent, although those at the back were pestering to know what was happening at the front. 'I think you had better start doing something before they get restless. It's Vortexdamned hot out there. When you have anything to report, either of you, I will be in Bator's private quarters.'

With that she walked towards the palace doors. She wasn't immediately aware that Gevenan had signalled a dozen of his men to follow her.

She did hear Valorian ask Gevenan, without realising just how well his voice carried, 'Who the sweet hells *is* that daughter of a bitch?'

Gevenan, who knew exactly how loud to speak in order for her to hear him, gave an audible sigh and said, 'You know what, Legate? Take my advice: you really don't want to know. Let's just say that she's stubborn and cantankerous and as hard as a hobnail. She has powers that could send you to Acheron with a flick of her wrist. But she'll also make the best damned Exaltarch this country has ever had.'

Ligea smiled.

Now if only I can get inside without falling flat on my face with fatigue . . .

'Exalted One?'

She woke with a start, the name bringing her up from sleep into an instant state of terror. But it was only Gevenan who had woken her. '*What* did you call me?'

'Exalted One.'

'Call me that again and it'll be your head on a stake at the gate.'

He smiled. 'Nice to know you're not going to change your nature just because you've become the greatest despot of the known world. Lord of Tyr, High General of Tyrans, Exaltarch of the Tyranian Empire, and all that.'

'I wish you'd grow sweeter-natured with age, Gev.' She glanced around, still a little befuddled by her sudden awakening. 'Is everything all right?' It was dark outside; she must have slept for hours. She sifted through her memories of what she had done before that. She had spoken to the palace slaves, had a bath, eaten yet another large meal. She'd been looking through the Exaltarch's papers, when she must have fallen asleep at the desk. Anyone could have killed her and she wouldn't have known a thing about it.

No ward put in place, no senses to tell her where people were, or what they were feeling. It was as if she had been rendered deaf and blind all at once. How could she ever survive without those skills? She looked at her cabochon. It was almost clear in colour, but she thought it might be a shade less transparent now that she'd eaten and slept.

It will be all right, she thought. *It will come back. It must.*

Because there was one thing for sure: if she didn't have Magor power, she'd be dead within days. If she wasn't able to tell a lie from the truth, she'd never be able to know whom to trust.

'It's about Arrant,' Gevenan said. 'We've found him.'

'Oh, good. Is he here?'

'Well, he's just had a bath. He needed it.'

There was a peculiar tone to his voice, and even without her abilities she knew there was something wrong. She stood up. 'What is it?'

'Foran is dead. We don't know exactly what happened, but the two of them got caught up in some of the fighting. Apparently Arrant tried to help Foran but he couldn't control his power properly.' He ran a hand through his hair. 'Ligea, there's no good way to say this. My men found him just outside the North Gate. Everyone was too scared to go anywhere near him. He was standing in the centre of a circle of . . . disintegrated people. Bits of flesh and fragments of bone. And blood. A lot of blood. The ground was *red* with it. So was Arrant. We think he killed our own men, as well as the legionnaires who were attacking. And the gorclaks too. And probably Foran as well.'

She felt all the blood drain from her head, and sat down abruptly. 'Is he—?' She stopped. Her mind couldn't think of the right question to ask.

'He's in a state of shock. He's not speaking. I asked the slaves to lay out a meal for him in that end room through there, next to your bedroom, but he hasn't eaten it. There's a bed in there for him, too. But – er, he doesn't seem to know who I am. He doesn't seem to hear when anyone speaks to him. I'll go and fetch him, if you like.'

'Yes,' she whispered. 'Please.'

When he had gone, she sat frozen in place. *Victory. Shouldn't I have known it? Victory always comes at such a terrible price . . .*

She looked up to see Gevenan leading Arrant into the room. Eyes unfocused, he looked straight through her, as if she weren't there. She rose and crossed to where he stood. She tried to gather him into her arms, but he stood rigid, unbending. Unseeing.

'Arrant – are you all right? Arrant? You are safe now. I'm here. Mater. And Gev. You're in the Exaltarch's palace. The war is over; it's all over and we have won.'

He didn't look at her. Gevenan tried speaking to him too, but nothing had any impact, and in the end Gevenan led him away.

She covered her face with her hands. This was the price of victory? She didn't want to pay it.

Don't let me lose my son. Please don't let me lose Arrant.
Not him too.

PART FIVE

SON OF THE
EXALTARCH

CHAPTER THIRTY-TWO

Arrant decided he hated banquets. This one was his first, but two hours into the evening and he had already made up his mind he didn't like the people who attended them. They weren't his mother's friends; in fact many were people who hated her. Men who would have killed her if they had known how to do it.

People had tried, at first. Fifteen assassination attempts in the first two years of her rule; he'd counted them. Ligea hadn't told him about the ones that didn't happen under his nose, but Arrant knew anyway. He hadn't needed Magor senses; he'd heard the palace gossip. Individual assassins with a dagger hidden in their wrap, archers shooting from a rooftop as she passed, poison in her food, even on one memorable occasion an attempt to drown her at the Public Baths. Thanks to her Magoroth abilities, she'd never been as much as scratched and, finally, as her reputation for invulnerability grew, and with all the assassins dead one way or another, the number of attempts in the following two years had diminished. The last one was, what – six months ago?

He looked around the banquet hall, cursing himself for having pleaded to come. True, the food was good. He regretted Tarran's absence – his brother would have loved the pheasant pie and the sweetbreads and the honey cakes – but when he'd called him, there had been no reply.

I wonder how he knows when I am desperate and when I am not? He's always come when I am in real trouble.

Part of him despaired. Tarran's visits purely for fun were becoming rarer and rarer.

A woman he didn't know was staring at him from the other side of the room. She was elderly, but still beautiful in a regal, haughty way. She wore an ornate pendant to match her gold-trimmed wrap; Arrant had never seen such a large item of jewellery. Pieces of it dangled almost to her waist. Her eyes flicked from Ligea to himself and back again, as though she was comparing the two of them, her gaze arrogantly contemptuous. She bent to speak to the man next to her, and he knew she was talking about him. The man murmured something and shrugged.

Arrant blushed hotly. *The bitch*, he thought. She had no right to look at him like that, as though he was an unwashed street urchin. He looked away, deciding he would ignore her.

Fortunately the two men seated to his right weren't too bad. The Reviarch Javenid and Arcadim Asenius, moneymasters. Arrant didn't mind them. They didn't patronise him, nor did they try to slime their way into his confidence. He suspected they didn't much like banquets either. Assorians didn't eat meat of any kind, for a start, and the feasting table was full of suckling pig and lamb, goose and swan, dormouse and sea slugs. The Reviarch ignored the meat and picked at the fruit and bread and cheese; crumbs clung to his beard, mixed in with his pearls. Arcadim just looked sick and uncomfortable. He sliced the cheese on his plate into smaller and smaller pieces, but none of it ever reached his mouth.

The moneymasters may not have enjoyed an imperial banquet, but they came when asked. Arrant knew why: it was their way of paying homage to Ligea, their way of showing everyone she had the support of Assorian money. She had granted the vassal state of Assoria its freedom almost immediately after she had become Exaltarch, and they were repaying the debt.

He also knew that an independent Assoria paid just as much money into Tyr's public coffers now as they ever had. They had to buy Tyranian protection, or end up losing their newfound freedom to the tattooed barbarians on their borders. Doubtless they would eventually have their own army, but in the meantime they paid for the use of Tyranian legions. The irony of that delighted Arrant, especially when he realised his mother had banked on just such a situation arising, not just in Assoria, but along all the borders of the old Exaltarchy.

The moment the new Tyrans had granted the provinces and vassal states their freedom, all the barbarians and vagabond nomads, whether they were the blue-bearded desert marauders of the south, the fur-clad bear people of the north, the corsairs of the Wild Waters, or the tattooed peoples to the east, had seen it as a sign of weakness and attacked. Kardiastan was strong enough, and Altan prepared enough, to defend themselves, but other freed provinces and vassals, now sovereign states, were forced to invite the old enemy back in to patrol and defend their boundaries. And for a little extra, Tyranian engineers would also build or repair paveways and aqueducts and border walls, just as they had back in the days when the Exaltarch had lorded it over a huge empire. Arrant loved the symmetry of that.

He watched as one of the Tyranian highborn came across to talk business with the Reviarch, while Arcadim continued to play with his cheese. The noble was wanting a loan to pay the labourers on his country estate. He wanted a promissory note against the value of his wheat and grape harvest, and grumbled audibly about his hardships now that he was not allowed to own slaves. The Reviarch shot Arrant a glance and tried to subtly inform the man that he was making indiscreet remarks in front of the Exaltarch's son, but the man continued, oblivious. Few people actually knew who Arrant was.

Arrant knew the moneymasters weren't too happy about the slavery issue either. Keeping slaves was illegal everywhere in Tyrans now, though everyone tried to circumvent the law, much to Ligea's exasperation. 'Those Vortex-blamed Assorians,' she'd said to him once, 'I *know* those god-worshipping moneymakers still keep slaves. But what can I do about it? Not one of their slaves will admit they are still enslaved!'

Arrant wondered about that. He caught the eye of Arcadim

and asked, 'Do you Assorian moneymasters still have slaves, Master Arcadim?' He tried to look innocently naive, but he was being mischievous. He was well aware the moneymaster believed, erroneously, that Arrant could tell a lie from the truth. He would therefore be forced to dodge the question, or be honest.

The moneymaster shot an agitated glance at the Reviarch, who had finally managed to get rid of the highborn man, but the Reviarch was sipping his wine, oblivious. Arcadim agitatedly tore some bread on his plate into smaller pieces. He said, looking at the bread without really seeing it, 'All Assorians in Tyrans pay their slaves now, Arrant.'

The Reviarch heard that remark and jerked his goblet, spilling some of his wine. Arcadim amended hastily, 'Pay their *servants*, I mean, of course.'

'How much?'

'Er . . . um.' He cleared his throat. 'Each servant gets a silver sestus coin per year, plus food, a pallet and two sets of clothes. And a new pair of sandals when needed.' He sounded a little shamefaced, as well he might. A silver sestus was not enough to live on independently for even a month; it certainly wasn't enough to get a man home to Assoria.

'And can they leave whenever they want?' Arrant asked.

'Yes. Naturally.' His bread was joining the pile of cheese crumbs.

Arrant asked innocently, 'Would they find employment in another Assorian household?'

Arcadim shrugged and looked away.

They wouldn't, of course. That was the catch. And they couldn't go to non-Assorian employers, because they thought it a sin to live in the house of an unbeliever.

Arrant glanced away from the moneymasters. He knew the slavery issue had been his mother's greatest problem as Exaltarch. How do you persuade people to pay for something they've always had for free? How do you do away with all the other litter of the old system dragging in slavery's wake? Slaves hadn't even been acknowledged to exist in the previous Exaltarchy's legal system! And what do you do with all the slaves no one could now afford to employ? How do you keep a country prosperous when the whole scaffolding of its economic life had depended on its having free labour and the looted wealth of the provinces, for as long as anyone remembered?

He looked at Ligea, sitting with the most important guests, smiling at something said by the head of the Gracii merchant family.

Why doesn't she talk to me any more? he wondered.

He learned all he knew of Tyr and the new Tyrans from his tutors, not his mother. She never included him in any of her negotiations with the merchants, or the diplomatic meetings with envoys, or her discussions with her advisers. He had thought that would change once he reached the age of twelve, officially now a youth wearing a wrap, not a boy in a tunic, but that had been a year past and she had continued to exclude him.

He thought, distressed, *She always will. Because I am not really a Magoroth. Because I'm nothing at all, just a Kardi youth with a cabochon that only works when it feels like it . . .*

As he acknowledged the truth of that, the shrunken mass under his breastbone contracted. He knew what it was, that shrivelled-up bit of himself: the ball of atrophied feelings and grim memories that he couldn't afford to think about because they hurt too much. They sat there in his midriff as ugly as dead weed on a beach, waiting for him to bring them out and pick them over.

He pushed the ball back down.

She's not my mother any more, either, he thought. *Not really. She's the Exaltarch.*

He took a deep breath, trying to grow in courage. He had to accept what she was, what he was. Even if there wasn't really an empire any more, she was a ruler with no time for a son who was of no value to her.

He looked up from his plate and caught the eye of the woman with the ornate pendant. She was still staring at him, her eyes as hard and cold as marble.

'She's a clever woman, our Exaltarch,' the Reviarch said and added, almost as though he had been following Arrant's previous line of thought: 'Who would have dreamed that inducting freed slaves into the army and navy would have solved so much of Tyrans's monetary crisis?'

'Who would have thought she would be able to sell a *Tyranian* armed force as an agent of peace?' added Arcadim.

Arrant pulled his thoughts away from his personal pain and nodded politely. 'Rent an army,' the sarcastic had called it. His politics tutor had explained how she'd had even more success with the Tyranian navy by converting part of it into the greatest merchant fleet the world had ever seen. And you could 'rent a navy' too, if pirates were a problem along your coastline.

Marvellous what you can do when you have a cabochon and a Magor sword, he thought, his cynicism curling his lip. Especially when she'd had help. Temellin had finally sent a delegation of the Magoroth under Garis, not to Tyrans but into the fledgling states, to aid them with the establishment of a new order around the Sea of Iss. And there had been the moneymasters, of course, prodding and tweaking the traders and the merchants and the highborn to act in ways not inimical to their own interests.

'My biggest fear,' the Reviarch said, reflecting Arrant's thoughts again, 'was that the old Exaltarchy would disintegrate into anarchy.' He glanced at Ligea. 'Yes, a clever woman, your mother.'

Arrant didn't reply, suddenly feeling out of his depth. In comparison with these two men, he knew nothing about the complex world of finance, commerce and trade. He changed the subject. 'Who is the woman opposite, the one with the big piece of jewellery around her neck?'

The Reviarch glanced across. 'Ah. That's Antonia, priestess of the Cult of Melete. She serves at the temple on the Via Galetea. No friend to your mother.'

'The pendant is the insignia of the Meletian High Priestess,' Arcadim added.

'Why doesn't she like Ligea?'

The Reviarch and Arcadim exchanged a glance. 'Ah,' the Reviarch said again, running a hand down his beard. 'You should ask your mother that. But it has a lot to do with the Domina Ligea taking the temple on the Forum Publicum away from the Cult of Melete, and giving it to the Unknown God. Antonia was the High Priestess there before. The temple on Via Galetea is half the size and not nearly as beautiful.'

'She's lucky she lived,' Arcadim added. 'She deceived the followers of Melete for years with a false Oracle.'

'Yes, I've heard that,' Arrant said, anxious not to appear too uninformed. 'When my mother became Exaltarch, she persuaded Esme, the Selected of the Oracle, to tell everyone what she knew.'

'That's right. When people heard what Esme had to say, there were some who pressed for Antonia's death, but Domina Ligea was merciful. Not always a good thing. The cult lost at least half their following over the affair,' Arcadim added.

There was an uncomfortable silence. The Reviarch cleared his throat noisily; Arcadim excused himself and disappeared in the direction of the lavatories; Arrant fidgeted and stared at his plate.

I shouldn't have come, he thought. *I don't belong here. I don't want to be here.*

And this was such a silly way to eat, lounging about on divans, picking things off the low table instead of sitting at a proper bench. And there were all the rules about how to eat. Fingers of the right hand only, never the left. Don't get the palm of your hand dirty, either. Wash the fingers in the fingerbowl between each dish. Stupid. Back in the Stronghold or on First Farm, they'd sat at a board table on upright chairs, and they'd used spoons. And your own dagger to cut the meat and bread.

He looked around the room once more, wishing that Gevenan could have been there. Although Gevenan would never have attended something like this, at least not voluntarily. Anyway, he was no longer in Tyr. He was now General Gevenan, the Military Governor of the Western Region of Tyrans, a post he had taken up two years after Ligea became Exaltarch.

He missed Gev. You always knew where you were with the General.

He was thinking about getting up and leaving when a youth

came and sat next to him, taking Arcadim's place on the divan. He looked bored too and pulled a sympathetic face at Arrant. 'They drag awfully, these banquets, don't they? Father insisted I come. If it wasn't for the food . . .'

'Try the stuffing in the goose,' Arrant advised. 'Water chestnuts, I think. It's really good.'

'Yes, I have. Are you really the Exaltarch's son, Arrant? Someone over there was saying you were.'

Arrant nodded. *Not someone else who wants something . . .*

'My name's Martecian,' the youth said chattily, oblivious to Arrant's wariness. 'Magistrate Pereus is my father – that's him next to the Legate Valorian over there. He said I should come and talk to you because you looked as bored as I did!' He laughed, and Arrant found himself grinning back. 'Are you training for the army yet?' Martecian asked, snatching a wine glass from a passing servant.

Arrant froze. 'Not – not officially.' *A blinding flash of light. Screaming . . . Don't think about it. Don't remember.* 'They won't take you before sixteen. Not into the officer training anyway.'

'How old are you, then?'

'Thirteen.'

'Oh. I didn't know. I thought you were older. I heard talk of you fighting during the fall of Tyr, and that was already four years ago. I'm sixteen. I'm going off to join the army this year. Are you going to do the same when you're old enough?'

Arrant shook his head.

'Why not? If you want to be the Exaltarch after your mother, you ought to be a military man first. Or are you going to the Academy to study politics instead?'

'I'm not going to be the next Exaltarch.' He thought he couldn't have imagined anything worse. And then did just that. *Being the Mirager of Kardiastan when I have no control over my power, that could be worse. A lot worse.* His hand shook as he reached blindly for some grapes.

'I suppose there's nothing to say the next Exaltarch should be the child of the last one,' Martecian agreed. 'In fact, I don't think it's happened like that in the past, has it? We are not a kingdom, after all. But people say you and the Exalted One are different from others. Because you have that.' He pointed at Arrant's left hand, indicating the uncovered cabochon.

The flash that came into Arrant's head was detailed, every piece of the scene stitched into the tapestry of his mind, embroidered with the vividness of perfect memory, as though he were there now, seeing it anew.

The chunks of flesh. The shower of red rain, blood falling, drenching. The stickiness of it on his face, trickling like honey down his cheek. The head of a man turning in the air, without its body. The splat of it when it hit the ground. The smell of meat . . . only the meat was human. The stink of human innards. All around him, the death of others. Men he had killed. None with the time to scream before they died. Foran obliterated. A bloody stream, oozing thickly into the drain of the paveway. The wounded men Foran had been treating nowhere to be found . . .

How many had he slaughtered? He had no idea.

Afterwards, there were some who said he'd killed Foran. That he'd killed some soldiers of Ligea's legion as well. And all the wounded. But he hadn't. Well, not all of them. Foran had died with a spear in his chest, and the legionnaire gorclaks had trampled some of the wounded. The others . . .

He dug his nails into his palm, hard, seeking pain to haul him back into the present. It took so little to bring on those horrible flashbacks, and so *much* to push them away.

Martecian gave him an odd look, and Arrant knew his abstraction would be construed as a further indication of his strangeness. He was, after all, the son of a woman many regarded as being a living goddess. Didn't she shoot lightning bolts from her hand and sword? Wasn't the very touch of her fingers said to be curative to the ill?

He's wondering if all they say about my instability is true. Wondering if the Exaltarch's son really could blow people to pieces with a look, just because he lost his temper. He's wondering if the Exaltarch's son should be feared, not befriended.

Everyone wondered that, sooner or later. Everyone had heard the rumours. Which was one reason why he had no friends of his own age. No parents would risk their offspring spending time with him alone; he might disintegrate them. Even now, Martecian was looking uncomfortable.

'Excuse me,' Arrant mumbled, and left the divan, left the banquet hall. Outside, he slipped away in the direction of his own quarters. Goddess, how he *hated* everything about the palace in Tyr! About this sterile life he led. Where nothing was true, where nothing showed its heart on the surface.

He dodged the servants bringing more trays piled high with steaming dishes. The smell was suddenly nauseating. He ran on up to the first floor, hoping to reach his room unobserved, but bumped into Narjemah coming from his mother's apartments. She was more Ligea's servant – no, more a companion than a servant – now that he was too old for a nurse.

She clicked her tongue when she saw him. 'You should be downstairs at the banquet,' she scolded. 'You wanted to be there! Nagging your mother like that . . .'

'No one will miss me.'

'Your mother will.'

'She didn't want me to go in the first place.'

'She likes you to be unknown. It's safer.'

He shrugged. 'I thought it might be interesting, but I was just bored. I don't have anything in *common* with those people. I can't even be myself. I dare not say anything – anything *normal*, for fear others will use it against my mother.' He took a deep breath, knowing he was beginning to sound like a spoiled child. 'You know what's really funny, Narjemah? When we first came to Tyr to fight the war, I thought that after it was over, we'd all go home. All of us: Ligea, you, me. Even Gev, to Inge. Oh, I knew Mater talked of being Exaltarch, but I thought that was just for a few months at most. After all, if we won the war, there'd be no need for her here, would there?' He looked at her, half rueful, half miserable. 'I was such a child then.'

She sighed. 'I know. I even thought the same thing myself,

although I might have extended the time frame a little. And I was no child.' She laid a hand on his arm. 'Come, let's go to your rooms and we'll have a mulled wine and a chat. It's been too long since we sat and had a talk.'

He nodded, pleased. And then felt scornful of a thirteen-year-old who was so lonely that talking to his nurse sounded like a good idea.

The wine, when it came, was watered – his mother insisted on that still – but deliciously tainted with anise and honey, cardamom and sultanas. 'Remember when we used to drink this up in the Stronghold on those cold snow-season nights?' he asked. 'Only back then you used to put a few drops of wine in the water rather than the other way around.'

She smiled. 'You were much younger.' Then she added, more seriously, 'Arrant, you do realise why your mother can't go back to Kardiastan, don't you?'

'I might have known nothing then, but I am not such an idiot now,' he said. Misery dragged at his voice, so he made an effort to sound more cheerful. 'I don't have a chance to be. I have six different tutors, remember? History, philosophy, rhetoric and politics, geometry, natural science and geography. And that's not including the chief scribe of the Asenius Counting House who comes once every ten days to teach me accounting and trade.'

He fiddled with his goblet, eyeing the sultanas at the bottom, swollen with wine and spice. He had so loved them when he was younger. 'I know if my mother leaves before her changes are properly fixed in place, the whole' – he searched for the right word – 'edifice will crumble. Cominus litters his rhetoric lessons with statements about how, without her, Tyrans would either degenerate into chaos and civil war, or it would have another despot like Bator Korbus.' He swirled his wine without drinking it. 'I know he's right. There are so many things that can go wrong. Gev has never managed to find Favonius or half the Jackals and Brotherhood compeers. They are still out there somewhere, causing trouble. Rathrox Ligatan too.'

Narjemah nodded. 'The changes she wants are so, um, funda-
mental, only she can achieve them. Because she is the only person
with Magor power. Which means she's the only person who can
choose the right men to implement the changes. She's very clever,
you know.'

'I know.'

'No, I don't think you do. Not really. For all your tutors and
your fancy education, I don't think you really see her as she is.
The Exaltarch part of her, I mean. Look at the way she manages
the Advisory Council and the Senate. She had to get the highborn on her side when she became Exaltarch. But why would
they support her, when she spoke of freeing slaves and vassal
states and conquered nations, which would destroy their income?
So she enticed the most powerful families by setting up another
Advisory Council, and seating their representatives there. Then
she used them unmercifully as scapegoats when people
complained of conditions. When the Council complained about
what she was doing, she gave them more power, more work –
which made them even more responsible if schemes failed. "If
they want power, they have to earn it," she told me once.

'What she did split the highborn families right down the middle,
between those who had power and those who didn't, and that divi-
sion halved their strength. Then, when she'd milked as much as
she could from that, she reassembled the Senate. And brought more
families into power, and balanced that by including the military
and the commercial traders.' She smiled at the look on his face.
'Never expected to hear me speak like this, did you? I'm just your
old nurse, who knows how to kiss a skinned elbow better, but
wouldn't know a philosophical treatise from a trade treaty, right?

'Ah, Arrant, before I was your nurse, before I was a slave, I
was one of the ruling class of Kardiastan. The Magor were well
educated, you know. Even Theuras. We were taught to read and
write and figure. Taught to think. Taught to think of ourselves
as – as *rulers*, in fact.

'Well, my world fell apart when Kardiastan was. When you
came along, the best thing I could be was your nurse, the woman

who was there for you when your mother couldn't be. That didn't mean I stopped thinking.'

He found himself blushing. It was true, she had never been more to him than the nurse he loved. He had never thought about her in any other context – only as she related to him.

She swirled her drink and took a sip, then put the goblet down. 'I resented your mother terribly when we first met. Did you know that?'

He shook his head.

'Because she had her cabochon, and I didn't have my powers any more.' She fixed her gaze on him. 'You don't know what it is like to be a real Magor, because you have never had a cabochon you could rely on. But when you've grown up knowing how the people around you feel, as I did, when you've been surrounded all your life by people who could speak together on two levels, using emotions as well as speech, when you know from young how to hear and see things with special clarity – it's like being a god. I suppose that's what made the Magor so arrogant, so ready for a fall. But for all that, it still made living – well, *magical*. Being without that power is like being blind and staggering along in the dark with your hands tied behind your back.

'It was wrong of you, Arrant, to refuse to allow your father to send you another Magor tutor when Foran died. You just wanted to punish Mirager-temellin for not sending for you once the war was over, and that was childish. And stupid.'

Arrant bit his lip, but didn't reply. It wasn't true, anyway. Not really.

Yes, Ligea had written to Temellin shortly after she became Exaltarch, telling him she had no time for her son. She was too busy and Foran was dead. With Kardiastan free, and at peace, it was better he went to his father. When Temellin wrote back insisting she keep him until he was of an age to receive his Magor sword, Arrant had been shattered all over again. *His father still didn't want him.* Nor, for that matter, did his mother.

But that wasn't why he had refused another tutor. No, he had done that because he was never again going to seek out the power of his cabochon. How could he, when he could kill people, people he didn't even *want* to kill, so easily? When he could turn people into mush and liquid as thoroughly as a mill grinder turned wheat to flour, even though he didn't want to? He wanted nothing to do with such power. He didn't want to feel the whisper of it in his cabochon. When he did, he tried to suppress it. And if that meant he could never be Mirager, then so be it. He didn't care. Ocrastes' balls, even sitting here *thinking* about it, he was sweating . . .

'It's a joy,' Narjemah said, 'to feel that power. It's a wondrous thing. And you are cutting yourself off from it.'

He kept silent.

'A Mirager needs to be able to use his cabochon.'

'We both know I'll never be the Mirager,' he blurted. 'And I think Ligea and Temellin know that too.'

'None of us knows any such thing.' She sighed. 'Arrant, you need to forgive your parents. You need to forgive yourself. None of this is anyone's fault, you know. It just happened.'

He reverted to his silence, knowing she was talking about a lot of things. His situation in Tyr. His separation from Kardiastan and his father. What had happened outside the North Gate . . .

She gave an exasperated grunt. 'You and Ligea, you are so alike sometimes. Mirage take the two of you! Do you know how much she blames herself for your lack of Magor skill?'

He was startled, although he thought maybe he had heard that before, from someone, somewhere. 'Why would she do that?'

'Because of what she did when she was carrying you. She drained herself of power on more than one occasion. Because she fell into the Ravage and it might have poisoned you. Because she made you become an essensa. Any one of those things might explain your problems; she's very good at blaming herself, is the Magoria. Whatever the explanation, *it was not your fault.*'

'Oh!' He thought about that. And came to the conclusion that it really didn't matter. How it had happened didn't change his situation.

'She did her best for you,' she said. 'She knew, right from the beginning, that she wouldn't be the best of mothers. How could she be? She had no memory of a loving family. As she was growing up she was encouraged to be self-contained, without sentiment, to be cold and calculating, to keep people at a distance. They were the virtues that Gayed valued and tried to inculcate in her.'

'You weren't there,' he said. 'Did she tell you all that?'

She shook her head. 'No, Brand did. Do you remember him?'

He nodded, and felt a cold twist of dislike. Memory came flooding in, unwanted, yet vivid in a way only a child could have remembered it.

Brand hugging Ligea. Brand speaking to him, trying to be friendly. Arrant pinched up his face and hid behind his mother until the big man retreated, baffled.

Ligea scolding later, annoyed, 'I don't know what's the matter with you. You've been acting very strangely lately. I'd like to know just why you treated Brand as if he were a Brotherhood Compeer about to haul you off to the Cages. You are behaving like a three-year-old!'

'I don't like him,' he muttered. 'And I don't like Altan.' They had been given a room in a dark, dank hut facing a water channel; it smelled of mouldiness and rot and damp. The ground was wet and mud oozed up wherever he trod, squishing between his leather sandals and his toes. He looked at his muddy feet in disgust. 'I hate this place. When can we leave?' he whined. 'I wanna go home.'

He pushed the rest of the memory away.

Narjemah said, 'Ligea's strength was that, in the end, she recognised Gayed's values as failings, not virtues. Her tragedy has been that she had so little time for you.'

'I don't blame her for that.'

'It left a legacy, though. It means that you two have only a shaky foundation on which to build a relationship now, and that's difficult. You have to make an effort to chat to her more.' She caught the expression on his face and sighed. 'I know, I know. Thirteen-year-olds hate confidential chats with their mothers!' She rose to her feet. 'Well, I'll be going to bed. We ought to talk more often, you and I. The Magor should always stick together, especially two incomplete Magor like us.'

He nodded. The conversation may not have changed anything, but still it felt good to have someone who cared what happened to him. Especially now that he didn't hear nearly often enough from Tarran.

'I envy you, Arrant,' she added as she paused in the doorway. 'You have a chance to obtain what I lost forever – the wonder of being one of the Magor. Don't throw it away so easily.'

But she didn't explain how it was possible to throw away something you had never got a grip on in the first place.

He continued to sit, sipping his wine, wishing for things that were never going to happen. Wishing Tarran came every day, the way he used to, and that his mother had time for him. Wishing his father wanted him and wishing he understood, really understood, why he didn't. Wishing he had control over his power and that he hadn't killed all those people. Wishing everyone believed him when he said he hadn't killed Foran.

The Illuser had taken a javelin in the chest and died. He'd seen it. He remembered it. It was just that afterwards no one had been able to find his body, just a few rags that had been his clothes.

Arrant looked at the fruit, plump with wine, remaining in the bottom of his glass. If he wanted, he could have asked for mulled sultanas to be sent up to him whenever he felt like them. Servants would have brought him all he wanted. He could have had it all – and he wanted none of it.

He put the goblet down, sultanas uneaten. Suddenly he had no appetite.

CHAPTER THIRTY-THREE

The day after the banquet, Arrant was restless and bored and filled with an odd sort of impatience to be up and doing something, although he didn't know what. When the mathematician from the Academy, Lepidus, arrived to give him a geometry lesson, he sent the old man away. He felt mean, knowing how difficult Lepidus found it to move around when he was half crippled by arthritis, but he did it nonetheless.

So I'm an arrogant bastard, he thought. *Who cares?*

He did, of course. He threw himself down on his bed, hands behind his head, and stared at the ceiling. A jumble of voices leaped up at him:

'– not even one sestus. Goddess, sometimes I wonder if we weren't better off as slaves. At least we got enough to eat then—'

'– do it today, I promise—'

'– those snail-nibbled bastards wouldn't work to please the Exaltarch herself—'

'– so they say. But I think—'

'– Councillor Trabus, I understand the problem—'

Vortex, that last was his mother's voice. As usual, his Magor ability was being as unpredictable as a gorclak on heat and somehow he was picking up conversation from within the palace. Trabus was one of the Advisory Council, a fussy little man as rotund and bald as a pomegranate, his unctuous tone like olive oil slipping over a warmed pan.

Arrant snatched his hands away from his head, hoping the

voices would disappear. They didn't. His mother was saying, 'I will not countenance anything that resembles the Brotherhood. It was an iniquitous organisation—'

'Perhaps, Exalted One. But it kept citizens in line. Now, when Tyrans seethes with unrest, the only thing that maintains stability is fear of the Exaltarch, of you personally, of your abilities – but you can't be everywhere, Domina Ligea.'

'I never wanted to rule by fear.' He heard the touch of wry humour behind the tiredness of her voice.

'You have done nothing to merit fear from the honest, Exalted One.'

Obsequious bastard, Arrant thought.

'Nonetheless,' Trabus continued, 'your powers are great enough to frighten even such as me, let alone the ordinary citizen of Tyrans.'

This was followed by a short silence that made Arrant wonder if he had at last lost the conversation, until Trabus said, 'But if you won't consider reintroducing a secret brotherhood of some kind, then perhaps you will give some thought to how to deal with what's left of the old one. There is reason to believe the Brotherhood still operates, with your downfall in mind.'

'Councillor, I'm delighted to find that you are worried about my welfare—'

Arrant lost the next couple of minutes to an argument between two children on the relative merits of the bats they used for their games of roundball, but then the conversation in the palace audience hall jumped back into focus. Ligea was saying, 'I'm aware of the rumours. There is nothing I wish more than that he hadn't escaped our forces. I don't need proof to know he's the one who tweaks the gorclak's ear because he can't reach the horn. But it has been four years, Councillor, and he hasn't managed to do any lasting harm yet.'

'Exalted One, one day he will reach the horn. He will reach you and find your vulnerable spot and attack you through that.'

'Then I shall have to make sure I remain invulnerable. I am

not defenceless. Rathrox can't get within two hundred paces of me without me knowing. Councillor, you may—'

Then she was gone again and all Arrant could hear was something that sounded like cartwheels over potholes and an unidentifiable metallic racket, as if the contents of a tinker's wagon had been subjected to a minor earthquake. When the audience hall did pop back into his head again, Trabus had gone and Ligea was speaking to a servant, saying, 'Bring Dominus Arrant to me.'

Arrant winced. She couldn't have known he was listening, could she? Vortex no, that was impossible, surely. He scowled. *Dominus!* How he hated that word. He wasn't a lord of Tyr who had earned such a title. He was a Magori, Mirager-heir to Kardiastan. But Tyr didn't know that.

Aloud, he said, 'Goddess, how I hate this place!'

Ten minutes later, a servant ushered him into the audience hall as if he were a petitioner being graciously granted an interview. As he crossed the marble floor, he noted Ligea had finally ordered those awful carpets ripped up. Doubtless she'd had them sold, just as she had earlier disposed of the lion skins and all the more ostentatious furniture. She wasted nothing.

She was dressed as she usually was these days, in a fine silk wrap woven through with gold thread. Her crinkled hair was highlighted with gold to match. He supposed she looked regal, but she didn't look like his mother. She didn't look like Ligea, who'd led an army, either. She was Ligea Gayed, Exaltarch, and he didn't really know her any more.

Ocrastes' balls, I hate this place. I hate it, I hate it . . .

He had another flash of memory. That first evening, as he was entering the palace for the first time. Tarran had been with him, trying to calm him down after what had happened. Trying to bring him back from the dark place he crouched in, silent and refusing to remember. Refusing to *think*, because thinking was agony. Thinking made him the murderer of innocent men.

There had been blood on the marble of the portico, and a sticky puddle of it right in the doorway, reflecting the light of the burning torches. *Blood. More blood.* He'd looked up, wiping his hands on his tunic as if he could rid himself of the stickiness that clung, only to see a man's head impaled on a spike over the doorway. Nausea crept up into his throat, to be swallowed back.

One of the soldiers with him, noting the direction of his gaze, said cheerfully, 'That was the Exaltarch. Bator Korbus, that was.'

Sweet cabochon, Tarran had remarked, *your mother doesn't believe in sinking only half the boat, does she?*

She didn't do that, Arrant had replied, utterly certain. *She wouldn't. Not Ligea. She's not like that.*

Tarran had remained unconvinced and Arrant had sunk back into his dreamlike state, where he was somewhere else, a time when he hadn't killed all those people.

But now he wondered if Tarran hadn't been right. He wasn't sure he knew his mother at all any more.

She waited until the door closed behind him before she greeted him. Then she smiled and came forward to take his hand, cabochon to cabochon. He knew she would feel nothing of his emotions. She'd always had trouble reading him and he'd been utterly hidden from her ever since the moment he'd killed the men outside the North Gate. It wasn't deliberate. It was just all part of the shrivelling that had started that day. All part of the barricade, and the loneliness.

He remembered the moment it happened: the stark instant when he knew what he had done, and knew that if he wanted to stay sane, he had to not be there. And so he had gone away. Closed up, like a shopkeeper putting up the shutters. He had come back, of course, but slowly, opening one shutter at a time, one sense at a time, one sliver of memory at a time, letting in just enough tragedy for him to cope with each time. There was nothing conscious about the decision to return, any more than there had been anything conscious about going away in the first place. It had just happened. It had taken him a year to reassemble all the memories into one indigestible lump of guilt.

But somehow, ever since then, his feelings had never re-emerged to be sensed by Ligea. Or, he assumed, by any Magor. He had wrapped them all up, tight inside himself, a ball of pain and scars and self-loathing, the canker beneath his breastbone. It never went away. It tainted him.

But at least he could hide himself – and his lies.

'You wanted me, Mater?' he asked. She gave the faintest of sighs and he wondered if she had unleashed her pleasure at his presence, hoping he would feel it and reciprocate.

'Yes,' she replied. 'Firstly, I've had a letter from your father that I thought you'd like to read.'

She handed him a papyrus scroll and he couldn't help the sick, angry pain in the pit of his stomach as he took it. He sat down on one of the divans to read. It was mundane news for the most part, and much of it concerned people he didn't know, yet it was enough for him to conjure up Temellin's face and hear his voice once more.

It ended with his usual expression of affection for him, and then a few words for Ligea that seared him with their poignancy.

I have never ceased to love you. This separation is a darkness in my soul. I beg you, come back. If you cannot stay, then just come to visit. How can I live any longer without seeing you?

The sentiment made him feel uncomfortable, as if he had been peeping into their bedroom. He wished he hadn't read that part. He hadn't wanted to know. 'Are you going to go?' he asked.

She shook her head, not meeting his eyes. '*I can't.*'

He stared at her, shocked. He had never heard that much pain in her voice. In *Ligea*? Controlled – that was his mother. Not a woman whose words spoke of the rawness of wounds, of a life lived so close to the emotional edges that she could fall too badly to rise again.

Yet when she spoke again, she was matter-of-fact. 'If I were to leave Tyrans, there'd be a revolution in my absence. Everything people died for would vanish into chaos. How can I – who caused the deaths of so many – allow my personal wishes to bring more tragedy? Arrant, I'm the only thing that's holding the country together.' She made a gesture with her hand. 'I knew the problems would be great. I just never realised how long it would take to solve them. If it hadn't been for the food Temellin sent last snow-season, people may have starved. We didn't have enough labourers to work the grain fields because farmers won't or can't pay them.' She sighed. 'I must go to the western cities soon, to talk to some of the civic leaders there. Gevenan tells me my presence might make a difference.'

'Ah. I suppose so,' he said, handing the scroll back. 'What about Tyr? At the banquet, the Reviarch hinted that you should be wary of the Meletian High Priestess.'

'Oh? Believe me, I am wary of her. She thought nothing of deceiving the religious to further the Exaltarch's power, and thus her own position.'

'Why does she hate you?'

'I made a fool of her, the same way she fooled others. I pretended to be the Oracle, among other things, and Antonia believed I was, until Bator Korbus and Rathrox finally managed to disabuse her of that notion. She has never forgiven me.'

'So why allow her to continue as High Priestess?'

'It's not so easy to get rid of a High Priestess. Some people believe she is chosen by the Goddess herself. I barely got away with forcing the Cult of Melete out of the Forum Publicum temple.' She shrugged. 'I could have killed her, I suppose, but it seemed a better idea to keep her where she was. She knows what I am, and what I can do. That fear keeps her honest. More or less. But this is not what I wanted to talk to you about.' She took a deep breath. 'It's something . . . more personal. And disturbing. I have heard rumours that you disappear from time to time. That you simply cannot be found. Arrant, have you been leaving the palace alone, without your bodyguards?'

'Aren't I entitled to some privacy, Mater? Do I have to be available all the time? If I have found a way to be alone sometimes, does it matter? And I was unaware I could leave the palace even *with* bodyguards.'

It could hardly have escaped her that he hadn't answered her question, which probably told her something anyway.

She said softly, almost gently, 'I hope I don't have to remind you that until such time as you can control your cabochon at will, it would be incredibly dangerous for you to leave the palace alone. There are still too many people out there who would be only too happy to hurt you because it would hurt me. Rathrox Ligatan among them.'

He nodded. 'I know that. I'm not stupid. Do you think he is here in Tyr?'

'I don't know. I haven't felt his presence, but then sorting out just one person from a city full of people is hardly possible anyway. He would have to be close by for me to do that. Just because I have not felt him, doesn't mean he's not out there, awaiting his chance.'

'We both sensed him that time we were on the boat, heading for Kardiastan.'

'He was close by, and furious. I may not feel him now, but I sense his fine touch behind much of this unrest – he is at his best when it comes to manipulating people, and the citizens of Tyrans are being manipulated.' She added harshly, 'He would love to get his hands on you, Arrant.'

'Don't worry; he won't,' he said. When he was out on the streets, no one recognised him. No one. He was too wily for that. He took too much care. Why didn't she have confidence in his good sense?

'I need to know how you are leaving the palace.'

'Ask the guards if I leave at all.'

'I have. And no one will admit to letting you out. And yet two of the servants swore they had glimpsed you in the crowds of Marketwalk.'

He didn't reply.

'I think it would be better if you didn't come to any more of the banquets,' she added, after a long silence. 'It's better that people don't recognise you. Better that they don't know what my son looks like.' She sat down beside him on the divan and glanced at the letter still in her hand. 'I have written back to your father telling him that it is time you went to him. I will not take no for an answer this time. You *must* go to him. And soon. You must be given your Magor sword. You have to learn what it is like to be a Kardi. When I come back from the west, I will arrange it, even if I haven't heard from Temellin.' She stood up, and he knew it was time for him to leave.

Audience over. Usher the petitioner out.

He turned to go, but then turned back. 'That day we first came here – did you order Bator Korbus' head to be placed over the palace doorway?'

'Why in all Acheron's mists would you want to know that?'

So I understand you better? I don't know why! I don't seem to know anything any more . . .

When he didn't reply, she said, 'Yes, I did. I slit his throat, and gave the order for his head to be removed and put over the door. I wanted everyone to know he was dead. I wanted all to see that *I* had killed him.'

He met her steady gaze. Finally he nodded, accepting. Yes, she was a woman who didn't believe in sinking just half the boat.

'War changes people,' she said. 'It changes us all.'

He thought of the boy he had been, before the attack on Tyr. Pleading with Foran to get closer to the gate. Because he wanted to *see*.

He nodded. 'Yes,' he said, 'it does.'

The canker under his breastbone suddenly seemed to have moved to his throat. He turned away so she wouldn't see just how close he was to tears.

When he had gone, she sat again and covered her face with her hands. That look on Arrant's face . . . So cold. He had not thought her barbaric, until now. *Now he knows, Goddess help me.* He had found out, and thought it a betrayal.

I never wanted to be Ligea Gayed again, but that's what I am becoming . . .

A compeer bitch.

Cabochon take it, Temellin . . . I can't do this alone.

* * *

Arrant returned to his rooms.

He sat for a while, looking at the chest on the floor. Then he knelt, unlatched it and extracted the clothes hidden at the bottom under his best wraps: a servant boy's tunic with the imperial insignia stamped around the hem, a servant's cap, a pair of rough-made sandals, a cheap leather coin-pouch. Apart from the insignia, the outfit was not unlike the garb he had worn as a younger child, and he felt more comfortable wearing it than the silk wraps the palace servants laid out for him every morning.

'It's silly,' he'd told Tarran once, 'but it's the servants who want me to dress in the clothes left behind by Bator Korbus and those who lived here. I don't care what I wear, and I don't think Ligea does, either. And yet we both end up wearing all this fancy stuff.'

Now, four years later, he found himself obscurely ashamed to find how effortlessly he had accepted what was given to him, no matter whether it was service, or unearned respect, or finely woven garments. It was so easy to make use of the servants' willingness to obey without question, to play on the fear his cabochon and his reputation engendered. Easy to be an arrogant little bastard.

That was how he had obtained the clothes, a year earlier. He had simply demanded them, without giving a reason. At first, he'd had no ulterior motive. He'd worn them around the palace just to shock the palace staff, but there was no point in doing that more than once or twice. Gradually the idea had grown on him that they would make a good disguise. A way of leaving the palace, of exploring the city.

The problem would be to pass through the gates. Earlier, as a young boy exploring his environs, he'd discovered a small kitchen entrance used only by the most menial of servants. It was guarded by an old man called Cosamini, who was nearly blind. Better still, it was not difficult for Arrant to reach that entry unremarked via the Exaltarch's personal garden and a gardener's passageway through to the kitchen garden, and hence to where Cosamini sat, his sole job to make sure that no one except servants on legitimate business came and went.

When Arrant put on the servant's tunic and jammed all his hair under the cap, he was no longer the son of the Exaltarch. He was just Urban, a nondescript fellow, one of hundreds who worked in the palace, who no one ever bothered to look at properly, especially if he timed his coming and going to coincide with the times of day when servants were at their busiest. Cosamini soon came to know Urban, the Dominus Arrant's cup-bearer. The lad stopped by to chat every now and then, when there was no one else around. And once Cosamini knew him, Urban started leaving the palace, once or twice every ten days, supposedly to run messages. For whom, Cosamini never asked. It wasn't his business.

CHAPTER THIRTY-FOUR

Tarran? Tarran – are you there?

Yet another call to Tarran went unheeded.

Arrant worried. And sometimes, when Tarran did come, he arrived trembling in Arrant's mind, unable to speak, his thoughts curled into a foetal ball that was a raw mass of hurting in Arrant's head.

Arrant found the best way he could help his brother was not to try to understand what was happening inside the Mirage, nor to ask about the Ravage that so scarred Tarran's thoughts. The best thing he could do was provide a refuge where his brother could get away from the horror, where he could *be*.

He tried again. *Tarran?*

He wanted his brother to enjoy his clandestine outing; having escaped the confines of the palace, he was already heading across the Forum Publicum.

One of these days, you are going to get caught, brother of mine, Tarran said. He sounded almost cheerful.

Hey, good, I'm glad you're here! Caught? Probably. Ligea will have a fit. She just lectured me about safety and stuff. But it's worth it. By all that's holy, I get so sick of the damn mausoleum of a palace.

That kitchen guard must surely realise who you are one day.

Arrant snorted. *Nobles do not wear these kind of garments and half-blind guards do not look overly close at servant boys. Those are the sad facts of life, Tarran, and I intend to exploit them to the full! The fellow has never laid eyes on Dominus Arrant anyway. Cosamini doesn't venture out of the nether regions, and the imperial princeling does not enter anything as mundane as the kitchen!* He remembered with nostalgia the times he had spent in the cavernous warmth of the kitchen at the Stronghold, or the cosy country kitchen of First Farm, and wished with conscious futility that those times had never ended.

What are you going to do today?

I thought I might wander down to the wharves.

How about buying a handful of deep-fried minnows on the way? I love the taste—

Vortexdamn, Tarran, do you ever think of anything but my stomach?

Well, I don't have one of my own to think about.

Yeah, and if I listened to you, I'd be as fat as a pregnant goat. Do you have money today?

Luckily for you, old Arcadim pressed some coins into my hand last night at a banquet. And so did the Reviarch. They can have no idea how much I appreciate this Assorian custom of giving spending money to the children of the house when visiting. Although where either of them thought I was ever going to spend it beats me. Hey, will you quit trying to take over my feet!

I thought of taking a shortcut through the Snarls.

Arrant hesitated. *I shouldn't. It can be dangerous in there.* He remembered his mother's concern, her distaste for even mentioning Rathrox Ligatan by name. A childhood image insinuated itself into his thoughts: the spider who was the blackness at the centre of his web, long dark limbs manipulating the strands, the city dancing to his rule.

Oh, come on. That's the most interesting part of Tyr! The Mirage doesn't have a city any more. The Ravage took it. And even when we did, it wasn't like this.

Guilt. Why did he always feel guilt when Tarran spoke of his life within the Mirage Makers?

I'll be with you, Tarran reassured him. *Nothing will happen. It never does when I'm around, does it?*

Arrant capitulated, unable – as ever – to withstand his brother's wheedling. *Oh, all right then.*

But it felt wrong. And he was uneasy, even as he told himself there were plenty of people about; that it was daylight. Nothing was going to happen.

The alleyways of the Snarls were crowded with houses, misshapen things so squashed together it seemed they squeezed their inhabitants out into the street: the poor and stateless, the old and weary, the freed slaves who had been thrown out of the only homes they had ever known once the Law had freed them.

I like the smell, Tarran said. *It's interesting.*

What? Arrant found that hard to believe. The Snarls had its very own odour. Not dirt exactly, or even rotting rubbish. Ligea insisted on the cleanliness of all the city, and she had abolished the shame that had been the heart of the Snarls – the Cages. But still the place had an unwashed smell, like schoolboys at the end of the day, as if a certain level of grubbiness went hand in hand with poverty. Arrant wrinkled his nose.

It was that time of the day when everyone seemed to be returning from the markets with their purchases. No one paid Arrant any attention except a beggar who kept pace at his side, whining, 'Young sir, spare a coin – just a copper—' The man hobbled along with the aid of a stick. Someone jostled him and he had to make a grab at Arrant to save himself. He smelled vile and Arrant thought he saw something rather loathsome crawling through the mat of his hair. He tried to shake the fellow off, but the taloned grip was a vice around his hand. 'Just a few coppers, lad—'

'Oh, all right,' Arrant said and fumbled at his pouch. The man took the proffered coin and vanished into the crowd. Arrant wiped his palm on his tunic.

Squeamish? Tarran teased. *Got too used to the princeling's perfumes, you have.*

Oh, shut up, Tarran. You can't tell me you enjoyed that encounter either.

Believe me, he's nothing compared to being gnawed by the Ravage.

Arrant's insides lurched like a drunk.

Tarran apologised. *Sorry, I shouldn't have brought that up. I come here to forget that sort of thing.*

Tarran, have you seen Temellin lately? Do you ever see him?

No. He doesn't come to the Shiver Barrens, and we can't see into Kardiastan proper. Why do you ask?

I want to know more about him. To know if he is all right. To know what sort of man he is.

Tarran was distracted by the antics of two lads hitting an inflated bladder against a wall with flat pieces of wood. He swung Arrant's head around to follow their progress. *Hmm? Oh, well, I have told you lots of things about him from when he lived in the Mirage.*

Yes. But none of that is recent. And you never told me about the two of them, not really.

Ligea and Temellin? Tarran was silent for a moment while Arrant threaded his way through a crowd gathered around a fishmonger's stall. Then he said, *Well, yes, that's true. But, Arrant, there are some things you should not be told. What happened between your mother and father is private. In fact, you wouldn't want to know. Truly.*

Arrant thought about that. Their courtship, their arguments, their loving. He shuddered. Goddess, no. *I suppose not*, he admitted. *But what about now? I feel as if I don't understand him. I don't understand why he hasn't asked for me sooner than this.*

He felt Tarran's concern, but any empathy from his brother was also tinged with a Mirage Maker's exasperation. Tarran didn't understand why it worried Arrant so. Why he felt this awful need to be wanted.

Well, Tarran said, *we had Lesgath – one of Korden's sons, just a bit older than you – in the Shiver Barrens recently, to get his sword. We asked him about what was happening in Madrinya. Everything is fine there now. You already know that the Tyranians have all gone, and that the Kardi people welcomed the Magor back, cheering in the streets when our father said he would rule as Mirager again. They are rebuilding the Pavilions, you know. That's the Kardi version of a palace and senate and all those sorts of places, I guess. Everything is fine. I didn't like him, though.*

Who, Temellin?

Worm-brain! Lesgath. He may be almost the same age as you, but he's not like you.

Arrant stopped dead, without any volition on his part. *Hey!* he growled at Tarran. *Will you stop taking over my body, you daft Mirage Maker?*

Look, over there. Cooked minnows. You were going to walk right past them!

All right, all right. But, Tarran, leave my body alone. If you keep doing that sort of thing, I'm going to end up having a heart attack.

All right. But it is fun . . .

The longing in his tone sent Arrant hurrying to buy and eat the minnows; at least Tarran could enjoy the use of his taste-buds. A few minutes later, however, with a suddenness so characteristic of his comings and goings, Tarran slipped out of his mind.

Just the thought of where his brother had gone made Arrant grow cold. How could Tarran bear it? What did he *not* say, about the way he suffered? What was it really like, the Ravage? He had asked Ligea once, and she had told him as best she could. He now knew the scar on her face had been put there by a Ravage creature. He knew Brand had pulled her out and his arm had been withered by the poisons in the Ravage ooze. He knew he had once become an essensa with Ligea in order to seek help to escape the Ravage. But he suspected that she hadn't come anywhere close to telling him what it was really like.

He had his Ravage dreams, of course, and they alone were enough to tell him he didn't ever want to meet those creatures face to face. *I don't have that kind of courage. I'm glad I'll never see the Ravage.*

He reached the last of the alleyways and emerged once more onto a main thoroughfare that headed down to the wharves. As he neared the first of the docks, he realised people were hurrying

in one direction as if there was something special to see at the
dockside. He was about to ask someone what was going on, when
he was stayed by a voice in his ear. 'Lad, wait a moment.'

He turned to find a large Tyranian man grinning at him.
'Sweet hells, lad – you're a tough one to catch. I've been trailing
you halfway through the Snarls!' He held out a coin-pouch and
waggled it. 'This is yours, I believe?' Blue eyes twinkled in a face
that looked as though it had been used as a battering ram at
least once, the kind of face that indicated its owner had lived a
very full life. He did have a nice smile, though, Arrant decided,
and his voice was pleasantly mellow with the faint tinge of a
country accent. Still, Arrant knew enough to know that you didn't
trust someone just because they had a pleasant smile.

Then he recognised the pouch and his eyes widened as his
hand groped at his belt where it should have been hanging. 'Why
– yes, yes.'

'It was after you bought the minnows; you didn't tuck it away
properly and someone took advantage of your carelessness.' The
man showed him the cut ends of the thong. 'Luckily for you, I
happened to see what was going on and caught up with the thief.'
He gave him back the pouch. 'He'll think twice about doing
something similar again, the thieving bastard.'

Arrant mumbled an embarrassed thanks and, while he checked
to see that the contents were still there, considered briefly whether
he should offer the man a coin as reward. No, he decided. The
fellow was too well dressed to be in need of money, and he might
be offended if he were offered any.

The man was already distracted, looking around at the
hurrying crowd. 'What's happening?'

'I don't know,' Arrant admitted.

'There's a ship in, I think. Must be a vessel out of the ordinary, though, for there to be a ruckus like this. Want to go and
have a look?' He turned without waiting to see if Arrant was
going to follow.

Arrant was intrigued enough to hurry after him, but soon
lost him in the crowd. Two large galleys were manoeuvring their

way into the docks. They weren't Tyranian, but that was hardly enough to interest the crowd that was gathering. It was more the general appearance of the first of the ships. The ornate figure-head on the prow, carved and painted, scowled arrogantly at the crowd gathering on the wharf. The face was repeated on the red-painted sails of tightly woven reeds, now being lowered and stowed. A colourful banner flew over the stern, and both vessels had standards tied to the mast.

Arrant squeezed to the front of the row of people lining the wharf, only to realise a moment or two later that the man who had recovered his purse was standing at his shoulder.

'Ocrastes' blessings,' the man murmured, 'I haven't seen one of those ships for years!' He sounded bemused. 'That's an Altani Delta vessel. They used to ply the Altani coast . . .' He shrugged. 'Impressive ships, aren't they? The figurehead represents the river god – Kaliamus.'

Childhood memories came slipping back: the all-pervading smell of water, the man his mother had liked so much, water and greenery meshed in unexpected combinations, flat-bottomed boats poling through water channels so narrow you could touch the reeds on either side. He had been used to Tyrans, where the desert-season was long and hot, and grey-green vegetation battled the dry sweep of winds for half a year. Altan had a brightness to it: blue skies reflected in water; greens of a vividness he had never seen before in nature. He hadn't liked it. To him, it had appeared false, exaggerated – like one of the Tyranian port ladies with their red lips, blushing cheeks and blue eyelids.

'I spent two summers there once,' the man added. 'With the legions.'

'You were a legionnaire?'

He nodded. 'Under the old Exaltarch, yes. I was an officer, once. But I just go by the name of Thracius these days. Thracius Macellian, originally from Corbussia.' He stood a little straighter, his pride in his service obvious. 'Ever thought of joining the legions, lad? It's a fine life!' He indicated Arrant's palace tunic with a wave of his hand. 'Better than a servant's any day. Bowing and scraping and fetching – that's no life for a boy with ambition.'

'I don't have any ambition.'

'No? Then you ought to have. What's your name?'

'Urban. And if I were to join the army, I'd probably still be a servant. I don't s'pose many ex-slaves end up as officers.'

'Hmm. Maybe not. Well now, will you look at that?' The wind had caught the banner at the stern of the first vessel, unfurling its patterning on the breeze. 'Do you know what the symbols on that banner mean?' He didn't wait for Arrant to answer. 'The sheathed sword says the ships come in peace. The tied bundle of reeds, that's the symbol of the Altani rebels. The third symbol, that's the papyrus plant. That's more interesting. It's the symbol for a messenger, or an envoy. It means that whoever is in that first ship comes with the status to act on behalf of the ruler. This is a very important man in Altan, whoever he is.'

Arrant hid a grin. Thracius took for granted that the envoy would be male, the kind of assumption that always annoyed Ligea, even though it was usually – always? – correct. *Goddessdamn, not even having a woman as an Exaltarch seems to change the way people think about things like that.*

'Never did like the sea much, myself,' Thracius said. 'I like the paveway under my shoes. Or under my horse's hooves, better still.'

He chatted on as they watched the vessels dock. The gangplank was run out and port authorities hurried up and onto the deck. 'Fees to be paid,' he told Arrant, 'and formalities to be observed. I hear the new Exaltarch makes foreign vessels pay through the nose. Says it's to help the competitiveness of our own merchant navy, but I think it's more to put money in her coffers. You can't do away with slavery and expect taxes to remain as they were!'

Arrant flushed. It was difficult to listen to his mother being so casually maligned and be unable to do a thing about it.

'Ah, listen to me, then!' Thracius continued amiably. 'You can't possibly be interested in all this. Sorry, lad. It's just that you're the same age as my nephew back home. Miss the boy. Used to tell him all manner of stories about my army days. Was teaching him to fight. With a sword. Throw a javelin, too. I don't suppose you'd be interested in that, would you? I mean, I'd love to have a lad to teach again.' He sounded wistful.

'I'm not interested in fighting,' Arrant replied, and felt his insides go rigid. He forced himself to relax. Not to think. 'Besides, I only get one half-day off every month.' He tried to look sheepish. 'I'm supposed to use the time to go to the temple.'

'Yes, of course. Silly of me. What about fishing? Do you like to fish? My cousin, down past the docks, has a small boat. Just a little thing. But there's plenty of fish if you get out into the middle of the bay. How about we meet up next time you are free and I take you fishing?'

Arrant felt a flare of remembered pleasure. The feel of a sea breeze ruffling his hair, the thrill of the line jerking in his fingers, the fascination of the way fish scales pockmarked his skin after he had wrestled his catch off the hook. At five he had wondered if the scales had meant he was changing into a fish. Now, his younger self seemed absurd. He found himself grinning. 'Yes,' he said. 'I'd like that.'

People had begun to disperse, and they could see the ships better now. A man stood on the deck of the main vessel, surely the envoy. He was huge and richly dressed in the Altani style. He wore his reddish-brown hair longer than was the Tyrianian fashion, and a lock of it over his brow was a brighter red, a bold flash of colour, in the sunshine. Arrant wasn't sure if that was natural or not, but he found it hard to imagine this man tinting his hair the way Ligea did now she was Exaltarch.

'Got the figure of a galley slave, hasn't he, though?' Thracius mused. 'Broad as an ox and the shoulders of a gorclak. Ugly brute. Urban, I have to be off. Got things to do.' He gripped Arrant's arm, hand to forearm, the legionnaire's traditional gesture of greeting and farewell. 'It's been a pleasure talking to you. Shall we meet here on your next half-day off, on this wharf, exactly a month from now would that be? Say, two hours past dawn?'

'I'd like that,' Arrant said, and his heart suddenly felt lighter. He doubted that he would turn up, but at least he could if he wanted. 'And thank you,' he added, 'for the money-pouch, I mean.'

Thracius lifted his hand in farewell and disappeared into the remnants of the crowd. Arrant turned back to watch the first of the galleys.

By this time, a detachment of the palace's mounted guard was approaching down the wharf, doubtless sent by Ligea once she had learned of the envoy's arrival. Someone would have sent word the moment the ships had come through the booms. Arrant shrank back behind some bales; the last thing he wanted was to be recognised by one of the palace guard.

They had brought spare mounts with them and the Altani and his attendants were soon riding through the crowd escorted by a Tyranian guard of honour.

Arrant had a good look at the envoy as he rode past. He had a withered arm.

It was Brand.

Ligea ordered that the Altani envoy and his small entourage, as representatives of one of Tyr's closest allies, be given quarters inside the palace rather than a villa in Tyr's diplomatic quarter. It was a mark of special favour, but not without precedent. The palace was spacious, containing numerous apartments and atriums with attached private gardens, far too many for the needs of an Exaltarch who had no love of courtiers, no interest in courtesans or catamites or gigolos, and no patience with hangers-on.

A day after the envoy's arrival, the Exaltarch accepted the envoy's credentials in a public ceremony, attended by many of the city's highborn and public officials. Immediately afterwards, the envoy requested a private audience, which was graciously bestowed by the Exaltarch in her private apartments.

When the servants flung open the doors for Brand, Ligea was standing in the middle of her audience room, dressed in her regal best and outwardly in command of herself; her scribe

Narbius and her handmaiden, Narjemah, were in attendance. As the envoy approached her, she dismissed the two attendants, and asked them to shut the doors on their way out. Narbius looked at her reproachfully as he left, but she ignored him. Narjemah gave Brand a broad grin, and he responded with a wink as she pulled the doors closed.

Alone, the two of them stood for a moment in silence. Brand moved first, crossing the room to her, to seize her hands, unspeaking. Their eyes sought the traces of the years, the scarring of tragedies, the laughter lines of a life lived well. They searched, and saw – and grieved. There had been little laughter, few joys and so much pain.

'Almost nine years,' she whispered. 'So *long*.'

He released her hands and enclosed her in the fold of his embrace, the strength of his right arm compensating for the weakness of the left.

'Oh, dear friend,' she murmured into his shoulder, 'I have been so lonely for so very long! So damnably *alone*.'

And for the first time in more years than she cared to measure, the Exaltarch of Tyrans cried.

CHAPTER THIRTY-FIVE

Arrant hated Brand.

He hated the way he and his mother smiled at one another. He hated their conversation, recalling this and that from the days before he'd been born, conversation that excluded him by virtue of its content.

The Altani towered over everyone, a giant of a man, confident in his size and strength, even though he had a withered arm. Everyone *liked* him; even the servants couldn't do enough for him. The man's mastery over himself annoyed Arrant; he was always so in control, so calm, so confident. Arrant despised the readiness of the sneer behind the man's smile, the way he subtly mocked anyone who said something stupid, the way no one else could see through the charm to what lay at the centre of this man's sardonic heart.

Worst of all, the Altani was there, in Tyr, and Temellin was not and never could be. Arrant wished that Gevenan was around to put this man in his place, but from all his mother told him, Gevenan had his hands full and she had no plans to bring him back to Tyr yet.

When Tarran became aware of his antipathy, he tried to remonstrate. *Brand's all right*, he said. *His love for your mother is genuine*.

It was the wrong thing to say. Arrant didn't want to hear about a man's love for his mother, any more than he wanted to hear about how close they had been in the past. Damn it all, she still professed to love his father, if his letters to her were any indication. He cut Tarran short and refused to talk about the matter, or even to think about it when Tarran was with him.

From this, he closed his brother off.

Sometimes, Tarran muttered, frustrated, *you have a tight-arsed mind, Arrant. Mirageless soul, I've more chance of growing hair on my chest than understanding you humans!*

Brand had come on behalf of the ruling High Lord of Altan, once a rebel leader called Hotash, to sign a new treaty of trade and cooperation with Tyrans. The signing ceremonies were duly carried out with much pomp and formality – Ligea hadn't managed to rid Tyrans of its propensity to overindulge in ceremonial – and Arrant expected Brand would then sail for Altan. He didn't. His ships returned with copies of the treaty, but Brand stayed on.

Ambassador Brand, High Plenipotentiary of Altan to Tyr.

It was hard to find Ligea without Brand at her side. At official functions, he was just one of the plenipotentiaries, but inside the palace he was always there. His apartments in the palace were a mark of Tyrans' friendship with Altan, so it was said officially. Unofficially, she slept with the High Lord's ambassador, and within days everyone in the palace knew it.

Arrant tried to avoid talking to Brand, which was difficult when Ligea insisted that the three of them have a meal together almost every day. Arrant retaliated with silence unless he was addressed directly. Then he would reply, careful to be scrupulously polite. Brand would have had to be both blind and stupid not to have known he was being snubbed.

After several weeks of this treatment, Ligea was fed up and, in a rare private moment, told Arrant so.

'What's wrong?' he asked innocently. 'I have never behaved disrespectfully to the Plenipotentiary! I hope I know how to behave with someone who represents his country to your government. Lepidus has schooled me in how to correctly address all ranks and nationalities.'

'Don't get smart with me,' she snapped. 'I can feel your attitude clear across the other side of the palace.'

'No, you can't,' he said. 'You haven't been able to read me from the day we arrived in this building.'

She stared at him, nonplussed. Her voice dropped to a whisper. 'How did you know that?'

He shrugged. 'You're my mother. I know. In fact, you know more about the servants who pick up the pisspots than about me.'

He knew he had struck a sensitive spot. And with sudden insight, he realised something else. When you came to rely on what your cabochon told you, you were lost when it failed you. *At least that's not a problem I'll ever have*, he thought with amused bitterness.

She shook her head at him. 'Goddess damn you, Arrant. I can have seasoned legionnaires tremble in their sandals when I walk past – why in all Acheron's seven hells can't I get my own son to behave?'

He thought of a clever answer, in fact several of them, but only after she had left the room.

A day later, Brand came to his door. 'May I come in?' he asked when Arrant answered his knock.

Arrant hesitated just long enough to make Brand feel uncomfortable, and then said, 'Yes, of course. Won't you please have a seat? It is an honour for me to have a plenipotentiary come to my private rooms! None of the others have ever done that.'

Brand took the divan offered. 'No, I don't suppose they have. Our relationship is, um, special.'

Arrant raised his eyebrows as he sat opposite. 'I was unaware we even *had* a relationship.' *Ocrastes' damn. I am getting good at this rhetoric stuff . . .*

'I *have* known you since before you were born, in a manner of speaking.'

'Well, I have no recollection of that, obviously. I do remember when we went to Altan when I was five or so. I didn't like you.'

'No, that's true. You were jealous, I think.'

'Doubtless I had reason.'

'Arrant, I have the deepest respect for your father—'

Arrant stood up abruptly. *How dare he!* 'No, you don't. Or you wouldn't hang around my mother like a dog sniffing for whatever he can get.'

Brand climbed to his feet, much more slowly, and had the advantage of towering over him. 'Arrant, Ligea and I have known each other since we were younger than you are now. You know that, surely. Ligea has not seen Temellin in more than eight years. That's a long time for a woman to be alone. She needs a friend.'

'She has Gevenan! Or Narjemah. Or me. Why doesn't she come to me?' His chest was heaving and he didn't seem able to unclench his fists. He knew he had lost control of the conversation. He sounded like a petulant child.

Brand echoed that last thought with his next words. 'Arrant, you are no longer a child. You *know* what I am talking about.'

'Stop right there! You have no right to even bring this up with me! How *dare* you even mention—'

'No – *you* stop right there. I've loved your mother long enough to have earned the right to speak of matters which concern her happiness and wellbeing. And what she needs right now is a son who cares enough for her, and who is man enough, to put her wellbeing before his own selfishness. You have no right to demand further sacrifice from her because you aren't secure enough within yourself to see her as a woman with needs. Right now, she needs you to be an adult about this. I don't mean even half as much to her as Temellin does; I know that and I deal with it. You ought to know that too, and if you don't, I'm telling you. But Temellin is not here, *and I am*. For her sake, be thankful I am.' With that, he turned and walked out of the room.

Arrant ran and slammed the door shut behind him. He turned and leaned against it, but his knees didn't seem to want to hold him up. He slid down until he was sitting on the marble floor, his back to the door. 'The *bastard*!' he said. 'The bastard . . . the sodding bastard!' His voice cracked as sobs shook his body. He wanted to be adult and cold and calculating, but the tears came anyway, making a lonely, lost boy of him all over again.

When the tears finally ceased, he rested the back of his head against the door and closed his eyes. *Tarran*, he thought. *Please come, Tarran. I need you. I am so lonely . . .*

But Tarran didn't come.

And that made him fear for his brother. He *always* came when Arrant was upset or frightened. Didn't he?

Ligea called Arrant into her audience room early the next morning. His stomach churned. *That bastard Altani wouldn't have told her about that conversation, would he?*

He need not have worried. She just wanted to tell him she had settled on a date for her departure to the western border region. 'I've just had word from Gev. He says the sooner the better, so I am leaving tomorrow.'

'*Tomorrow?*'

'Yes. To tell you the truth, the idea of escaping Tyr for a while is enticing. If I make preparations, everyone would know, of course – so it seems better if I just go. Take everyone by surprise. Gives them less time to plan mischief. What I want to know is this: do you want to come with me?'

He was wary. 'Is Brand going with you?'

'Yes.'

'Then no.'

She was surprised. 'Why ever not? I know you don't like living here, unable to step out of the palace much—'

'Mater, if you're going whoring around the countryside with Brand, I don't want any part of the trip.'

She went very white, except for two red spots in her cheeks. Mercifully, his cabochon didn't enlarge on her emotions.

'Arrant,' she said, 'please try to understand—'

'Oh, I understand all right. I understand perfectly. I *am* old enough for that.'

She paused, then said quietly, sighing, 'Somehow I think you're not.'

'I loathe being in the presence of that man.' He made no attempt to conceal the savagery of his disgust with her. Then, to sharpen the cutting edge of his words, he added, 'Couldn't you at least have waited until I had gone to Kardiastan before you invited that – that sneering, self-satisfied, *smug* bastard under your wrap? You're like some silly servant girl who can't keep her eyes off the backside of one of the palace guards!'

Her face went from white to dark, and he knew he had the power to enrage her as never before. She snapped, 'How *dare* you presume to insult me on a subject you know *nothing* about!'

They stood facing each other across the room, and it was he who looked away first. Tears pricked behind his eyelids and his throat seemed to have swelled so large he could scarcely breathe.

He hated her. He *hated* her. How dare she do this to him? How dare she put him in this humiliating position where everyone mocked her as a whore, where everyone was laughing at her?

There was a long pause while she took a deep breath and controlled her rage. When she spoke again, she sounded calm. 'You will go to your father soon. It won't be long; a matter of months at the most. And while I am in the borderlands, please have a care. Tyr is not safe for either of us yet. I forbid you to set foot in the city while I am gone, even with your guards.'

She gestured with a hand, dismissing him. He turned on his heel and walked out, back in control.

In his anger and hurt, he had not heard her pain.

That night Arrant had another Ravage dream.

He dreamed he was submerged beneath the stinking ooze and was being attacked by its creatures – nothing new about that – but when he woke up he was not in his room on his pallet. He was somewhere else. And he had no body.

In fact, he was not human. Nor did he seem to have any limits.

He was an immensity of matter and he was aware of it all, all of it him: vast, huge, sensitive, every part aware, every part capable of sensation, of pain, of joy. He was here and there as well. He had no eyes or ears or nose or skin, yet he saw and heard and smelled and felt. He was all senses—

Appalled, he realised he wasn't a person; he was a land . . . trees, lakes, animals, flowers, rivers, beauty. His vastness overwhelmed him. He was deluged with sensations too numerous for his mind to catalogue, drowned in stimuli too vivid for his brain to absorb. He could not cope with his own enormity.

His mind was going to burst: this was too much! *I am not this – this is not me!*

And then, suddenly, he felt a terrible tearing agony. He wanted to rip himself up, rend himself to pieces, destroy what he was, anything to rid himself of what ate at him. *Devoured* him. Oh, sweet Mirage—

Arrant! What in the name of the Magor are you doing here? Get out! You'll go mad—

Where am I?

You're in the Mirage – you've joined us! You must get out of here—

And he was back on his pallet, flung back by the Mirage Makers, dragged back by Tarran, jolted into his own reality. He lay gasping, his whole body still aching with the memory of an intensity of pain that seemed almost incomprehensible.

Shit, Arrant, you gave me a fright.

'Tarran – damn it, what happened?'

Skies above, who knows? You did what I do, I guess. You came to me, the way I come to you. You were there, with us, in the Mirage. You were one of us – one of the Mirage Makers . . . I thought you were going to die—

'So did I. By all that's holy, how can you stand such pain?'

There was a pause before Tarran answered. Then: *We are not human, Arrant. We – we have each other. And it's not usually so bad. It's just the past few weeks the Ravage has been trying to expand itself. Brother, I must go. They need me. We must withstand this, or we are—*

He didn't tell him what they would be but Arrant knew anyway. Dead. Doomed. Torn to pieces. Sweet Melete, now he *knew*.

Tarran left, leaving Arrant feeling as if every cranny of his mind had been pounded.

He was still shaking with shock when his door opened and his mother came in. She had flung a wrap over her sleeping gown but she was barefoot and breathing hard as if she'd been running. She held her Magor sword in her hand and it glowed.

'*Arrant*?' she asked, her voice panicked in a way he hadn't heard for years. 'Goddess, what *happened*? What's the matter?'

'A dream,' he said. 'I thought I was attacked by the Ravage.' Vortexdamn, this time his emotions must have had the punch of a rampaging gorclak. She'd felt him clear across the palace to her sleeping quarters. So much for never reading his emotions . . .

Using the tip of her sword, she lit the small oil lamp on the low table by his bed. 'A dream? But your pain was so *real* – I thought, I thought – oh, hells, I don't know what I thought! I haven't felt you for four years, and now, when I do, it was to be slammed with something so, so *stark* and agonised . . .' She dragged in air, slowed her breathing, took his hand in hers.

'I know,' he said dryly. Vortex, he could feel it still. 'I'm all right now. It was just a dream.'

She sat on the bed at his side, not relinquishing her hold on his hand. 'Are you *sure*?'

He said, with a vehemence that welled up from inside him, 'You gave my brother into that horror. He's there still, suffering—' He stopped, and could have bitten off his tongue. He hadn't intended to make such a pointless accusation.

She released his hand and stared at him, expressionless. And then, finally, flat-voiced: 'How did you know that?'

Too late he remembered: no one had ever told him about how Pinar had died, or about his brother – except Tarran. He lay still, thoughts skittering this way and that as he wondered what he could possibly say to explain it. He even considered telling her about Tarran. But how in all the seven layers of Acheron did you tell someone that you heard voices in your head from a being who lived in another country on the other side of a mountain range?

Could I prove Tarran's existence? he wondered. *I could show her I know a lot of things I shouldn't be able to know – about the past, about the Mirage and the Ravage.* The idea of sharing his knowledge of Tarran's pain was suddenly overwhelmingly attractive. He wouldn't have to shoulder the burden of knowing all by himself . . .

And then he remembered something Brand had said to him. *What she needs right now is a son who cares enough for her, and who is man enough, to put her wellbeing before his own selfishness.*

If he told her about Tarran, how on earth would she feel? Tarran would no longer be a nebulous embryo she had given to the Mirage Makers, but a real person, the suffering brother of her son. She would understand the consequences of what she had done.

A fitting punishment for her behaviour, surely.

A horrible thought, *horrible*. How could he even *think* it? He shuddered, hating himself.

He withdrew, closing off every part of himself that he could find, pushing all feeling down into that dried-up ball of pain and memories in his centre. 'I, er, suppose—' he began, and hoped that once again he was unreadable to her, 'I suppose someone must have mentioned it when we were in Ordensa.'

When she sighed, he knew he had succeeded.

She said quietly, 'It was either Pinar's son or you, Arrant. I made a choice, and I don't regret it.' He heard the other words she didn't say: *And it was either Pinar or me . . .*

He was subdued now. 'Yes. Yes, I know. I do know. I don't blame you.'

They were both silent. Somehow there didn't seem to be anything either of them could say, no way either of them could explain themselves, or explain what had happened to them. They were as far apart as the sands of Kardiastan were from the marble walls of Tyr.

He closed his eyes, and a moment later heard her move away and let herself out.

Loneliness closed in once more, the chill of it enfolding him. He knew he had just made an adult choice. He knew it had been the right choice.

So why do I feel so utterly miserable?

CHAPTER THIRTY-SIX

The day after Ligea and Brand's departure was the day that Arrant had arranged to go fishing with Thracius.

Still reckless with an anger that had not dissipated in spite of Ligea's visit to his room, he didn't think twice about leaving the palace to meet the Corbussian ex-legionnaire. And she didn't care anyway, did she? All she wanted was to crawl into bed with her lover. Anyway, Thracius was no danger to him. The man had no idea who he was. And Arrant had not sensed that the fellow was the kind of man who, er, liked boys; Thracius' eyes gleamed whenever his gaze lit on an attractive woman. Arrant had begun to notice things like that.

I will go, he thought. The truth was, his loneliness was eating him alive. If Tarran had been around, it wouldn't have mattered so much. Just thinking of his brother produced a nauseating lump of worry in the pit of his stomach, but there was nothing he could do about it.

Yes. I will go. It will be fun to go fishing again.

Yet once he reached the wharf, he was beginning to regret the impulse that had brought him. It was foolish, surely, to think that a man who must be older than his mother would really be interested in a lad he thought to be a palace servant. He must have another reason. Arrant had heard stories of boys enticed away from their homes only to vanish, to be used for who knows what purpose . . .

When he spotted Thracius, though, his uncertainties vanished.

The ex-legionnaire flashed a grin of pure delight and greeted Arrant with a cheery, 'Well met, Urban – I'm glad you came.' He held up a basket to show him. 'Fishing gear and lugworms as bait. And, of course, something for us: flat meat-cakes, with sauce. And a flagon of watered wine. There's a clink in my pockets nowadays,' he added happily. 'I have a job as a night guard with some moneymasters. Dangerous work in these Goddess-forsaken times, and it's not the same as being a legionnaire, but the pay is good.'

Arrant's cabochon gave a twinge in his palm, and chose that moment to tell him that what Thracius had said last was the exact truth. Unfortunately, unasked, it also decided to give him a rush of information involving, apparently, the conversation of every individual in the neighbourhood. An awful lot of them seemed to be liars. He sighed as they turned to walk in the direction Thracius indicated.

'Something wrong?' Thracius asked.

'No, no. But, if it's hard to find a good job, why didn't you stay in the army?'

'And serve the present Exaltarch? No.'

His bluntness took Arrant aback. 'Why not?'

'Because she destroyed the Exaltarchy. She brought down the greatest empire the world has ever known. Tore it into pieces. And now we have a ruinous policy of a slaveless society, and every petty group of peasants who once benefited from our rule now governs themselves.' He smiled ruefully at Arrant. 'I'm sorry. I shouldn't gabble on like this to someone who works in the palace!'

Arrant shrugged. 'It doesn't matter. I'm not going to tell anyone. Besides, you are quite safe. This Exaltarch doesn't throw people into the Cages for expressing an opinion.'

'No, that's true,' he conceded. 'But you see, Urban, I was a *legionnaire*. We fought and sacrificed so much for Tyrans to rule from one end of the Sea of Iss to the other. Friends *died* beside me in battle for those ideals – and when Ligea Gayed became Exaltarch, she chucked it all away.' He gave a shrug and another smile, as if he laughed at himself. 'But it's all in the past now. Little point in being bitter about what I cannot change, right? Perhaps you and me should agree not to discuss politics, all right?'

Arrant found himself smiling back. He knew he should have argued, said all the things about how slavery was wrong, and that Bator Korbus had been a cruel and violent man, and that it was his wars of acquisition, fuelled by greed, that had killed Thracius' friends, but he didn't. It was hard to dislike Thracius. He was so open, so unabashed about what he thought and what he believed in, so proud of his achievements, of what he had been.

They walked on through the bustle of the commercial port, past the fishing fleet on the other side, and so to the fishing village on the outskirts of the city, outside the walls. Here, Thracius' cousin had his small mastless boat, homemade and cumbersome, beached on a bay along the River Tyr. 'We don't even have to leave the safety of the bay,' Thracius said. 'I'm no sailor, and the tide out in the centre of the river can have you halfway to the Issian Isles before you know it, or so I'm told. Here, help me get this thing launched . . .'

Out on the water in the sunshine fifteen minutes later, catching the occasional fish, where the only threat seemed to be the avaricious eye of a seagull, and the only tension that between fish and man, Arrant felt the perfection of a peace he had not encountered since leaving the Stronghold. For a while he could pretend to be just a child, enclosed in that childhood illusion of safety. For a brief hour or two, he knew a happiness he had not felt for years.

In between the excitement of hauling in each catch, Thracius chatted, describing what it had been like to be a soldier in an Exaltarchy that stretched through all the known world – not stories of battle and death, but tales of the absurdities of military life, stories of the places and people he had seen. Arrant listened, enthralled.

'Did you know,' Thracius asked, 'that the women of inland

Fastiglia take a new husband each time they have a child, discarding the old one like a worn-out skirt? And what about Asagon! Now, there's a strange place. There, the wise men tattoo male genitals on their foreheads to show that they have renounced sexual pleasures in exchange for wisdom.'

Midmorning, they shared the food Thracius had brought and Arrant sighed with contentment.

'How old are you, lad?' Thracius asked suddenly.

'Thirteen.'

'Born what month?'

'The last month of the snow-season. Why?'

'Ah – just comparing you to my nephew, back in Corbussia. He's around the same age. Wish sometimes that I had a lad of my own, one that I know about.' He gave one of his grins. 'Not too late yet, though, is it?'

Arrant smiled back.

'I suppose we had better think about returning. You only get a half-day off, right?'

Arrant nodded. ''Fraid so. I have enjoyed myself, though, Thracius.' He began to pick the fish scales off his skin, remembering doing the same thing long ago, Temellin sitting beside him.

Thracius stared at Arrant's bandaged hand and gave a quick frown. 'What did you do to yourself there, Urban?'

'What—? Oh, this. A cut, that's all.'

'Must have been bad to take so long to mend. You were wearing the bandage last time I saw you.'

Arrant felt himself flushing. 'I knocked it before it was healed. Ripped it open again.'

A moment earlier the look on Thracius' face had been one of concern. Now his expression could have been chiselled marble. Arrant's flush deepened. Then he felt the twinges of fear.

Thracius' left hand flashed out to grip his, the hold as powerful as a vice, his eyes black with a deep, killing fury. Arrant knew he had made a terrible mistake. Thracius was groping for his dagger, and there was nothing he could do.

The man was all muscle and sinew, a trained fighter. Even as Arrant struggled to pull his hand free, Thracius slashed with the knife.

Arrant looked down. The bandage on his hand fell off, neatly cut away. Instinctively he curled his fingers over his palm. With ridiculous ease, the ex-legionnaire forced his grip open.

The cabochon lay quiescent and visible, a golden gem in the middle of his palm. Ligea had cut the skin free of it not long after they had come to live in the palace. 'I won't hide what we are any longer,' she'd said.

Thracius' sharp intake of breath contained all the horror of a man condemned. 'Ocrastes' balls! You are the Exaltarch's bastard *son*!' He looked up to meet Arrant's gaze, his voice an appalled whisper. 'Holy Goddess! My head will be stuck on the palace gate for this! Are you mad? What have I ever done to you that you would do this to me?'

'I haven't done anything to you!' Arrant protested.

'Sodding son of a bitch you haven't! *You're the son of the ruler of Tyrans.* I'll be accused of kidnapping or worse. Who the sweet hells is going to believe I took Urban – whatever-your-name-is—'

'Arrant.'

'—Arrant out fishing because I thought you were a pisspot servant boy from the palace? For all I know, just *thinking* you were a servant might be enough to see me burned at the stake.'

They stared at each other, in a stillness so long a seagull was emboldened to come and sit on the bow of the anchored boat. It eyed the heap of bait.

'My mother is not like that,' Arrant said finally. 'No one will harm you. I will not let her, for a start. And no one is going to find out anyway. I have been leaving the palace like this for a year or so and no one has ever found out. Row me back to the shore, Thracius, and I shall walk back to the palace. You will never hear of this again. And if you are wise, you won't mention it to anyone.'

There was another long silence. The seagull made off with

some of the lugworms. The agonised look on the man's face did not diminish.

'I – I can't do that,' Thracius said miserably. 'What if you came to harm on your own? I would be responsible.'

'You're not responsible for me!'

'I am now. I know who you are and what you do.'

'I don't understand.'

'Urban, er – Dominus, I have to take you back to the palace, and tell the guards what you've been up to. You can't wander the streets of Tyr alone. It is too bloody dangerous. I have to take my chances that the Exaltarch won't have me scourged for this.'

'Why should what I do worry you? You despise my mother for what she has done, for a start!'

He looked shocked. 'Yes, but she is still my Exaltarch! I despised that son of a bitch Bator Korbus, too, you know, as a *man*. But the Exaltarch – whoever it is – is Tyrans. I would *never* do anything to harm Tyrans. And having the Exaltarch's son loose on the streets of the city could bring disaster!'

'Nonsense! Who cares enough about me?'

'Are you so very stupid, boy? If someone who didn't have Tyrans' best interests at heart was to find out, they could kidnap you and force Domina Ligea to do something foolish. Always assuming she does care what happens to her idiot offspring!'

Arrant flushed. *He's right*, he thought, despairing.

Thracius heaved a deep sigh, and some of the tension dissipated from him. 'I'm sorry, lad. I shouldn't have said that.' He gave the ghost of a smile. 'Quite apart from the fact that it's bloody stupid to call the son of a ruler an idiot, it isn't true. You aren't an idiot – just very young and inexperienced in the ways of the world. And it can't be easy, shut up in the palace all the time, surrounded by men sucking up to you, not knowing who to trust. It's no life for a lad.'

'You – you understand?'

'I was a tribune once. That was enough to get invited to a lot of banquets and the like when we were in Tyr and other cities.

THE SHADOW OF TYR 401

I know about tedious protocol, about having to watch your tongue. I know you rode with the rebels, just as I rode with the legions; you were raised to be a soldier, like me, not a courtier. Yes, I know how you must feel. Still, it's not safe for you to wander the streets at will.'

'Please, Thracius, don't tell anyone about this.' He heard the whine in his tone, and hated himself for pleading.

'Are you going to stop sneaking out of the palace?'

Arrant's glimpse of the future was crushing. No escape from the palace walls. Nothing absorbing or distracting to offer Tarran when next he came. It was all very well for his mother to talk of sending him to Kardiastan, but she'd been speaking of that for years and it hadn't happened yet. What if it never did? What if his Father decided he didn't want a son who couldn't manage his Magor power?

He was silent.

Thracius sighed. 'Well, thank you for not lying, anyway. All right, we'll make a pact, you and me. You promise never to leave the palace without telling me, and I won't say anything. If you want to be alone, I'll just follow you to make sure you are safe. But no more wandering around alone. Ever.'

Arrant considered that, knowing in his heart that the man was right. He risked too much on his own in the city. It would be different if he could rely on the power in his cabochon.

Thracius frowned as if he'd had a sudden thought. 'Or am I the one being stupid and naive?' he asked. When Arrant gave a questioning look, Thracius indicated the cabochon. 'That,' he said. 'Everyone knows now what the Domina Ligea did with that thing the day she took Tyr. Not to mention having a sword that scares the piss out of brave men. Come to think of it, I heard stories about you, too. About something that happened at the North Gate. I wasn't in Tyr myself, at the time, but people talk.' He eyed the cabochon. 'They say you killed legionnaires with that thing.'

Arrant nodded. The seagull had come back for a second helping of the bait and glared at him with a bright yellow eye. 'Yes. I did,' he said quietly.

'So I am just being the stupid dolt, am I? You are quite capable of looking after yourself. And right now you're laughing at me.'

Arrant shook his head.

Thracius bent over his dagger, apparently examining the blade for nicks. 'I'm a soldier and I'll fight – bravely – any man who stands against me. But someone who pours out light and magic and spells—?' He shook his head. 'That's not the kind of thing that a *man* likes to deal with. Our legions lost too many men to numina magic in Kardiastan.'

Arrant sighed. Thracius felt Magor power was a coward's way out, but he wasn't quite blunt enough to say it. 'You haven't seen me do any of those things,' he said.

'No, I haven't, but you could if you wanted to, I suppose.'

'No, I can't. My c— the gemstone in my hand doesn't really work any more. It never has worked well, and ever since the day we entered Tyr—' He swallowed, trying not to remember. 'I can't use it. I just – can't.' He stirred uneasily. It didn't seem right to speak about it to a non-Magor. Ligea would have been furious if she had heard him.

'So what *can* you do?'

'About the only thing I can do with any reliability is to shield myself from my mother,' he said, not bothering to hide his bitterness. 'I don't even have to think about that. It just happens.'

'Can't you sense a lie? I did hear rumours about that being one of the Exaltarch's skills—'

'Is that common knowledge now?' Somehow that depressed him. 'I suppose that's not to be wondered at. But me? No, I can't.'

Thracius considered him with sympathy. 'Ah, lad, don't take it to heart. Me, I like you the better for being ordinary!' His look softened. 'All right, what's it to be? I either take you back to the palace and tell the guards I found you wandering about the streets, or you make me a promise that you will only leave the palace when I can meet you. You can pay me for my services, if that makes you feel any better about it.'

Arrant nodded. 'All right. I promise. We'll make arrangements to meet.'

Thracius looked pleased. 'Excellent. What about right now? I don't suppose you really have to get back to start work.'

Arrant smiled slightly. 'No, but I do have one of my tutors coming. I have to return, otherwise I'll be missed.'

'Then we had better get that anchor stone up. Can you pull on that rope, lad? Hells, what the Vortex am I going to call you? I can hardly keep on calling the Exaltarch's son "lad"!'

Arrant shrugged as he moved to haul up the anchor. The seagull, coming back towards the boat for another meal, veered away, giving an indignant screech. 'I don't mind. Out here I'm just Urban.'

'All right then. That's fine with me. And I hope you won't hold what I said about your mother against me, either. Didn't mean to be disrespectful.'

'Yes, you did.' Arrant heaved the dripping stone aboard as Thracius inserted the oars into the rope loops on the gunwale. 'You don't respect her because of what she did. You don't have to pretend with me.'

'I've always been loyal to my Exaltarch,' Thracius said formally, 'and your mother's the Exaltarch now.' He shook his head sadly. 'Though I'll admit this new world of ours is hard to like. Sometimes I wonder if she couldn't do with better advisers.' Thracius paused. 'Forgive me. Shouldn't have said that.'

'It's that wretched Altani who's advising her now,' Arrant said savagely.

'The High Plenipotentiary?'

'Yes. Ambassador Brand. Pompous fool.' In his heart he knew that was a lie; Brand was neither pompous nor a fool. And although he had heard Brand and Ligea discuss policy and strategies at length over the lunch table, even once talking about how best she could manage the more recalcitrant members of her Advisory Council and Senate, Brand's influence was not untoward. Ligea was far too strong to give anyone too much sway over her decisions.

Thracius took up one of the oars and sculled the boat to face the coastline. 'Yes, I did hear some gossip along those lines in the streets. And the fellow's only been here a month! Didn't waste much time, did he, then? And it's not wise of her,' he said. 'People are saying that Tyrans is running in front of Altani horns now; there's a lot of resentment.'

Arrant was shocked. He had no idea that Brand's influence was being criticised by the public; it seemed ridiculous. He wished he hadn't said anything.

'Don't let it upset you,' Thracius said kindly as they headed back to shore. 'The Exaltarch has far too much sense to allow such a man to be seen in her company too often. After all, he used to be her slave, so they say.'

Arrant reddened. As he sat facing Thracius, there was no way the man could not see. 'She has taken him to the western border-lands with her,' he said, looking away.

Thracius' eyes widened and he stopped rowing. 'Oh. *Oh.*' For a moment he seemed at a loss for words. Finally he started the boat moving again, saying, 'Goddess, lad, it's like that, is it? I did hear rumours – I'm sorry.'

Arrant's flush deepened. *Papa,* he thought, *you had better get me out of here soon. I don't think I can stand much more of this.*

CHAPTER THIRTY-SEVEN

'So your mother's back in Tyr.' The two of them were seated in a small pothouse – there were only four tables – and Thracius had just handed Arrant a mug of soft ale, a suitable beverage for someone only just a man, or so he'd once informed Arrant. The place smelled of spilled mead and the unwashed bodies of the clientele; of roasting rats and the fat that dripped from the spit to sizzle on the hot hearth stones.

Once every ten days during the two months Ligea had been gone, Arrant had left the confines of the palace to meet Thracius for a couple of hours' freedom. What they did varied. They had been fishing again; once they'd attended a chariot race; once they'd gone to see some wrestling. On other occasions they'd just wandered through the markets, or the port, and ended up in an eating house or a pothouse somewhere.

Arrant enjoyed Thracius' company. The Corbussian could speak intelligently about so many things: the skills of a sculptor, the design of a mosaic floor, the lines of a horse or the pedigree of a gorclak; he could recognise the origins of a ship by the way the crew set the sails; he could hold a conversation in half-a-dozen different languages and tell a ribald joke in them all; he had been to all the better-known plays and heard the best of the bards.

In some ways, though, it had proved to be an uncomfortable relationship. Thracius always spoke his mind, and his point of view was often not one Arrant wanted to hear. And now his mother had returned and he was wondering if he would be able to sneak out so often. 'Yes,' he said in reply to Thracius' query, 'she's back. And Brand with her.'

'Ah. I've heard the Altani didn't make himself too popular in the west.'

'Really? I hadn't heard.' But then, who would tell him anyway?

'The Exaltarch's friendship with him is not doing her any good, lad, and it's not doing the country any good either.'

'It's none of your business,' he snapped, and was immediately ashamed. It wasn't Thracius who'd made him angry, but his mother and her infatuation with that hulking Altani. Damn them both.

Thracius stirred on his stool and then leaned forward, arms on the table, facing him across the time-polished boards. 'It *is* my business. It's the business of all loyal Tyranians.'

Arrant was silent.

'We must protect her from herself. She's just a woman, and she's easily led astray. What kind of men are we if we let her be fooled?'

Arrant stared at him. Easily led astray? *Ligea?* 'You're joking, Thracius. My mother is more capable than any man I know. She could gut you as easily as most women chop vegetables. She doesn't need protection, and she wouldn't take kindly to being described as "just a woman", either.' He grinned at the thought of what she would have said if she'd heard his condescension.

'She's a woman,' he said stubbornly. 'She lets her heart rule her head. And that's no good in an Exaltarch.'

'So what would you do about it?' he drawled, accepting that Thracius' prejudices were not going to be changed by him, and probably wouldn't budge even if he had the proof chiselled in stone right under his nose.

'Urban – no, *Arrant*, just give me the word, and I'll get rid of him for you.'

Arrant stared at him, astonished. 'Get rid of Brand? How? Get the Altani rulers to recall him, just like that?'

'Well, no, obviously. I was thinking of more direct means.'

Arrant tried to hide his shock. 'You mean – *kill* him?'

'Yes, if it was your wish.'

'You're mad! Of course that's not my wish.' Yet something inside him stirred at the thought, and that response appalled him. Hurriedly, he pushed the thought away.

Thracius didn't appear to notice. 'All right then, I could arrange for him to be kidnapped, and given a scare and a warning he wouldn't forget in half-a-dozen lifetimes. He'd be off to Altan like a bolt of lightning, and he wouldn't come back, I promise you.'

'That's not necessary.'

The Corbussian shrugged. 'As you wish. But don't forget the offer if you change your mind.'

And he didn't forget. When he saw Brand and Ligea laughing about something together, when he saw the way his look caressed her body – he remembered.

He hid those rogue thoughts from Tarran, on the several occasions his brother came. His visits were brief anyway, just a moment or two to say he was all right. Arrant didn't even have a chance to tell him about Thracius. He regretted that; he would have valued Tarran's opinion on the Corbussian. But these days, Tarran could think of nothing but what was happening in the Mirage.

In the past, Arrant had at least been able to provide distraction for his brother. Now, his inability to help wounded his spirit. At night, lying on his bed, staring at the shadows blurred by his tears, he reflected that all he could do for Tarran now was cry.

It wasn't enough, not for either of them.

When he saw Thracius next, the Corbussian suggested a shortcut through the Snarls in order to get to the port, taking a route that passed by the new jail built to replace the Cages. Ligea had told Arrant about the horror and stink of those barred coops. He hadn't been surprised she had ordered their demolition and replacement. Doubtless the prisoners had approved, but oddly enough the public were angry at the change, saying the new jail pampered criminals. Apparently the honest citizens of Tyr preferred the stench of the vermin-ridden cages to the present stone building.

That day, a crowd surrounded the new building, blocking the streets and forcing Arrant and Thracius to halt. A glance showed Arrant the whole throng consisted of the scum of the Snarls: the misfits, the thugs, the unwashed beggars.

'I don't like the look of this,' Thracius muttered.

Arrant knew what he meant. The crowd was saturated with such an intensity of ugly passion that it stimulated his cabochon. He tried to shut the gem down, but it stubbornly glowed and force-fed him a stream of emotions. The crowd swayed to an orchestrated rhythm that he could almost hear: a drumming passion of hate. No longer a group of individuals, it had become a united beast, with a single unreasoning mind. And someone was driving it, goading it, conducting it. Arrant briefly sensed the triumph of a subtle mind and then it was gone, hidden and anonymous in the crowd.

The cabochon glow faded. He cursed its limitations, even as he shuddered at its possibilities. Why did it do this to him? He would rather have known nothing!

And then he caught some of the shouts: 'Down with the Altani! Down with the Exaltarch! Free Garcius!'

Thracius turned to the man next to him. 'What's all this about, then?'

'The Imperial Guards have thrown Garcius the Nab in the clink,' the man told him angrily. 'On the Altani Ambassador's say-so. We'll tell 'em all what we think of that!'

'Come,' Thracius said, taking Arrant's arm. 'We'll take another route.'

'Who's Garcius?' Arrant asked once they'd left the crowd behind.

'Ah – no one important. A petty criminal, but he's popular enough in the Snarls. He's just an excuse. The crowd are angry about . . . a lot of things.' He was going to say more, but apparently thought better of it. 'Don't worry about it,' he said finally, but the way he said it made Arrant worry all the more.

Just outside the main gate of the palace, they ran into another throng of people. 'What in the Vortex is this?' Thracius growled, taken aback at finding a second crowd so soon after the first.

'The Exaltarch's there,' Arrant whispered in warning, glimpsing his mother's chariot. She had just arrived at the foot of the main stairs together with her mounted bodyguard. The crowd pressed in on her as she dismounted from her chariot, but when her guard moved to form a barrier, she gestured them back and allowed people to approach. Doubtless she had sampled their mood and knew there was no hostility there.

'Can she sense you?' Thracius asked nervously.

He shook his head. *At least I hope not.* But with an unpredictable cabochon, how did he know what would happen?

Thracius wanted him to circle the crowd to the kitchen entrance, but Arrant lingered, watching. A man holding a wrapped child in his arms reached out in supplication towards Ligea. She spoke to him, then pulled back the wrapping and placed a hand on the child's face. Her cabochon bathed the three of them with gold; the rest of the crowd drew back, awed and reverent.

'What's she doing?' Thracius hissed.

'It's probably a sick baby,' he said.

'Can she heal it?'

'Maybe. But any kind of healing takes time and saps energy. I doubt that what she's doing now will do much other than start the healing process.' A thought came unbidden: *I wish I could do that.*

Thracius seemed to be struggling with a confusion of feelings. Arrant couldn't sort out any of them, but was aware of his agitation. Anything to do with Magor power seemed to unsettle the ex-legionnaire. *Which makes two of us . . .*

'Arrant,' Thracius said, 'I'm off. I'll see you in another ten days, all right?'

He had time only to nod his agreement before Thracius was gone.

*   *   *

Arrant couldn't mention the incident in front of the jail to Ligea without revealing that he had left the palace, but he made a point of having dinner with her and Brand that night and she brought up the matter herself.

'I think I can see Rathrox Ligatan's skinny fingers manipulating this one,' she remarked after she'd given the two of them the gist of what had happened. 'Although I'm not sure why he'd want to drag your name into it, Brand.'

'Brand didn't order the man's arrest?' Arrant asked, looking not at the Altani, but at his mother.

She gave the faintest of pauses before she replied, just to let him know that his rudeness in directing the question to her instead of to Brand had not gone unnoticed. 'Of course not! Wherever did you get that idea? The man is just a common criminal, arrested in a perfectly normal way. But rumour has it that he is some kind of hero, seized for throwing a stone at Brand. It never happened. The whole thing is ridiculous! I ordered the demonstration to be ignored and finally the crowd drifted away, but I doubt that that will be the end of it. There's been a lot of unrest in Tyr while we've been gone,' she added. 'I feel Rathrox is behind it: I know his style so well. Besides, I sensed him today. Favonius too. They are both in the city somewhere. Cabochon, how hard it is to combat rumour! It's like trying to pick up a live fish by the tail . . .'

She smiled at Arrant. 'Oh, I forgot to tell you some news. Gev is coming back to Tyr.'

He brightened. 'He is? Why? I thought you needed him in the western borderlands.'

'I do. Come to think of it, I need him everywhere. But he wants to retire. To go home, to Inge. So of course he must. He will sail from here.'

'A mistake,' Brand muttered. 'There are times when it's better not to go back. When there have been too many years.' There was a wealth of meaning in his words, but Arrant wasn't interested.

'I'll admit I was surprised,' Ligea said. 'He never wanted to return before. But people change, and he has grandchildren now whom he's never met. Maybe he hankers after family.' She lounged back on the cushions of her divan. The food on the low table in front of her was largely untouched. Arrant never usually thought of such things, but it suddenly occurred to him that she looked tired and strained.

Brand must have had similar thoughts because he asked gently, 'Ligea – is it worth it?'

There was a pause before she answered. 'I made a vow when I agreed to the Covenant,' she said, and Arrant had an idea that she spoke for his benefit, not Brand's. 'I swore to serve the people of Kardiastan. To protect the country, and them.' She cut a guava into two and then into four. 'I still believe this is the best way I have of doing that. If I were not Exaltarch, Rathrox would soon have one of the more pliant of the highborn in the Exaltarch's seat, someone who would reinstate slavery and think once again in terms of conquest. Especially in terms of the conquest of Kardiastan.'

'Why?' Arrant asked, puzzled. 'Kardiastan is no threat to Tyr.'

'That's not necessarily the way Tyranians see it. Kardiastan is both strategically important and a very uncomfortable neighbour to have.' She gave a wry smile. 'Full of numina and people with magic swords, you see. A country to be feared. Why, one of their number – and a woman at that – even managed to gain the throne of Tyrans and bring a great empire to its knees . . .

'If I were to die tomorrow, some in Tyrans would ache to rip out Kardiastan's throat, if not in this generation, then in the next. Perhaps they wouldn't succeed, but they could bring the hell of war back to us.

'And so I must establish the kind of institutions that will prevent both slavery and a military-minded state from existing here again – ever. Once I have, and this land is stable, only then can I think in terms of retiring. Of having a life of my own.' The guava was now in eight pieces. She looked up at Brand with a vestige of her quick humour. 'Besides, I like all this, you know. In some ways, the tougher it is, the better I like it. And one day I'll have the pleasure of bringing that bastard Rathrox down. It's just not so easy, not when you must have scruples – and a

Senate full of its own importance, trying to curb my powers.'

Something in the rueful honesty of her smile brought home a truth about her to Arrant: she was afraid. Afraid of her own love of power. She reined herself in deliberately. The insight was a revelation.

'However,' she went on, 'I *am* tempted to put on a disguise and hunt out that insect Rathrox myself, just as I would have done to someone I wanted, back in the days when I was a Brotherhood Compeer.'

'Too dangerous,' Brand said quickly. 'In fact, I wouldn't mind betting that he has his watchers out there at the gates waiting for you to do just that. He knows you as well as you know him, after all. He knows what you'd like to do. An arrow would be all it takes . . .'

She sighed. 'Yes, I'm afraid you're right. In fact, I know you're right. I've felt them. He has his spies everywhere, just as he always did. They watch everyone who comes and goes, and any disguise would come under his scrutiny sooner or later. But still I'm tempted. How can I bring him down if I don't confront him?' The guava was now so much mince on her plate and she'd eaten none of it. 'Damn it, Brand, sometimes I feel I'm more of a prisoner now than when I was back in the Mirage, warded under Temellin's orders.'

Arrant froze in place. Spies watching the gates? Did they watch the kitchen entrance? Commonsense told him that of course they would, if they were looking for Ligea. They'd expect her to try a servant's disguise or similar. But would they be on the lookout for *him*? He tried to convince himself that they wouldn't. And anyway, very few people knew what he looked like.

I wish I hadn't attended that banquet.

Fear ruffled the surface of his mind like a breeze across water. He closed off the channel of his thoughts, and paid attention to what Brand was saying instead.

'It may make the present situation harder for Rathrox if I went back to Altan. He's obviously using my presence here to stir up trouble.'

'Ah, no, Brand. I couldn't bear it if you left.' She reached out and wrapped her fingers around his.

Arrant's hands clenched so tight under cover of the table he thought he'd drawn blood with his nails. How *dare* she say such a thing in front of him?

'Excuse me,' he said, coldly polite. 'I wish to go to my room.' He didn't wait for permission but rose and walked away, his back sword-straight, his eyes full of furious tears.

He wasn't due to meet Thracius again for ten days, and during that time, Arrant heard no more about trouble on the streets of Tyr. His tutors kept him busy and Ligea had insisted that he resume his military training as well – every day. He did not enjoy the lessons, although he knew and liked the teacher she sent; he had taught Arrant before in the Stronghold.

The next time he met Thracius, the man seemed tense. 'I need to talk to you,' he said. 'Urgently.' He walked Arrant away from their usual meeting place at the fountain in the Forum Publicum, hurrying him into the Snarls, back to the same small pothouse they had visited before. He chose a table in the corner, separated from the only other occupants, a couple of rough-looking road-menders sitting near the door.

'Arrant,' he said, 'I'm worried. I've heard something – someone tried to involve me—'

He was edgy; Arrant caught an underlay of excitement, or was it fear? He couldn't tell. His cabochon was silent on the matter. 'What is it?' he asked.

'A plot. Against the Exaltarch. I've heard rumours but no details, and I'm not likely to, either. I refused to join, and they're not going to trust me now. Goddess, lad, this is serious this time! They are gaining support; if half what they told me is true, the Exaltarch herself is in danger. They are using this matter of the Altani, Ambassador Brand, to whip up a furore of hate; they are making the Exaltarch seem disloyal to Tyrans. "She's a foreigner," they say. "She destroyed our empire and now she listens to foreign advisers."'

He fell silent as the pothouse-keeper came up and asked what they wanted to drink. He ordered a soft ale for Arrant and wine for himself, and waited for the man to disappear into the back room before he spoke again. 'Lad, the only way to pinch off the shoot of this thing before it takes root too deep to die is to get rid of the Altani. People blame him for half the current troubles. If he disappears, then they'll think she did it, and she'll regain some of the credibility she's lost. Do you understand what I'm saying? We've run out of time.'

Arrant stared at him, aghast. 'It's not that bad, surely. I would have heard something!'

'Your mother probably doesn't want to worry you. I hear, though, that she's insisting you be trained in the use of a sword. If that's true, then it should tell you something.'

'I thought it was because I'll be going to my father soon—' He was about to ask how Thracius knew anyway, when the Corbussian interrupted.

'Your *father*? Who's that? He must be a Kardi, surely!'

Arrant nodded.

'Sweet Elysium!' Arrant couldn't interpret the odd look on Thracius' face, or the strange tone he used when he added, 'We have to do this all the quicker then.'

Thoughts whirled through Arrant's mind, loose ends tangling. 'Do *what*? I'm not going to let you kill Brand, so you can forget that for a start. Don't even *suggest* it.'

'Well, that would probably produce the best result. But I wasn't going to say that. You made it clear you won't let me organise it. Fair enough. And I don't suppose you're going to let me scare Hades into him, either.'

Arrant shifted unhappily in his chair. 'Somehow I don't think Brand scares easily.'

'All right, I won't try. But I do want to talk to the man. If he is loyal to Ligea – in love with her, even – he won't want to cause her any harm, right?'

Arrant nodded. 'In fact, he suggested to Ligea not so long ago that it might be better if he returned to Altan. She was the one who wouldn't have it.' He couldn't keep the bitter rage from his voice.

'Women can be extraordinarily silly when affairs of the heart are concerned, you know.' There was just a hint of scorn in Thracius' words. 'A hard fact for a son to accept about his mother, but it's true nonetheless. I can speak to the Altani, though, man to man, and I suspect he will listen, especially when I tell him the details of the plot I heard. When he hears the truth, he'll do the sensible thing.'

'All right. Let me go back to the palace. I can speak to Brand and have him inform the Guard to let you in.'

'No, that wouldn't work. People are watching the palace. If I go near the entrance, they'll know I am going to betray them. It's doubtful I'll get in the door. Brand will have to come out to see me.'

'How am I going to get him to do that?' He felt that he was on the back of a runaway horse. Everything was rushing past him too fast; there was no time to think. 'He'll be as suspicious as a street cur.'

A group of schoolboys paused in the shade of the doorway, their hands full of wax tablets and half-eaten hot meat-cakes; they smelled of the schoolroom and spiced gravy. They couldn't have been any older than he was, and all they had to worry about was whether they could read their letters well enough to please their tutors. Arrant envied them.

Thracius didn't even notice them. He was taut with emotion. 'It shouldn't be too hard. You write him a note asking him to come here, and we'll ask the pothouse-keeper's boy to send it to the palace.'

Arrant frowned. 'A note saying what? Once he realises I'm out in the city, worse still, in the Snarls, he'll tell Ligea and she'll have a contingent of Imperial Guards here – plus herself – before you and I have time to finish our ale. I'll be hauled off to the worst lecture of my life, and you'll be in trouble and still wouldn't get to talk to Brand.'

'It depends how you word the note,' Thracius said. 'Look,

you've told me that Brand has tried to be friendly. Now's his chance to get on your good side. Believe me, he'll think hard before he passes up the opportunity. What you do is this: you write that you sneaked out of the palace dressed as a servant. Make it sound as if this is the first time you've done anything so silly. Tell him you are now in this pothouse in the Snarls, but don't have enough money to pay for the meal you've eaten. Say they won't believe who you are and won't let you go. Then ask Brand if he would mind coming to get you. And you ask him – no, you *beg* him – not to tell your mother or anyone else. Say you'll tell her yourself.'

Arrant thought about that. Thracius could be right. Brand would like Arrant to be under an obligation to him. He was silent again as the pothouse-keeper delivered the ale and wine.

'He may still tell my mother,' Arrant said, once the man had moved away.

'Not if he wants you to look kindly on him. Anyway, the Exaltarch shouldn't be a problem for us this morning. She's busy at her usual monthly audience with the trademasters and merchants.'

Before Arrant could ask how he knew that, he added, 'Lad, if we don't act now, then this movement will spread like fire in dry brush and your mother is doomed. If I can convince Brand to leave the country, it will be a step forward. But I think I can do more than that. I think I can convince him to talk sense to your mother. Lovers can say things others can't. And I know how to speak to a man like this Altani.'

'She's not so easily defeated. Nor is she without support. There are those who worship her—'

'Gullible lowlife,' he said, dismissive. 'Believe me, those who condemn her grow in number every day!' He dropped his voice and glanced around to make doubly sure no one could hear him. 'Urban – Arrant, the old Brotherhood is involved. Under the man who used to be the Magister Officii, Rathrox Ligatan. He's as clever as the guardian at Acheron's gate. No amount of numen magic will save her if he can turn enough people against her.

There's even grumbling within her own troops, all stoked by Rathrox Ligatan. He's been four years in the planning of this.' He reached inside his belt pouch. 'Look, I have brought a scrap of cheap papyrus and pen and ink to write with. We don't want anything too fancy, not if it is supposed to be supplied by a pothouse.' He grinned and showed Arrant the back of the paper. It was an order list of wines and prices, written in an ill-educated hand. 'If we fail, and Brand sends guards to fetch you, no damage is done.'

'Except to my freedom,' Arrant replied, sighing.

Thracius laid a hand on his shoulder, his voice intense with passion. 'Arrant, whatever happens, remember that I am a loyal servant of Tyrans. And when I look at you – I see a son I might have had. Remember that . . .'

Propelled by Thracius' urgency, Arrant took the papyrus and began to write.

CHAPTER THIRTY-EIGHT

'More wine?' Brand asked. 'Or would you prefer juice? I can send a servant for orange juice.'

His visitor laughed, lounging back in his chair so he could swing his legs up onto the low table in front of them. He crossed his ankles, scattering dishes. 'One of the perks of living in the palace, eh? Whole bevy of people tripping over themselves, just to serve you.'

Brand surveyed the mess the General had just made on the table. 'Or clean up after *you*, Gev,' he said.

'One could get used to this highborn life, you Altani barbarian. You're getting soft, I'll bet.'

'And why not? I'm not a slob of a soldier like some I know. Don't I deserve a bit of luxury at my time in life?'

'A bit more than luxury, from what I've seen. Cosying up to the Exaltarch may not be my idea of a fun roll on the pallet, but I have no doubt it has compensations. Good lay, is she?'

Brand sighed. 'Same old Gev. Tongue as subtle as a blacksmith's hammer, and the manners of a vulture at a carcass. The wonder of it is that no one has ever run a sword through your innards in some pothouse brawl. I'll certainly be tempted if you continue to talk about Ligea like that.'

'I have every intention of dying in bed at eighty, stabbed from behind by the cuckolded husband.'

Brand snorted. 'And that's not an unlikely scenario, I suppose. Gev, you're not wearing your uniform. You really have relinquished your position as High General of Tyrans?'

'In everything except my signature on the papers. I am going home, Brand. To Inge.'

'I don't know what she'll do without you.'

'She can promote Valorian to general, for a start. He's a good man.'

'I heard you didn't like him!'

Gevenan chuckled. 'I don't like anybody much. And that fellow smells of perfume, wears his hair in curls and manicures his nails. Huh! But he's got a mind like a sinkhole. Absorbs everything. Never forgets a thing. And the result is a tactician second to none. He's wasted here in Tyr. She should promote him.'

'Val likes life in Tyr. He has a fondness for beautiful young women hanging on his every word at banquets, and more than a fondness for handsome young athletes in his bed at night—'

A knock at the door interrupted him. It was one of the palace guard, handing over a grubby scroll addressed to him, delivered, the guard said, to the main gate.

'Love letter?' Gevenan asked as Brand closed the door.

Brand grinned, but the grin vanished as he read. He wrenched open the door and called the guard back. 'Find Dominus Arrant,' he ordered, 'and get him here on the double. If you haven't found him in five minutes, come back and tell me. Snap to it, man!'

The man nodded and was gone.

'What is it?' Gevenan asked, sitting upright and swinging his feet to the floor.

Wordlessly, Brand handed him the note.

Gevenan read it and laughed. 'The brat!'

'I hope this is no more than what it seems.'

'You think he might be pulling some sort of trick on you because you're humping his mother?'

'It's possible. But unlikely. He's not that sort of lad.'

'No, that's true. More the serious type. Takes things to heart. Still, this' – he shook the note – 'is understandable. Ocrastes' balls, Brand, you were the one who was telling me that the boy didn't have much of a life here in Tyr, confined like an Assorian wife because of the danger he would be seized by Ligea's enemies. Is it any wonder he's broken out? He doesn't have much idea of the value of money, though, by the sound of it, does he?'

Brand frowned. 'You know, if there's one thing I would have said about Arrant, it was that he had enough brains to know you don't buy a meal without having enough money to pay for it.'

Gevenan looked at him sharply. 'Ah. You could be right. Hmm . . . so, if the guard doesn't turn him up in his bedroom, do you want me to go with you?'

Brand thought about that, and shook his head. 'No, I think not. Ever since that riot at the jail, Ligea has asked guards to dog my footsteps every time I leave the palace, so I won't exactly be alone. But . . . if I'm not back with him in an hour, check out the pothouse mentioned in his note, will you? And tell Ligea.'

It wasn't much fun sitting in the pothouse waiting for trouble. And Arrant was sure trouble was on its way. Even if Thracius and Brand had an amicable conversation, no one was going to be happy with Arrant, least of all Brand. And so he sat, his thoughts turned inwards, miserably wishing the day was already over.

Several more people came into the pothouse, taking the tables near the door. They comported themselves like soldiers, although they weren't wearing uniform.

Arrant tried to look inconspicuous. He didn't want to be recognised by an off-duty palace guard. 'Thracius,' he said, 'I – I really don't want to be here when Brand arrives. I think I want to go back to the palace.' He went to stand up, but Thracius yanked at his wrist so hard he flopped back down into the chair.

'No. I want you to hear what I have to say to Brand. Just sit down, Arrant, and wait.'

Another man walked in, and took a chair at the table next to them, so Arrant dropped his voice. 'Thracius, I'm going to be in a lot of trouble, and I'd rather go and see my mother and explain, than talk to Brand about it first.'

'Don't be childish. This is important, Arrant. Stay where you are.'

The newcomer looked across at them curiously. He was old, with limbs as thin as a gazelle's, and a wiry body that seemed little more than skin over sinew. Thracius frowned at Arrant, warning him to be quiet, so he subsided. He was beginning to wish he'd never had anything to do with the Corbussian. Tears threatened, but he wouldn't give in to them. He was thirteen, for gods' sake, not some thumb-sucking crybaby. He knew he was feeling sorry for himself, and was shamed.

Cabochon damn it, I wish Tarran were here . . .

The thin man at the next table was staring at him. His eyes had an unsettling intensity, as though they could see Arrant's most hidden secrets. Arrant turned away and kept his left hand curled up tight over his palm. He regarded the pothouse with sudden aversion. The tables were dirty, slopped with ale and wine. Flies blackened the edges of each spill. The bodies of several squashed cockroaches adorned the broken tiles of the floor. The walls, pocked by patches of peeling paint, were scratched with vulgar graffiti and even more salacious drawings.

Other men now filled the adjacent tables, all well armed. The road-menders had left.

'Men like me,' Thracius explained, when he noted the way Arrant was eyeing the weaponry of the newcomers. 'Ex-legionnaires who left the army because they weren't going to serve with the same men they once fought against. They take the same sort of work as I have – as guards. Guarding the rich, guarding the money-masters, guarding trade caravans, guarding merchant ships. A step down for prideful men. You are looking at a tavern full of resentment, Arrant.'

Arrant was about to remark that Brand would not be happy entering a place like this, when the words froze on his lips. *Goddess*, he thought. *This is deliberate.* And then: *Arrant, you fool. You utter, utter fool. Thracius is going to threaten the Altani. These men are his friends . . .*

He had never felt so sick. His face felt drained of colour. He turned to Thracius. 'I need the privy,' he said and started to rise. Once again, Thracius pulled him back down. 'I said, *don't move.*'

'Thracius,' he protested in injured tones, trying to sound like the naive boy he had been five minutes earlier. 'I really need to go—'

'It can wait,' Thracius snapped and his hand was still tight around Arrant's wrist.

Two more men walked into the pothouse and, without asking, took the only two empty seats – at their table. One of them winked at Thracius. Arrant wrenched his hand free, sent his chair flying and made a wild dash for the door. His concentration was all on reaching the street before Thracius.

He never came close. The thin man at the next table stuck out his foot. Arrant flew through the air to land hard on the floor between the tables. The breath whooshed out of him. Someone immediately trod on his left hand, grinding his cabochon into the floor. Arrant gasped and tried to pull away. Swords left their scabbards all around him. There were two more sandalled feet in front of his nose. He raised his head still further and looked up.

Brand. It was Brand. One of the armed men held a blade to his neck.

Behind them, someone slammed the pothouse door shut.

Arrant stared, aghast. Any confidence he'd ever had melted into a childish need for comfort, but there was no one to give it. 'I'm sorry,' he mumbled. 'I'm so sorry.' Pain shot up his arm but the foot pinning his fingers down did not budge.

Brand unwisely ignored the sword at his neck. He kicked out to dislodge whoever had been standing on Arrant's hand. With his good arm, he hauled Arrant to his feet. The sword was chopped down in anger, slicing through his tunic to open a cut across his collarbone. Someone else seized his withered arm and twisted it up his back. With astonishing speed and strength, he bent double and heaved. His assailant went sailing through the air over his head, to crash into a table. He reached for his own weapon, yelling, 'Run for it, Arrant!'

Arrant dived for the door, but it had been barred. He grabbed the bar and lifted. Behind him Brand was bellowing for help, so he started yelling as well.

Brand always goes out with guards. If we make enough noise—

Glancing over his shoulder as he heaved, he saw Brand had managed to draw his blade. A man was clutching a stomach wound. Arrant threw the bar aside, and tried to push open the door, only to realise it opened inwards. Someone slammed him against it. Eager hands grabbed him, holding him there, pinned like a banner to the boards. A muscled arm clamped his left palm flat to the planks. He winced; his hand was bruised and still paining him. He couldn't move, so he yelled some more. The pothouse-keeper pinched his nose closed with dirty fingers until he opened his mouth. The moment he did, a cloth was stuffed in. It smelled of ale slops and tasted of sour vomit and yeast. The pothouse-keeper let go of his nose, chuckling.

He looked over his shoulder again, and his despair was a pain slicing into his ribcage. Brand was bent over a table, vanishing under attackers. He'd lost his sword, but was still struggling. Thracius leaped over a fallen chair, coming at Arrant. He had a knife in his hand and pressed the blade of it to the side of Arrant's throat.

'Hold it right there, Altani,' he called. His voice was so thick with loathing Arrant didn't recognise it. 'Not a move out of you, or the boy dies.'

The men gradually stepped away from Brand where he lay on the tabletop. He sat up, dabbing at blood that ran down from a cut on his head into his eyes. More blood soaked the shoulder of his tunic. He looked at Thracius.

'Well, well, well. Favonius Kyranon. Still threatening children, I see. I heard about what you did at Prianus.'

Arrant, trying to work the cloth out of his mouth with his tongue, stilled. *Favonius?* The Jackal who had tortured the children?

'Prianus?' Thracius blinked, sounding genuinely puzzled.

'You don't even remember the name,' Brand said softly. 'Maybe you never even knew it . . .'

Arrant's mind didn't seem to want to work. The thin man grabbed him, forced his hands together, palm to palm behind his back. He then tied them that way, using thin twine. He had a claw-like grip, that man, and he was rough. The ties were too tight. He turned Arrant to face the room and pulled the cloth out of his mouth. 'Scream and this goes back in,' he said. He smiled, showing yellowed teeth.

But Arrant was still dealing with what had preceded. He turned his head towards Thracius, disbelief and shock denying the information of his senses. 'Prianus?' he whispered. '*You* did that? Thracius——!'

'Thracius?' Brand asked, and gave a low laugh. 'You poor fool, Arrant. He's no one called Thracius. That's Favonius Kyranon, one-time Stalwart, more lately legionnaire of the Brotherhood Jackals. Gevenan's been chasing this fellow all over Tyrans for years.' Brand's gaze slid on to the thin man now standing beside Arrant, and the rage in his eyes glowed like coals in a brazier. 'And that soulless strip of flesh and evil there, that's Rathrox Ligatan, once Magister Officii, head of the Brotherhood.'

But it was to Thracius that Arrant's gaze kept returning. 'Prianus,' he said. '*How could you do that?*' Dark red lines, carved into a girl's body with an artist's eye for pattern. *While she was alive.*

'Don't worry, lad,' Thracius said roughly. 'You'll come to no harm if you do as you're told.'

But there was nothing he could have said that Arrant could believe. Not now. Not ever again. This was the man who'd ridden into a village and left a message for Ligea written in the blood of its children. Thracius, who'd told him stories, taken him fishing, taught him how to appreciate the beauty of a sculpture or a fine mosaic. Favonius Kyranon the Jackal, who had taken the heart out of a four-year-old boy and left it on the stoop for the child's brother to find.

Arrant closed his eyes and turned his face away.

Thracius – no, Favonius, with steely fury, hissed in his ear. 'Blame your bitch mother. She did this to me, she made me what you see.'

Anger swelled in Arrant, bursting through his veins into a roaring in his ears, a haziness in his vision, a pounding in his heart. He reached out to the power of his cabochon, not caring what it would do to his hands if it came. Not caring if it mutilated or killed them all: himself, Brand, everyone in the room. Not caring anything, except that he use it, that he have enough to kill this man who stood beside him and blamed Ligea for the evil he had done. He pulled, deep and sure and raging.

And nothing happened.

No light, no gold, no feeling of salvation. He shook, his whole body shook with his concentration – but found only a void. He knew then that he strove to draw something out of a pit of nothingness as deep as the ocean.

'Goddess,' Favonius was saying to Brand, 'I wonder if you know how much I enjoy seeing you here like this, you bastard thrall. How much I've looked forward to this day. I haven't forgotten the Mirage, you see. I haven't forgotten the Stalwarts and how they suffered. Do you know how many of us returned, you shrivelled-arm helot? Do you?'

'Get on with it, Favonius,' Rathrox said quietly. His face seemed grey in the lamplight of the closed room. His eyelids drooped over a look that assessed them all, a look that absorbed or discarded what he needed with the ease of experience.

Favonius collected himself. He took a deep breath and began to speak, still addressing Brand. 'Listen carefully,' he said. 'You are going to do something for us, and you are going to do it well, do you understand?'

Rathrox, who had left his side and gone to sit down, added, 'And if you think there's help waiting for you outside, forget it. We are aware that you are normally followed by guards when you leave the palace on foot, and we have taken precautions accordingly. They have been, um, redirected.'

Favonius continued, 'In a moment you are going to go back to the palace with me, helot. The minute you and I leave this building, Arrant will be taken elsewhere. When we return, it will be to his new location. In the meantime, you will walk with me as if I am your best-loved crony from your past. You will get me into the palace, and you will get me in to see Ligea. Once there, you will ask her quietly to get rid of anyone else who happens to be with her. You will see that there is no fuss. Once us three are alone, you will tell her Rathrox here has her boy, and that Arrant will be killed if she doesn't do all we ask.

'And this is what we ask: she will leave her sword in the palace. She will keep her magic stone flat against her body, over her heart. She will ask to have her usual chariot and mounted guards brought around to the palace steps. She will act in every way completely normally. She will speak to nobody, not even you, unless I hear every word. Us three will leave the palace in the chariot. I will give directions. Be warned that outside the palace there will be other watchers to make sure that all goes well. When the chariot stops in front of the place we take her to, she will dismiss the driver, the guards, everyone. Understand? If she doesn't, Arrant here will die.

'We will enter that place. Once she does that, Arrant will be safe – unless Rathrox has the merest suspicion that anything is not the way it should be. If he has, then a knife goes into the boy's throat. You must persuade Ligea not to think that she can torture the position of Arrant's new location out of me and then come and rescue him. If I don't get back on time, or if there is any unusual activity outside the building where Arrant is kept, the boy will die. As for you, thrall—' He smiled an anticipatory smile that was edged with cruelty. 'Your wellbeing will depend on your cooperation.'

'No.'

The single word was said calmly and firmly. Brand looked across at Arrant. There was no condemnation there; no reproach. And no hope. 'I'm sorry, Arrant. But if I do what they ask, all three of us will die. This way, at least one of us lives.'

Arrant knew what he was saying and felt an odd rush of relief. He was going to die. It was no more than he deserved, and if they could keep her safe – it was enough. He nodded his agreement.

'Good lad,' Brand said softly.

Rathrox rose to his feet and moved across to Arrant's side once more. 'I don't think you've explained things all that well, Favonius.' He turned to Brand. 'I don't give a damn about you one way or another myself, but Favonius here wants your head on a plate, so he'll get it. But I have no intention of killing Arrant, quite the contrary – if we can get our hands on Ligea. Once she is dead, this lad is our new Exaltarch.'

He laid skinny fingers on Arrant's arm, digging into the flesh. Laying claim to him, body and soul. 'Who better? A lad we can manipulate, who can't retaliate. The gullible will think he is some kind of god because he has a gemstone in his palm. We know he has no magic to use, but it's a secret we will keep. He will be our figurehead.'

'And you think I will go along with this?' Arrant asked.

Rathrox was utterly contemptuous. 'You won't have any say in the matter, lad. Not if you want to stay alive. The merchants and trademasters and the highborn and the Cult of Melete will all support us because of what we can offer them. They know we will bring back slavery. Oh, doubtless the Senate and Advisory Council will jog along for a while. But we – we the Brotherhood and our Jackal Legion – will run the Exaltarchy.' He ran his tongue over his thin lips. His discoloured teeth were displayed in an unpleasant smile as he looked back at Brand. 'You will tell Ligea that her son will be safe if she comes to us without trouble. Favonius will tell her the same thing, and she will hear the truth in his promise.'

For the first time Brand showed some emotion. 'You bastard. You want her to die knowing you have her son; that you will use him the way you once used her—'

He smiled. 'That's right. The perfect revenge for what she has done. I see you appreciate the exquisite irony of my plan. There is no greater pleasure than to have one's enemies die despairing of all they have ever lived for.'

'You can squirm whichever way you like, thrall,' Favonius added, 'but there's no way out of this for you. Ligea will come because it's the only way she can save her son. And she will know she can save him because she knows Rathrox. She knows how much he will enjoy raising the boy. And even as she knows the kind of life her son will lead, she will have to let it happen, because the alternative is worse. Death for him.'

Brand looked across at Arrant, the agony of his indecision in every line of his face. He could save Arrant or he could save Ligea. He couldn't do both. Either way he was doomed and he knew it; but Arrant read compassion, not censure, in the glance Brand gave him.

Sweet cabochon. What have I done?

'I'd rather die,' Arrant told him, but his voice broke. 'Don't do it, Brand. *Please*, don't do it.' *How could I live with myself, knowing it was my foolishness that ruined everything?* How could he have ever hated this man?

'Perhaps I can make the decision easier for you, helot,' Rathrox said, the purr of his voice an obscenity. 'If you don't cooperate, if you don't return with Favonius unhurt and with a compliant Ligea, Arrant will die slowly. I shall carve him up, piece by piece, and I'll send the pieces to Ligea, one at a time. I know how to make a person die very slowly. It can take months . . .' He raised a hand to Arrant's face, and ran grey fingers down his cheek in a gesture of sensual pleasure that clenched Arrant's heart with terror. He wrenched at his bonds and twisted his face away. Rathrox laughed.

Favonius refused to look at him but Arrant saw his hand shake on the knife he held. Perhaps there were still some things the ex-Stalwart found hard to stomach, after all. Arrant couldn't be that wrong about him, could he? Thracius had called him the son he might have had . . .

But then there had been Prianus. Maybe there was nothing at all Favonius would not do.

Brand shrugged. 'That will not be necessary. I will go with the – the jackal-hearted bastard.'

Rathrox nodded and smiled, Favonius let his blade drop away from Brand's neck, the two men who had held Arrant released their hold. 'Give him his cloak to cover that wound, someone, and let's go,' Favonius said simply.

'*Brand*—' Arrant said.

The Altani looked back at him from the doorway.

'I'm sorry.' Arrant was crying, unable to see him through the tears. 'It's my fault. All my fault. And I'd still rather die.'

Brand nodded. 'Yes, but I have to be able to live with myself. Or rather, I have to die knowing how I have lived. And so does Ligea. Courage, lad. Courage. And never forget. That's all I ask of you.' And he turned and walked out of the door with Favonius.

Arrant was frozen with horror at what he had done. Brand was going to die. Ligea was going to die.

She is going to throw away all she has achieved to save me.

How could he have been so stupid? How could he have been such a baby – he who had lived with intrigue and deception and plotting all his life? Why hadn't he seen the kind of man Thracius-Favonius was? How could he have ever believed no one would find out he sneaked out of the palace in disguise?

Unwanted fragments of memory crowded into his mind in illustration of his idiocy. The banquet. The way Antonia the High Priestess had stared at him. Perhaps she was the one who described him to Rathrox Ligatan's spies. The beggar who had grabbed his hand, his left hand, that day he'd first met Favonius. The 'stolen' purse. Favonius' careful approach. Never pushing himself forward. One slow step at a time. The talk of his nephew. Maybe they had intended to seize him that first day – except Brand had arrived, and Favonius, fearing he'd be recognised, had left.

Probably most of what he'd said at first had been the truth. He would have been scared of being caught out in a lie, until Arrant had obligingly told him there was no need, that he couldn't read a lie. Even the way Favonius had said 'I just go by the name of Thracius these days' had been carefully worded to be the literal truth. They'd risked much, not knowing just what Magor capabilities he had. What a relief it must have been to Favonius to find out Arrant's cabochon didn't work as it should. Maybe they'd wanted to seize him then, only he'd obligingly informed Favonius that Ligea had left for the western borderlands. They'd had to bide their time until she returned.

Ligea is going to give herself up to her enemies to save me.

And how carefully they had planned their trap! The way Favonius had uncovered his cabochon, as though he hadn't known it was there all along. His feigned shock. How he had played on Arrant's dislike of Brand, fed his jealousy, stoked his fear of Rathrox Ligatan. That demonstration in front of the jail – they'd orchestrated that, just for his viewing. And he'd obliged them, as naively and as arrogantly stupid as a grasshopper trusting the friendship of a hawk. All because in his heart he'd wanted Brand dead.

Betrayer. Arrant the traitor.

Deep inside, Arrant had despised his grandfather, Miragersolad, scorned him for his treachery. But at least the Mirager had done it for another. Arrant had done this for himself.

The guilt he felt was a corrosive acid in his stomach; the self-disgust a suffocating blanket that choked his breath.

Brand is going to die today.

Kardiastan could be threatened again, because of me. People could be enslaved again, because of me. The Exaltarchy could be racked by war again, because of me. Ligea is going to sacrifice herself to save me. They will torture her to death, of course. He'd seen the look in their eyes when they spoke of her.

He wanted to die. Oh, cabochon, how *much* he wanted to die.

CHAPTER THIRTY-NINE

Ligea left the audience hall through her own private door, glad the audience was over. The merchants and traders were a prickly bunch, always full of complaints because their profits were too low, or their taxes too high. They tried hard to make her feel she was a fraudulent interloper pretending to be the ruling emperor. It didn't help that in that room she remembered all too clearly a time when she was the one kneeling at the foot of the Exaltarch, touching her fingers to the hem of his robe in submission.

'Domina?' Narbius, her scribe, approached. 'General Gevenan has arrived back.'

She felt pleasure ripple through her, lifting her spirits. And that made her laugh. It was hard to say why someone who irritated her as much as Gevenan did could also make her feel suddenly happier because he was around. 'Where is he?'

'He went to see Ambassador Brand, Domina. I think they are probably still in the Ambassador's quarters.'

'Ask them both to join me in my apartments.' She turned to walk that way, then stopped dead. 'Narbius, wait!'

He came back obediently. She stood stock still, shock coursing through her body. 'Tell – tell the General I want to see him on the double. Say Favonius is in the palace. Quickly.'

Narbius had no idea who Favonius was, but he heard the urgency in her voice. He ran.

So did Ligea. The first thing she needed to do was something completely practical. She wanted to change out of the ornate wrap she wore and into something she could fight in. As she ran, she assessed all she could sense of what was happening. Brand and Favonius were definitely together, side by side. That didn't make sense. The two men hated one another. What possible reason could either of them have for this?

She dashed into her quarters and made straight for the chest where she kept her old clothing. Narjemah, busy with some mending, looked up, startled.

'Trouble,' Ligea said, flinging off her wrap. 'Favonius is here with Brand. They are heading this way. When they arrive, show them into the atrium.' In desperate haste, she pulled on her trousers and tunic. 'Then you go to the handmaiden's room, but leave the door slightly ajar. Go out into the passageway from there, and when you see Gev arrive, get him unseen into that room. I want him to hear my conversation with Favonius.'

'*Conversation?* With that bastard Jackal? Mirageless soul, Ligea – I thought you would be more likely to burn a hole in his guts and out the other side after what happened to Prianus.'

Ligea strapped on her Mirager's sword, then reached out briefly to touch Narjemah, not in reassurance, but in warning. 'I've got such a bad feeling about this. Brand is sick with fear. He is spilling everything out – Brand, who usually keeps himself as well armoured as a tortoise.' Her voice wavered and emerged in a broken whisper. 'His horror is so strong it slams against my soul. He doesn't know how to tell me what he must. Goddess, Narjemah – there is so much fear in his mind!'

Narjemah's eyes widened. 'And – and the Jackal?'

'He's not the man I once knew. Oh, Vortexdamn, Narjemah – where is Arrant?'

'I don't know.'

They had a bare second to exchange a look of sick fear before the knock came at the door.

When Brand and Favonius entered, Ligea was standing on the other side of the atrium, with her back to them, looking out into the garden. She didn't turn around, and Narjemah slipped away without speaking after opening the door.

She said, as calmly as she could, 'You have the gall to come here, Favonius, and assume that you will walk out again, alive?'

'Oh, I know I shall. Your time here is over, Ligea. It ends today. You were a fool to ever assume that the Magister and I would let you stay in the Exaltarch's seat.'

She turned then, but didn't look at him. It was Brand's eyes she sought. For him, she gave a look of love, and tender regard. But the desolation she found in return shook the foundations of her courage. It took all she had, to say calmly, 'Brand, you had better tell me what all this is about.'

Gevenan placed the palace guard on high alert before he raced up to Ligea's quarters. Narjemah beckoned him into the hand-maiden's room, a pokey hole of a place meant to be a slave attendant's sleeping quarters, and indicated the slightly open door. He nodded and went to put his eye to the crack of the opening. Brand was speaking, a recital that made Gevenan's blood run cold.

And standing beside him, with a half-smile on his handsome face, was a man he'd never seen before. It didn't matter, Gevenan would have known him anywhere. He'd chased Favonius Kyranon and his Jackals from one side of the country to the other, and spoken to hundreds of people who knew him. *A handsome man, even though his face looks as if he's had a head-on collision with a gorclak.* They had been Ligea's words. *Women find him attractive. His self-assurance appeals to them. His nose is crooked at the tip . . .*

And he killed children.

By the time Brand finished speaking, Gevenan knew he was in trouble. Ligea would never forgive him if he did anything that resulted in Arrant's death. Already she was using their battle sign language, fluttering her fingers to indicate he was to take no action.

What in all Acheron's hells was he to do?

Jumping Ocrastes, Ligea – how can I let you die? Without you, we are lost!

Panic was not something he normally felt. He was the cool, cynical soldier, a bloody general for gods' sake. The product of years of tough training, the cruelty of the rowing bench and the harshness of slavery. A commander, with a mind given to careful planning and calm assessment. Yet he was frantic as he left the handmaiden's room. His head told him he would fail. No matter what he did, he would fail. If he – or any of his men – followed Ligea and Brand and Favonius, then Arrant would die, and Ligea would never forgive him.

And yet that was the better solution. In the broad scheme of things, Arrant didn't matter. He would never rule in Tyr, and there were many others who could take his place in Kardiastan's hierarchy. It was *Ligea* who mattered. If she died now, all she had put in place would disintegrate, especially if Rathrox Ligatan was there to ensure it happened.

Ergo, Ligea had to live. And if that meant Arrant had to die, then die he would, if Gevenan had any say in the matter.

In theory, it was all clear cut. The sort of difficult decision a general was supposed to be able to make without giving too much thought to the tragedy it would cause. But Gevenan had lost children of his own to the separation caused by the realities of war and invasion and slavery. Besides, he *knew* Arrant. Deep down in a place generals weren't supposed to consult when making decisions, Gevenan loved the boy – and, if he were truthful, his affection for Ligea ran just as deep.

He had to make a terrible decision in a hurry, and he suspected that whatever the outcome, he was going to have trouble living with it.

For the first time in years, Gevenan of Inge felt sick at heart.

They removed Arrant from the pothouse through the back door. They stuffed the dirty cloth back in his mouth, rolled him inside a carpet and carried him through the streets. If anyone saw them, well, it was only a couple of men hefting a floor rug, a common enough sight.

Inside the roll, Arrant fought to breathe. The more he tried to drag in air, the worse the cloth in his mouth felt. And in his panic, he did what shame had prevented him from doing earlier: he screamed for his brother.

Tarran. Tarran—!

Tarran heard his panic and came.

Mirageless hells, Arrant, why in the name of the Magor are you so uncomfortable? Where are you? What's that smell? What have you got in your mouth? What the ravaged hells is happening? Why is it so dark and stuffy?

Tarran. Arrant choked on his name. He couldn't speak, not even inside his head. He opened up his memory to Tarran instead, and let him know everything that had happened, right from the first day he'd met Thracius. Favonius. He felt Tarran reel under the knowledge.

Mirageless soul, Arrant, what are we going to do? Not a word of blame. Just a wash of love and concern and the idea that they were in this together.

Arrant had never loved his brother more. He had never liked himself less. *I don't know,* he said. He had to have air. The smell and taste of pothouse slops and carpet dust blocked his throat. His head was pounding, and there were strange flashes in front of his eyes. *Help me . . .*

Shivering sands, Arrant, you are suffocating. Keep calm. Slow down. You're a Magoroth. You can slow your breathing down to almost nothing, remember?

Only if I have power . . .

Call on it.

Tarran, you know what happened last time I deliberately used my power. I killed everyone who happened to be standing within twenty paces of me. No, more than that. I disintegrated *them.* His stomach churned at the memory although in reality the very last time he'd reached for his power, back in the pothouse, he had achieved exactly nothing. Nothing at all.

That was four years ago, Tarran replied. *You're older now. And you don't have any choice. Try.*

I already have, he admitted, struggling for breath. His head continued to pound. *Just before you came. There was nothing there. Just . . . emptiness.*

Try again.

Tentatively, he reached out to touch the power. This time he felt it stir. Then, suddenly, a spate of sensation and emotions from those around him. Anger, fatigue, frustration, glee . . .

Calm it down! Tarran said. *You're getting too much. Too wide an area. Concentrate on yourself. On your breathing. Slow it down!*

He was choking. Drowning in dust and foul air.

Carefully he reduced the power and extent of his reach. He sensed the men who carried him. He could feel Rathrox close by; the man's emotions seeped into the air the way a foul-smelling midden stank out its surroundings. His gloating triumph drifted outwards in swirls of darkness. And Arrant knew just from the feel of him that he didn't intend Ligea's death to be an easy or a swift one. His intended revenge was a hideous monster, groping through his mind like the Ravage in the Mirage. Torture, degradation, abasement, despair, suffering: he intended it all. Had planned it to the smallest detail. He also wanted her to know what was done to him, Arrant; wanted her to see it.

Culpability washed through Arrant, paralysing thought. He choked.

Stop that, Tarran said. He sounded like one of Arrant's tutors in a moment of exasperation. *Miragedamn, you humans waste so much time on your emotions! Come on, Arrant. You've got to get your breathing right.*

He concentrated. Slowed everything down: his mind, his body, his breathing. Slow, shallow breaths. His surroundings slipped away into a fog, together with his discomfort. Nothing mattered except each breath. Breathe. Slowly. Wait. Exhale. Slowly. The world seemed to stop. Only his breathing continued, so very, very slowly.

And then he was dumped on the ground. Hard. The jolt restarted everything. *Tarran?*

I'm here. I'm not leaving. Not this time.

Tarran, if I call up destructive power, will I burn a hole through my other hand?

Tarran was silent while he shuffled through his Mirage Maker memories to find the answer in things that had happened before either of them was born. *A cabochon can't hurt its owner,* he said at last, *any more than their sword can. But . .* He hesitated. *But the power has to find a way not to enter your body. It will slip out any way it can, and that means it could burn your clothing. And that could set fire to your body. Just normal burns.*

Normal burns. Arrant snorted at the thought of burns being 'normal'. *I'll have to do it anyway, I guess,* he said bleakly. *If I can.* He felt himself fading as he tried to drag in breath. The gag was choking him, rasping the back of his throat. He tried to concentrate, but his head ached badly. His mouth was dry. Every breath was laboured. He closed his eyes but still his vision danced with sharp-edged shards of colour.

He felt the men pick him up once more, and then they were moving again.

Oh, Tarran, what a Vortexdamned mess I've made of things.

Tarran said, *Favonius was once an honourable man and he loved your mother. Perhaps there's some hope in that.*

You saw what they did in Prianus. He tortured the children, Tarran. We saw the bodies.

We'll think of something. Is that your sword that's digging into your hip?

No, just my dagger. They never even bothered to take it from me. He wanted to weep. *That's how frightened they are of me . . . !*

Let them misjudge you. Calm down, Tarran said. *But you have to make a decision. Do we try now or later?*

It was hard to think rationally. To keep his mind clear. He could feel himself drifting away into the fog. *I think I'll wait until we've reached wherever we're going. Otherwise – otherwise we might never find out where they are bringing Ligea. She'll already be on her way. If I'm free but she doesn't know it, she'll still be in their power.* That was logical, wasn't it? He was no longer sure. It took such effort to think.

Yeah. I think that's best too. Arrant—

He struggled for breath. *Can't breathe . . .* Panic closed in with the darkness.

Arrant!

But he was gone.

He was vaguely aware of the moment he was unrolled from the carpet. The cloth was at last pulled out of his mouth. He tried to drag in air, but wasn't sure he had. Someone lifted him. Carried him. Dumped him. Somewhere, a long way off, he heard an alarmed voice expressing concern that he was dead. He wanted to contradict that, but couldn't wake up enough to speak. His head rolled drunkenly. He felt weird, as though someone else was doing his breathing for him.

Yeah, me, Tarran told him. *Are you all right?*

Don't know. Feel weak. Can't feel the power any more. He started to panic again. *I've lost it!*

You won't find it while you're still weak. Rest. Concentrate on your breathing.

He tried to obey. A voice said, 'I think he'll be all right. He was choking on the gag. He just blacked out, that's all.' Water trickled into his throat and he swallowed.

He lay, blessedly undisturbed. *Breathe. Just breathe.*

When he finally opened his eyes, he found himself in a squalid room, dim with daylight filtering in through mean slits high on the wall. The floor was rough stone, the furniture basic and battered. There was weaponry everywhere: spears, javelins, shields, bows. And two guards, men who had been in the pothouse.

He was lying on a divan. He tried to sit up, but didn't seem able to move.

'Stay where you are, boy,' Rathrox Ligatan drawled. He sat close by, playing with his dagger. Arrant knew why: it was to use on him if there was the slightest hint that Ligea hadn't obeyed the instructions given to her by Favonius. But not to kill. It was to carve a piece out of him. Where, he wondered with sick horror, would Rathrox start?

So he stayed where he was, curled up on his side. His hands were still bound, palms together behind him. Everything ached. He looked up at Rathrox and hated.

Try your power, Tarran said.

Did. Too weak. Nothing there.

Arrant, we should be ready to do something before Ligea gets here!

Think I don't know that?

But he was so tired. Pain lanced through his head accompanied by pulsing jags of light. He couldn't *think*. He groped once more for power, but his weakness mocked his attempt.

He dragged in more air. Concentrated. Two men besides Rathrox, armed, standing against the wall. Fighting men; they had as many scars on their muscular bodies as chisel marks on a wood carving. Swords and knives tucked into their belts. Alert, professional. The cuirass embossed with a dog's face might be missing, but he would have bet anything that these men had once been Jackals.

Then Rathrox Ligatan. No sword, just the knife. He played with it. A Tyranian-made weapon, designed as a throwing blade, but it could be used just as effectively to slit a throat or stab a man. Rathrox handled it as though he was familiar with all its uses. Gevenan had taught Arrant to see things like that: 'Watch how a man holds his weapons, Arrant. If he fondles it like a man fondles his lover, then he loves using it. And knows how to make it respond to him. Such men lack conscience.'

He thought about his cabochon. If it failed him in a splutter of colour and sparks, it would alert his captors that he could possibly be dangerous. That he was worthy of being more closely watched. And if he called up too much power and it escaped his control, he could bring the whole building down on top of them all. Which was fine as long as Ligea and Brand weren't there . . .

Safer to use it before Ligea came, then he wouldn't have to worry about hurting her. Tentatively, he tried to sense Rathrox's emotions.

The ex-Magister Officii was enjoying himself, savouring the taste of sweet victory and revenge. That, Arrant could tell without feeling a thing; it was obvious from the smile playing on that lean grey face of his. Now he even leaned forward from his seat to lay the coldness of his blade against Arrant's cheek. 'You and I are going to be seeing a lot of each other in the future, boy. You will dance to my music for the rest of my life. Even the women you take to your bed will be of my choosing . . .' He pressed the blade down with his thumb, opening up a thin bloodied line across the skin.

Arrant flinched. It was hard to hide his fear. Rathrox saw it, of course, and laughed.

Beetle-faced bastard, Tarran muttered with uncharacteristic savagery. *Make sure you turn his smile inside out afterwards, Arrant. He reminds me of the Ravage.*

There was a knock at the door and one of the men went to open it. A new voice said, 'All's well, Magister. Legate Favonius gave me the nod. She's done everything exactly as yer wanted. We watched and nobody left the palace after they did. Nobody at all, not even a servant. They'll be at the other house in a minute or two.'

'Excellent. Now go back outside, Telios. Check that the chariot and her mounted guard really do go away, then come and tell me.'

'Yes, Magister.'

Rathrox turned to Arrant with his feral grin that stretched the skin over the bones of his face. 'Favonius is bringing them to an empty house. They enter, walk up to the roof, traverse the length of the street and then enter here from above. So if anyone has followed her, they won't be able to find us. Your mother is doomed, lad. How does it feel to know you will soon be the new Exaltarch?'

'I won't do what you say,' he whispered. It was all he could manage.

'Boy, that's irrelevant. You will just be on display, nothing more. A pretty, pampered youth with as many toys as you like.'

Relax. You're too tense, Tarran told him.

Of course I'm tense! Tarran, what the sweet hells can I do?

Rathrox ran a finger along his blade. The gesture reminded Arrant of a mantis rubbing its forelegs as it waited for its prey. There was something very insect-like about him: the greyish tinge to his thin body, his watchfulness, his lack of anything that resembled human compassion as he watched Arrant with slitted eyes. He knew how much he repelled and his smile broadened.

Never mind, Arrant. Bugs can be squashed, Tarran remarked sourly. *You've got to relax. You need strength to use the cabochon.*

Arrant swore at his brother. Panic wove through the fabric of every thought. The more he reached for his power and failed, the tighter the weave became, crushing his ability to think. He was running out of time.

Narjemah followed Gevenan out of the handmaiden's room and ran after him down the passage. 'Gev – what are you going to do?' she asked.

He turned, annoyed, knowing he had little time, but something in her face, begging him for answers, had the power to start him thinking instead of panicking. He had to leave the palace before Ligea did, and his departure had to look innocuous. 'You can help, Narj. Find me a whore. A servant girl who'll hop into bed with anyone and pretend she likes it for just a few coppers.'

She didn't feign ignorance of what he meant, or protest that the palace didn't employ servants with loose morals, or ask him why he wanted a girl like that. 'Anrianna,' she said immediately. 'She'll be cleaning along here somewhere.'

Within moments she was back with a sultry-eyed girl from the Issian islands, who looked up at him from under her lashes – a come-hither look he guessed she had spent hours practising. He grabbed her by the arm and pulled her towards the guards' entrance gate. At the same time, he fished in his pouch for a coin. He gave her the first one he found – a silver. 'Anri-what-ever-your-name-is, I want you to hang onto my arm for the next ten minutes as if the Goddess of Love has answered your every prayer. After that, you can have the whole day off. Can you do that?'

She grinned up at him, already clutching his arm and simpering. 'Oh, General, that's going to be the easiest silver I've ever earned.'

Gevenan gritted his teeth, and hurried her to the exit. As they stepped outside, he slowed down to a stroll, chatting calmly, a smirk on his face, even though every nerve in his body was screaming at him to run, to hurry, to *do* something. *Oh, gods, Arrant, why did you do this?*

'Stay here in the barracks for at least half an hour,' he said as they entered the gate, saluted by a legionnaire who only just managed not to snigger. 'Then you can do whatever you like.'

She beamed. 'Thank you, General. Y'want anything more any time, you have only to ask this girl!'

But he had already turned away, forgetting her existence. He strode straight to the office of Legate Valorian, the one man he could be sure knew how to think on his feet. He burst into the room without waiting to be announced. Valorian was seated behind his desk, speaking to his second-in-command, Tribune Descalis.

Good. That was a stroke of luck. 'Val,' he said, 'I need you. Now. And two of your best soldiers. As soon as possible, at this address, armed but not in uniform, on foot and unobtrusive.' He slammed Arrant's note down on the Legate's desk. Valorian didn't so much as blink. 'That's the first thing. The second thing is this. The Exaltarch is about to walk – knowingly – into a trap. I need a mounted force, horses, ready to move at a moment's notice. The Exaltarch, with her personal escort and her chariot, are going to leave the palace any time now. She doesn't want to be followed.'

He looked at Descalis. 'Tribune, I want her followed nonetheless. Use your best man, just one. He's got to do it so unobtrusively that no one will ever know, especially not the people who are watching the palace gates and possibly the barracks as well, to see who leaves. He's to find out where the Exaltarch goes and then double back here. You then get a couple of hundred men to that place on horseback as fast as you can. Surround the building and let no one in or out. I'm hoping that by the time you get there, Valorian and I will have already rescued the Exaltarch and her son. If not, it's up to you. Don't wait for us. In the meantime, I want every legionnaire in Tyr to be put on the alert – *without* it being obvious. Remember, *we are being watched*. Is all that clear?'

'Perfectly lucid, General.' Valorian turned to Descalis and added calmly, 'Get me three non-military tunics and tell the Mendorian twins and that guide from Turion, the one with the beard and the limp – I forget his name – that I want them here on the double. And not a word to anyone about what you just heard.' He turned back to Gevenan. 'I'll be there.'

But Gevenan was already on his way out.

Fortunately, Gevenan knew the pothouse named in Arrant's note from his days as a slave in Tyr, so he didn't have to waste time searching for it. As he expected, it was empty of people when he arrived; even the pothouse-keeper was missing. There was blood on the floor. A lot of it.

It took him five minutes and a copious supply of coppers doled out to street urchins before he discovered that two or three men lugging a rolled-up carpet had earlier exited from the back door. If there was one thing Gevenan was certain about, it was that a pothouse in the Snarls would *never* have had a carpet on its floor. His hopes shrivelled. Had they already killed Arrant and this was the way they had removed his body? 'What way did the men with the carpet go?' he asked one of his small informants.

The boy, sensing the urgency of Gevenan's need, held out his hand again. Gevenan sighed and gave him another copper, instead of the clout about the ear that he felt like dispensing. The boy pointed to a laneway snaking deeper into the Snarls.

'General?'

Gevenan turned to see Valorian arriving with a set of identical

444   GLENDA LARKE

twins in tow, all of them bristling with weapons. Gevenan groaned.
'Ocrastes' balls, you look like a bloody walking arsenal! Didn't I
ask you to be inconspicuous?'

Valorian gave a sweet smile. 'Unobtrusive was the word, I
believe. And I am not sure I would know how to be either. For
whom are we looking?'

'At the moment, it's not who, it's what. A rolled-up piece of
carpet. I hope you have a stack of coppers in your pouch, Val,
because this is going to take a small fortune paid out to every
scummy-looking urchin you see.'

CHAPTER FORTY

Rathrox rested his knife against Arrant's throat. Occasionally his hand wavered and the edge of the blade pricked the skin. Arrant tried not to move. Time edged by, an agony of waiting. Telios returned briefly to reassure Rathrox that Ligea's guard had gone away. He was sent back out to watch the street.

When Arrant finally heard Ligea coming down the steps from above, he took advantage of Rathrox's distraction to twist around and look. She had her left arm bound with cloth flat against her chest, the cabochon over her heart. Favonius walked beside her, his sword pressed to her side. Two men, ex-legionnaires, walked behind them, each with a blade in their hand.

They were followed by Brand, guarded by another two armed men. Their expressions were hard enough to have been hacked from a rock face. More Jackals, Arrant guessed. Both had their swords out; the tip of one rested against Brand's back.

'Try to free that hand and I swear I'll sever it, my sweet,' Favonius said to Ligea as they reached the bottom of the steps.

Damn them to the Ravage, Tarran said. *The Magor die if they're separated from their cabochons. It's a horrible, lingering death. Takes days. He must know that.*

Arrant felt sick. He couldn't imagine a world that didn't contain his mother.

Ligea ignored Favonius' words as though he hadn't spoken them, and he flushed as if she'd slapped his face. She looked around the room, assessing the situation, even before she allowed her glance to rest on Arrant. She sent out a wave of love when she saw he was untouched.

I felt that! Tarran cried.

So did I, Arrant said. Relief suffused him. Not only was his cabochon beginning to work, albeit a little later than he would have liked, but he was feeling better. The intense throbbing of his headache and the moving zigzags in his vision were ebbing away.

The room was crowded now. *Eight of them if you count Favonius and Rathrox. And only three of us,* Arrant thought.

I wonder if she knows she won't kill herself with her own cabochon? Tarran asked.

She will use it anyway, whether she knows or not, he answered with conviction. *She's just waiting for the right moment.*

She was tightly controlled, her face expressionless. If she despised him for what he had done, she never showed it. He wanted to tell her all that he could by way of his own emotions, but didn't know how.

Try, Tarran said. *Your power is growing every minute. Tell her you have it!*

How? It was a cry of despair. He didn't know how to show his feelings. The ball inside him was huge, grown larger with guilt, everything confined within, compressed, twisted tight. How could he ever rip the fabric of something so hard and galled?

Love her enough to tell her, Tarran said. *That's all.*

Arrant stared at her, and something of his guilt and despair and self-loathing fell away. *Love her enough . . .*

'So,' Rathrox said to her, 'we meet again.' He tapped the handle of his dagger with the forefinger of the hand that held it. The tip jabbed deep enough to open up a trickle of blood down Arrant's neck. 'Be careful what you do, because the first person to die will be Arrant here.'

She stared at the ex-Magister, expressionless. 'You would be the second.'

'Ah, but I would get such pleasure from knowing I had stolen your son from you first, Ligea.'

She inclined her head and, incredibly, the corners of her lips curled up in a half-smile. And somehow, with that faint twitch of the lips, she managed to mock him. 'Rathrox,' she said, 'd'you know, I think I would prefer that you use my title when speaking to me?' Her voice was silky, yet full of menace.

'Ah, no,' he said. 'I'd rather choke than name you Exaltarch.'

'Oh,' she returned, her tone bland, 'I didn't mean Exaltarch. I meant Miragerin. Miragerin-sarana.'

Love her enough? At that moment, Arrant thought her magnificent. He wept inside, and the love he felt for her was more than forgiving; it was accepting. His own fault was so huge; how could he find fault with others? He not only didn't care that she had sought something in Brand's arms, he was glad she had found it. Something inside him tore. He felt emotion flow away from him, a river of it escaping. The relief was enormous.

Rathrox was startled by her words. An eyebrow shot up. 'So, you actually found out who you are – amazing.'

'That's right. Bear in mind that you face not only the Exaltarch, but the Miragerin of Kardiastan.'

He shrugged. 'What difference does it make? We have the means to keep you docile.' He indicated Arrant by prodding him contemptuously with his free hand. His eyes never left Ligea's. 'As you can see, your ill-gotten bastard brat is alive and well. And he will stay that way, as I have promised – but always under my heel.' He smiled. 'Ah, Ligea, you'll die piece by piece, knowing what we are going to do with your son. Can you have any idea of how much you are going to suffer?'

But she was looking at Arrant, giving the faintest of nods, acknowledging that she had felt all he had tried to tell her. She knew he had access to his powers. He moved his hands slightly to show her the way they were bound palm to palm. Her lips tightened.

Arrant felt Rathrox pour out a stream of triumph and loathing like a deluge of floodwater filled with debris. 'Do it now,' the ex-Magister said, nodding to Favonius.

It was a moment before Brand or Arrant or Ligea understood,

a precious sliver of time lost to their incomprehension. Both Arrant and Ligea felt the nastiness of Favonius' emotions before either realised his exact intention: to sever her hand. Everything happened at once then, a whirl of movement that lasted less than a minute, yet which seemed to stretch forever.

Tarran shouted in Arrant's mind, *You can do it!* But even as Arrant called up all the power he had, two Jackals grabbed Ligea by the arms. Favonius cut through the cloth that held her hand flat to her body, and twisted her arm so that her palm faced the floor. Still holding her by the wrist, he swung his sword, aiming at the fold of her elbow.

A great flash of colour swept out of Arrant's cabochon. The ties that bound his hands burst into flames and his arms flew apart. Rathrox jabbed at him with his blade. It never connected. The power slammed into the ex-Magister and hurled him across the room to hit the stone of the opposite wall. Arrant screamed in pain as his clothing caught fire. Flames licked his hair, his face. Yet his horror at being burned could not obliterate the sight of what was happening to Ligea.

Held tight by the two Jackals, with Favonius holding her left wrist in a grasp of iron as he swung his sword, she must have known that to struggle was futile. She did the only two things that could possibly save her: she let her power free – and she lifted her feet off the ground. A swathe of her gold power blasted the stone slabs of the floor. Stone chips exploded under their feet, unsettling their footing. The sudden weight of her body unbalanced those who held her, but still Favonius' sword stroke connected. They all crashed to the floor. Blood sprayed them as they fell.

Simultaneously, Brand turned on one of the Jackals who held him, punching him in the stomach with a balled-up fist. He head-butted the other, and took a sword cut on his thigh in return. He grabbed the first man's sword right out of his hand while he was still gasping – and killed him with it. The second Jackal, nose broken, blood pouring down his face, stumbled back into a defensive position, preventing Brand from helping Ligea.

One of the Jackals near Arrant whipped off his cloak and wrapped Arrant in it. He lost sight of the fight. He felt the man beating his hands on the cloth to put out the flames. He rolled across the divan, away from him. Tarran screamed advice into his head. He thumped onto the floor and flung off the cloak. He rose on one elbow and killed his rescuer with a shaft from his cabochon. He misjudged the force necessary, and the beam went right through the Jackal's torso to blast a hollow in the wall behind.

Arrant looked around. Brand had killed the second man he had been fighting, but another had taken his place. The Altani was limping badly from his wound and he was losing the duel. Rathrox, apparently dazed and uncomprehending, was on the floor next to the wall, his dagger lying beside him. Even as Arrant glanced at him, the ex-Magister's conscious mind blanked out and he slumped back.

Ligea's blast of power had killed the two Jackals who had been holding her, but Favonius' sword stroke had caught her across the forearm, opening a gaping slash from elbow to thumb, baring the bone. She was clutching the cut, but blood splashed onto the floor. She faced Favonius, with her cabochon shedding a glow onto his chest. He still had his sword in his hand. He said her name and smiled. He didn't believe she would kill him. And the light in her cabochon flickered and died. She staggered back, gripping her arm, as blood and power drained away together.

Strength, Tarran said. *She's losing strength with the blood.*

Arrant tried to stand to go to her, forgot his feet were still tied, and crashed to the floor. He stared down at himself. His hands shook. His tattered clothes smoked. He smelled burned hair. Everything hurt. He had red rings burned around his hands. And he had no time to think about any of it. He grabbed his dagger and cut the twine that tied his ankles.

Favonius' triumph was potent in the air. Arrant read his intention in his emotions: he was going to kill her – and enjoy it. Without thinking, Arrant held up his hand, palm outwards. For once, his cabochon did everything he asked of it. A short burst of gold bathed Favonius in pain. His sword fell to the floor.

'Tell that man to drop his sword and stand against the wall,' Arrant said, and his voice sounded harsh and adult to his ears. When Favonius hesitated, he increased the pain. From between clenched teeth, Favonius gave the order, and the man who had been fighting Brand obeyed. Arrant widened the breadth of the gold light to include him. It was quicker than building a ward and right then he didn't care how they felt.

Brand limped towards Ligea. 'Ocrastes' balls – Ligea!' he said. '*Your arm—!*'

Oh shit, Tarran said. *She'll bleed to death if she doesn't stop that—*

'Help me carry her to the divan,' Brand said, and then added to Ligea, 'hold your arm up, above your head.'

'Arrant can get the bleeding under control,' she said as they laid her down. 'Will you stop *fussing*? I'm not going to die.'

Arrant held her arm and poured in his healing power, subduing her pain almost as an afterthought. 'What about your power—?' he asked.

'It'll come back. I'm just weak from loss of blood right now, that's all.'

That was exciting, Tarran said. He was bouncing around in Arrant's mind like an excited puppy.

Shut up. Let me concentrate. He was having trouble believing everything was going to be all right. He'd been such a fool, and yet they were all safe. Somewhere in his head was the thought that his stupidity didn't deserve this ending.

'Brand, you're hurt,' Ligea said. 'Your leg—!' She struggled up into a sitting position.

Brand cradled her against him. 'I'll attend to it in a moment. It's not serious.' He ripped a piece off his own tunic to bind her wound, but Arrant had already stopped the blood flow and pulled the ends of the broken blood vessels together so they could mend. He wondered how the magic of his cabochon knew how to do that when he himself didn't.

That's me, you dolt, Tarran said. *The Mirage Makers know all sorts of things.*

That interested Arrant, but he couldn't consider it then. His focus was all on Ligea – until Rathrox's burst of triumph broke inside his head.

By that time, it was already too late.

The dagger had spun out of the ex-Magister's hand, aimed at Ligea. And she was too weak in power to sense it, too weak in body to dodge it. But Brand, who had no powers at all, saw.

He had just tied off the ends of the makeshift bandage on her arm. He flung himself in front of her, even as he pushed her down. The ward Arrant erected was just a second too late.

Brand took the blade meant for her in the side of his neck. His life began to ebb even as he toppled; in horrified silence, Arrant felt it fade.

The world fell apart.

Ligea knelt by Brand on the floor. Her grief and outrage sent Arrant reeling. 'Ward Rathrox!' she snapped, and he obeyed without thinking, trapping the man where he stood, propped up against the wall.

Ligea gathered Brand into her arms with infinite gentleness. 'Heal him,' she gasped at Arrant. 'For pity's sake, heal him. *I have no power left.*' She eased the dagger out.

Arrant grabbed Brand's hand, but Tarran's Mirage Makers' knowledge told him there would be no healing this time. The blade had severed too much. The spinal cord was cut. He was choking on blood. The rise and fall of his lungs was stilled.

Arrant let Brand's hand fall and stood, his arms loose by his sides. His mind refused to absorb the truth. Repeated words in his head spun in senseless circles: *he can't die, he can't die, he can't . . .*

Oh, Mirageless soul, Tarran murmured. *Oh, Arrant, I'm sorry.*

'It's all right, love,' Ligea was saying, stroking Brand's brow, uttering the lie as if that would make it truth. 'We're safe, all of us. It's over.'

Incredibly, Brand spoke. How he managed it, Arrant never

knew, but the words were real, not just a movement of his lips, as his dying gaze fixed on Ligea's. His lips quirked up. 'I can think of worse reasons to die,' he said. He sounded amused. His love spilled from him, and his life followed.

Arrant felt the abrupt absence of his living, the blank space where once there had been a man. He himself dragged in a shuddering breath, knowing that the death was his fault, knowing that he had destroyed what little happiness his mother had in her life.

'No,' she said. 'Oh no.' She raised her eyes to her son's, her gaze barren of hope. 'How will I ever live without him?' The words held the stark simplicity of truth.

His remorse was bile in his throat, bitter and self-accusing. She touched his hand, and he felt her compassion for his own anguish. In the midst of all her pain she could still tell him not to condemn himself.

He didn't answer that touch. He couldn't.

My fault. My betrayal. I listened to Thracius because I was jealous. I should have warded Rathrox.

Arrant—

Shut up, Tarran. I know what I did.

She said, her voice little more than a whisper, 'He was my closest friend. We were children together.' She stood and walked over to Rathrox where he slumped, pressed against the wall by the ward. 'Release him,' she said to Arrant.

He opened up the ward, and the ex-Magister sprawled to the floor. She stood over the remains of that once-powerful man, her rage blistering. Rathrox's fear crept around the room like a ground mist.

Arrant thrust the thought of Brand from him. He mustn't think of Brand. Mustn't look at him. He couldn't cope with that. *What have I done?*

She said, 'I want you to understand exactly what I'm going to do, Rathrox. First, I'm going to kill you with my Magor power. With this.' She supported her wounded arm with her good one, and showed him the cabochon in her bloodied hand. She had managed to call up a faint light into it, which she focused on his face. He tried to flinch away, but couldn't. Still she didn't kill him, not then.

She went on, 'And then I'm going to continue what I've been trying to do in Tyrans. First, I'm going to consolidate my power by hunting down every one of your compeers and your Jackals until there's not one left. Then I'm going to build up the strength of the Senate still more and make them answerable to the citizens of Tyrans. The arbiters are already recodifying the Law on my orders, and I intend to make every citizen answerable to that Law. And the people who enforce the Law will answer to the Hall of Justice and the Senate. There will never be another Brotherhood, Rathrox. There will never be another Magister. And finally I'm going to limit the power of the Exaltarch. I'm going to make sure that there is never another Bator Korbus. And then I shall go home to Kardiastan, to live out the rest of my life in the land you stole from me.

'And I'll succeed in all that. I'll succeed because I have this.' She indicated her cabochon once more. 'Are you ready to die, Rathrox?'

She increased the pressure of her remnant power and he grovelled at her feet. Grovelled, like a frightened child. Spittle dribbled from his mouth. One hand clutched at her sandal in submission, his fingers clawed.

'This is for my mother, Rathrox. For the Magoria called Wendia, who died in an ambush.' She jabbed him with power. 'And this is for my father, for Solad, whom you twisted into a traitor. And this is for Brand, who was a far better man than you could ever be. And this is for me, because of what you did to me and what you wanted to do to my son.' Each time she mentioned a name, she increased the pressure inside the light.

'No—' He held up a hand, as if he could stop her. His fear stank like damp rot. 'Please, Exalted One—'

Her face twisted in disgust. The flare from her cabochon was short and sure. His face melted and he was dead.

She began to fall, overwhelmed by her weakness, but Arrant

was warned by his senses and caught her. He lowered her to the floor, cradling her head on his lap, while he channelled more power to her healing.

She'll be all right, Tarran assured him. *She just needs time and rest. And food. She must eat. You should too.*

She was limp in his arms, yet it was an effort to touch her. His guilt was a physical thing inside him, a creature with a mind of its own. It crippled his thoughts, sickened his stomach. He glimpsed Brand's body on the floor out of the corner of his eye, and felt that creature inside cut him off from future, past and present. He was Arrant, despicable in what he had done. Alone. Always to be alone because of what he had done.

I'm here, Tarran protested. *I'll always be here.*

'But you can't make things better. It will never be better,' Arrant murmured. 'You can't bring somebody back.'

Still his power stayed with him, strong and sure and true, doing all he asked of it. When he was sure Ligea would be all right, he rose to his feet and looked around. Almost to his surprise, Favonius and the other Jackal were still there, immobilised with pain. He drew back the power into his cabochon and released them. The Jackal staggered back, his face reflecting his terror. When Arrant did nothing, he turned and stumbled to the door. Arrant let him go.

Favonius didn't move. He knew it was useless to try. The expression on Arrant's face told him he had reached the end of his road.

Arrant knew exactly what he was doing. Thracius had fooled him, but that wasn't why Favonius was going to die. He said, 'You shouldn't have called him thrall.'

Favonius whispered, shocked, 'You'd kill me for *that*?'

'Yes. But more for a village called Prianus.' He felt as if he were a hundred years old. 'It's a matter of what is deserved. But I don't expect you to understand why.' He raised his left hand.

'No,' the man protested, his revulsion spilling from him. He drew himself up, shrugging away the last of his pain, controlling his fear. 'I'm a soldier, damn it! I was once one of the

Exaltarch's Stalwarts. I don't want to die of – of desert-numen magic. Use my sword, so I can die on a good Tyranian blade, as a legionnaire should.'

Arrant paused.

'I could have been your father,' Favonius said. 'Arrant, you could have been my son. Don't kill me that way. Please.'

Tarran tensed inside his head, but said nothing.

Arrant said, 'You – or your men – carved the heart out of a child, and left it on the doorstep of his house. Would you rather I killed you like that?'

Favonius's voice was hoarse and wretched. 'Better that, than to die by sorcery.'

Arrant was tempted to cruelty: to bring the power back into his cabochon and see the terror in the ex-legionnaire's eyes – but he couldn't do it. He shrugged. 'As you wish.' His brother's approval shimmered across his mind.

He picked up Favonius's sword from the floor, weighed it in his hand. His gaze met Favonius'. And suddenly it wasn't easy any more. To plunge a blade into a man's chest and know he was going to die in pain.

He hesitated.

'You know what?' Favonius drawled, smiling. 'I am *so* glad I killed that Altani thrall. It will pain your numen bitch of a mother for the rest of her life—'

Arrant drove the sword in as hard as his arm could force it. Favonius Kyranon fell at his feet, but it took a while for him to die. Arrant watched, and hated it. And wondered at the fleeting look of amusement he'd caught on the man's face as he fell.

I'll never be a soldier, he said, sharing the thought with Tarran. *And he should have been happy with the cabochon. I could have killed him instantly then, without pain.*

He forced himself to look one more time at Brand. He'd killed the Altani, too, as surely as if he'd been the one to throw the knife into his neck.

I didn't deserve to know him, he told Tarran.

CHAPTER FORTY-ONE

Standing at the door, Arrant looked down at his charred and blood-spattered clothing. When he rubbed a hand over his head, pieces of burned hair crumbled under his fingers. Exposed skin was raw and weeping. He hadn't thought about it, but his magic had already set the normal processes of healing underway, and lessened his pain.

Why didn't my power work as well as this earlier? None of this need have happened!

He looked across at Ligea. He had to get help for her, and quickly. Her wound needed stitching. But it was possible Rathrox and Favonius had a lot more ex-legionnaires or compeers at their command and they could be arriving any minute, called by the man who had just left.

Careful when you go outside, Tarran warned.

He took a cloak from the hook near the door, flung it over his blackened clothing and let himself out into the street. He blinked, surprised to find himself under a midday sun. Somehow, he had thought more time had passed than that. Time enough to sunder his world.

Brand is dead. An hour ago, he was walking these streets, just like anyone else. It didn't seem *right* that it should still be the same day, that the sun should be shining, that other people should be laughing as they passed by.

Gevenan's here! The thought popped into his head without him even being aware that his positioning power was working.

He turned, and saw the Ingean general striding towards him, his worry dominating the air like a coming storm. Further away, a contingent of guards blocked the roadway. They were led by Legate Valorian, his curls looking unusually tousled, his charm in abeyance. Telios and the Jackal who had rushed out of the house in such a hurry were now sullen-faced and stationary in the grip of several of the guards. Valorian had a tight grip on Telios' ear and, by the look on the man's face, his hold was painful.

Arrant felt a rush of gratitude as Gevenan came up; the General would know what to do. And then gratitude slid into burning shame.

'Arrant? Gods, lad, are you all right? Where's your mother and Brand? Were we in the wrong house?'

Arrant pointed to the door behind him. 'In there,' he said. *Brand is dead. If I had done things differently, he'd be alive.* He wanted to say the words aloud, but nothing came out. He wanted to say he was sorry, but how could you say sorry to the dead?

Gevenan gestured to Valorian to bring up his soldiers, then turned back. 'What happened to you? You look awful! You look as though someone decided that barbequed Magor meat should be on the dinner menu.'

'I'm fine,' he said, astonished to hear how firm and normal his voice sounded. Brand was dead, and he'd caused it. There should be *something* different.

'Are there any more Jackals in there?'

'Not that I know of. You'd better check the roof, though. That's the way they came in.' So in command of himself. He could have been a soldier, reporting to his commander. A lie, all of that. He was a stupid child. A traitor.

'Ah. That would explain why we couldn't find you. We were beginning a house-to-house search. You'd best go and wait with those soldiers down there, the ones guarding those fellows, while we check the place out.'

Arrant nodded, but once Gevenan and his men had entered the house, he walked away in the opposite direction, into the serpentine twists of the Snarls.

Are you all right? Same question, but from Tarran this time.

I don't think I'll ever be all right again. He was shaking inside and his fingers trembled, even when he kept his fists closed tight. Splinters of memory danced through his mind. Brand's sightless eyes staring at nothing. His mother, risking everything for him. The way the blade had slipped into human flesh and the light had gone out of Favonius' eyes because he, Arrant, had decreed it so.

Arrant? Where are you going?

Tarran's puzzled touch in his mind was tentative. Guilt was not an emotion that bothered the Mirage Makers too much.

He replied, *Just . . . walking. I'm all right. And I think I want to be alone now.*

Arrant, you can't blame yourself—

He cut his brother short. *Ah, but I do, Tarran. I do. Please, I need to be alone. I can't face anyone who – anyone who knows. Not – not at the moment. Just go.* He was too ashamed.

Bewildered, hurt, Tarran withdrew.

Arrant walked on at a steady pace, without any real aim, looking neither right nor left. He kept himself wrapped in the cloak; he avoided meeting the glances of those in the street; he wanted so desperately not to face anyone. How could he ever look his mother in the eye again?

Mater, I'm sorry. I was jealous. I couldn't let you be happy. And now I've taken it all away.

If it had been possible, he would have torn all that had happened that day from his mind and cast it from him. He didn't want to face it. It wasn't *bearable.*

Brand was dead. He'd been everything Ligea had said he was: an honourable, decent man who had loved her. Loved her enough to die for her, die gladly. Even past his last breath, he'd found the strength to tell her how worthy he felt she was of that death – to make a joke of his devotion.

How can I live with what I have done? If he hadn't been so jealous, this never would have happened. If only he had warded Rathrox, Brand wouldn't have died.

* * *

An hour later, he stood on the narrow arch of a bridge that crossed over the River Tyr. The water below was swift and dark, skeining out from the city sewers towards the sea in writhing cords. A little further downstream the river broadened into the port waterways and was lined with wharves and warehouses; here, however, there were only narrow stone buildings, their backsides jutting over the black water, their midden shutes stuck out of the walls in an untidy stinking row.

I can't endure this.

Thoughts going round and round. The same thing, different angles, each glimpse as painful as the last. With his stupidity, he'd killed a man who hadn't deserved to die. *I can't live with this. I can't.*

He looked down at the water. He could jump and let it carry him out to sea until he was too tired to swim any more. There was no one around. It would be so easy ... He'd heard that drowning was not such a bad death. So easy to do. He could just drift along out to the ocean. Drift into death, and peace. The water slid past so fast, the tide must have been on the ebb; he'd be out to sea in no time. With nothing to worry him.

And Tarran will have nowhere to go. Nowhere safe from the Ravage. *And Ligea will grieve.* How could he add to the pain she would have to face when she woke?

He clutched at the stone balustrade of the bridge, wanting to weep, but had no tears. He must bear the unbearable, because he was needed, because he had a brother and a mother. He couldn't erase one error by committing another.

Tarran, oh Tarran, I was wrong – I do need you.

His brother came immediately, as if he'd been waiting, and enfolded Arrant in the embrace of his mind.

Arrant felt Tarran's flicker of horror when he realised what Arrant had been contemplating. Yet his brother didn't try to speak. There was no way he would ever understand why Arrant had been about to jump off the bridge, but he did know what was needed: unquestioning love. And he gave it willingly.

Arrant wasn't sure how long he stood there with Tarran in

his mind, but at last he said, *I'm all right now, Tarran. I'm not going to do anything silly, I promise you. I might be able to do it to myself, but I couldn't do it to you.*

He felt his brother's relief. *I'm glad. I couldn't do without you, not really, you log-headed lump of a human. There's too much of this piss-weak humanness in me still. I'd – I'd go mad with the Ravage pain if I couldn't come to you sometimes. Quite apart from that, I, um, I happen to like your company. Arrant, you're as odd as a shleth's hairy backside but . . . I like to have you around, you know.*

'Yeah. I know.'

It's – it's more than that even. Arrant, I need you. We – we may not have much longer. Come home.

He was appalled and tried not to show it. 'What – what do you mean?' He choked. How could he go on if Tarran was gone? 'Gods, Tarran, I will do anything to help!'

Just come home.

'You mean Kardiastan?'

Yes. Maybe – maybe, if you came, you could think of something . . . some way to help us. And then, with an apologetic farewell, he was gone again, pulled into the troubles of the rest of his being.

Arrant didn't move. Without Tarran, he felt cold. He didn't know where to go. How could he face his mother? Or Gevenan? Or Narjemah? *How can I face myself?*

So he just stayed there, looking down at the water. Going over and over what had happened, as if he could change anything just by wanting it so. Weaving back the gall in his middle into that tight, hard lump with its impenetrable skin. Reducing pain down to something that was manageable, that didn't stop his breathing in his throat . . .

And after a while he became aware that he was no longer alone.

Several people had crossed the bridge since he'd come here, but they hadn't given him more than a curious look and he'd hardly noticed their passing. This time someone stayed. He glanced up to see a man standing a few paces away, a pack hefted on his shoulder.

Shocked, Arrant stared, thoughts jostling. The man was Kardi. He was even dressed Kardi-style, with no concessions to Tyranian fashion. About thirty years old, or a little more, a strikingly handsome man, almost femininely beautiful. A finely featured face, and a lithe, athletic body, although he was short. *A head for a sculptor to model*, was Arrant's stray thought. And then: *Brand's dead, and I'm thinking about sculptures? What kind of person am I?*

The man spoke first, his words an echo to Arrant's thoughts. 'It's strange, isn't it,' he remarked, 'how the world goes on, even when you think yours has come to an end.' He held up his left hand and showed him the cabochon there.

He was Magor! No, more than that. *He was Magoroth.*

'Did you know,' he added quietly, 'that you've been searing my brains with your emotions for hours? A pretty dance you've led me, lad! And now when I do find you, you seem to be contemplating putting an end to all your troubles by jumping into the River Tyr.'

He came towards Arrant and looked over the balustrade at the blackness below. 'Quite frankly, I wouldn't advise it. That water's filthy. It's so thick with rubbish, you wouldn't sink and think of what a fool you'd look then.' He gave a crooked grin. 'Besides, you'd probably end up dying six months hence of some quite dreadful skin disease as a result of your dip, just when you'd decided life was worth living after all.'

Arrant tried to smile. 'I'd sort of decided not to anyway.'

The man nodded. 'Yes, I guessed you might have. You actually stopped totally scrambling my brains a little while back. Do you know what a mess you look? Your hair has been singed like a boar made ready for roasting. Your eyebrows are all frizzy. Your hands have been burned. They must hurt. In fact, you look as if you could do with some home comforts.'

Arrant shrugged indifferently. 'I'm fine.' *I deserve the pain . . .*

'Hmm.' He seemed unconvinced. 'I gather, from that, you don't want to go home.'

Arrant shook his head and shuddered. 'Not – not yet.'

'Ah. Well, I don't have a place to take you, because I only

arrived this morning, aboard a Kardi coastal trader. I *was* intending to go straight to the palace. Nothing like a bit of luxury after a couple of weeks crammed into a ship with a cargo of freshly tanned shleth pelts. Tell you what we'll do, Arrant; we'll take a room in an inn. No, that's not what they call them here, is it? Taberna, that's right – we'll take a room in a taberna. I noticed one back along the street towards the port. Then you can clean up a bit. I'll scrounge some clean clothes for you as well, if you don't mind wearing a Kardi outfit. I'm short and you're tall for your age – we may be able to fix something up.'

'I – I think that sounds like a good idea,' Arrant said, struggling with the bleakness in his head. With the desire to sit down and do nothing except be swamped with misery. 'How – how do you know who I am?'

'You have the look of your mother. Besides, there's not all that many thirteen-year-old Magoroth lads gadding about Tyr. One tends to have heard of the one there is.'

'You know my mother?'

'Once upon a time. In fact, when I was a youth not that much older than you are now, I was even a little in love with her, in a worshipful sort of way. And your father is a close friend.'

'He sent you to fetch me,' Arrant said flatly, guessing. He had wanted it so long; why now did he feel nothing?

'Yes. My name's Garis.'

Arrant's insides skidded sickly. 'Ligea's mentioned you.'

'I should hope so. We have shared much, Sarana and I, good and bad.' He put his hand lightly on Arrant's shoulder and guided him off the bridge. 'This way.'

They walked in silence. Garis didn't volunteer anything, and Arrant didn't ask anything. Half an hour later, he was sitting in a rented room, washed and dressed in clean clothes, staring list-lessly at the food Garis had ordered for them from the kitchens.

'Can't eat anything?' Garis asked.

He shook his head.

'I think we'd better talk. Maybe you could start with telling me why it is that, when I mentioned my name, you reacted as if

I'd pronounced a sentence of death on you? I'm not really such a bad sort of fellow, you know. I don't beat my servants, starve my shleths or even kick other people's brats. So what's wrong?'

Misery welled up in Arrant, black and threatening. 'You were a friend of Brand's,' he whispered.

'Yes, that's right. He's probably the best friend I've got.'

'He's dead. I killed him. And almost killed my mother too.'

Garis sat motionless for a moment, trying to contain his shock. All Arrant's sensing powers had dissipated, but he didn't need them anyway. He could see Garis' reaction. The man was biting his bottom lip, hard. His hands were coiled fists on his knees. 'But *she's* all right?' he asked.

Arrant nodded miserably. 'Wounded. And weak. But she was regaining strength when I left her.'

'I think you'd better tell me everything.'

Arrant hesitated. A wave of nausea had him fighting not to heave up the contents of his stomach.

'You need help,' Garis told him. 'If I know what happened, I will help, I promise you. No matter what you did.'

And so Arrant began the whole sorry story. He stumbled and repeated himself; jumped from one thing to another, then had to backtrack to make it all clear. He didn't mention Tarran, and although he said he was jealous of Brand, he avoided saying exactly why. Garis listened carefully, only occasionally asking a question to clarify something.

When he'd finished, Garis said quietly, 'That's a heavy burden to learn to live with, Arrant. You will have to have courage. And you're too hard on yourself, as well. You did something stupid, and you were prompted by ignoble motives, but there are very few people who haven't done something equally stupid and sordid at some time in their lives. Most are just lucky that nothing terrible comes of it.' He fiddled with the wineskin he had in his hand. 'Like you, I am also one of the unlucky ones. I was responsible for the death of my wife and my unborn child because I did something foolish. I have to live without her always, my first child has no mother, my second child was never born – and my wife has no life at all. You're not alone, although I don't suppose that is any comfort to you right now.' The pain of his remembering hung in the air between them.

'How – how do you bear it?' *How will I bear this?*

'You live one grain of sand through the hourglass at a time. One grain, and then the next, and the next, and the next. Until an hour has passed. And then you live the next hour, and the next, and the next. And then you find you have lived the first day. That's how you do it, Arrant. One grain of sand at a time.' He sighed. 'Mostly you learn to accept that what's done cannot be altered. My wife died years ago. Is it still painful? Oh, yes. Some things will pain you for the rest of your life. But you learn to live with them. You learn to accept. The pain *does* grow more bearable with every passing year. The guilt never goes away, but you survive it. And somewhere along the line you'll even learn to laugh again.'

They sat in silence for a moment, then Arrant said, 'I'm sorry. About Brand and you, I mean. You've lost a friend, and I've just been thinking about myself—'

Garis wasn't about to denigrate his regard for Brand just to lessen Arrant's pain. He said simply, 'He was one of the finest men I've ever known. We didn't just know each other back in Kardiastan before you were born, you know. We travelled together throughout the old Exaltarchy. Plotted rebellion together to free the vassal states and the provinces. We had many good years. He was the one who pulled me together after my Tavia died. I'll grieve for him. I'll miss him.'

Arrant started to cry, terrible racking sobs that came from a place too deep to have a name. Garis pulled his head down onto his shoulder and held him tight. He said, 'Brand liked you, Arrant, and I'd back Brand's judgement in a thing like that any day. Don't be too hard on yourself.'

The sobbing should have been cathartic, but it wasn't. It was just another scourge to his back.

Four days. Brand had been dead four days, and she still couldn't absorb the reality of the truth: she would never see him again.

He wasn't coming back. She woke each morning, and had to tell herself, all over again, that he was dead. All over again, that sinking feeling would hit the bottom of her stomach. And then the grief would start.

Not just grief for Brand, but for Arrant. And she couldn't help him, either. She had no words to assuage such pain, not hers, not his.

Goddess be thanked Garis had arrived when he had. Garis, so much older and wiser and saddened than the youth she had once known, but still Garis for all that. Looking after Arrant this time, instead of her. Garis who was going to take her son away . . .

She was waiting now to say goodbye. She leaned on the balustrade of the palace loggia and looked out over the city. Her city. The breeze played with her hair, tickled her neck. *It ought to be grey*, she thought. *Or white*. But it wasn't. Underneath the gold highlighting, she still had hair of a Kardi brown.

Fiercely, she told herself she was glad Arrant was going to Temellin. It was where he should have been all along. It had been a mistake to bring him to Tyrans. And now she was sending home a troubled youth who didn't know how to be a Magor, a young man who didn't know his father at all.

Temellin, she whispered to the wind, *it was a mistake, my love, and now you have to set it right . . .*

She thought she felt Temellin's presence there, behind her, but when she turned, it was Arrant who faced her. Alone, and so vulnerable. She stepped up to him, took him into her arms and hugged him, but she felt the resistance of his body even as he put his arms about her.

'Your wound?' he asked.

She showed him her arm. 'Fine. Look! You did an excellent job.'

He didn't answer.

'I am going to miss you, more than you could possibly know,' she said. 'I wish . . . I wish I could come with you.'

'I am so sorry,' he said, and he wasn't talking about his departure.

'I know.' She stood back to look at him, her hands on his shoulders. 'It – it wasn't just your fault, Arrant. We all could have played it differently. We just have to live with the decisions we made, and the results. Neither Rathrox nor Favonius would have behaved the way they did, if I had not incurred their anger in the first place. I had the chance to kill both of them, on different occasions, and didn't do it. I would do anything, anything at all, to change that. But I can't. And you have suffered for it. Brand *died* for it.'

He swallowed. 'Favonius said he could have been my father . . .'

The words were a lance into her heart. *Was everything she had ever done going to add to his burden, his pain?* 'No,' she said vehemently. 'He couldn't have been. You are who you are, because you are *Temellin*'s son.'

'Were you lovers?' There was no accusation there, just a striving to understand something beyond his comprehension.

How was it possible to explain her liaison with the man responsible for Prianus?

The words were so hard to say. 'Yes. Before I met your father. Favonius wanted to marry me. But in the end I humiliated him, and that he could not live with and still be the man he had been.' She sighed. 'Sometimes being a man has nothing to do with being a good fighter, or a fine athlete. Sometimes the greatest men are those who know how to live with their adversity, or be courageous in the little things day after day. Brand was a slave. So was Gev. They were both ripped from their homes, badly treated and humiliated on the slave blocks of the Exaltarchy. And they still stood proud. That is what it is to be a man. In the end, Favonius never came close, for all his soldier's bravery.'

She drew in a deep breath. 'These things are difficult to talk about with you, Arrant. And I suppose it is equally embarrassing for you. All this happened before I met Temellin. Be assured of this: I – I have never ceased to love your father, to love him beyond all other men.'

He nodded, not meeting her eyes. Instead, he dug in his belt pouch. 'I want to give this back to you,' he said. 'I guess I won't need it any more. I'll have the real thing.'

She took what he offered. It was the lump of Mirage Maker clay. In her hand it re-formed once more into Temellin's head, smiling at her. 'He looks older,' she said, and then snorted at the absurdity of her remark. 'But then, he is. Thank you, Arrant. I – I shall treasure it because it will remind me of you both.' *Oh, Goddess, how can I do without you too?*

She took a deep breath, gathered her courage one last time. 'There is something else I have to tell you. Several things, in fact. I wish I didn't have to, but you need to know. Just in case.'

He looked up at her, the wounded sorrow of his look both an accusation – although doubtless he did not mean it to be – and a plea not to hurt him, not to burden him with more knowledge that was too much to bear. She swallowed and plunged on, hating all she had to say.

'Your troubles with your power. It could be as a result of all the things that I did when I was carrying you. I've always blamed myself. It's not your fault; it was mine. I went to fight the Stalwarts and I fell prey to the Ravage. And then I overused my powers, again and again. I think all that harmed your power.'

He nodded. 'Narjemah told me. You should have told me earlier. I always thought it was because I was too stupid, or not trying hard enough, or something.'

She heard his unspoken words: *It hurt.* 'I – I always wanted you to have hope. I thought if you believed it was because of damage done before you were born, you'd give up. And you shouldn't.'

'So I should go on hoping it will miraculously get better one day? Why are you telling me all this now, then?'

She winced at his bitterness. 'Because you need to have all the facts to help you make decisions. There's something else your father and I did not tell you, about how we met. Your father had lost his Mirager's sword to the Tyranians. That meant there could be no more cabochons bestowed. He made up his mind to die if he couldn't find it, so someone else could become the Mirager and be granted a new sword. Fortunately, I was able to return his sword to him.' She smiled faintly. 'It's a long story, and one day I'll tell the details.'

'What is it you are trying to say?' He sounded so adult, so composed, but she heard the pain.

'Soon you will walk the Shiver Barrens and be granted your Magor sword. One day – gods grant it a far distant day – you will have to do it a second time in order to swap your Magor sword for a Mirager's sword. I want you to be very careful about doing so, Arrant, if you haven't learned by then to control your cabochon and the Magor sword you will have.'

He regarded her, his head tilted to one side, hearing what she hadn't said. 'Because if I can't make cabochons with my Mirager's sword, I'd have to kill myself.'

She nodded and looked away from the bitter shock in his eyes. 'Yes. It – it would be better that you renounce your position as heir than take up a sword you could not use.'

'I see. I understand.'

'It – it may not come to that.'

'No. It might not.'

There was an awkward pause, and then they spoke of other things: practicalities, messages, discussions on trade and monetary matters that Temellin needed to be informed about, on wars still being fought in other parts of the old Exaltarchy. She gave him packages to be sent to Kardiastan. Gifts for Aemid and Temellin.

In Ligea's ears their conversation sounded so stilted. *I've lost him*, she thought. *He sees me now as a woman grieving for her lover, rather than his mother. As a woman who destroyed his future before he was born, because of her ambition. Ah, sweet Melete, we pay a terrible price for love.*

She kissed him on the brow, embraced him once more, and he left. She would see him again before his ship sailed, but this was the last time she would see him alone. She had wanted to tell him so much, and had said so little.

'Nothing much you can say to a boy who's just had his first brush with adult guilts, is there?' She jumped, startled. She'd been so wrapped in her thoughts she hadn't been aware that Gevenan had come up behind her, entering the room through the door Arrant had left open.

She turned and said, matching his sadness, 'Oh, Gev, he's been a grown man these four days past. His childhood is gone.' *And why is that so damned* hard *for a mother to take?*

He nodded. 'He will carry that load on his back for the rest of his life. But there are very few good men – or women – who don't have a pack that's too weighty to heft at times. That's what life is.' He gave a dry laugh. 'Ocrastes' balls, listen to me! Gevenan of Inge, spouting philosophy? I must be ill.'

'I would shoulder all of that pack for him if I could.' She sighed. 'I guess that's what mothers are, even this one. I was pretty rotten at the whole parent scenario. I hope his father can do a better job. Goddess, Gev, if I'd known motherhood would be so damnably *painful*—!'

He snorted. 'You wouldn't have changed a thing.'

She shook her head, more as an expression of her uncertainty than in negation. 'If I could go back, I'd change everything,' she said, and the fervour of her desire surprised even herself. 'Gev, I told myself I was doing all this for Kardiastan, to keep my nation safe from the Exaltarchy. It wasn't true, not really. You were right: I did it because I wanted revenge on Rathrox and Bator Korbus. On my father, even though he was already dead. Well, I got my revenge. Rathrox Ligatan and Bator Korbus and Favonius Kyranon – they all died with the bitter knowledge that they had failed and I had won. There can be no greater triumph. And you know what that victory tastes like. You warned me.'

He didn't reply.

'Ashes, Gev. Ashes on my tongue. The ashes of those who died. The dead coals of the years I've lost to war.' *The dying embers of lost opportunities. I could have married the man I loved and shared his life and his rule. I could have spent time knowing my son. I could have had other children. And Brand could be alive.*

'I threw it all away for vengeance.' She shook her head again. 'It wasn't worth it.'

'Oh, stop it,' he said crossly. 'Wallowing in self-pity like some broken-hearted adolescent. Brand would say it was worth it – his people are free! He spent years fighting the Exaltarchy because you made it possible for him to do so, by what you did here. He never regretted that, not a moment of it. He risked his life every day to help bring it about! Vortexdamn, if you'd ever bothered to ask that great hulking Altani son of a bitch what was the best way to die, he probably would have said, "Saving Ligea's life!" Which is exactly what he did do in the end.

'And what of people like me? I was tied into a slave's existence until you came along. Now I'm the High General of Tyrans! Ocrastes' balls, Ligea, there are thousands of us out there who would bend down and kiss your feet in gratitude. You've suffered, it's true, and so have others. But the vast majority of us who survived, we *know* it was worth it.' He waggled his forefinger at her. 'And I'd say that, even if I was stone-cold dead, with Bator Korbus' lance through my arse!'

She stared at him, her mouth open. There was a long silence. And then she began to laugh. He glared at her. She covered her mouth, but couldn't stop, until finally his mouth twitched, and he joined in.

'Goddessdamn, Gev,' she said at last. 'You are so good for me. I had thought I'd never laugh again.' She wiped her eyes with the back of her hand, knowing the tears contained more than just mirth. She added, suddenly sober, 'Do you know what the irony of all this is? It was Brand who taught me to feel compassion. And what I learned was what killed him. I should have slain Favonius while I had the chance, in Kardiastan. I should have wiped the damned Stalwarts off the face of the land. And I didn't. I had the opportunity to kill Rathrox, hesitated – and lost the chance. And so, years later, Brand died.'

'Compassion is never wrong, Ligea. And Brand would be the first to say it.' He waved a hand out over the vista of the city. 'Would you bring back the Cages and jam-pack them with everyone who might just possibly cause you trouble in the future, the way the Exaltarchy and the Brotherhood used to? That's no way to govern! Cruelty may give you short-term victories, but they don't last. And what comes in the wake of tyranny is always worse than what follows compassion. Always.' He gave a bark of laughter. 'And I never dreamed I would ever say that! Gevenan of Inge speaking of the benefits of compassion? Melete's tits, old age is making a milk-and-water weakling of me.'

'You're not old, not you.' And he was right. Or she had to believe he was right. No, both of those things. She sighed. 'I don't know what I shall do without you.' She wanted desperately to ask him to stay. Vortexdamn, she needed him! How could she run this recalcitrant land without a general she could trust by her side? But she wouldn't ask. He had a right to his own life. *Sweet Elysium, Brand, she thought, that's your doing, you Altani barbarian. There was a time when a thought like that would never have occurred to me.* She blinked away more tears.

He feigned surprise. 'Without me? Me?' He rubbed a hand over his head, and she noted his hair was thinning. And it was grey, too. 'You know, I don't know about this going home business. I'm a lousy sailor. And it's an awful long way over land. To ride all that distance, for a man of my age? My knees hurt.' He pulled a wry face. 'Let's face it, Ligea, my wife married again and my boys were raised by another man, my daughter married a Tyranian legionnaire who settled in Inge – I know all that already. What's there for me to go back to? Besides,' he added, offhand, 'we still have some more Jackals to track down, don't we? They have to be plucked out and squashed. Now's our chance, while they are headless . . .'

She smiled, and felt once more the stirring of excitement, the pull of danger.

Some things never changed.

Glenda Larke is an Australian who now lives in Malaysia, where she works on the two great loves of her life: writing fantasy and the conservation of rainforest avifauna. She has also lived in Tunisia and Austria, and has at different times in her life worked as a housemaid, library assistant, school teacher, university tutor, medical correspondence course editor, field ornithologist and designer of nature interpretive centres. Along the way she has taught English to students as diverse as Korean kindergarten kids and Japanese teenagers living in Malaysia, Viennese adults in Australia and engineering students in Tunis. If she has any spare time (which is not often), she goes bird watching; if she has any spare cash (not nearly often enough), she visits her daughters in Scotland and Virginia and her family in Western Australia. Visit the official Glenda Larke website at www.glendalarke.com

Find out more about Glenda Larke and other Orbit authors by registering for the free monthly newsletter at www.orbitbooks.net